Advance praise for

DARK
SEDUCTION

"Brenda Joyce mesmerizes....[The] Masters of Time
[series] is intense, compelling and wickedly erotic!"
—*New York Times* bestselling author Virginia Henley

"Brenda Joyce has consistently written high-quality
romance. Now she's adding a chilling touch of the
paranormal. It's a 'keeper'—I loved it."
—*New York Times* bestselling author Heather Graham

"In the mood for timeless danger and passionate
adventure? *Dark Seduction* is sensual paranormal
romance by a master! Brenda Joyce delivers a book
you won't want to put down."
—*New York Times* bestselling author Christina Skye

"*Dark Seduction*...a scorching sensual read
that leaves you breathless for more."
—*The Mystic Castle*

"*Dark Seduction* is...a deliciously dark, daring, sensual
tale that seduces readers. Allow yourself to be drawn
into this spellbinding tale and savor every moment
with a Masters of Time [novel]."
—*Romantic Times BOOKreviews*

BRENDA JOYCE

DARK SEDUCTION

HQN™

ISBN-13: 978-0-373-77233-9
ISBN-10: 0-373-77233-5

DARK SEDUCTION

Also by

BRENDA
JOYCE

The de Warenne Dynasty
A Lady at Last
The Stolen Bride
The Masquerade
The Prize

The Deadly Series
Deadly Kisses
Deadly Illusions

Watch for the next book in
Brenda Joyce's de Warenne Dynasty

The Perfect Bride

Coming August 2007

Brenda Joyce and HQN Books
are also excited to introduce

Dark Rival

The second book
in the thrilling new Masters of Time series
Coming October 2007

For my son, the genius who brainstormed the original concept with me—without the "hot" parts, of course!

ACKNOWLEDGMENTS

This book would not have been possible without many different layers of support and faith. I would like to thank my agents, Aaron Priest and Lucy Childs, who suspended their own uncertain feelings toward the paranormal genre and got solidly behind the original concept for The Masters of Time, allowing me to "sell" the concept to HQN. I must also thank my editor, Miranda Stecyk, for her lavish support. Although uncertain of some paranormal elements, she was open-minded enough to let me "go for it," and became a great cheerleader for the work in progress, encouraging me as a writer, while sharing her enthusiasm in-house, and for both I am indebted. And of course, my assistant and proofreader, Laurel, once again offered priceless support, enthusiasm and encouragement. Thank you all!

DARK
SEDUCTION

PROLOGUE

The Past

WHEN CLAIRE AWOKE, it was the dead of night.

For one moment, she was disoriented and confused. It was raining heavily outside. She lay in a canopied bed in a room she did not recognize. As she blinked in the darkness, she saw a fire in a stone hearth and two small, narrow windows. Instead of glass, iron bars bisected them. Through the bars, she saw a torrential night sky. And then she heard him.

Claire...come to me.

Claire bolted upright, alarmed. Instantly, she recalled Malcolm's near brush with death. But he wasn't with her in the room; she didn't know where he was. Was Malcolm all right? How long had she been unconscious? The sky had been cloudy earlier, but there hadn't been any sign of rain.

Claire...upstairs...above ye. I need ye...

Claire froze, breathing hard. She was very much alone, but he was using telepathy to communicate with her and his thoughts were as clear as if he'd spoken them. He was somewhere above her. She could feel him. Claire faltered, her insides hollowing with terrible urgency. *He was hurt, close to death. They had locked him up somewhere. She could save him.*

Claire jumped from the bed. She was warm, but not from the small fire—her blood was running hot in her veins from his potent summons. She had to find him. She was choking on desperation. Claire tore the brat from her body and flung it aside, but she found no relief from the feverish heat. *She had to be with Malcolm.* Swallowing, she became very still, listening for him.

It took but a moment to get past the sound of her pounding heart. And then she felt his torment. He was weak from the battle, his body savagely cut, and he was in pain. He could not even sit up. She had to find him. He needed her. He needed to be deep inside her, taking power from her.

Claire tensed as heat flared between them. He had heard her. He knew she was coming and he was waiting for her.

She looked up at the ceiling. Aidan had told Royce to take Malcolm to a tower. There were four towers, one on each corner of the curtain walls of the castle. Both gatehouses had towers, too, but she was certain he was directly above her. Claire jerked on the neckline of her leine, the linen sticking to her wet skin. It did not become easier to breathe.

She ripped the offending gown from her body, panting hard, clad only in her denim skirt and T-shirt. *Where are you?*

Claire. Upstairs. Above ye. 'Tis the East Gatehouse.

She smiled, her heart pounding with renewed urgency. *I am coming.* Claire tried the doorknob and realized it was locked. She was instantly enraged. They had locked her in the chamber!

Hurry, lass.

Claire inhaled and caught his scent. She could smell sex. His lust filled the room from the ceiling above. Frenzied, she pulled on the old-fashioned door handle. Her fear had given her superhuman strength, because the door blew in, the lock snapping.

Panting, she peered into the corridor and saw that it was empty, a single torch burning in one wall sconce. Barefoot, she soundlessly ran up the narrow, winding stone staircase.

Her flesh felt as if it might explode from her body if she did not leap into his arms soon.

Another landing faced her, one torch burning in the hall. Claire didn't stop. She went to the next level, where she found a small round antechamber instead of a corridor. A heavy wood door faced her, bolted from the outside, an iron padlock on it.

A throbbing tension filled the anteroom. *Malcolm's.*

He was on the other side of that door, hard and hot, promising her a universe of ecstasy. Claire now knew she would eagerly die for his touch.

Claire moaned and found her dagger stuck into the waistband of her skirt, jamming it into the padlock. In New York City, she would have never been able to pick such a lock. But now she viciously thrust the dagger into the lock and it sprang open. Moisture began to trickle down her legs. Claire flung the bolt aside and yanked the door open.

His silver gaze slammed into hers.

Malcolm lay naked on his back on a pallet at the far wall, a pale linen bandage glaring in contrast against his swarthy skin. His head was turned toward her and he was watching her carefully. He was fully erect. Claire understood; he had become the hunter lying in wait for her. She was eager to be his prey.

Claire wanted to run to him, but at the sight of so much beauty and the anticipation of so much pleasure, she simply could not move.

A smile began as he sat up slowly, grunting with pain. The bandage was stained with red blood. "Come t' me, Claire."

Claire stumbled forward as he carefully stood, clearly weak from the battle and loss of blood. She caught him, wrapping her arms around him, and when his entire naked body came into contact with hers, tears of desire began.

"Lass," he gasped, holding her in a viselike grasp. He flung his head back and his power fell over her like a huge cloak. Claire was cocooned in warmth that began an invasion from the outside, in. She was acutely aware of a soft, sweet draining sensation—and as aware of Malcolm, groaning uncontrollably, head flung even farther back. Suddenly she felt his terrible pleasure begin.

He cried out thickly. "Aye, Claire!"

She met his gaze as he seized her arms and she saw the triumphant lust there. He smiled savagely, spread her thighs, his mouth against hers. He thrust deep, gasping. "Ye taste *good*."

A huge wave broke and Claire wept in more pleasure than she had dreamed, but Malcolm moved now, draining her and coming at the same time, and the wave kept breaking. Lightning comprehension shocked her as the universe became solidly black and filled with exploding stars, each one another one of her climaxes. This time she would be lost in this galaxy of endless pleasure, she was never coming out and she didn't want to. Every climax was more violent, more brutal and better than the one before. It didn't matter. This was how she wanted to die, giving Malcolm her life, while riding his huge hardness into eternity.

His seed streamed and burned. He roared his pleasure as he took her, the sound that of a beast, not a man.

Claire wept and begged for more, and more always came. She somehow knew she could not withstand this, but she wanted it anyway. Another terrible wave broke, crushing her with ecstasy.

Suddenly Malcolm roared a final time—and thrust himself away from her.

Claire wanted to protest but she couldn't. She was in a vortex of pleasure and pain and spinning away so rapidly now that she realized she was really dying. She could feel the last essence of her life spinning out of her, faster and faster, like a whirling top about to keel over....

Claire began to settle, limp and empty, fading away. She

looked down on her nearly naked body, sprawled out on the stone floor, and saw Malcolm standing by the window, staring at her in horror. Aidan and Royce bent over her now. And suddenly the tower was filled with blinding light. Suddenly she saw the Ancients faintly outlined and crowding into the room....

"Is she alive?" Malcolm cried.

CHAPTER ONE

The Present

CLAIRE WAS AFRAID of the dark.

It was dark now—and something had just thudded downstairs.

She stood absolutely still in the bedroom that was above her bookstore. Claire sold old and rare books and manuscripts, as well as the occasional used but rare tome, and because of the quarter-of-a-million-dollar inventory she kept downstairs, she had a state-of-the-art security system, a Taser and a gun. She knew she hadn't left a window open, as it was sweltering in the city in July, and she would never leave a window open anyway. It was too dangerous. Crime was out of control in the city. Last month, her neighbor, a wannabe model, had been murdered, and although the police weren't saying so, she suspected it had been a pleasure crime. She strained to hear, debating getting her Beretta from her bedside drawer.

But she heard nothing now. As she stood there, clad in a pair of cotton candy-striped boxers and a thin ribbed tank top, her bedroom looking as if a tornado had cycled through it, the stray cat that had appeared earlier that day wandered in from the hall outside. She was flooded with relief. The cat had knocked something over! She shouldn't have suspected the worst— after all, her motion-detection sensors hadn't gone off—but even after all these years, she hated being alone at night.

Terrified, the child crouched by the door, as a dark, deathly shadow drifted by.

Claire scowled at the handsome black cat, refusing to allow a single thought of her mother's long-ago murder to invade her consciousness now. "You! I shouldn't have fed you, now, should I?"

Purring, the cat slithered between her ankles, rubbing sensually there.

Claire scooped him up, the first time she had done so, holding him tightly to her chest. "Rascal," she whispered. "I need a dog, not a cat, but if I didn't know that someone was missing you, I'd keep you."

The cheeky creature actually licked her face.

Claire wiped her chin, dropping the cat to the floor, knowing she'd have to post some Found notices in her Tribeca neighborhood before she left for the airport tomorrow. She was in the midst of packing for a long-overdue vacation. Tomorrow, she was bound for Edinburgh, and on Friday she would be driving across the Highlands. This time, her first stop would be the starkly beautiful island of Mull.

Excitement filled her. The cat had made himself comfortable on her bed, and Claire stepped away to return to her packing. She went to her antique bureau, purchased on a previous trip abroad in Lisbon. She traveled extensively for her business. Smiling as she tossed her dark auburn hair over her shoulder, she pulled out a pile of tanks and tees. She was twenty-eight years old, soon to be twenty-nine, and she ran an extraordinarily successful business, with half of it conducted on the Internet. Since graduating from Princeton with a master's degree in medieval European history, she'd taken exactly two personal vacations. Her first had been to London with a tour of Cornwall and Wales. At the last minute a friend had told her she had to spend a few days in Scotland, and even though she was not a creature of impulse—Claire liked to be in control—she had changed her itinerary the day before departing to do so. The moment she had passed Berwick-upon-Tweed, an odd excitement had filled her. She had instantly loved Scotland.

It had almost been like coming home.

She'd given herself the standard tour that time—Dunbar, Edinburgh, Stirling, Iona and Perth. But she had known she would come back to explore the Highlands. Their stark majesty and rugged desolation called out to her in a way she had never before experienced. Two years ago, she had returned, spending ten days in the north and northwest. On her last day, she had discovered the small, craggy, beautiful island of Mull.

She had traveled to Duart on the sound of Mull, the seat of the Maclean lairds for many centuries past. An intense need to explore and discover the history of the area had overcome her, but wandering through the castle hadn't satisfied her at all. Just before leaving the island, she had stumbled across a charming bed-and-breakfast in Malcolm's Point, and she had been directed to Dunroch by its owners. She had been told Dunroch was seat of the Macleans of south Mull and Coll and that the current laird remained in residence, although he was rarely seen. He was a recluse, they said, and unwed, a terrible shame. Like most aristocrats, financial reasons forced him to open the grounds and a few rooms to the public.

Intrigued, Claire had rushed over to Dunroch an hour before closing. She had been so overwhelmed by the gray castle that the moment she approached the drawbridge that lay over the now-empty moat, chills had begun to run up and down her spine. She had been breathless as she passed under a raised portcullis and through the short, dark passageway of the gatehouse, realizing it had been a part of the original castle, built in the early fourteenth century by Brogan Maclean. She had paused in the inner bailey, staring not at the bare courtyard, but toward the sea and the keep. She didn't have to be told to know that the tower, looking out over the Atlantic, was a part of the original fortifications, too.

All of the rooms were closed to the public except for the Great Hall. Once inside, Claire had stood there, oddly mesmerized. It had seemed familiar, although she had never been there before. She had stared at the large, sparsely furnished chamber, seeing not the three elegant seating arrangements, but a trestle table, occupied by the lord and his noblemen. No fire burned in the massive hearth, but Claire felt its stifling heat. When another tourist had walked past her, she had jumped, almost expecting the see the laird of Dunroch. Claire could have sworn she felt his presence.

She could still recall the sight of the imposing castle from the road below the high cliffs as if she had been there yesterday. She'd thought about the castle a lot and she'd even done some research, but the southern Macleans were mysterious. A Google search and her online research library hadn't brought up any reference to any of the southern Macleans since Brogan Mor, and he had died in 1411 at a bloody battle called Red Harlow. The lack of information only whetted her appetite, but Claire had always been insatiable when it came to history.

Claire sorted through a pile of jeans, breathless now. This trip, she was spending one night in Edinburgh and driving directly to Dunroch. She was staying at the bed-and-breakfast, Malcolm's Arms, and she had given herself three entire days on the island. But there was more. As a seller of rare books, she intended to ask the present-day laird if she could have access to his library. It was an excuse to meet him. She didn't know why she was compelled to do so. Maybe it was because there was no history on this branch of the Macleans since Brogan Mor. Claire had decided the current laird was probably sixty years old, but she had an image of him in her mind, like a mature version of Colin Farrell.

Claire tossed a few pairs of jeans into her suitcase,

deciding that she was almost done. She was tall for a woman, standing five foot ten in her bare feet, and she was incredibly fit from kickboxing, running and weight training almost every day. Being strong made her feel safe. When Claire was ten years old, her mother had gone to the corner grocery store, leaving Claire alone in the one-room apartment, promising her that she'd be back in five minutes. She'd never come home.

Claire tried not to remember about that endless night. She'd been a fanciful child, believing in monsters and ghosts, annoying her mother to no end with her claims that creatures lived in her closet and beneath her bed. That night, she'd seen terrifying shapes in every shadow, every drifting drape.

That had been a long time ago. Still, she missed her mother. To this day, she wore an odd pendant which her mother had never taken off—a highly polished pale semiprecious stone set in four arms of gold, each arm intricately detailed with an obviously Celtic design. Whenever Claire felt particularly sad, she would clasp the pendant in her palm, and her grief would ease. She didn't know why her mom had been so attached to it, but she suspected it had something to do with Claire's father. The stone was the dearest memento Claire had.

Not that she had a father. Her mother had been painfully honest, explaining that there had been a single night of passion when she had been young and wild. His name was Alex, and that was all Janine knew—or said she knew.

After her mother's death, Claire had gone to live with her aunt and uncle on their upstate farm. Aunt Bet had welcomed her with open arms, and growing up, Claire had become close to her cousins, Amy and Lorie, both near her own age. When Claire turned fifteen, Aunt Bet had sat her down and told her the gruesome truth.

Her mother hadn't been murdered for the money in her purse or her credit cards. She'd been the victim of a pleasure crime.

That knowledge had changed Claire's life. Her mother had been murdered by a perverted madman. It confirmed her worst fears—bad things were out there and they happened at night.

And then, in her sophomore year of college, her cousin Lorie was murdered while leaving a late-night movie not far from campus. The police had swiftly determined that Lorie had been the victim of yet another pleasure crime. That had been five years ago.

She didn't know when the nation's oh-so-clever press had first coined the phrase *pleasure crime,* but it had been around for as long as she could remember. Social commentators, psychiatrists, liberals and conservatives alike all claimed that society was in a state of anarchy. Eighty percent of all murders were now sexually related, and every year it was getting worse. Lorie had died like a thousand others. She'd had sex. Bodily fluids had shown that she had been very aroused and that the perpetrator had climaxed several times. There had been no struggle, and to this day, the police had no clue as to who Lorie had been with. A witness had seen Lorie leaving the theater with a young, handsome, athletic-looking man. She had seemed happy, even smitten. A police sketch had been circulated but no one recognized him and, as usual, there was no match in the FBI's criminal database.

But that was why pleasure crimes were so shocking and disturbing. These perverted murderers always seemed to be complete strangers, yet they somehow seduced their victims, and to this day, no one knew how. There were all kinds of theories. Cult theory claimed that the perps belonged to a secret society and used hypnotism to entrance the victims. Sociologists called the deaths a pathological trend and blamed it on everything from video games, rap and the culture of violence, to broken homes, drugs and even blended families. Claire knew it was bull. No one knew how and no one knew why.

It almost didn't matter. Every victim was young and attractive and died in the same way. Their hearts simply stopped beating, as if overcome by the excitement and arousal.

Ever since her cousin's murder, Claire had made certain she was strong enough to do some damage should one of the city's criminally perverted think to assault her. Amy had decided to take martial arts, too. In fact, Amy had been the one to suggest the self-defense course and she had encouraged Claire to learn to shoot. Both young women kept guns in their homes. Claire was glad that Amy's husband was in the FBI, even if he sat behind a desk. She felt certain he did have some inside information, because Amy was always talking about how evil the crimes were. She never said more and Claire suspected she wasn't allowed to. That was okay. Pleasure crimes were evil. Maybe there was a sick cult after all. Claire kept her gun loaded in her bedside night table. No one was ever going to hurt her, not if she could help it.

Her packing almost concluded, she decided to make herself a light supper. She smiled at the cat, who was curled up on the pillow she slept with. "Rascal, not my pillow, please! C'mon. You can have some catnip while I eat. A glass of wine is definitely in order."

As if he understood her perfectly, the black cat leaped from the bed and approached.

Claire bent to stroke him. "Maybe I should keep you. You are such a handsome thing."

The words were barely out of her mouth when the motion detectors chimed and someone began banging on the front door of her shop.

Claire jumped a foot and then froze, instantly flooded with adrenaline. The pounding continued. She glanced at the clock by her bed. It was half past nine. This was either an emergency or a loon. And she damn well wasn't opening the door to a crazy. There were too many madmen on the loose.

Claire ran to the nightstand, taking her Beretta from the

drawer. Sweat gathered between her breasts. Her two neighbors had her number, just in case there ever was an emergency. This had to be a stranger. She started barefoot down the stairs.

She tried not to think about all the heinous crimes being committed in the city.

She tried not to think about her neighbor, Lorie or her mother.

"Claire! I know you're in there," a woman cried, sounding pissed off.

Claire faltered. Who the hell was that? She didn't recognize the voice. The person who was so impatient to get in that she was rattling the door, as if to break it off its hinges. That, of course, was impossible. The door was thick as all hell and the hinges were cast iron.

There was a small hall with a console table at the bottom of the stairs where she always kept a single desk lamp lit. Her office was across the hall. To the left of the stairs was her kitchen, with its breakfast area, and to the right, the large room that served as her store. Claire entered the store, hitting the light switch and flooding the shop as she did so.

The black Venetian blinds were drawn. "Who is it?" Claire demanded, not going to the door.

The banging and rattling stopped. "Claire, it's me, Sibylla."

Claire tried to think. She was almost certain she did not know anyone named Sibylla. She was about to tell her to get lost—in a polite way, of course—when the woman spoke. "I know you have the page, Claire. Let me in."

Claire wasn't curious, not now, not with a loony stranger banging down her door, not when it was black as Hades out. "I have twelve thousand books in stock," she said tersely. "At four hundred pages on average, there's a lot of pages in here."

"It's the page from the book of healing." Sibylla was sounding very annoyed, dangerously so. "It's from the

Cladich and you know it." She pushed the door open and stepped inside, something snapping as she did so.

For one second, Claire was in shock. Only the Terminator could break her door open that way, and the red-haired woman stepping determinedly into her shop was not the Terminator, not by any stretch. She was of medium height and frame, no more than five foot six, probably not much more than a hundred and ten pounds. Claire realized she was dressed all in black, like a cat burglar, and that she had clearly picked her state-of-the-art locks.

Tomorrow she was installing a new security system.

Claire pointed the gun right between her eyes. "Stop right there. I don't know you and this doesn't feel like a bad joke. Get out." Her hand wasn't shaking and Claire was amazed, because she was afraid. She had never looked into such cold, soulless eyes before.

Sibylla smiled at her without any mirth and it transformed her beauty into a mask of malice. Her smile spoke of threats. For one moment, Claire's heart went wild as she realized this strange woman wasn't going to listen. But the woman did not appear to be armed and Claire had at least twenty pounds on her.

And then Sibylla laughed. "Oh, my gods! You don't know me... You haven't gone back yet, have you?"

Claire never wavered, keeping the gun trained on the middle of the woman's forehead. "Get out."

"Not until you give me the page," Sibylla said, striding directly to her.

"I don't have any page!" Claire cried in disbelief. Her hand began to shake. Claire started to squeeze the trigger, lowering the gun to point it at Sibylla's shoulder, but she was too late. Sibylla took the gun from her with the speed of a striking snake. Then she raised her fist.

Claire saw the blow and tried to block it, but the other woman was amazingly strong and her braced forearm fell away. The fist felt like brass knuckles as it slammed into the side of her head. Pain exploded and Claire saw shooting stars. Then there was only blackness.

CLAIRE CAME TO SLOWLY, layers of blackness receding, replaced with thick gray shadows. *Her head hurt like hell.* That was her first coherent thought. Then she realized she lay on the wood floor. Instantly, she remembered everything.

A woman had broken into her shop and assaulted her. For one moment, Claire lay still, pretending to be unconscious, listening acutely to the night. But all she heard were the cars passing and horns blaring on the street outside.

Slowly, Claire opened her eyes, realizing she had been moved. She now lay in the area between the kitchen and the shop, not far from her office. The desk lamp remained on. Claire slowly turned her head to gaze into the store. She almost cried out. It was empty, the front door thankfully closed, but it looked as if every single book had been thrown onto the floor. Her store had been ransacked.

Claire sat up, rigid with dismay and disbelief. The woman had most definitely been looking for a page from that book she had mentioned. She touched the side of her head, finding a huge lump behind her ear, and hoped against all odds that her most valuable inventory hadn't been stolen. She needed to call the police, but she also needed to know what Sibylla had taken.

She had never heard of the Cladich. But in medieval times, there had been references to books and manuscripts which contemporaries had believed had various restorative and healing powers. In spite of her aching head, she became excited. She would do a Google search on the Cladich as soon as she got her bearings. But why would that intruder think that a page from that book was in her store?

The intruder could be a simple nutcase, but Claire was uneasy. Sibylla had seemed to know her and she hadn't seemed crazy, not at all. She had seemed vicious, ruthless and deter-mined. Claire reached up and clasped the pendant she wore, taking a moment to recover her composure. Of all the nights for a burglary and an assault! But she wasn't really hurt. If she was lucky, the woman hadn't found what she wanted. If she was really lucky, that page was actually in her possession!

Claire stood, beginning to calm, the throbbing receding to a dull ache, while a familiar excitement tingled in her veins. Her instinct was to rush into the store and take inventory, but she knew she ought to ice her head first and then call the cops. And she also wanted to check to see if a book called the Cladich had ever existed at all.

But security came first. Claire went into the shop to lock the front door. As she crossed the store, carefully stepping over books and manuscripts, she retrieved the Beretta from the floor. The door had a double lock. Tomorrow, when she had triple locks put on, she'd also add a bolt. As she turned the lock, the reassuring click sounded, but when she tested the door, it opened.

Her heart leaped with dismay. If her locks no longer worked, she was going to a hotel. Claire hesitated and opened the door a crack to look at the lock. Her eyes widened as she stared at the gouges in the wood door frame. It almost looked as if Sibylla had pushed the locked door open, ripping the teeth of the locks through the wooden jamb to do so.

But that was impossible.

She slammed the door closed, refusing to panic. The street outside had been relatively quiet except for some passing cars, but she had no security now. *Every night, dozens of pleasure crimes occurred.* She had made it her business to know.

She hurried to her desk, skipping over piles of books, grabbed the chair and put it under the doorknob. When the police came, she'd ask them to help her move a bookcase in front of the door. That should add enough security for the moment.

But how could she leave town tomorrow, as planned? Her trip would have to be postponed, Claire realized. She was going to have to take inventory of her stock. The police would demand it. And what if someone had put a valuable page in one of the volumes?

The lure of her vacation and Dunroch warred with her excitement over the possibility of making such a huge discovery. Claire ran into her office, not even turning the lights on. She tapped the space bar on her laptop to bring it out of hibernation, her pulse pounding now. She raced into the kitchen, hitting lights, and began filling a Ziploc bag with ice. The pain in her head had dulled to an unpleasant headache. Maybe she would skip the hospital after all.

From the store, she heard the chair scraping across the floor just as she heard a man curse.

Claire was in disbelief. It could not be another intruder! And then the fear began. She moved, grabbing the gun from the counter, checking wildly to see if it was loaded and then slamming off the kitchen lights. She faded into the wall behind the open kitchen door. Trying not to panic, she listened intently for the man again but heard nothing.

Yet it hadn't been her imagination. She had heard a curse, nearly inaudible. Claire's heart pounded with frightening force. Had he left? Or was he even now ransacking her store? Was she going to be assaulted again?

Was he looking for that page from the Cladich? Because this could not be a coincidence. She hadn't been burglarized in the entire four years she had been open for business.

The phone was on the other side of the kitchen. She knew she should call 911 but she was afraid the intruder would hear her and turn his attentions on her. She gripped the gun so hard her fingers ached, her palms sweaty now. Anger began. This was her store, damn it. But the fear was consuming and no amount of righteous anger could chase it away.

Afraid her shallow breathing was audible and would expose her, Claire began creeping into the hall. The damn desk lamp remained on, making her feel horribly exposed.

She could see across the store to the front door, but no one stood in there.

As she passed the stairs, she was seized from behind.

Claire cried out as a powerful arm locked her in place against what felt like a stone wall. Panic made it impossible to think. She became aware of being held, viselike, against a huge, obviously male body.

Her heart was thundering, but suddenly it slowed and Claire had a shocking sense of familiarity. In that moment, fear vanished, replaced only by her acute awareness of stunning male power and strength.

He spoke.

Claire did not understand a single word he said. Her heart raced and fear clawed at her again. Her instinct was to struggle and she began to squirm, grasping his arms to wrench them off. She wished she had spike heels on so she could jam one into his booted foot. Her bare legs came into contact with his thighs and she froze. His legs were absolutely bare, as well. Claire inhaled harshly.

He spoke, jerking on her with his thick arm, and she did not have to understand his language to know he was telling her to be still. And as he pulled her closer, she felt him stiffen against her backside.

Claire froze. Her captor was aroused, shockingly so. The sensation of a great, hard length pressed against her was terrifying—and electrifying, too. "Let me go," she gasped desperately. And two words blazed across her mind: *pleasure crime.*

She felt his grip tighten in surprise. Then he said, "Put yer weapon down, lass."

He spoke English, but there was no mistaking the exaggerated Scottish accent. Claire wet her lips, too dazed to even try to consider what that meant. "Please. I won't run. Let me go. You're hurting me."

To her relief, he relaxed his hold. "Put the weapon down,

be a good lass." As he spoke, she felt his stubble against her jaw, his breath feathering her ear.

Her mind went blank, and she could only think of the powerful pulse pounding against her. Something terrible was happening, and Claire didn't know what to do. Her body had begun to tighten and thrum. Was this how those women died in the middle of the night? Did they become dazed and confused—and aroused? She dropped the gun and it clattered onto the floor but did not go off. "Please."

"Dinna scream," he said softly. "I willna hurt ye, lass. I need yer help."

Claire somehow nodded. When he removed his arm, she ran to the other side of the hall, whirling and slamming her back against the wall to face him. And she cried out.

She had expected anything but the masculine perfection facing her. He was a towering man, at least six inches taller than she was and hugely muscular. His hair was as black as midnight, his skin bronzed, but he had shockingly pale eyes. They were trained upon her with unnerving intensity.

He seemed just as surprised by the sight of her as she was by him.

She shivered. God, he was handsome. A slightly crooked nose, perhaps broken once, achingly high cheekbones and a brutally strong jaw gave him the look of powerful hero. A scar bisected one black brow and another formed a crescent on one cheek. They merely added to the appearance that this man was battle-hardened, experienced and far too strong for anyone's good.

But he was a loon. He had to be, because he was wearing clothing she instantly recognized—a midthigh, mustard-colored linen tunic, which was belted, and over that, covering one shoulder, a blue-and-black-plaid mantle pinned with a gold brooch. He wore knee-high, heavily worn, cuffed leather boots, and a huge sword was sheathed on his left side, the hilt sparkling with paste jewels. He was costumed as a medieval Highlander!

He looked like the real deal. He had the bulging arms that could have wielded a huge broadsword effortlessly in the kind of battle one read about in a history book. And whoever had made his costume had done their research. His leine looked authentic, as if it had been dyed with saffron, and that blue-and-black mantle looked hand-loomed. She had to look at his strong thighs again, where his muscles bulged, thighs that looked rock hard from years of riding horses and running hills. Her gaze crept upward to the short skirt of the leine, where a rigid raised line remained. Claire realized she was ogling him, perspiration running in a stream between her breasts and thighs. She was breathless, but that was because she was afraid of him.

And then she saw that his eyes had lowered to her legs. She blushed.

He lifted his unmistakably heated gaze to hers. "I didna think to see ye again, lass."

Claire's eyes widened.

His smile became seductive. "I dinna like me women t' vanish in the night."

He was most definitely mad, she thought. "You don't know me. I don't know *you*. We haven't met."

"I be insulted, lass, that ye didna recall the event." But his satisfied smile never wavered and he kept glancing at her legs and her tiny, midriff-baring tank top. "What manner o' dress is that?"

Her color increased and she felt it. She prayed he was not one of those pleasure-seeking murderers. "I could ask you the same thing," she retorted, shaking. "This is a bookshop. You must be on your way to a costume party. It's not here!" She had to appease this man at all costs and she had to get him to leave her store.

"Dinna be afraid, lass. Temptation ye may be, but I have other matters on me mind. I need yer help. I need the page."

She exhaled now loudly, but not in relief. She didn't want to be alone with this man. Her mind raced. "Come back tomorrow." She forced a smile and it felt sickly. "We're closed. I can help you tomorrow."

He sent her another seductive smile, clearly used to charming women to his way—and his bed. "I canna return on the morrow, lass." And he murmured, "Ye wanna help me, lass, ye do. Leave the fear. It dinna serve ye well. Ye can trust me."

His soft tone sent a spiral of desire through her. No man had ever looked at her in such a manner or spoken so seductively, much less a man like this. Claire could not look away from his gaze. The wild pounding of her heart eased. Some of her fear receded. Claire actually wanted to believe him, to trust him. He smiled at her knowingly.

"Ye'll help me, lass, an' send me on me way."

For one moment, she was going to agree, but her mind was screaming at her oddly, confusing her. Then the sirens of a fire engine blared on the street outside, passing in front of her shop. He jumped, turning toward the door, and she came to her senses. She was covered in sweat now. She had been about to do all that he asked!

"No."

He started.

"My assistant will help you tomorrow." She swallowed. She was as firm as she could be and it felt like a huge feat. She wiped her bangs from her eyes, her hand trembling. It was as if he had almost hypnotized her. She avoided his gaze now. "If it's important, you'll come back. Now, please leave. As you can see, I have some cleaning up to do—and you are likely late for your party." She wished her voice hadn't cracked with the terrible tension and fear filling her.

He did not move, and it was very hard to tell if he was annoyed, angry or surprised. "I canna leave without the page," he finally said, and there was no mistaking his stubbornness then.

Claire glanced at the Beretta, which lay on the floor in the hall about an equal distance from them. She wondered if she could seize it and force him out.

"Dinna think to try," he advised, his tone soft.

She stiffened, knowing she could not best this man and that it would be dangerous to attempt to do so. He didn't seem to be violent, but he was obviously a nut. She'd help him if that would get him to leave. "Fine. I doubt I have what you are looking for, but go ahead, tell me what you want." She glanced very briefly at his face and when she took in his hard beauty again, her heart did a double somersault.

A look of triumph flitted through his eyes. "Ancient wisdom was given to the shamans of Dalriada long ago an' put in three books. The Cladich be the book o' healin'. It was stolen from its shrine. It's been gone fer centuries. We ken a page be here, in this place."

Claire started. What the hell was going on? "Your lady friend was already here, looking for a page from the Cladich, or so she said. But I hate to tell you this, it's bunk. No books existed in the time of Dalriada."

He stared, and then fury glinted. "Sibylla was here?"

"Not only was she here, she whacked me over the head. I think she had brass knuckles in her fist," Claire added with a wince. Was he in cahoots with the first burglar? But if so, why on earth would he be dressed in such a costume?

The moment she had spoken, she wished she had not. He crossed the narrow hall before she could take a breath. Claire cried out, but it was too late. His arm was around her again and briefly, their gazes met.

"I said I wouldna hurt ye. It would benefit ye greatly, lass, t' trust me now."

"Like hell," Claire cried, her heart thundering in alarm. But she could not look away from his magnetic gray eyes. "Let go."

"God's blood," he finally snapped, jerking her. "Let me see the wound!"

Claire understood his intentions then and she was shocked. He only wanted to see if she was hurt? But why would he care?

"Ease yerself," he said with a smile, his tone coaxing.

And when she allowed herself to relax just slightly, he released his hold, as well. "Good lass," he murmured, the words as sensuous as silk upon her bare skin. Then he was threading his long, blunt fingers through her hair, brushing the shoulder-length strands aside, finding her scalp. Claire stopped breathing. His touch was like a lover's caress, the barest flutter of his fingers across her hot skin, causing her body to tighten. For one maddening moment, she wished he would run his hand down her neck, her arm and over her breasts, which were tight and peaked. He gave her a brief glance that was almost smug, telling her that he knew. *Tha ur falt brèagha.* His tone had dropped into a soft, seductive whisper.

Claire breathed. "What?" She had to know what he had said.

But he had found the lump. She winced as he touched it. He said more firmly, "'Tis a good-sized robin's egg, I think. Sibylla needs a lesson in proper manners an' I have the mind t' be the one to teach her."

She had the oddest feeling he meant his words. She stared into his gaze, trying to understand who and what he was, when he lifted the pendant she wore. Surprisingly, she did not mind. He held the pale grayish-white stone in his hand, his knuckles firm against her skin, there beneath the hollow of her throat.

"Ye wear a charm stone, lass."

She knew she couldn't possibly speak. This man was too potent, too mesmerizing.

"Be ye kin, then? Do ye hail from Alba? Be ye a Lowlander?"

His hand had moved lower, so that her heart was thundering beneath it. Alba was Gaelic for Scotland. "No."

He let the pendant fall against her skin, but as he removed his hand, his fingers deliberately brushed a path along the top of her breast, trailing fire in its wake.

Claire gasped, looking into his heated and bold eyes. She could see them entwined, there in the small hall of her home. "Don't." She didn't even know why she protested, because protesting was not on her mind.

An eternity seemed to pass. There was no doubt he was seeing the same image she was. She had the feeling he was debating giving in to the huge tension knifing between them. Then his expression changed and he smiled, but it was self-deprecating. "Ye need," he said thickly, "a new manner of dress. A man canna think clearly with such a fashion afore him." And he turned away from her.

It was a relief. Instantly, Claire came to her senses, jumping away from the wall. Her body was on fire. This man was dangerously seductive. Finally she said, "Who are you? Who are you, really? And why are you dressed that way?!"

A twinkle came to his startling eyes and his face softened. And he smiled at her, the smile so genuine he became beauty incarnate, revealing two deep dimples. "Ye be needin' a pretty introduction? Lass, dinna be shy. Ye need only have asked." His voice rang with pride. "I be Malcolm of Dunroch," he said.

CHAPTER TWO

FOR ONE MOMENT, Claire was in disbelief, and then she got the joke. Amy! Her cousin was her best friend. Amy knew she was on her way to Mull, where she would stay at Malcolm's Arms, and she also knew that Claire had fantasized about meeting the laird of Dunroch. Her cousin had decided to play a prank on her by sending this wannabe actor to impersonate a medieval Highlander. And Claire laughed.

Normally, she would not be amused, but she was so relieved.

The man pretending to be Malcolm of Dunroch stopped smiling. He stared at her, first in suspicion, and then his expression hardened, becoming dark. "Be ye laughin' at me, lass?" he asked too softly.

"Amy sent you!" Claire cried, still having one last chuckle. "God, you are good! You had me for a moment—I thought you were a loon. The truth is, I almost believed, just for a second, that you were the genuine article." She grinned at him.

He scowled. "Ye be mad, lass. An' you accuse *me* of bein' the loon?"

His quick anger almost seemed real. "I know you're not mad," Claire said quickly, instinctively appeasing him. "Just one damn good entertainer."

"I dinna ken ye, lass." His regard was piercing.

His theatrics were no longer amusing. He was an actor, not a loon, not a burglar. Her cousin had hired the most gorgeous hunk she had ever seen as a joke. And not only was he gorgeous, he was clearly attracted to her, too. She became still. She hadn't been with anyone in three years, not since her last relationship had ended. Claire began to think hard about the fact that he was not an insane burglar and that men like him were not a dime a dozen. But what was she going to do, exactly?

He was as still. "Lassie?"

Then she came to her senses. He was a stranger. In a city filled with vicious murdering criminals, only crazy or desperate women met men without a friend's introduction. She wasn't crazy and she wasn't desperate. She should not be thinking about sex.

But she was.

Claire wet her lips, aware that her body was turned on, no matter her common sense. "Enough with the brogue. Cat's out of the bag." She turned away from him and as she did so, she was faced with the devastation in her store.

Her attention was instantly diverted. Claire stared at the precious books littering the floor. Her cousin would never condone such destruction.

That woman had *not* been a joke. *He* might be an actor, but Sibylla had been a burglar. She had ransacked Claire's store and assaulted her, and Claire still didn't know what she had taken. Suddenly, Amy's joke wasn't funny anymore. Malcolm had scared her, considering what had happened before he had appeared. And it didn't even make sense. Sibylla had also asked about a page from the Cladich. What did that mean?

As she tried to make sense out of the events of that evening, he walked past her and began retrieving the books.

"What are you doing?" she asked tersely, riddled with tension all over again. This wasn't right; everything was still wrong.

He faced her, a dozen books in his arms. The imitation leine had short sleeves, and his biceps bulged. "I will help ye, lass, but ye need to help me in return." He sent her that engaging and alluring smile.

Claire steeled herself against his magnetism, jerking her gaze away. It was almost too late, as her body heat was climbing. She hugged herself defensively now. "That was improv, right? I told you about Sibylla and the page from the Cladich and you went with it. That's what actors do." That was the only possible explanation…except she wasn't certain she had mentioned Sibylla before he had asked her about the page.

He slowly shook his head. "I dinna ken. But if ye be thinkin' I be an actor, ye be wrong, lass. I be the Maclean of south Mull an' Coll."

Claire became angry. She folded her arms against her chest, then regretted it, as his gaze moved to her breasts. "Please stop," she said harshly. "This has been a terrible night. I know Amy sent you as a joke, but Sibylla assaulted me and ransacked my store."

"An' that be why I wish to help ye now. Where do ye want me t' put the books?"

Claire shook her head. "No. I appreciate the offer, but I'll clean up by myself." She wanted him gone. She needed to think and she needed to call the police.

But he ignored her, placing the books in a neat pile on the floor, as if he understood there was no point in putting anything back on the shelves. He glanced at her as he straightened.

Clearly he intended to stay and help. Did that make him decent, as well as gorgeous? Softly, she said, "The joke's done. Really. You can go now."

He muttered something in Gaelic and she froze. "You're really a Scot."

"Aye." He held another armful of books.

Claire told herself not to panic. He could be a Scottish actor, just like Sean Connery, and some Scots continued to speak Gaelic. "Amy did send you, didn't she?"

He didn't answer. Instead, he stacked the books next to the first pile.

She shook her head, her unease about to become full-blown panic again. If Amy hadn't sent him, then who and what was he?

He bent to retrieve more books, and Claire was faced with the sight of the leine riding high up on his powerful, corded hamstrings. The fact that he was so masculine didn't help alleviate her confusion. Her body continued to vibrate with all kinds of tension, but she wasn't as frightened now as she had first been. If he wasn't going to leave, what should she do?

She should call her cousin and find out the truth, but damn it, she was afraid of what Amy would say.

He straightened and caught her staring. "Ye be too hungry fer such a beauteous lass," he said softly. "Where's yer man?"

"There isn't one." She was flushing.

He stared blankly at her. "I dinna ken this world," he finally said, shaking his head. "Ye live here alone?"

Claire nodded. "Yes, I do." They were having a conversation that was almost normal. She debated how to innocently make that phone call without his becoming alarmed. There was no way to avoid it.

He was incredulous. "And who's t' protect ye in danger?"

"I protect myself." She smiled weakly.

He made a sound. "With that weapon?" He nodded disparagingly toward the hall, where her Beretta lay on the floor.

"I also have Mace, pepper spray and a Taser."

His eyes narrowed. "More weapons?"

Surely he knew what Mace and pepper spray were, at least. "I am hardly the only single woman in the city."

"A woman needs a man to keep her safe, lass. 'Tis the way o' the world, the way o' men." He was firm.

Claire was briefly speechless. This man spoke as if he were from a past century. "It's not the way of my world," she finally said. "And you're scaring me. I admit it. I'm a wuss and you need to get out of character." Her cheeks were hot.

"I dinna wish to frighten ye, lass," he murmured. "But what man in his good mind would leave ye to yerself?"

She couldn't help being flattered. And the way he was regarding her now, from beneath thick black lashes, left her in no doubt that he was oversexed. Claire swallowed. She couldn't just sense the sexual tension coming from him, she could actually feel it. It was almost a third presence there in the room with them. She had not a doubt he would be an amazing lover.

"Ye need a man, lass," he said softly. "'Tis a shame it willna be me."

She stiffened. Was he reading her mind? Was that a rejection? She was only thinking about what was terribly obvious!

She stared at him and he stared back. "Why not?" Her tone was hoarse. She could barely believe herself. She had never even had a casual affair.

And his gaze intensified. "Ye be intent on seduction, lass? Ye wish to seduce me?"

Claire was mortified. "No." She couldn't think, so how could she even begin to know what she intended?

He smiled—a soft, heartbreaking smile—and then he spoke with vast regret. "In another life, *momhaise,* I would gladly accept such a beautiful invitation."

Only this man could make a rejection so utterly sexual. His words should have hurt her. Instead, she stood there aching.

He turned away. Claire glimpsed the very evident ridge of his arousal beneath the tunic and she almost expected her store to go up in flames.

He spoke brusquely now. "I need the page afore another takes it. It belongs in the shrine with the Cathach. I expect yer help an' then I'll be gone."

It was another moment before Claire came to her senses. "This isn't a joke, is it? My cousin didn't send you here. You are from Scotland."

His gray gaze was steady. "Aye."

She began to shake. "The Cathach is in the Royal Irish Academy. Every scholar knows, because it's the oldest illuminated Irish manuscript that anyone has ever found."

As emotional as she was becoming, he was as calm. "The Cathach be enshrined on Iona, lass."

Claire shook her head. Was he a nut after all? "There is no shrine on Iona—it is nothing but ruins!"

His face settled into hard planes and taut angles. "Maybe in yer time."

"What the hell does that mean?" she cried.

"It means I ha' been to the shrine many times. I have guarded it meself."

She swallowed, backing away. "I believe you are a true Scot, but why the costume? Why the absurd story—the lies? And who is the woman who broke into my store?"

His eyes flashed. "Dinna accuse me o' lies, lass. Men ha' died fer less." He shook his head. "I dinna ken what book is in yer academy, but 'tis nay the book o' wisdom, which I ha' seen with me own eyes."

"That's impossible!" Claire cried, terribly agitated now. "You believe it, though, don't you?"

"I speak the truth." He folded his massive arms across his chest.

Her mind was racing now at an alarming speed. There was no way to rationalize his behavior or beliefs. The genuine Cathach was in Dublin, on display. It was not enshrined on the island of Iona. There was no shrine on Iona! She had been there. The monastery and abbey were in ruins. Had a shrine existed there, she would have seen it. And what about the Cladich—and the page that both he and Sibylla claimed they were after? She was a scholar, but she had never heard of such a book before.

"Tell me about the Cladich," she said.

His gaze narrowed, as if he was wary. "Fergus MacErc brought the book to Dunadd. When St. Columba established the monastery on Iona, it was enshrined there with the Cathach. 'Twas stolen from the Benedictines," he said.

She wet her lips, her heart racing. He was definitely mad, because he believed his every word. "If you are telling me that a manuscript predates the Cathach and the establishment of St. Columba's monastery on Iona, you are *wrong*."

His eyes darkened. "Do ye accuse me o' lies again?"

"I don't know what to think! There was no written tradition among the Celts until St. Columba's time—*none*," she cried. "The Druids prohibited writing. Everything was oral."

His smile was smug. "Nay. The books were written, because the Ancients wanted it so."

"The Ancients?"

Softly he said, "The old gods."

Beyond mad, she thought. She prayed for the strength to dissemble. Then she looked right at him. "All right, I concede. I am only a bookseller, so maybe I'm the one who's wrong." She smiled. "I'm cold. I am going upstairs to change, but I'll be right back. Go ahead, look for the page. I'll help you when I come back downstairs." She didn't bother to tell him that such a page, if original, would be in fragments if not carefully preserved.

He smiled back at her, a smile that did not reach his gray eyes.

He knew she was up to something. It didn't matter, as long as he let her leave the room. Claire walked slowly out of the front store, when what she wanted to do was run. His gaze burned holes in her back. She darted into her office, pausing at her small desk, and unplugged and snatched up her laptop. No sound came from the front. Holding the laptop to her chest, she started up the stairs, tripping in her haste.

In her bedroom, she leaped onto the bed, lifting the computer's lid. Shaking, feeling ill with dread, she went to the Internet and did a search for the Cladich, then lifted the phone. But before she could even dial 911, the information she wanted appeared on her screen. Claire forgot all about calling the police.

The Cladich was a myth. There was almost no proof that it had ever existed, except for a reference to the holy manuscript that had been found on the effigy of a tomb in the tiny village of Cladich, Scotland. Three scholars believed the claim. They all held that it had been a book of healing, belonging to a secret society of pagan warriors. However, they were divided after that. One claimed the brotherhood and scripture dated to the Dark Ages; another, to the birth of Christ. The third opinion was that the secret brotherhood had survived into the Middle Ages, although it was doubtful the book had.

Claire began to tremble with excitement. She had to remind herself that the book was a legend. But both Malcolm and Sibylla believed a page was in her store. What if it wasn't a myth?

As she scanned the article again, she felt him.

She slowly looked up, across her bed. Malcolm stood as still as a statue in the doorway of her bedroom. His silver gaze was fastened upon her.

She couldn't move. She stared at him, forgetting all about the Cladich and its missing page. His gaze moved over her face, her breasts, her legs. Her skin fired and flamed. Slowly, vaguely aware that she was no longer herself, Claire leaned back against her pillows. She needed him.

His voice cut the trance like a whiplash. "Get up."

Claire jumped from the bed. His face was so tight it looked as if it might crack. He strode past her, to the bed.

"Who are you?" Her heart was thundering madly.

His hand swept over her favorite pillow and he turned to look at her with astonished and furious eyes. "Goddamn it," he exclaimed. "Aidan slept here? In yer bed?"

She did not know what he was talking about. "There was a cat...a stray...but I haven't seen it in hours." She was babbling. Her heart refused to slow. Worse, her body continued to ache for fulfillment.

He was thunderous. "There be nay time left." He looked her up and down, scathingly. "Change yer fashion an' come down now. Yer comin' with *me,* lass." It was a statement, not a request. He spun past her and left.

Claire stood there in shock. All of her fear returned, and with it, a vast confusion. There had been no mistaking his urgency. He had perceived some threat, real or imagined— but he was the threat, wasn't he? And who the hell was Aidan?

Claire felt as if she was in the path of an oncoming hurricane and that her life was about to be blown to hell. She ran to the top of the stairs. "I'm not going anywhere with you!" Even as she insisted, she had the dreadful feeling that he was going to have his way. But where did he think to take her? And why would he want to take her anywhere?

He didn't answer. He had walked into the kitchen but hadn't turned on any lights.

Claire raced back into the bedroom. She slammed the door and frantically ran to the phone. She dialed 911. The operator was calm and in no hurry, which infuriated Claire. "There is a burglary in progress!" she screamed at the man, and slammed the receiver down. At least the police should be there within five or ten minutes.

She ran to her suitcase, leaping out of her boxers and tank top as she did so. She shimmied into a thong and pulled on a bra. Her hands were shaking and it took her three tries to hook it closed. What was he up to now? She was almost afraid to find out. But she wasn't going anywhere with him. She'd stall until the police came and carted him away and then she'd start researching. She seized the top garments from her open suitcase and quickly pulled on a denim mini and a cap-sleeved tee. Stumbling into a pair of really worn cowboy boots, she grabbed a cotton cardigan and ran to the bedstand. She seized the deadly Taser, slipped it in her pocket and flew down the stairs.

The kitchen remained dark but the refrigerator was open, shedding light, and he was staring into it. Claire hit the lights and he whirled to face her, his sword ringing as he unsheathed it.

Claire leaped back so quickly she fell against the stove. She'd never heard a genuine sword before, but she knew immediately that his weapon was real.

He held the sword high, his eyes black with fury, as if she was his mortal enemy and he was an instant away from cleaving her in two.

He lowered the sword. "By the gods, lass," he said hoarsely. "Dinna sneak up on me that way!"

She wet her dry lips, unable to look away, her heart hammering so hard she felt faint. For one instant, she had been afraid he was going to kill her on the spot.

A madman with a sword. She was in deep shit.

"I'll never hurt ye," he said, a strange expression twisting his face. His gaze had slipped to her legs again.

"You scared me," Claire managed to say, beginning to tremble. That was a vast understatement. If that sword was genuine, what did it make the man?

"Be ye impoverished? Ye have no garments but rags?" His gaze lifted to hers.

Claire didn't even try to answer. She stood there, overwhelmed with what her mind wanted to tell her.

"Dinna fear, lass, I'll see ye clothed soon enough." He began to smile reassuringly at her, when she could not possibly be reassured, but then his gaze jerked past her and widened. Before Claire could really register that something or someone was in the hallway, he shoved her behind him. "Get back," he commanded.

Claire stumbled from the force of his push as his sword rang, unsheathed once again. The sound was answered by another sword's terrible echo behind them. In dread and disbelief, she turned and cried out.

Another towering man, dressed almost exactly as Malcolm, faced him, a huge sword raised threateningly in both hands. He was dark haired but fair skinned, impossibly handsome, and his eyes were filled with malicious delight. *"Hallo, a Chaluim."* He spoke softly in Gaelic, his words clearly taunting. *"De tha doi?"*

Malcolm roared, *"A Bhrogain!"* The battle cry was ancient, barbaric and deafening. It was also terrifying. Claire cringed as Malcolm wielded a blow that would have cleanly sliced the other man's head from his neck had his adversary not met it with equally great strength and skill. The two swords locked and rang again.

And in that moment, she knew *everything* was real. These men wanted to kill one another and it was not an act. Malcolm's adversary no longer smiled, his expression primitive, feral. As Malcolm went on the offensive, his enemy parrying every blow, she saw that they had the kind of ability that only came from years of practice—and years of actual battle. They were not in costume. They were medieval warriors intent on murder, mayhem, death.

So much testosterone filled the store that she felt ill and faint. Blow after blow sounded.

Someone was going to die soon. *Malcolm could die.*

And Claire thought about the Beretta.

She had left it in the hallway. Both men were in the midst of their battle in the center of her kitchen. Claire edged toward the door, skirting the breakfast area as she did so, making certain she stayed far from the battling men.

And then she ran into the hall as their swords rang again and again, the violent battle clearly reaching a savage crescendo. She saw the Beretta and seized it. She wanted to turn and flee, but instead, she ran back to the kitchen and pointed the gun at Malcolm's enemy.

"Stop," she tried, but her teeth were chattering.

Malcolm had seen her. His eyes had briefly widened. "Lass, nay!"

"I'll shoot!" she cried. "Malcolm, tell him I will kill him if he doesn't stop!"

Malcolm and the other man were braced against one another, sword to sword. Malcolm smiled coldly. "Ye heard my lass, Aidan. Surrender, afore she murders ye with her weapon."

Claire prayed he would surrender. She didn't know who he was, and she didn't know why she was defending Malcolm, but she would put a bullet in the intruder if she had to. She was a very good shot, but she had never fired a gun under such circumstances, or in such fear. Her hands were shaking, and while she would try to only wound the man, she wasn't confident that she would not kill him by mistake.

The dark-haired man visibly relaxed, although for one more moment he and Malcolm remained braced like two horned stags. Then, as one, both men disengaged, stepping farther apart.

Claire sidled past Aidan, who turned to smile at her. Her heart turned over at the sight of so much male beauty and strength.

Aidan murmured, "Ah, beauty, ye let me live another day." He grinned, clearly enjoying himself and not in the least bit shaken by such a violent fight. "Rascal that I am, I be eagerly awaitin' our next meeting," he added.

Claire rushed to Malcolm's side, barely comprehending him. He stepped protectively in front of her, and in doing so, he briefly blocked her view of Aidan. "There willna be another time," he growled back at Aidan.

Then he turned to Claire, his gaze searching. "Did he hurt ye?"

Claire was shaking like a leaf. She was about to tell him that she was fine—a monstrous lie—when she realized that Aidan was gone. "Where did he go?" she gasped.

"Give me the weapon, lass," Malcolm said softly, taking the gun from her. He set it on the counter and put his arms around her, pulling her into his embrace.

And dear God, he felt safe. Claire clung, shocked by the overwhelming sense of security his huge body was giving her. "Who was that? Where did he go?"

His gaze seemed to melt as he looked down at her. His huge hand stroked down her hair to the small of her back, and everything changed. His body was so strong and male, his scent was so heady and sexual that her knees buckled. Her bare thighs were molded to his equally bare ones, but his tough leather boots were a startling and not unpleasant contrast against her shins. In her cowboy boots, she was still shorter than he was, and her breasts were crushed against the solid wall of his chest.

And he was massively aroused, his erection standing hard and high against one hip.

Claire's insides hollowed. She wanted this man and it had nothing to do with any trance.

"Have no fear, lass. The bastard's gone." His hand moved lower, over her denim-clad bottom, his fingers spreading firmly there. "I be wantin' ye, lass."

She wet her lips. "I know." She dared, "I want you, too."

He smiled at her and she felt his hand caress her bottom, low near the hem of her skirt. "Can ye wait an hour or so?" he murmured.

Claire was overcome with pulsating desire. Ordinarily she was hard to please, but she felt that if he touched her—really touched her, right then, between her legs—she was going to climax. Maybe it was the battle she had witnessed. "Take me upstairs," she heard herself whisper, and she was too hot to be horrified by her forward behavior. She had never felt this way before.

She would worry about who and what he was another time, later, after they had used each other and pleasured each other again and again.

His jaw tightened. "Ye dinna listen well, do ye? It's nay safe and I canna protect ye here. But I will protect ye, lass. Ye be *my* Innocent now."

"I don't understand," Claire whispered, pressing closer. The only thing she did understand was that he was refusing her offer. She leaned her face against his chest and her desire escalated out of all control. In his arms, she shook with an intense, consuming hunger. She ran her hands down to his waist, barely able to bite back a moan. He seemed to rise higher and harder in response.

His grip on her tightened. "I be sorry, lass," he said.

Once again, Claire just couldn't understand. It was as if they were from two different worlds, speaking two different languages—except for the language spoken by their inflamed bodies.

And then they were catapulted across the room, through walls, past stars.

Claire screamed.

CHAPTER THREE

'TWAS HIS FOURTH LEAP, but he was still unprepared for the pain.

Holding the woman, her screams renting the night, he fought to withstand the excruciating torment. It was as if his skin was being flayed from his body, as if his scalp was being torn from his skull, as if his limbs were being wrenched from their sockets. He knew he would land whole. It did not matter. He had never known such agony and torment could exist. He choked on his own sobs, too.

And then they landed.

'Twas with the force of being thrown from the highest cliff and landing upon a jagged rock face. Malcolm grunted, pain exploding in his back and head, bright lights blazing. But he did not release the woman. He thanked the Ancients that he had somehow kept her with him and then he prayed that she was strong enough to live.

The woman wept now, softly, against his chest.

A Master shall not use his powers for his own gain.

He tensed. Although the torment had lessened, it remained. He had been told that the strange limbo of being weak and defenseless lasted mere minutes, and had he been alone, he would have had patience. But he wasn't alone. The woman was in his arms, and as the pain faded, his body hardened. He wanted sex.

But he hadn't brought her back because he wanted her. He had followed Sibylla to the future, hunting both her and the page. The woman was an Innocent, caught between evil and good. He couldn't leave her in her time, alone and without defenses, not with both Sibylla and Aidan nearby. He had taken vows to protect Innocence through all ages. His life was no longer his own.

Three years ago he had been chosen. He had been summoned to the monastery on Iona, only to learn that the monastery did not exist. Instead, a secret Brotherhood lived behind those stone walls. He had been told that he came from an ancient line of princes, descended from the old Celtic gods, and that he must follow in his father's footsteps, defending mankind. He had taken the sacred vows, vows that had irrevocably changed his life. *Defend God. Keep Faith. Protect Innocence.* His war was not with kings and queens or the clans, his war was with evil. There had been shock—but somehow, there had been relief and an utter comprehension, as if he'd known that one day, the summons would come.

For now, his entire life made sense. His unusual strength, his keen intellect, his compassion and endurance had always awed others, and he had always felt different, even from his own people. He was different. He had been destined from the moment of his birth.

With the Abbot's blessing, he'd read the ritual pages, and he had come into most of his powers. They were powers which no mere mortal could ever possess. Other powers would mature more slowly. He no longer had a human life span. And while the vows were simple and straightforward, the Code was long and subject to interpretation. However, the most basic tenet of the Code held that no Master could use his powers except to uphold his vows.

And that did not exclude his sexual powers, which were greatly enhanced now.

He did not have to look down at the woman in his arms to know she was beautiful, and somehow different from the others he'd taken to his bed. The urge to move over her was consuming. He could so easily mount her, sliding long and deep, pleasuring them both. He was hugely virile and rarely sated—it was almost a curse. Apparently, every Master suffered such extreme manhood. Carnal pleasure was not forbidden, and no Master would tolerate it if it were. But there were different kinds of pleasure that were forbidden, pleasures that were evil. He finally looked down at her. Her sobs were softer now and she turned her gaze up to his.

Her eyes were a shocking shade of green.

He watched her carefully. Her torment was fading and he saw no reason to deny himself. Although he had patience in politics, diplomacy and battle, with women he had none. And why should he? He was the Maclean and a Master and he had never met a woman who did not wish to eagerly share his bed.

Those who hesitated were so easily entranced.

He felt the moment she thought about his embrace, his body, his manhood and what he could offer her. He felt her quicken, and her genuine surprise at her own response. She was not accustomed to desire but she desired him. That pleased him.

Her eyes widened.

He smiled, caressing her bare arm to reassure her, about to promise her great delights. He did not have to focus on the black Highland night to know they were alone and safe. Evil brought an intense chill with it, one far different from that of a northern summer evening. Danger was not near—not yet.

"Ye did well, lass." He leaned over her, aware of a tremor passing through him. Anticipation made him feel almost faint. "There's nay more danger—an' we be very much alone."

Her eyes turned bright with hunger.

Although already thick with blood, more heat rushed to his loins. He had never seen such a tall woman, with such endless legs, and the way she was sculpted with such taut muscles maddened him. He wanted those legs wrapped around his waist—*now*.

"Lass," he murmured in his most enchanting tone. He had lurked in her mind and knew that she had been celibate for three years. He knew the passion he would receive. The woman was sexually desperate and he did not blame her.

He ran his hand down her arm, taking a good look at her scantily clad bosom, and then at the hem of the rag she wore, which was just a handspan from the wet treasure he would soon plunder and possess. She looked up at him, her eyes shimmering. He slid his hand to that hem and hesitated. Their gazes held, and his heart did a strange flip. "I be glad," he whispered, "that ye survived the fall."

She inhaled, trembling. Her hand crept up between them to his chest. Another tear stained her cheek and she whimpered softly, restlessly shifting. He recognized the nuances in the sound and he swelled further, pleased.

He shifted deliberately, the leine riding high, his cock thrusting past it, and he slid his hand down her thigh, and then upward, lifting the rag. He pressed her closer so that he could throb against her sex. She gasped in pleasure, her gaze flying to his. "I want to pleasure ye, lass, an' ye been denied. Let me come inside ye."

He brushed his mouth over her ear, breathing there. She gasped, bucking up against his hardness, spreading for him— the answer he wanted. He lifted her leg over his waist and as he did so, there was consuming desire. His veins ran with so much hot, pulsing blood, he could not stand it.

As he moved over her, lifting up the short rag she wore, she clawed his shoulders, rearing up to kiss him. But kisses were of no interest now, not when he was pulsing so fiercely and so hard. He stabbed forward and cried out. Her flesh was soaking wet and burning hot and it seized him tightly, a perfect vise; he gasped from the force of such blinding pleasure.

She cried out in elation, too.

It was so *good*. He could barely think rationally now. He wanted to watch her come; he drove deeper, steadily, then paused to stroke her distended sex. She wept. He smiled triumphantly and plunged within her throbbing flesh again. She met him savagely, desperately, and he felt her pent-up hunger from years of denial become a swirling cocoon of energy and passion. He had known it would be like this. He pinned her wider. *Look at me, lass.*

She did, crying out in a shuddering, endless climax.

His mind went blank, black. He needed release, too. He came, spilling all he had into her, spinning in ecstasy as he did so, and as he shouted in pleasure and triumph, the urge overcame him completely.

The desire was dark. Demonic. It was the urge to take far more than her body.

Because his pleasure could be enhanced so easily—with one taste of her power.

His mind froze even as his body kept streaming.

Nothing compared to the rapture of such power.

He looked down at her as she wept in ecstasy, aghast with his desire.

But it was forbidden. He was a Master, not a Deamhan. He had vowed to protect Innocence, not to destroy it.

Malcolm staggered away from her, reeling. He leaned against a tree, dizzy from the prolonged climax and the realization that she tempted in him in an unspeakable, evil way.

"No!" she gasped, frantically reaching out for him. And then she fell back, eyes closing.

She lay still now, as if dead.

But he hadn't done anything but pleasure them both. He swiftly knelt, lifting her into his arms. He was still thoroughly aroused, but it did not matter. He could barely believe what he had wanted to take from her. He wanted it still. "Lass!"

Her eyes fluttered. She had fainted from the excitement of such a huge release. He laid her face against his chest, where his heart thundered, holding her there, relieved. The lass was fine. But he was not fine, not at all. The horror remained.

And he was hardly done with the woman. He wanted her still, in his bed, in every sexual way. But how could there be another time when he did not dare trust himself?

And then he felt the chill.

Like an Arctic breeze coming off the highest mountain, the cold crept closer, instantly dropping the temperature of the pleasant summer evening. The blades of grass, the thistle and wildflowers around him froze. Malcolm became rigid, straining not to see but to feel.

The chill settled over the glen.

It was hunting him again.

CLAIRE BEGAN TO REALIZE that she was in a man's arms, being swiftly carried and then laid down on the ground. It was hard and cold. She was weak and dazed, disoriented. What had happened? Where was she?

"Dinna speak and dinna move," the man said. "Ye stay with yer back to the boulder, ye ken?"

Claire heard him. She realized her back was pressed unpleasantly against a rock face of some sort while her nails dug into wet, cold dirt. She stared down at the ground, seeing not a tiled kitchen floor but leaves, branches, dirt and grass. Images and sensations scrambled together in her mind—stars and agony, a terrible force, Malcolm and ecstasy, his power huge. And then she heard that bloodcurdling war cry. *"A Bhrogain!"*

She cried out as numerous swords rang, being drawn from their sheaths. She stumbled to her feet, so weak she staggered. In a panic, she looked for her gun and an image assailed her, of Malcolm in her kitchen putting the gun aside. They weren't in her kitchen now. Goddamn it. She was in the woods somewhere!

Leaning against a tree, she seized the pendant at her throat, her heart fluttering wildly with fear. It was cold out and the stone was hot. And then she saw Malcolm, a few steps from her, his back to her, holding a branch aloft, his stance defensive and belligerent at once. Her gaze moved past him and she choked off her cry.

A dozen knights faced him. The men were giants, clad in chain-mail shirts, steel chausses, gauntlets and helmets. The eye plates were closed, making them look evil. They were armed with lances, swords and axes. Their huge warhorses snorted and pranced, white-eyed. Wildly, Claire realized that they were in a clearing, surrounded by black woods. Beyond the woods she saw the dark shadows of numerous mountains. The night sky was the most brilliant she had ever beheld.

Malcolm said, not turning, "Get back to the rocks."

Claire didn't move. Did he think to face down over a dozen huge armed men himself? And he had no shield! Before she could even begin to think about what was happening, the first few knights charged, howling terrifying Gaelic war cries.

Claire bent and seized the first rock at hand and ran to stand beside Malcolm. He cursed in his tongue but did not look at her. Claire didn't think twice. As the first rider came upon them at a gallop, his lance couched under his arm, she flung the rock at the man.

Malcolm thrust his makeshift staff as she hurled the rock. The rider ducked and the rock missed, but Malcolm knocked him from his horse, then used his longsword to sever the man's head from his body as if the man were a rag doll. Claire backed up against the tree, seeking the Taser. Malcolm used his staff to parry another lance, flinging a mail-clad warrior to the ground. In one violent motion, he thrust his sword at the prone knight, instantly beheading him, too. Claire choked.

He turned to face another warrior, this time tossing the staff aside. He locked swords, shouting. "Lass!"

But she had already seen the third warrior-knight riding right at her, as if he would simply run her down. His black helmet had sinister eye slits. Certain she was about to die, Claire leaped forward, below the lance he held, thrusting the

Taser against the horse's shoulder. The horse reared, screaming, as the rider swung his lance at her. Claire ducked; she
had ruined his aim. And she felt his savage fury.

There was no time to run. The horse reared again and
Claire went after it. It was in midair as she shocked it in the
chest. The man cursed while the horse flipped over onto its
back, crushing its rider, and then the animal leaped up and
galloped off.

The mail-clad giant lay still, his neck at a grotesque angle,
clearly broken.

Claire knew she was not alone. She whirled and held up
the Taser threateningly, two mounted warriors having come
up behind her. They hesitated, clearly uncertain as to whether
to attack her or not. Beyond them, Claire saw Malcolm
fiercely slaying man after man. In spite of the odds, he was
definitely in control of the situation.

"Lass," he roared. "Get back to me."

That was a great idea, Claire thought, except that one of
the two warriors was between her and Malcolm. He was
smiling at her now, smugly, clearly anticipating her death. He
tossed his lance aside and drew a steel rod with a spiked ball
dangling from its chain.

Claire was terrified. He could take her head off easily with
it. That ball, whirling wildly, could flay her body into pieces.
She had to attack or she would die.

Claire bristled and stepped forward. Evil had killed her
cousin and her mother and if it killed her, she'd take as many
of the bastards down as she could. She'd get his horse, too,
or die trying.

"Damn it, lass!" Malcolm was shouting at her.

Too late, she realized she was putting an even greater
distance between them, but she didn't dare take her gaze
from the warrior. She was certain he smiled, backing his
mount just out of her reach.

"Coward," Claire hissed.

He said something to her in Gaelic, and Claire knew it was a taunt.

His buddy had ridden his horse to the side, clearly thinking to watch her murder or to get behind her, just in case. Claire knew she couldn't defend herself against them both. Letting him sidle behind her was not a good idea.

"Fuck you," Claire said. She ran at the knight with the ball and chain and jabbed the horse in the face.

It screamed, rearing, the rider spurring it viciously to bring it back to the ground. Claire grabbed his leg, pulling on him. He was glued into his saddle. Claire had read about how the saddles knights used were designed so they were as secure as if strapped in. She gave up. The horse had come down and the rider swung the ball viciously. Claire ducked entirely beneath the horse, aware she could be trampled, and as she came out the other side, the ball was flying there, at her. She dived for the ground and the ball ripped open his horse's hind-quarter. The horse screamed, rearing. Claire glimpsed his bare knee above the plates on his armor. She leaped and jabbed the Taser there.

He stiffened.

Claire didn't wait. She stunned him again in the only place she could—the knees. He fell from the horse, crashing to the ground at her feet.

But before she could feel any triumph, he jumped up when he should have been stunned senseless, the ball and chain in hand. Claire didn't think twice. She kicked him as hard as she could in the head, snapping his head back and then she jammed the Taser into his neck.

This time he went down.

And she felt the beast coming. Claire whirled to face the bulging whites of the other warrior's destrier as it galloped toward her. Claire dropped and rolled as the horse thundered past. Malcolm shouted at her again.

And when she leaped up, he was striking her attacker.

Claire watched Malcolm cleave the man's arm from his shoulder. Her stomach protested violently and then the man's head went flying through the air. Her stomach churned even more.

Thundering hooves sounded in the distance.

More warriors, Claire thought frantically.

"Lass!" Malcolm roared, leaping onto the riderless steed. He galloped toward her and held out his hand. Claire didn't hesitate. More riders were approaching and she had no wish to stick around to find out if they were friends or foes. She gave him her hand and he pulled her up behind him, suddenly halting the charger. Shocked, Claire saw the rest of their attackers fleeing at a gallop, while from a different direction, a smaller group of horsemen came cantering toward them.

She felt all of the tension leave Malcolm's huge body.

She was gripping his waist, still clutching the precious Taser. "Friends?" she gasped, beginning to shake. She was about to throw up.

"Aye, Ruari Dubh, me uncle."

Claire collapsed against his back, shaking uncontrollably. Worse, tears came. She was in such shock she could not think. But nothing had ever felt better than his wool brat under her cheek and nothing could be more reassuring than his musky male scent.

He slid from the horse, turned and pulled her down, right into his powerful arms. "Ye be brave, lass. But by the gods, when I give ye a command, 'tis t' be obeyed!" His eyes were silver, and they blazed.

She couldn't speak. Now she understood the scars on his face. She just shook her head and leaned her face against his chest, shaking like a leaf.

But his tunic was wet and sticky against her cheek. Claire pulled away, instantly afraid he was wounded and bleeding. Their eyes locked.

"'Tis nay mine," he said softly, the same softness coming to his eyes

Relief made her knees buckle. He put his arm around her, allowing her to stand upright against his powerful side

And then she saw the bodies—and body parts—lying scattered about them. She really saw them. And every single moment of that awful battle raced through her mind. Claire pulled away, ran a short distance, dropped to the ground and vomited violently. *What in God's name was happening?*

A medieval man—knights welding swords and axes—a night sky the likes of which she had never before seen.

Claire couldn't breathe.

There were no electric lights anywhere, no telephone poles, no cars, no sounds at all except for trees whispering in the breeze and the horses snorting, bits jangling.

"Lass." His huge hand was on her back. "'Tis over now. Ye got a good weapon there an' I ken ye can use it. Ruari and his men will see us safely on."

Claire closed her eyes, wanting to vomit again, but she had nothing in her system to heave. They weren't in her store. She recalled being hurled by a huge force through walls, past stars, almost like being thrown from an airplane without a parachute. There had been so much pain.

She struggled for air, panting hard now.

He was the real deal. There were a dozen bodies in the clearing to prove it. Oh, God.

His arm went around her. "I ken ye never been in battle afore. 'Twill pass. Ye need t' breathe deep."

'Twill pass.

He'd said that before. He'd said that in the exact same way, as if to reassure her—but he hadn't reassured her. Instead, there had been so much desire, and the next thing she knew, she was on her back and he was inside her, impossibly hard, impossibly deep, and she was coming.

Claire was in disbelief.

Something terrible was happening.

He was speaking in French now, over his shoulder, to his friend. Claire was fluent, but she didn't hear what he said. She did not want to be there and she didn't want to believe that they had had sex. She turned and struck him as hard as she could.

Her blow landed on his cheek and echoed. He didn't move, but his eyes went wide.

Claire backed as far from him as she could get. She hit a boulder. "Don't come near me," she warned. "I want nothing—*nothing*—to do with you!" She hadn't asked for any of this, damn him!

His face was expressionless, but she saw his chest rise and fall more swiftly now, a sign of some agitation. Well, let him be pissed, she thought wildly. She was pissed!

"Lass, tell me yer name."

"Go to hell," she cried. "Where am I?"

His nostrils flared, his jaw flexed. A terrible moment passed before he answered, making Claire wish she hadn't cursed him. "Alba. Scotland," he amended. "Morvern." He tried a smile on her, but it was cool. He was angry with her. "Not far from me home."

The irony made her laugh shrilly. She would have been at Dunroch by Sunday, and now she was just a few miles away!

"We'll be goin' to Carrick Castle fer the night. Come, lass, ye be tired, I ken." His tone was cautious now.

She shook her head, shivering, even though the night was pleasant once more. Her teeth chattered as she spoke. "We're in your time." She had no doubts.

His expression remained deadpan. "Aye."

She swallowed. "What time is that?" When he did not respond instantly, she yelled, "What year is this, damn it?"

He stiffened. "1427."

Claire nodded. "I see." She turned her back to him, hugging herself, aware that her entire body was shaking as if with convulsions. She had always wanted to believe in time travel. There were scientists who said it was possible, and they had put forth theories of quantum physics and black holes to explain it. Claire hadn't even tried to understand, as science was not an easy subject for her. But she understood the basics: if one traveled faster than the speed of light, one would go into the past.

None of the theories or what she had thought or even currently believed mattered. She knew with every fiber of her being that Malcolm was the medieval laird of Dunroch. No Hollywood set would ever be able to replicate the battle she had just seen—and had been a part of. Her knees went weak all over again. She was sick and she was exhausted. She wanted to get as far from this man as she could. And she was also afraid.

The last place she wished to be was medieval Scotland. She wanted to be home in her safe apartment, with its state-of-the-art security system. In fact, right now, she'd give just about anything to be in her kitchen, sipping a glass of wine and watching the reruns of *I Love Lucy* or *That '70s Show*. She slowly turned and their gazes clashed.

"We need to go," he said flatly, with no compassion in his eyes. "There be evil in the night, lass. We need to be behind solid walls."

Claire started. Unfortunately, she could not agree more. She told herself not to think about her mother now, but it was impossible. On the other hand, she did not want to go anywhere with him. What she wanted was to go home.

"I didna give ye a choice. Ye come with me." His eyes were hard now.

"Send me home," she said harshly.

"I canna."

She stared and he stared back. "You can't—or you won't?" she finally said.

"'Tis nay safe," he said flatly.

Claire began to laugh hysterically. "Like fighting a bunch of medieval knights armed with swords and axes is *safe?*"

His expression became thunderous. "I ha' tried to ken, lass," he said grimly. "I ha' nay more patience left."

Claire thought about the way he had looked at her and used his powerful legs to spread hers, without even an if you please. *Wham, bam, thank you, ma'am.* It didn't matter if this was the fifteenth century, she was a modern woman. She wanted to curse him again. She knew better than to dare.

A man rode forward. "Maybe I can be o' help. Black Royce o' Carrick, at yer service, Lady."

Claire looked up at him and a frisson of shock went through her. "Black" Royce was actually dark blond, with the hard but nearly perfect features of a Viking. He was in his early thirties, and he was as tall as Malcolm, with broad shoulders and bulging arms. He was clad like the knights who had attacked them. He wore a shirt of mail that reached his upper thighs, with gauntlet, elbow cups, chausses, knee cups and a helmet, the visor up. He carried a lethal-looking lance under one arm, wore two swords, long and short, and over the mail shirt, he wore a brat. It was impossible not to wonder if, like Malcolm, he went bare beneath the leine he surely wore under the chain-mail tunic.

He smiled slowly at her, as if he was aware of her admiration and her suspicions. His eyes flickered as he spoke. "Yer name, Lady?"

She knew Malcolm was watching her. She glanced at him. He was furious—which was fine by her, as he damn well deserved it. She didn't know what had set him off. "Claire. Claire Camden," she said. She forced her witless mind to work. "I need to get back to my time," she said. "Can you help?"

He did not seem taken aback by her question. "I would dearly love to take ye home, but that duty is nay mine."

"He has abducted me," Claire cried. But she flushed as she

spoke, because she was beginning to recall a few pertinent facts—like being whacked over the head by Sibylla and that warrior Aidan's intrusion, as well.

Malcolm stepped to her side, his expression purely black. "Ken as ye will," he said darkly. Then he stared coldly at Royce. He spoke in French. Claire wasn't surprised, as she recalled that most of the nobles in England and Scotland spoke the language of the European court. "She is my Innocent. She is under my protection and it stays that way until I decide otherwise."

Claire pretended not to understand.

"I understand," Royce returned softly in the same language. "She has been through a shock. She is very upset. If you wish, I'll escort her back to Carrick. I am sure by then she will have calmed." His smile was dry.

Malcolm spoke. "I have already taken her, Royce, and I will not share."

Claire flushed, turning away so neither man could guess that she could understand them. She was enraged. How dare he tell the other man what he had done! But he hadn't been bragging like a boy in a locker room. Were they fighting over her like two dogs over a bone? She was stunned, but what did she expect from a pair of macho medieval warriors?

Royce shrugged and turned to Claire. "Malcolm wishes to protect ye, Lady Claire. He be strong an' powerful an' the chief o' Clan Gillean. Ye be in good hands."

A sarcastic quip formed. She held it back. She was shocked, angry and frightened, but she wasn't foolish enough to think that she could survive for very long in fifteenth-century Scotland without someone to look out for her. She slowly faced Malcolm as Royce rode ahead, his men forming in two lines behind him. "When can I go home?"

"I dinna ken."

"Great," she retorted, trembling.

He gestured. Claire preceded him to where a man was

holding two of the steeds taken from the dead. He paused, taking the reins of the gray horse. "Can ye ride?"

"I grew up on a farm," Claire said tersely. She hadn't been on a horse in years and the horses she had ridden back then had been plow horses, not warhorses. But after the events of that evening, getting up on the huge, blowing animal seemed like a piece of cake.

How had her life come to this? And what was she going to do? Despair consumed her. *What if she couldn't get back?*

A big, callused hand settled on her shoulder.

Claire slowly turned, a familiar tension vibrating within her. He was powerful and sexual and she did not want to be aware of him as a man. But she was, especially after the brief interlude they had so unfortunately shared.

How could she have done such a thing?

His hand left her and he unpinned his brat, deftly draping it around her. His every accidental touch made it harder to breathe. He pinned the plaid closed just below the hollow of her throat, where her pulse was pounding like mad, belying her intentions to be indifferent to him and pretend she didn't want him. His hands stilled there and he raised his gaze to hers.

Claire's heart lurched at the sight of so much heat. Very, very vividly, she recalled his breadth, his length, his hardness and power. Desire made her feel faint.

His hands dropped away and his smile began, smug and satisfied. He nodded at the horse.

Claire mounted, his brat shielding her thighs from view.

CHAPTER FOUR

WHEN HE FELT SATISFIED that she could control the charger somewhat, Malcolm left Claire with two of Royce's men and rode to the side of the column so he could be alone. The forest was thick and dark around them, but he could smell the sea as they approached Loch Linnhe. There was no scent in the world like that of the woods mingling with Highland sea, he thought, except, of course, for the scent of her.

But now he could not touch her. He must not touch her. With her, he had no control.

Royce rode over to him. "What's botherin' ye, Calum?" he asked softly, speaking in Gaelic.

Malcolm hesitated, aware of his cheeks heating. Fortunately, Masters respected one another and did not lurk upon each other. He spoke in their native tongue, grim. "Sibylla has the power to leap time, Ruari. Moray has given it to her when she was but a lowly Deamhan all these years."

Royce's eyes widened; he was clearly dismayed.

As he should be, Malcolm thought. The powerful, demonic earl of Moray was the overlord of evil in Alba. It was said that, long ago, in the beginning, Moray had been a Master, until evil had corrupted him, stealing his soul. There was no doubt his line came from the Ancients, for his power was so great that no Master had been able to vanquish him, not in a thousand years. His quest was power and control, his means, destruction, anarchy and death. He had a great title, great lands, huge armies of both Deamhanain and humans.

Those he sent easily into death's jaws. And he was so charming, so handsome, so clever that he was favored by the royals—especially the current queen, Joan.

Many of the Deamhanain were simply humans possessed—like the knights that had just attacked them, giants among men, their powers enhanced by the demonic possession. Sybilla was human, but Moray had made her his lover, taken her soul, given her his children. And now, he had given her one of the most coveted powers of all, the power to leap the ages.

Royce glanced at him. "I dinna think ye be broodin' about a Deamhan, even if she be Sybilla, whose time has come."

"Aye, she must die. If she can leap like a Master, she has too much power now." The most powerful Deamhanain were always to be hunted and vanquished. It was too dangerous to allow them their lives. "But she may ha' the page. I followed her to the city of New York," he said grimly. "I followed her to Lady Claire's bookshop. She was there first. The shop was ransacked. Lady Claire doesna ken what be stolen, and what nay."

"If there be a page from the Cladich, it must be returned to the Brotherhood," Royce said firmly. "Moray has enough powers, an' he canna have the power to heal his own spawn."

Malcolm could not imagine a world where the Deamhanain could heal each other. The first Deamhanain, those who'd been seduced by the devil and stolen from the Brotherhood, were hard enough to vanquish without such powers.

"If Sybilla left Lady Claire alive, she has a use fer her," Royce added. "If Sybilla doesna have the page, she may think yer lady has it."

Unfortunately, Malcolm had just had that exact thought. His heart lurched with dread. The wife of John Frasier, a treacherous and powerful Lowland earl, Sybilla was even more dangerous than her husband, for he was simply an ambitious nobleman, while she was possessed and allied with Moray. She was almost as evil and cold-blooded as her overlord. Her reputation was vast. She loved to slowly torture her victims, both male and female, and then take pleasure in their deaths. He almost hoped that Sibylla had the page. Otherwise, Sibylla might believe that Claire knew where the page was, and she would hunt Claire. He was sickened, as he knew what Sibylla would do to Claire if she ever caught her.

"I think ye need make certain Sibylla kens Lady Claire be ignorant o' our affairs."

"She be ignorant." But she was not as ignorant as she had been, Malcolm thought grimly. He had brought Claire back to protect her from Sibylla and Aidan. Now he wasn't certain he had done what was in her best interests.

"'Tis nay safe to send her back, alone," Royce said suddenly. "Not yet."

Malcolm looked at him. "Do ye lurk?"

"I dinna have to lurk in yer head to ken yer fears fer her."

He hesitated, wondering what Royce had left unsaid. He hoped his lust was not obvious. "Aidan was also there." His blood boiled at that thought.

Royce's tawny brows lifted. "So he hunts the page, as well."

"He hunts whatever pleases him," Malcolm exclaimed, filled with fury. "He follows no command! The bastard was in her *bed*. I sensed him there."

"Aidan is a rogue," Royce said calmly, "but he is nay evil. Surely the Brotherhood sent him to the future, as they did ye. And Lady Claire is beautiful. If he had her first, ye may hate him, but ye canna change the past. 'Tis nay allowed," he warned.

The Code was not simple. There were many rules, some subject to debate, as well as interpretation, but never going back in time to change the past was one of the most important ones. No Master was allowed to change history. But if Aidan had even touched her, he'd be tempted to go back in time and do the forbidden. "He didna bed her. I'd have sensed him in her. But if he touched her—aye, a single touch—I will kill him."

Royce stared. "Ye be very possessive, lad."

Malcolm looked straight ahead between the stallion's pricked ears. "Dinna start."

"Ye dinna ken the lass."

"Aye, I dinna. Soon, when 'tis safe, when I ken that Sibylla doesna hunt her, then she will go back." And that way she would be safe from *him,* he thought grimly. He tried to imagine her at Dunroch, while not in his bed. It was impossible.

He could send her to Carrick with his uncle. Instantly, he dismissed the thought. His uncle was the least romantic man he knew, but like all the Masters, he could entrance a woman to his will and he always had a beautiful woman in his bed. He'd seen the way Royce had looked at her—the way he'd almost preened upon being introduced.

And by the gods, he became aware of a burning jealousy, because Claire had given his uncle a good lookover, in return. No, she was going to Dunroch, and he'd deal with his dilemma with an iron will when the time came.

As for Aidan, he had better keep his distance, too. Aidan was a rogue warrior, doing as he pleased, when he pleased. The world knew he was a hedonist. He'd had legions of lovers already. Beauty was his weakness. Did Aidan burn with lust for her, too? Malcolm did not trust him. Did he think to pleasure her and take her life while he did so? Malcolm felt certain Aidan had committed pleasure crimes because Aidan had but half a soul—and that half was black.

"Aidan invited ye to Awe once," Royce finally said, as if sensing his thoughts.

Malcolm jerked. "Aye—three years ago." Aidan had sent an invitation by messenger shortly after Malcolm's induction into the Brotherhood. He had ripped the missive to shreds.

Royce ignored that. "Ye should go to Awe and speak with him. Make a truce, Calum."

Malcolm stared, and said softly, "If I go t' Awe, I go fer one cause an' one cause alone. I go t' kill the bastard."

Royce's expression became hard. "Ye better cease such talk. A Master canna kill another Master an' ye ken."

Malcolm smiled coldly. "Really? That be one rule I dinna care for."

"I want to see peace between ye an' Aidan afore I die," Royce said sharply.

Malcolm stiffened. "What kind o' talk is that?" In truth, he didn't even know how old his uncle was.

"We're nay immortal." Royce said, his smile suddenly tired. "I been huntin' evil fer hundreds of years, Calum. My time will come."

Malcolm was aghast. "Do ye have a death wish? Yer a great Master. The Brotherhood needs ye, Ruari. The Innocent need ye." I need you, he added silently, but his uncle had to know that. Brogan had died when Malcolm was nine years old, and Royce had been more of a father than an uncle ever since, as well as a loyal friend.

Royce smiled then. "Ye be so young, Malcolm. I envy ye yer innocence—an' I pray ye'll never be without hope."

Malcolm became concerned. "Ye never speak this way. Is there something yer not telling me? Is something amiss?"

"After two hundred years, we have word of a page from the Cladich bein' near. The Deamhanain want it, and we must once again guard such a power for ourselves and Alba. I remember the first time the book was stolen, and the hunt to find it an' bring it back to the shrine. I remember when the Cladich was stolen the second time—an' we ha' not seen it since. I remember when Moray stole the Duaisean. The cycle of life never changes, like the sun rising an' setting, day after day an' year after year. It is a cycle of good an' evil, an' it will never end. Nothing changes—it is all the same. If a Master finally vanquishes Moray, there'll be another, greater Deamhan t' take his place."

Malcolm was very alarmed. "One day, Moray will be vanquished. No one will take his place."

"Ye stay far from Moray! I have tried to kill him a hundred times. Ye tried once, too, an' look at what it got ye."

Malcolm tensed. It had gotten him to Urquhart, where he had come close to losing his soul.

And then Royce smiled, revealing two dimples. It was the smile Malcolm had seen women fight amongst themselves to receive. "Dinna listen to the ramblings of an old Master like me. Ye protect the woman. She's yer Innocent now. Ye'll stay safely at Carrick t'night. T'morrow I'll be holding Moray's men back if they attack another time when ye go t' Dunroch. The MacNeil will want a report," he added.

"And he'll have one," Malcolm responded, relieved that Royce's odd, bleak humor was gone. "I go to Iona immediately."

Royce became grim. "Calum, Sibylla obeys Moray. If she let Lady Claire live, there be one more possibility. Ye will not care fer it."

Malcolm tensed.

"Mayhap the dark lord wishes Lady Claire to live."

Malcolm whirled his mount. "Dinna begin t' think that Moray has any idea the lass exists!"

"If Sibylla has the page, why else would she let her live?"

EVEN IN A CAVALCADE of armed men, Claire was afraid. She did not like the black forest they were riding through. She didn't need an imagination to know that all kinds of danger lurked in its impenetrable depths. And she wasn't thinking about wolves and mountain lions. What if there was an ambush? What if the men who had escaped returned to finish them off? They had meant to kill Malcolm—and they had meant to kill her. And to think she had been afraid of crime in the city!

She still could barely believe all that had happened. She

had gone back in time, which was shocking enough, and there had been a huge battle. She hoped she would never witness or participate in such a battle again. However, if she stayed in the fifteenth century for very long, the odds were she was going to find herself in such dire straits another time. Her expertise was medieval European history, not Highland history, but she had certainly dabbled in the latter. It was filled with intrigue, conspiracy, bloodshed, murder and warfare. Reading about it in a classroom had thrilled her. Living it was an entirely different matter.

Claire knew she had to set her fear aside and find calm in order to think. But her composure was in shreds. Two large, silent Scots, apparently assigned to escort her, rode on each side of her. Claire focused on deep breathing while trying to think happy thoughts. She thought about Thanksgiving at the farm and then gave up. She started to laugh, feeling hysterical, images of the bloody battle and severed heads vying with images of Malcolm's lust-ravaged face in her mind. She wasn't calm—she didn't think she would ever be calm again.

She recalled her insane behavior during the battle, when, instead of hiding as Malcolm had ordered her to do, she had tried to fight back. She was never going to understand what had motivated her. Claire Camden was not brave. She was afraid of her own shadow and everyone else's, which was why she had created such a little fortress in her shop. Except that fortress had been breached tonight. And she was not a Taser-welding female Schwarzenegger, even if she had acted like one. She didn't want to be a female version of Malcolm!

What if she couldn't get back?

Her tension increased. This was her greatest fear. Claire's heart lurched. If she started thinking about being trapped in the past forever, she wouldn't be able to think, period, and her mind was her only defense. Even in this violent, chauvinistic world, wisdom must surely prevail, even if it came from a female.

Her eyes had grown accustomed to the darkness. The night was lit by so many stunning stars and a brilliant half-moon, that it really wasn't all that hard to see. For one moment, as Claire scanned her surroundings, she allowed herself a grudging acceptance of the beauty of the night sky. Only in the fifteenth century could one see such a magnificent sight.

A few of the warriors also held torches, which helped illuminate the night. Her gaze moved to the pair of towering men who led the riders, then settled on Malcolm. He and Black Royce were silent now, but they had conversed for quite some time, clearly about grave matters. Claire grimaced. She knew they had been discussing her.

She stared at Malcolm's back. He seemed to be a superior warrior. In fact, if she thought about it, his prowess had been extraordinary. She was probably as safe as a woman in this particular time and place could be, considering that he seemed to feel obligated to protect her. But by God, she would feel a helluva lot better once they were at Carrick and behind solid stone walls.

And then what?

She had a hundred questions and she needed a hundred and one answers. She had to know that she could get back and when that would be. She had to know why they had been attacked. Had it been a mere instance of two clans feuding? She did not think so. And she did not like Malcolm's reference to evil.

Those warriors had been strange and different.

Claire shuddered. She didn't want to think anymore, but she couldn't stop herself.

Sometimes, while walking down the city streets, more frequently at night than during the day, Claire would pass by someone and feel thoroughly chilled. The first time it had happened, she had been so surprised that she had turned to look at the passerby. She had looked into hollow eyes.

It had somehow been terrifying, horrifying. She had been fifteen years old at the time, but it had been before Aunt Bet's stunning revelation about her mother's death. She had never looked at any such person again. Instead, she would duck her head, avoid all eye contact and keep on going.

She pretended it was a New York thing to do. Everyone knew New Yorkers were cold and strange, they weren't friendly and they didn't make eye contact. That was how one managed in the big city amongst millions of people.

The night her mother had been murdered, it had been so cold in the house although it had been an Indian-summer evening. It was the one fact she recalled with vivid, tactile clarity.

Claire stiffened and her mount danced in protest. One of the Highlanders reached out to seize her reins and Malcolm whirled to see what was happening. Claire didn't want to think about the past. Dealing with the present was bad enough.

But Claire breathed hard, the horse snorting now. *Damn it.* A terrible draft had chilled the glade just before the warriors had invaded, the same kind of cold that had filled the apartment.

Claire had spent her entire life avoiding overthinking the dark side of the city. She'd worked her ass off to make a small, secure and successful world for herself. When bad things happened to friends, neighbors and coworkers, she began supporting challenging political candidates. Crime was out of control and society was breaking down, so she worked harder. Work was a refuge. She wished she was working now.

But that world felt as if it had just gone up in smoke. And damn it, life seemed equally dark and chaotic in medieval Scotland. She didn't know what to think, and she certainly didn't know what to do.

Ye be my Innocent now.

She shivered. What did that mean?

Malcolm's tone had been filled with possession back in her apartment when he had first made that statement, and it had been as possessive when he had told Royce that he didn't share. She felt her cheeks warm. He had pointedly told Royce that he'd "taken" her. That was the point. He had taken and used her body, just like that, in one stunning instant, when she had been recovering from the torture of time travel. There hadn't been warm words, promises, declarations of affection. Love had not been involved. It had been pure, raw, carnal sex.

She was never going to believe that she had welcomed his attentions the way that she had. She still couldn't believe she'd actually wanted—desperately—his invasion. Traveling back in time must have altered her senses or her sensibilities, or both. Maybe it had changed her physically, too. She'd always been hard to please and finding a release had usually been a chore, but it had been shockingly easy with Malcolm.

She was old-fashioned and proud of it. She was not going to deny how attractive he was, but so what? She met attractive men in New York all the time, and even if they weren't as macho as Malcolm, there were some real power players out there. Power had always turned her on more than dumb good looks, but she had easily dismissed the men who had briefly tried to pursue her. Most of the men she met were highly dysfunctional. She had been celibate for three years because she insisted on affection, if not love, before intimacy. Power players weren't into affection or love, they were into conquests.

It sounded awfully familiar.

Claire did not want to continue to think about that brief, combustible act of penetration and climax. If she did, her dry mouth would get drier and her speeding heart would race even more wildly. However, she had better think about it and prepare herself for his advances. He still wanted her. It was more than obvious. She felt it every time he looked at her. His sexuality and desire emanated from him in hot, tangible waves. And he was possessive. He had been warning Royce away. She wasn't going to compromise her morals or her standards—or her dreams—just because she was lost in medieval times with the hunk of all ages. She had never had casual or meaningless sex. *Ever.* She'd had two relationships. She had been in love as a sophomore at Barnard, but her other affair had been more tepid. She'd wanted it to be love, but it had been hard to pretend, and in the end, she had given up.

And maybe that was half of the problem. He'd noticed right away that she'd been starving her body sexually. Crude and rude as he was, he'd commented openly. What had he said? He'd called her "hungry." Apparently, he'd hit the nail on the head.

The next time they spoke, she had to set some boundaries and make some rules. She was very alone and this was his world. If he was chieftain of his clan, he was used to doing what he wanted, when he wanted, all of the time. Claire knew enough about the structure and culture of the Highland clans to know that a laird was God and king, judge and jury, policeman and warlord. His word was law and it was final.

Her heart had picked up an alarmed beat. She didn't have to be rational to recall striking him and cursing him. She no longer knew herself, but she did know this. He might have deserved it, but it didn't matter. She didn't know him, never mind that he wanted to protect her. He was lord here, absolutely, and she had better appease him if she could. Otherwise, and maybe anyway, she was in deep shit.

Suddenly, Malcolm appeared at her side. Claire was so immersed in her thoughts that his appearance was as startling as that of a ghost. She flinched, her horse prancing. But he smiled, reaching out for her reins, steadying the charger. "I didna mean t' scare ye. Ye be all right, lass?"

Claire tried to ignore his powerful presence, his masculinity and what might happen later if she didn't find a way to keep him at bay. "We need to talk." That was the understatement of her life, she thought.

"Aye." He gestured ahead. "Carrick."

Claire followed his gaze and her eyes widened. The pale castle was perched high above them on equally pale cliffs. Her heart beat wildly, but not with fear.

The last time she had been in Scotland, she had almost taken the turn at the sign pointing to Carrick Castle. Her guidebook had said the scenery was breathtaking, and a tour of the grounds and castle was not to be missed. But in the end she had driven by, intent upon arriving at Iona by nightfall.

Maybe being thrust back in the past wasn't all that bad, Claire thought, excitement sweeping over her as she stared up at the imposing pale stone walls, the towers and the keep. If Malcolm kept his distance and she avoided any more battles, if she kept her head on straight and her courage up, this might just be an incredible and amazing, once-in-a-lifetime educational experience. She could probably even write about it, not that anyone would believe her. She was about to enter a fifteenth-century stronghold. She was about to see things that no historian had ever reported. And while she remained afraid, she wanted to go inside that castle.

If she could get back home in one piece, sooner rather than later, she might be able to manage this amazing twist of fate. She turned to look at him. "How long will it take to get there?"

"Less than an hour," he said. "And we'll discuss yer matters when we arrive."

THEY RODE UP the steep hill in double file, but had to go one at a time through the very narrow entrance of the walled barbican. Carrick was set on the top of a hill, overlooking steep cliffs on all sides, and the site had clearly been chosen because the hill was divided from the road by a steep, impassable ravine. Without the drawbridge, ladders or siege engines, no one was entering or leaving.

Claire shivered as she rode across the drawbridge, Malcolm still beside her. An outer bailey filled with huts and livestock was behind them, and she glanced down into the ravine. Hundreds of feet below, it was filled with sharp, jagged rocks. Attackers who were thwarted on the draw-bridge or trying to scale the curtain walls would fall to their deaths on the ground below.

As if reading her mind, Malcolm said, "No one has besieged Carrick."

Claire managed a sickly smile. A castle built solely to withstand assault and attack was, in a way, as unnerving as the battle they'd just survived. The sun was rising above the towers and the ramparts, and the sky was a pale gray, stained with fingers of crimson and pink. The sight would have been breathtaking, just as her brochure had promised, if she didn't know that each and every jagged rock had been put in that ravine by human hands, meant to inflict pain and death.

They now rode single file through the narrow, dark pas-sageway of the gatehouse and its four towers. Claire looked up. There were "murder holes" above her from which attack-ers would be doused with hot oil and arrows if they ever got this far. She looked down. Her horse was crossing a wooden plank set in the stone floor. She knew it was a trapdoor.

Claire looked grimly at Malcolm. "What's beneath us?" Whatever was there, she knew that anyone unfortunate to be riding or walking over the trapdoor when it opened would not survive.

"I dinna ken," he said. "Mayhap sharpened staves or beds of knives." His gaze was interested. "Ye ken the way of our warfare."

Claire was dry mouthed. "I've studied it a bit."

They rode past a pair of thick, studded, open doors and into the inner bailey.

She breathed. Although it was early, men and women were hurrying about the bailey, clearly intent on their morning tasks. Smoke was rising from two buildings that were directly ahead, built against the northern walls. She smelled baking bread and saw so many serving women going to and fro that she was certain that the smaller building contained the kitchens.

Beside it was the imposing, four-storied great hall. Black Royce was dismounting there, a small boy having materialized to take his horse. He patted the boy's head and headed up a wooden staircase, vanishing beyond a heavy wooden door.

She glanced around again, trying to absorb everything. A man in priestly robes stood in front of what had to be the chapel, a two-story stone hall built against the eastern walls. The rest of Black Royce's men were dismounting by the building she assumed to be their hall, which was above the stables. Women and children had appeared to greet them, the women wearing long leines, the children short ones. Some of the soldier's wives wore brats. Laughter and conversation ran rampant, as did hugs and kisses.

Claire breathed hard, overcome by the sights and sounds, the hustle and the bustle, and the emotion, of these fifteenth-century people. So far, all was as she had imagined, but she wasn't imagining anything now. She was at Carrick Castle, and it was 1427. Chills swept her. This was truly an amazing opportunity. Then she realized Malcolm was staring.

Unthinkingly, she smiled at him.

He started, and slowly he smiled back. "Ye be pleased."

She inhaled, because she was thrilled. "I am in a fifteenth-century fortress. I am very fond of history." She wasn't going to explain her degree to him. "I've read about what life is like in these times, but I am seeing it myself firsthand."

He was wry. "'Tis nay special." He slid from the horse, handed off his reins to a waiting boy and held up his hand for her.

Claire came to her senses. She was making the best of a bad situation, but taking his hand was not a good idea. She pretended not to notice and slid from the horse.

Malcolm thanked the boy, touched her back and indicated she would precede him up the stairs. Claire didn't understand.

She felt certain that men in his time did not allow women to go first, never mind that chivalry was a huge part of medieval culture.

He gestured impatiently. She gave him a grudging nod and then hurried up the stairs. She stepped through an oversize, paneled-wood door and into the great hall and blinked, surprised.

She had been expecting the very sparse furnishings of the period. She had been wrong. The walls and floors were stone, of course, and wood rafters supported the high ceiling. But there were several fine rugs on the floor, obviously from France, Italy or Belgium, instead of rushes. While there was a crude trestle table with two benches before a huge hearth in which a fire roared, there were also several arrangements of upholstered chairs, each finely and intricately carved by the best medieval craftsmen. A magnificent sword collection was displayed over the hearth. Several beautifully carved trunks served as tables. Oil paintings were on the walls, the portraits highly stylized as was standard for the period, and a stunning tapestry was on one wall. Claire had expected far more primitive conditions. She had expected dogs, mice, vermin and rushes on the floors. Black Royce's home was very well furnished for the fifteenth-century Highlands and as livable as a modern manor home. Still, something was missing—a personal touch. Claire would bet he was not married.

Royce had been helped out of his armor and was sitting in the room's largest chair, the upholstery burgundy velvet. A young woman handed him a mug of what Claire assumed to be ale. She now noticed that another young woman had taken his brat and mail and was carrying it away. Both females looked to be no more than twenty, if that, and they were blond and pretty. As Claire came to the realization that she was not the only young and attractive woman in the Highlands, a third woman appeared. She offered Malcolm a mug, smiling and blushing as she did so.

"Tapadh leat," he said, smiling back at her.

She was very pretty, with strawberry-blond hair, half Claire's size and nowhere close to twenty-one. Claire had always liked being tall, but suddenly she felt gawky and more like a giant than a woman. The blonde murmured, *"De tha sibh ag larraidh?"*

Claire's heart lurched with dread. Was this woman his love? And why did she care?

Malcolm shook his head, speaking softly in reply. His smile was terribly seductive.

The girl's color increased. She glanced at Claire and hurried from the hall.

Claire realized she was hugging herself. If he wanted to bed someone that young, it wasn't her affair. And of course he would. He was macho and oversexed. He was a medieval lord. He thought it his right and the dumb blonde probably thought it an honor to jump into his bed.

Claire was jealous. And that was even worse.

He took her arm but spoke to Royce. "I will show Claire t' her chamber."

Royce had stretched out his long, boot-clad legs and seemed to be utterly indifferent. He sent them both a lazy, knowing smile.

Claire flushed. If he thought she was Malcolm's lover, he was wrong. Claire carefully shrugged away from Malcolm's grasp. She followed him up a narrow staircase, trying to keep her distance from him while also trying not to stare at the back of his bare legs.

He pushed open a wood door and stood aside. "Ye can sleep here. We'll go to Dunroch t' morrow."

Claire wondered grimly if that would allow him a more leisurely romp in the hay with the strawberry blonde. She stepped past him into her chamber.

The room was very small, but there was a good-size fireplace on one wall and the bed had four carved posters and a fur coverlet. There was a single window, a slit without glass, the shutters open. As no fire had been started, it was icy in the room.

She knew she would never sleep. Her mind would race in circles.

The strawberry blonde appeared, sending Malcolm a smile before kneeling to start a fire.

Claire bristled. "Get a room." She smiled sweetly at him, belying her caustic tone.

He grinned. "Yer jealous o' the maid?"

Claire could not believe she had been so transparent. "Hardly. Oh, by the way, thank you for the loan." She fumbled with the brooch to give him back his plaid. She didn't want it. It reeked of his masculinity.

He reached out and grasped her hand, stilling it.

Claire stiffened, certain he was preparing to make a pass. That certainty increased when the blonde glanced at them and silently left the room, closing the door behind her.

Claire knew she should move away. Instead, the man's sex and heat pulled at her, encouraging her to step closer.

"'Tis cool and ye have nay clothes." He released her hand, moving to the single table in the room. There was one roughly carved wood chair there, along with a pitcher, a flask and two mugs. He poured liquid from the flask into a mug and handed it to her. Claire smelled the red wine and was immediately diverted. She was, she realized, thirsty and ravenous.

"'Tis a fine claret, from France," he said softly.

Claire saw the glitter in his gaze, and felt her own pulse escalate. She took a drink, wondering if he hoped to loosen her up, and then another. "It is good. Thank you."

He smiled, clearly having no intention of leaving the room. "Why do ye care if I bed the wench?"

His tone was casual but Claire almost leaped out of her skin. "I do not!"

"I dinna want the wench, lass," he murmured.

His meaning was beyond clear. He had the ability to speak

in such a suggestive tone that all she could do was think of sex. She had to do something before he put his hands on her.

He turned away, stunning her. She saw him pour another mug, his hand rock steady. When he faced her, he leaned one hip against the table.

"We ha' matters to discuss," he said bluntly, clearly aware of her discomfiture.

Claire inhaled. This was safer territory, indeed. But before she could ask a single question, his expression hardened. "I dinna ken the way o' yer world, Claire, but in my world, no one—not man, not woman, not child, not wild beast or dog, *no one*—disobeys me."

She stood at attention now. "I am sorry."

"Ye nay be sorry. Ye plot yer own causes!" he exclaimed.

She had been caught. "Sometimes I feel you can read my mind!" she said furiously.

"I can sense yer strongest thoughts as if ye speak them aloud," he shot back, standing. He set the mug down hard, hard enough that the table jumped. "In battle, I will protect ye. But that means ye hide if I say hide and run if I say run and ye dinna think, ever." His eyes flashed.

Claire knew she should not allow herself to debate him. She fought her temper and lost. "My lord," she said, meaning to speak demurely and failing. Instead, her tone was undeniably sarcastic. "In my world, women are leaders, warriors, queens without kings!"

"Ye argue now?" He was incredulous.

She flushed. Appease him! she thought frantically. "I am sorry. I don't know why I didn't hide. I am an utter coward. And I didn't intend to disobey you. It just happened."

His expression eased slightly. "Ye be nay coward, lass. Ye be strong an' brave." His gaze slid over the brat as if he could see through it. "I never seen such a body in me entire life."

He stared at her, his gray eyes fiercely intent.

This was the time to set some boundaries, Claire thought,

if she could. Her body raging just as it had in the woods, she took a long, deep breath. "In my world," she said carefully, "a man does not touch a woman without her permission."

His expression did not change.

"Do not pretend not to understand!" she cried desperately.

His tone was dangerous. "Oh, I ken, lass. I ken."

"What does that mean?"

Very softly, he said, "I took what ye offered an' I gave what ye wanted."

She gasped, outraged. But she also recalled wanting him desperately and having the best damn orgasm *ever.* She felt her cheeks burn. "I am not a…a…lightskirt! I have never… ever…jumped into bed with a stranger! Did you hypnotize me?"

"I dinna ken." His lashes lowered, fanning out on his high, beautiful cheekbones.

She swallowed, her mouth unbearably dry, while an ache raged between her thighs. Why couldn't she control her attraction? This wasn't helping matters—it was complicating them! "I don't throw myself at strange men. You need to keep your distance."

His gaze slid over her in a very suggestive manner. "I think," he said softly, "ye dinna throw yerself at any man, except me."

He was right. She was speechless.

He looked satisfied now.

"Did you hypnotize me in the woods?" she cried hoarsely. "Because the only other explanation for my behavior is that I have lost my mind—or it's been altered by what has happened!"

"Explain the word *hypnotize,*" he said.

She tried to speak more calmly. "It means mesmerize, entrance, enchant! When you look at me sometimes, it is very hard to think!"

"'Tis a small gift," he said smugly. "And a useful one."

"What, from Merlin the Magician?"

"Ye be so distressed an' angry, lass, an' why? Ye wanted it an' ye were pleased. 'Tis nay important now. Or be ye mad because I ha' decided not t' give over to such temptation again?"

It took her a long moment to decipher his words. *"What?"*

"I want ye, Claire. Dinna doubt me. But I be sworn to protect ye."

"Are you telling me you are not going to—" She stopped. She had been about to say make love, but if she did, he would laugh at her, she was certain.

His lashes lowered again. "Fuck ye?"

She inhaled. If a modern-day man spoke that way, it would probably be offensive. Coming from Malcolm, it only conjured up graphic and heated images of his driving his very extraordinary length into her repeatedly, with shocking power and stunning effect. If he did so now, right now, she would explode.

She swallowed. She had been certain she was going to have to hold him off. Now he was telling her he was not interested—except he was, because even now she felt him throbbing in the room. His lust was as tangible as the wine she could smell in her mug. Was he clever enough to be manipulating her? She was confused, and damn it, she was even dismayed.

"What would make you decide to be a gentleman?" she managed to say.

He looked up with a brief, self-derisive laugh. "I be nay gentle, lass, an' we both ken." His humor vanished. His gray eyes turned black. "I dinna wish to see ye lyin' dead beneath me."

Claire would have backed up if there was somewhere to go. "I don't understand." But the fear that had vanished during their conversation returned.

His gaze slowly moved over her, deliberately, and then it lifted to her face. "I want ye badly, very badly, but I dinna trust meself."

"What does that mean?" she gasped.

He was blunt. "I killed a maid. I willna do so again."

"You killed a woman?" Claire cried, backing up into the bed. The word *evil* went right through her mind.

"Ye be terrified," he said softly.

"No!" Her heart shrieked at her. Malcolm was not evil. She would bet her life on it. He had not just said what she thought he had. "You said you wanted to protect me," she breathed.

"Aye."

Claire realized she was panting. "Please don't tell me…!"

His face was hard. "She died in my arms, Claire. She died takin' her pleasure from me."

CHAPTER FIVE

CLAIRE REALLY NEEDED to sit down. Malcolm's gaze was hard, even angry, and entirely unwavering. But he was not evil—there was nothing evil about him. He could not have committed a pleasure crime.

"What happened?" she somehow said, seeing him not as he stood there, but with some woman beneath him, in the throes of her passion.

"I told ye!" He was sharp.

Claire finally sat down on the edge of the bed. "People do die during sex, I mean, normal sex. Even if it's not a pleasure crime, sometimes a man's heart stops. Or a woman's. It's from the excitement. If the woman's heart was weak, if she'd been ill, if she was older, feeble—"

He cut her off. "She wasna old. She was younger than ye. Her heart was strong."

This could not be happening. She did not want Malcolm to be an evil madman, but the parallels were glaring. *Strangers seducing the young and the innocent.* Malcolm was a stranger—and he was mesmerizing.

Had she been mesmerized in the woods?

"How well did you know her?" she asked carefully, fear uncoiling inside her.

"I dinna ken the lass." His gray gaze glittered.

"You were strangers."

"Aye."

She couldn't breathe. A challenge seemed to be in his

eyes, but she wasn't sure she could meet it. Sweat ran down her body in streams and she couldn't help but be afraid—and sickened. But somewhere deep inside herself, she refused to believe what he was telling her. "You killed her for *fun?*"

His eyes went wide. He said with great care, "I dinna amuse meself with death, Claire. I dinna ken me powers. I needed the maid, badly. I dinna wish to hurt her or see her dead."

In that instant, she saw the pain blazing in his eyes. *He was in the throes of guilt.* She slumped in relief, and sympathy swelled. "Malcolm, it was probably her heart."

He turned and lifted his mug of wine, draining it. "I didna stop when it was time to stop. I couldna think." He turned his heated silver eyes to her. "Like in the forest. Fer a moment, I couldna think o' anything but the pleasure I was takin' from ye."

She trembled, swept abruptly back to a vivid recollection of that stunning orgasm. She had stopped thinking in the woods, too. It had been impossible to be rational while in the throes of such desire. But now, she was uncertain. Clearly he regretted what had happened, deeply. As clearly, he was haunted by guilt. But he spoke as if he had killed the woman out of brute strength. And that sounded like rape.

His gaze was direct. "I didna rape her, or any woman. She wanted me."

Claire believed him. What woman wouldn't want the medieval stud facing her? And that only made it harder for her to understand what had happened. It had to have been the woman's heart, she thought. It could not be anything else. A madman did not feel guilt.

"Now ye ken why I willna bed ye," he said firmly.

She shivered. They were having a terrible conversation about a ghastly sexual death and she was having grave reservations about this man, but she still couldn't escape his sexuality. It seethed in the room and his words conjured up the image of her in his embrace, passionately entwined.

"That's fine," she said through dry lips. "I don't want to share your bed. Not now, not ever."

He gave her a disbelieving look.

Claire flushed. Her body no longer obeyed her will, but she did have a will. "When I sleep with a man, it is because he has my heart," she said slowly, and she felt her color increase.

His eyes widened. "Surely, ye be in jest."

Claire was mute. She wished she hadn't revealed herself that way.

He choked, but she realized he wanted to laugh. His face straight, he said, "An' ye have loved men, lass, aye?"

She became affronted and sought refuge there. "If you want to know how many men I have made love to, I am not telling you!"

"I begin t' ken, aye, I do." He smiled endearingly. "It be fine, lass, really. 'Tis a shame, though, to have only had a dozen or so men in yer life."

"There were two!" she cried.

He smiled at her.

Claire could not believe this medieval hunk had the wit to trap her into the truth. She stared, outraged and even insulted. At least he would never know the details of her love life. Her college lover had been gorgeous and smart, even if he had cheated on her. Her second lover, James, had been great to brainstorm with and debate, but rather lacking in the performance department. This man, of course, did not even know the definition of the word *faithful,* but he wouldn't have any performance problems, either. And she would never, ever reveal that it had been three years since she'd last had sex.

He was smiling as he turned away to refill his mug. Claire didn't like his knowing smile, either, except that it made him shockingly handsome. Maybe the real battle wasn't with him, but herself.

And Claire thought about the terrible battle in the forest. "We need to talk, but not about sharing a bed."

He set the mug down, facing her. His expression was stunningly serious. "Aye. Ye defended me fer a terrible crime an' ye defended me in the wood. We be strangers, Claire, not kin. Why?"

She bit her lip. "I don't know why."

Silence fell. His gaze slipped to her throat and she realized he was staring at the pendant she wore. "My father had a stone like that, lass. He wore it till the day he died."

Claire was immediately interested. Of course his father was dead, otherwise Malcolm would not be laird. She wanted all the information she could get now. She wanted to know everything about the man standing before her. She told herself it would help her survive this ordeal. "How did he die?"

"He died at the Red Harlaw, lass, a huge and bloody battle."

Claire went still. "Your father was Brogan Mor."

His gaze narrowed. "I didna tell ye his name."

Her heart was thundering in her chest. What kind of coincidence was this? "Do you want to hear something ironic?" She wet her lips, not waiting for his response. She didn't have to, for his regard was intensely riveted to her now. "I was on my way to Scotland when you came to my store. I was leaving the following night. And while I was arriving in Edinburgh, my plan was to drive directly to Mull and stay at Malcolm's Point, so I could visit Dunroch."

His temples throbbed. He did not say a word, but from his expression, he did not seem terribly surprised.

"Your father is in the history books. I read he died in 1411 at the Red Harlaw, but of course, I had no idea I'd be meeting his son shortly thereafter." She sat back down, shaken. Maybe, given the dates, she should have realized that Malcolm was Brogan Mor's son. "There's nothing on your line, Malcolm, after the death of your father."

He came forward. "He was a great man, lass, a great warrior, a great laird. Did yer books say so?"

"I'm sorry. They only mentioned the date of his death and that he led the Macleans in the battle."

"Not all of them," Malcolm said. "The Maclean of north Mull, Tiree and Morvern sits at Duart."

"Black Royce is not laird of his clan?"

"Nay. His lands were granted by a royal charter long ago. He be earl of Morvern, but vassal to me. He be a southern Maclean, lass."

Claire couldn't imagine Royce being subservient to Malcolm. He hadn't acted so, she thought. "Who became laird of your clan when Brogan died, Malcolm? You were obviously too young to do so."

"I was nine years old when Brogan died an' I became laird. Royce helped me, spending much of his time at Dunroch, until I turned fifteen. That day I needed no one beside me to rule."

Before Claire could assimilate that he had become a clan chief at nine years old, and the actual leader at fifteen, his gaze moved back to the stone she wore. "Tell me about the stone."

He kept going back to the pendant. "It was my mother's. Why?"

"Brogan lost his stone at Harlaw," Malcolm said, staring at her pendant. "'Twas black, not white, like ye have, but it be the same. 'Tis charmed with powers of healing. There are other lairds an' even clerics who wear a charm stone. But ye ken."

"This is a piece of moonstone set in gold," Claire cried nervously. "It isn't magical!"

"How did yer mother get it? It belonged to a Highlander, lass."

Claire went still. "I don't know. I never thought to ask. I was a child when she died. But she never took it off. The truth is, I always thought—no, I always sensed—it had something to do with my father."

His eyes widened. "If yer father gave it to yer mother," he began.

"She could have bought it in a pawnshop! Or my father could have bought it there, if it was even his." Oddly, she felt panic. Had her father been a Scot?

"Ye be distressed. Why?"

Claire shook her head, turning away, hugging his brat to her body. "I didn't know him and he never knew about me. I was a mistake, the result of a single night of passion." She whirled. "You're almost making me think that my father is a Highlander—a contemporary one, of course."

"Ye dinna look like any Highland lass, but I be thinkin' ye be connected t' me, somehow."

She sputtered, "I am connected to you because you ripped me from my time and brought me back here with you!"

He smiled grudgingly. "Aye."

"How? How do you travel through time?" This was the single most important question of all, if she was ever going to get back to the twenty-first century.

"I will it."

Claire stared and he stared steadily back. "Some wizard or monk, some shaman, must have found a black hole and figured out accidentally how to use it," she finally said. "And the knowledge was carefully passed along." It crossed her mind that if a medieval man could travel through time, surely peers of hers were secretly doing the same thing.

"Nay. 'Tis a gift from the Ancients."

She could not look away. "The ancient shamans?" Was he telling her that time travel dated back to pre-Christian times?

"The old gods, Claire," he said softly. "The gods most of Alba have forsaken."

She felt chills. Her theory had to be correct. Someone, perhaps in medieval times, perhaps much earlier, had stumbled upon time travel. Such knowledge would be carefully guarded and carefully passed on. Of course he believed that his ability was given by the gods. His culture was a primitive one. Throughout time, mankind sought explanations for events and phenomena they did not understand in religion.

But he was treading in dangerous waters with such beliefs. "Which old gods?" she asked, fear arising.

He just looked at her.

"If you believe you have powers from a god, any god, even Jesus, that's heresy."

His mouth hardened. "I be Catholic, Claire."

Claire shuddered. No Catholic believed as he did. Her mind raced. Heresy was a serious crime in the Middle Ages. In Europe, the Church had actively and aggressively prosecuted heretical movements, using the notorious court of the Inquisition to do so. Heretics were usually excommunicated and outlawed, not executed. On the other hand, a member of the Lollard movement had been burned for heresy by the Church, right there in Scotland. The date was unforgettable, because the great wave of prosecutions had come a century later.

"Have you ever heard of John Resby?"

His eyes widened. "Aye."

Claire tensed. "He was burned at the stake for his beliefs in 1409."

"I was a small boy."

Claire inhaled. "Then you know you should not be talking so openly about old gods and having powers a man should not have."

"'Tis a privy discussion," he said darkly. "I be trustin' ye, lass. Ye have no fanatical beliefs."

"How would you know that? But you're right. I'm not even Catholic, Malcolm. I'm Episcopalian." And that made her a heretic in his time, as well. "Your secret's safe with me."

He nodded. "If I didna trust ye, I'd never tell ye the truth."

She couldn't imagine why he would trust her, an absolute stranger. He added, "But ye'll come to the mass with me, Claire."

"Of course I will. I'm not a fool—I have no problem playing along with orthodoxy until I go home."

His gaze flickered oddly and he walked away from her.

"How many of you are there?" she asked grimly. The ramifications of his beliefs kept growing. A man who had extraordinary powers could be accused of witchcraft, sorcery, association with the devil. Thank God the great witch hunts were in the next century, not this one. "Can Black Royce travel through time? Is he one of you? Does he believe this power comes from the Ancients, too? And how have you kept yourselves secret?"

A cool smile flashed. "Why do ye care about Royce's powers?"

"He's different, like you," Claire said firmly.

"Nay." He turned away from her, his stance stiff and braced. "Royce be the earl of Morvern, nothin' more."

Claire hesitated, very aware that Malcolm was closing the discussion now. But they were treading upon dangerous and probably forbidden territory. His beliefs—and his ability to travel through time—were undoubtedly a very secret subject. But she was beyond certain that Royce had Malcolm's abilities, and probably his beliefs, too. She slowly walked up behind him. When he turned, she was aware that only an inch separated them, and that she should not use any feminine wiles to get the answers she wanted. She slowly laid her hand on his chest.

A huge jolt of desire stabbed her as her palm smoothed the linen shirt flat against his hard muscle. "Tell me. Finish it. You've already told me a terrible secret, one that threatens your life, so tell me the rest."

His smile was twisted. "Dinna play me, Claire." But his eyes blazed and not just with anger. Claire recognized lust.

"Why not?" Touching him was making her feel weak and faint. "You've played me from the start."

"Then ye play with yer life."

In spite of the pulse now throbbing against the silk of her thong, she felt more chills. "No. I trust you, too." Oddly, she realized she did. "How many of you can time travel? And why do you do it? Do you belong to some kind of religious order, a secret society?" But she knew the answer.

His stare hardened and his hand covered hers, pressing her palm even more firmly to his chest. "Ye ask too many questions. Ye dinna need so many answers."

"Not fair! You brought me here—I do need to know," she cried. And she did what would have been unthinkable in New York City—she slid her hand into the slit neckline of his leine, her fingers brushing a heavy cross and chain and then settling against his hot skin.

His smile was tight. "Fire, lass," he warned.

Something bumped her hip. Claire tried to breathe. "You said you trust me. You brought me here. I'm a historian, Malcolm, a scholar. That's why I know so much about your time. Please. I have to know." She looked at him imploringly.

He breathed hard. "The Masters are sworn to defend God an' the Ancients, keep Faith, an' guard the Books."

She gasped, trembling with the excitement of discovery.

"We are sworn to protect ye, Claire, an' all like ye. *Protect Innocence.* 'Tis the holiest of the vows after the vows we make to God."

She could not look away. "I knew it. You're not the first knight to belong to a secret order with heretical beliefs. Will you tell me the name of the order?"

His smile was like a snarl. "There be no name." And he jerked away from her, his leine bulging over his stiff manhood.

She could not retreat now. "What are you defending God from? What are you defending the Ancients from? What are you defending the Books and people like me from?"

He whirled. "Evil."

Chills broke out all over Claire's body.

"What be wrong, Claire? Ye look frightened. Or have ye asked too many questions fer that pretty little head?" He was cool, mocking and furious.

She swallowed. "I don't care how condescending you are. Yes, you have frightened me. We both know there is evil in the world. You just made it sound…organized."

His stare intensified, making her want to squirm. "Do ye nay believe in the devil, lass?"

And Claire thought about her mother. *She stared at the back of the frayed tweed sofa as she hid behind it, trembling with fear, wishing her mother would come home. A shadow drifted into the room…*

"No, I do not," she gasped, sweating profusely now. "Do you *want* to frighten me?"

His expression lost its ferocity. "Ye pushed me, lass. An' ye seduced me with a simple touch. I want t' protect ye, but mayhap this be best. Mayhap ye need ken the way o' life here."

She seized the opening. "How many Masters are there?"

He made a harsh sound, stalking over to the table to pour more wine. Claire realized he was not going to give up his fellow knights.

She changed tack. "Why were we attacked? Who were those men and what did they want?"

"They were Moray's men. Moray wants the page, Claire. He also wants me dead."

Claire tensed, suddenly sick in her soul. "Moray is your enemy."

"The earl of Moray be God's enemy, Claire. He sent Sybilla to yer shop t' find the page. He must not find the page or the book." He added intensely, "He be yer enemy, as well."

She could not shake the sick feeling. "I get it. The books are holy relics, really. You guys are fighting over them and you'll kill to discover them—and to prevent your enemy from taking them."

"The Cathach be safe in its shrine," Malcolm said. "I be sworn t' guard the sacred books, Claire. If the Cladich be near, I must use all me power to find it an' return it to Iona."

"You keep saying books. How many are there?"

"Three."

"I know the Cathach is the Book of Wisdom, the Cladich the Book of Healing. What does the third book offer?"

"It holds every power known to the Ancients."

Claire's insides lurched. Somehow, she knew this was not good. "I don't understand."

"The Duaisean holds the power to leap time, the power to take life, the power t' give it. In it is the power o' minds, o' slavery, o' dreams. There be many more powers, too." He was grim. "This book gives *anyone* its powers."

That sounded terrifying. Of course, no book could give anyone such powers. And while she didn't believe in these powers, he did, and so did everyone who was a part of his order. She knew the power of the mind. These Masters were probably empowered by their beliefs. Hadn't she seen Malcolm in action on the battlefield? He'd had superhuman prowess—or that was how it had appeared.

Claire sought calm and failed. "Where is the third book?"

He simply looked at her.

Oh, my God, Claire thought. She tried to remind herself that the book had no power, but she whispered, "Your enemies have it."

"Aye. It's with Moray an' it has been with him fer a long time." He added in warning, "He has great powers, Claire, an' nay Master has been able to defeat him."

And Moray wanted Malcolm dead. She did not want to care—this wasn't her affair, not at all—but if Malcolm believed Moray to be invincible, he would never defeat him. Suddenly she wasn't excited, not at all.

Instead, she was afraid, not for herself, but for Malcolm.

WHEN MALCOLM LEFT, Claire ignored his parting words to rest. Her head was spinning—sleep would be impossible.

She turned and slowly paced the small chamber, trying to sort through everything she had learned. Malcolm was a religiously motivated knight. There was no doubt he took his vows very seriously and would probably give his life to fulfill them. The Masters had to form a secret society, otherwise they'd be prosecuted for their heretical beliefs. Still, no matter their faith, they seemed to serve mankind. That was admirable and she admired him now, even if she wasn't sure she should.

And now she was beginning to fully understand. There was no question that the three books were incredible historical artifacts. But these men believed the books to have great powers given by the old gods. They were powerful and empowering holy relics. Of course, factions would form to fight over those relics and kill to acquire them, or to prevent them from falling into the wrong hands.

This power game had nothing to do with her—except that she owned a store filled with rare and old books and Malcolm had brought her back in time with him. And Moray's men had tried to kill her, too. She changed her mind. This war had everything to do with her now. Somehow, she was smack in the middle of it.

What are you defending God from? What are you defending the Ancients from? What are you defending the books and people like me from?

Evil.

Claire did not want to theorize about evil in the Middle Ages. Her plate was full. Moray was probably an ambitious, ruthless and clever nobleman, and nothing more. He had the Duaisean, but he did not have extraordinary powers, no matter what Malcolm claimed. And he wasn't her enemy—or was he?

She became grim. If she was under Malcolm's roof and his protection, then she probably was Moray's enemy. She did not like the thought.

Uneasy, Claire walked over to the narrow window and instantly, she was diverted.

The Highlands stretched away into eternity, a blend of the sparkling blue waters below and emerald-green hills beyond. The sun had risen, high and bright, in a cloudless, vividly blue sky. The water was almost iridescent, and the forests glittered, too. The view was majestic, breathtaking, and it made her suddenly feel that everything was almost worth it.

She gripped the sill. Last night she had been in New York, packing for her trip to Scotland. She had been bound for Dunroch and she had yearned to meet Dunroch's laird. And he had appeared in her store, whisking her back to his time. How could this be a coincidence?

Claire touched the stone pendant. Malcolm felt she had some connection to his world, other than the obvious one. She was starting to wonder if he was right. And every time he was near, there was that intense physical pull, mostly desire, but there was even more than that.

She did not want any more internal debates. She was missing a thousand answers, but she wasn't going to figure it all out now. This scene was exactly what she needed, a brief respite, a moment of cleansing beauty and peace. She left the chamber, determined to enjoy the view from a better vantage point. She really needed to chill out, big-time.

The ramparts had been a story above her chamber. She didn't hesitate, finding a small, winding staircase at the end of the short hall. She hurried up. The moment she stepped onto the walkway, not far from a corner watchtower, she inhaled deeply, finally smiling.

Claire walked to the crenellated edge of the ramparts, overwhelmed by the beauty of the land. Where in Morvern were they, exactly?

"Hello, Claire."

The voice was frighteningly familiar. Claire whirled to face Sibylla. Her heart skidded as she met the other woman's black, fathomless eyes.

Sibylla was smiling. She wasn't dressed like a modern

cat burglar, and Claire recognized the style of her gown. The style was popular in France among the wealthiest noblewomen and far more immodest than its English counterpart, low cut, the bodice and sleeves fitted. But now Claire saw the glitter in Sibylla's eyes. Her expression was one of sheer lust.

Sibylla had time traveled, too. "How did you get in here?" Had somebody been stupid enough to lower the drawbridge for her? Or had she leaped from the future into the past, right inside Carrick Castle? "Malcolm is inside."

Sibylla's smile stretched. "I don't want Malcolm, I want you. You don't have to be so frightened, Claire. I won't hurt you. I let you live, didn't I?"

"What do you want?" Claire cried, not reassured.

"I want the page," Sibylla said harshly, suddenly enraged. "You have it, I am certain. I went back—I went through every damn book. It's not there!"

Claire gasped. "I didn't even hear about the damn page until last night! Why do you think it's in my store, or that I have it? I don't!" She glanced over her shoulder at the tower. Where was the guard?

Sibylla laughed. "They're dead. And I have changed my mind. You did not tell me what I wish to know, so I will have to hurt you, won't I?" She smiled. "The pleasure is mine, Claire."

Claire turned to flee when she was seized from behind. Sibylla whipped her back around with stunning strength. Before Claire could react, she had her pressed against the crenellated wall with so much force Claire thought her spine might snap in half. And then she put one powerful hand on Claire's face, increasing the terrible pressure to Claire's back.

Her eyes shimmered with bloodlust. "I have waited so long for this, Claire." And she bent close and slowly licked Claire's pulsing jugular artery.

Claire couldn't breathe now. She was afraid she'd be broken in half if she struggled. She tried to stay still, as

Sibylla sent her tongue up and down her throat, but she couldn't stand it and she cried out, "Please stop!"

"Tell me where the page is or I will kill you," she murmured, her mouth close to Claire's. "After I make you weep in pleasure."

Claire felt tears begin because the pain in her back was unbearable. Just when a vast gray world began to descend upon her, Sibylla released her.

Claire straightened, gasping in pain, and then went down on her knees, reaching for the stone at her throat. The gray shadows receded, replaced by vivid blue skies and Sibylla's frighteningly dark, hollow eyes. "I'll tell you everything," she lied, her back against the stone wall. She slowly pushed herself to stand.

Sibylla smiled. "Take your time. No one will look for us here and I don't mind if you resist." Her eyes gleamed.

Claire closed her eyes, sweating in fear, her back throbbing. She had to lead Sibylla on and she needed help. The woman had superhuman strength and if she didn't need Claire, she'd probably kill her in the most unimaginable way.

The stone was scalding her hand. Suddenly she knew what she could do. She could tell Sibylla the page was hidden at her store, and the woman would take her back there to find it.

She would be home in her relatively safe world—but she would never see Malcolm again.

Claire realized there was no decision to make. "It's in my chamber just below us."

"If you are lying, I will torture you before I kill you. There will be so much pain, Claire. You will beg me to take your life, but I won't do so quickly."

Despite Sibylla's threat, her fear had entirely receded. Now she could think clearly, effortlessly. "No one was in the hall when I came up here. Malcolm believes I am sleeping. I doubt anyone will see us if we go inside."

"You go ahead of me," Sibylla ordered and she gripped Claire's shoulder, her nails breaking Claire's skin through all of her clothing. "If we are espied, you die."

"Fine." She walked slowly ahead, still holding the stone, which was cool now. When she realized she had been clutching it to her throat like a child's ragged security blanket, she dropped it. She started down the narrow, circular staircase carefully. Adrenaline began.

Sibylla was a single step behind her.

Claire whirled and seized her ankle, pulling her forward as hard as she could. As Sibylla fell, Claire dashed to the steps above her, screaming as loudly as possible for help. Sibylla started to leap up, her expression murderous. But as she straightened, Claire was waiting for her. She kicked her in the face, a front kick her personal trainer would have been proud of.

But Sibylla only teetered slightly backward and then she kept on coming.

Claire turned and ran, reaching for her Taser, thinking, holy shit! The woman was a female Terminator and she was two steps behind her. Pissing off that woman was not a good idea. And then she heard racing footsteps coming up the hall below them and Malcolm shouting for her.

Of course he would save the day! Claire burst onto the ramparts, then realized Sibylla was gone.

She turned, shocked, breathing hard, as Malcolm, Royce and six men leaped through the open doorway, swords ringing as they were unsheathed.

"She's gone!" Claire was in disbelief. Sibylla hadn't passed her and she couldn't have turned to flee back into the keep without running directly into the men. She had vanished into thin air.

Malcolm sheathed his sword, reaching for her. Claire didn't think twice; she went into his arms. "It was Sibylla."

He tilted up her chin, his eyes blazing, as Royce barked orders to the men. "She hurt ye."

"I'm fine." She began to tremble. "That woman has the strength of a dozen men."

His nostrils flared. "Yer bleeding on yer shoulder." But he was looking at her throat, as if he knew what Sibylla had done.

"I'm fine," she cried as Royce strode over, looking even more enraged than Malcolm.

"Sibylla will pay," he said. "No one enters Carrick without my pleasure." He turned to Malcolm. "Two men are dead."

That woman had so casually murdered the guards, Claire thought, shivering. But Sibylla was pure evil. She had seen the darkness in her soulless eyes—and she prayed she would never look into her eyes again.

But it was worse than that. Like Malcolm, she could time travel.

Royce turned to Claire. "If she wanted ye dead, ye'd be dead, as well."

Claire wet her lips. "She thinks I have the page."

Both men stared, eyes wide. Malcolm turned to Royce. "Sibylla does nay ha' it, but I ken who does."

Royce looked unhappy then. "Malcolm."

"Nay, dinna try t' stop me now."

Claire had no idea what the exchange meant. But now that her adrenaline was gone, she realized she was shaken and exhausted. She felt violated by what Sibylla had done—and what she had wanted to do.

Instantly, as if he knew, Malcolm turned, putting his arm around her and holding her upright. "Come, lass. We'll speak inside."

Claire nodded and they went back down the stairs. Images flashed and she saw her brief struggle with Sybilla and the woman's pale, furious face, her black, frightening eyes. "How did I make such an enemy?"

Malcolm guided her into the chamber and directly to the bed. Claire's insides instantly tightened and she glanced at him. His steady regard met hers. "This time, Claire, ye obey me." He threw the fur cover aside and took her arm, guiding her onto the down pallet.

Claire jerked off her cowboy boots and slid under the covers. He arranged the pillow behind her head, his expression deadly serious, his mind clearly not on his actions. But he was fussing over her and something melted in her heart. How could such a powerful, arrogant and presumptuous man reduce himself to fixing her pillows? Maybe she should not be so quick to stereotype him, she thought.

She touched his hand. Sparks ignited, but then, they were never really extinguished, not when he was nearby. "What is it?"

He met her gaze, hesitated, then sat down by her hip. "I have vowed t' protect ye an' ye almost died today. Not once, but twice."

Claire did not want to think about everything that had happened on the ramparts with Sibylla. "Why does she think I have the page? Because I own a specialty bookstore?"

"Because she didna find it in yer store." He suddenly lifted her cap sleeve. "'Tis a scratch."

Claire didn't care about the scratches. "So what? Why does everyone think it's there, anyway?"

"I dinna ken, Claire. If Moray sent Sibylla t' yer store, I believe the page be there—or was once."

Claire absorbed that. "How did she get into Carrick? She leaped time, didn't she? To get away."

"Moray dispenses the powers from the Duaisean with great care. He has made her strong so she can slay his enemies an' she can leap time in order to serve him well. Aye, she probably vanished into the near future."

Claire tensed. She didn't like the fact that the bad guys could travel through time, too. She began to realize that the woman could never be captured if she could simply leap away into another time. However, that was suddenly the least of her worries. She impulsively touched Malcolm's arm. "He can *dispense* powers?"

"Aye. Why do ye think his armies be so powerful? They nay be ordinary men, lass."

Claire began to breathe rapidly and shallowly. "I know you believe in the books, but I don't. His armies are ordinary— human. She's ordinary, even if her power was shocking." She realized she was near tears, but her near hysteria was from overload and exhaustion.

He remained grim. "I ken ye dinna wish t' hear the truth, but 'tis dangerous fer ye now, Claire. Ye need to ken the truth o' the world."

Claire realized she might lose it if he said another word. "Don't you dare," she cried.

His gaze was searching, then it softened. "Lass, t'morrow we go t' me home an' we'll discuss these matters. Ye'll be safe there." He smiled reassuringly at her. "Dunroch's walls are thick an' sure. I have affairs to attend, but I willna be gone fer long."

It took Claire a moment. She sat up. "You intend to leave me at Dunroch? Absolutely not! I am going with you!" she cried. And she realized that she did not wish to be separated from Malcolm. The issue was one of her safety.

"Ye canna come with me, lass. I willna be gone long. A few days, a week, nay more."

"A week," she gasped, horrified. "Where are you going? You are sworn to protect me! Sibylla may decide to make hamburger out of me while you are away! And what about Aidan—and Moray? Does Moray think I have the page, too?"

"I must speak with MacNeil. I go to Iona, and then, t' Awe."

She hardly cared. She seized both of his hands. "Take me with you," she cried. "Do not leave me behind."

His gaze locked with hers. His mouth turned down and his eyes filled with a torment she didn't understand. He suddenly touched her throat. "I'll be the one t' kill her," he said flatly.

And his fingertips stroked the exact place Sybilla had licked her. But the thick, callused pads caused a delicious shiver to arise.

Claire knew a tear fell. "She didn't hurt me. I'm a wuss. I'm tired. And I'll admit it—I'm in over my head."

"Yer afraid," he said flatly. "I'll die afore allowin' ye to be hurt, Claire."

Claire went still, and damn it, she felt a thrill. "Because of your vows," she somehow whispered.

"Nay. Because o' ye, lass. Because o' ye."

Her heart exploded in her chest.

Carefully, he looked from her eyes to her mouth.

So much desire made her feel faint. Claire felt the huge tension throbbing between them.

His gaze slowly lifted. And then he leaned toward her— and kissed her throat.

Claire gasped as his mouth feathered the skin where she had been violated. And as the pulse in her sex exploded with urgency, she clasped his hard, stubbled jaw. The promise of so much raw sex coursed in the room. Did it matter that he didn't love her and she didn't love him? Nothing had ever mattered less.

He straightened and stared.

"It's all right," Claire breathed, wanting to encourage him.

He was silent. "We play with fire, lass," he said quietly.

"I don't care!"

His gaze drifted again to her mouth and she knew he was finally about to kiss her. And she could no longer think of a single reason why he should not.

"Fire," he said harshly, "an' evil."

CHAPTER SIX

MALCOLM BRUSHED his mouth against hers.

Claire did not move. She had wanted to kiss this man for so long, and the featherlight caress of his lips sent such desire through her. She had never been kissed by such a powerful man and she had never known such a gentle kiss, either. Claire moaned softly, reaching for his huge shoulders. Dear God, she wanted him to deepen the kiss.

He had a hand on each side of her, pressed into the bed, as he played her lips, slowly but insistently, kissing her again and again. The pressure steadily increased, his tongue beginning to flick at the seam of her lips. Claire could not stand it. She cried out.

He became still. Claire did not care. She clawed his shoulders, moaning shamelessly, thrusting her tongue at his lips, demanding more while urgently spreading her thighs. For one more instant, he didn't move, not even to return the kiss, while she frantically tried to thrust her tongue past his strong, closed mouth. Why was he doing this?

And then he caught her head in his powerful hands. Claire went still and he kissed her hard and openmouthed, instantly reversing their roles. His kiss was so demanding that she felt the wall against her head through the pillows.

And Claire kissed him back, shocked that so much pleasure could be gained from a kiss. And damn it, a kiss was not enough!

As he sucked on her mouth, his tongue locking fiercely

with hers, Claire ran her hands over his hard chest, wanting the damn tunic to disappear. She wanted to feel every inch of his hard, powerful body, but not through coarse linen. She wanted to touch his skin, explore his muscles, taste every inch of him. She found the slit at the neckline and slid her hand through, shoving aside the large cross he wore, gasping when she felt his bare, hot skin under her palm. This was so good....

He grunted. She tried to move her hand lower but it was impossible, the neckline wasn't deep. She jerked her hand out and then frantically stroked down his rib cage and hard, tight abdomen, over the tunic, toward his navel. She cried out wildly when she felt the hot, huge, bulbous tip of his erection thrusting at her.

She was going to die if he did not take her with that hardness....

He jerked her hand away from his penis, his grip uncompromising, breaking the kiss as he did so. "Nay, lass," he breathed hard, his eyes savagely bright.

"Damn you," she wept, writhing in an urgency she could not bear. She managed to gaze at him through her tears, panting hard. Shocked, Claire realized he was standing firm to some dumb notion he had about not sleeping with her. Furious, desperate, she wanted to strike him, but he held both of her wrists now and there was no possible way to do so.

"I need t' leave ye," he said harshly, and he released her.

Claire reared up, fists flying, pummeling his chest. "Like hell!"

He used his forearm to brush the blows aside the way he might an annoying fly. Then he placed his hand abruptly on her bare knee, pressing her leg into the bed.

Claire went still, her heart almost exploding with comprehension, anticipation, more insane fire licking between her thighs. "Yes," she whispered.

His face hard and tight, his eyes glittering, he slid his hand up her leg and beneath her skirt, all the way to the wet cleft there.

She gasped, sinking back against the pillows, arching shamelessly for him. "Hurry," she said hoarsely.

His eyes flared brighter, and Claire blinked back hot tears when his knuckles brushed her silk-clad, throbbing sex. He moved his long blunt fingers beneath her thong, and held it suspended from her flesh. His knuckles lay deep where she was the most sensitive and distended.

"Oh, God," Claire gasped.

"Aye," he said thickly, and he jerked her skirt up to her waist, his gaze riveted on her. "Ye wear a string. A string with lace an' beads."

Claire whispered, "Please."

He edged his thumb slowly over one distended lip, then down the other one. Claire bucked as his thumb traced the swollen outline of her clitoris. She gave in and came, bursting into a thousand pieces, crying out in anguish, pleasure, ecstasy.

And then she felt his tongue probing her there.

The delicious and agonizing pressure renewed itself with stunning force, as his strong tongue tasted her, stroked her, circling her. It had been so long—and never like this! She broke apart again, weeping, moaning, flayed by his tongue, again and again, crying out in part pleasure, part pain. He did not stop, testing her threshold, pressing into her again, causing an even greater, more violent orgasm. Claire sobbed and his tongue finally stilled. She panted and breathed and finally she floated back to the bed.

Claire lay back, incapable of any movement now. She wasn't certain how long he had been performing oral sex on her, but she'd had so many orgasms she had lost count. Her body actually hurt now. And Malcolm hadn't come.

What had just happened? How had she let this happen? And what about his pleasure? She was finally sane again. She no longer knew herself. Was this his idea of foreplay?

Was he going to try to mount her now, when she was

finally sated, as she had never, not even once in her life, been sated by anyone?

She bit her lip, shocked when a surge of desire formed at the thought of his moving onto her, into her. But he was motionless. His cheek rested intimately on her thigh and she was now acutely aware of the huge tension in his stiff, rigid body.

"Malcolm." She did not recognize her own voice.

She finally realized he was in the midst of some kind of internal battle.

He breathed hard, harshly. His hand moved over her sex, just once, a sweeping caress.

He left the bed, throwing the fur over her, and their gazes met.

Instantly she sat up, alarmed. His eyes blazed with lust. The hunger she saw there was frankly frightening. His face was hard and his huge erection stood up against the linen, making her mouth dry, her heart race all over again. Claire tore her gaze from his blazing eyes, beginning to tremble.

She died taking her pleasure from me.

Maybe that woman had died because he was so sexual and so strong.

It was a horrifying thought.

He turned and left.

Claire gasped, wide-eyed. Her every instinct was to run after him, but to do what? He did not need comfort—did he? He needed sex, but he had given, not asking for a thing in return. She leaned back into the pillows, stunned. Maybe it was time to rethink her opinion of him.

HE STOOD ABSOLUTELY STILL on the ramparts between the two towers, the whisper of an early-morning breeze flattening his leine against his bare thighs, his hand grasping the hilt of his sword. Tension vibrated within. A glacial chill had cloaked Urquhart the moment he had passed through the gatehouse. Moray was waiting for him.

His stomach twisted into knots. There had been many warnings and he had ignored them all. He glanced up the allure and down it, but no one else was present. He looked below, first into the bailey at the peasants there, and then into the wide silver blue belly of Loch Ness.

A breeze shifted past him, whispering his name. "Calum."

And the voice was not the wind, but Moray. The lord of darkness—his mortal enemy.

He trembled with his rage and hatred, and pushed open the wood door of the stone tower.

Darkness wafted onto the ramparts like an oncoming storm, dulling the light of the rising sun, and for one moment, he could not see.

Moray smiled at him.

His teeth were shockingly white. His skin was bronzed from centuries of sun, but he seemed all of thirty and five, if that. He was dressed in the English-court manner, his hose scarlet, the black wool doublet trimmed in ermine, a red-and-black brat pinned over one shoulder by a ruby-and-gold brooch. Moray was Defender of the Realm and King James's favored counsel.

"I have been waiting for you, Malcolm," Moray purred, speaking English. He was laughing as he spoke.

"Tha mi air mo sharachadh." I am tired of this.

Moray seemed delighted, his smile widening. "Then what has taken you so long?" He lifted his sword and it rang as it slipped from its sheath.

Thought vanished. Sanity was gone. He drew his sword and thrust. "A Bhrogain!"

Moray easily met the blow, and when the two huge blades locked, he knew he faced the kind of strength and power he had never before imagined. He had never lost a battle, but in that single moment, he doubted his ability to defeat Moray.

Moray deflected every blow as if he were a child in napkins.

The battle became absurd. Moray played him while he had no strength left to wield his sword. He should have listened, he should have waited. His powers were too new, too unformed. And suddenly Moray thrust past his defenses and his blade sank deep into muscle and flesh, into bone.

He gasped as a terrible comprehension began, accompanying the blazing pain and heat.

Moray smiled, pushing the blade more completely into his body, through tendon and muscle, and he was completely skewered to the wall.

Moray withdrew, the blade dripping his blood.

He tried to fight the sudden and terrible wave of weakness, but it was impossible and he sank to the floor. The tower had become shockingly still. He choked on pain, fury, blood, realizing that Moray had vanished.

He closed his eyes tightly, but not against the burning pain in his chest. All he could think of were the sacred vows he had recently taken. He had vowed upon the ancient and holy books at the sacred shrine, to defend God and mankind. But evil had just left the tower and it would hunt the Innocent from one end of the realm to the other, in all times.

And in that stunning moment of clarity and comprehension, he knew he must live to protect Innocence as Brogan and his ancestors had.

A terrible lust began. It was the lust to live, and it raged.

Somehow he struggled to his feet, clutching his bleeding chest. His body screamed at him for life. Urges began which he suddenly, instantly, understood—urges to take power so he might restore his own. But he was alone and his life was rapidly draining away. As death crept over him, he prayed to the Ancients who had first brought the Masters to the earth.

A woman rushed into the tower, shouting his name in alarm.

He was near death. She was unfocused in outline, dancing before his eyes, the tower swimming in gray shadows. And he was shocked, because he knew she had been sent to him.

She ran to him. Before she even touched him, he realized that she was young, wholesome, healthy and filled with so much life force that he choked on it. He reached for her. She helped him stand upright and he felt her power flowing into his veins.

He cried out, relieved.

She staggered and he held her. With every passing moment of union, his strength returned, increasing, escalating. It was good…and he became triumphant.

And he threw his head back against the wall, crying out as power swelled inside his veins. And with the surging strength came a sense of invincibility, the comprehension that he would not die. Elation roared in him—he had never known so much power. He had never known such rapture. Shocked, he realized his loins had engorged, too. Even more rapture beckoned.

He pulled her close so she could feel his lust, and her eyes widened. "Aye," he said roughly. "Let me pleasure ye, lass."

"My lord," she whispered, throwing her arms around him.

He turned her back to the wall, moving aside his leine and her skirts. And he could not wait. He pushed her thighs apart and thrust hard, directly, deep. And as he came, he had to take even more from her—it felt too good not to.

He was blinded by the lust, the power, her ecstasy, his. Her life rolled from her in huge, slick waves and the power escalated a hundredfold. She was weeping and begging. He did not hear. He had been carousing since he was fourteen and he had never experienced so much ecstasy or known it could exist. He came again, his loins never slackening. He had more virility than any single man should ever claim.

This was a power he had not dreamed of.

And the power blinded him, kept him engorged, allowing him terrible stamina and endurance. He howled his pleasure at the sunrise. This time he would be able to kill Moray.

And then he realized the woman was finally still.

He glanced down at his chest. His leine was soaked with

blood, but the wound had closed. There was only a ridged scar above his left nipple.

He owed this woman his life. Cradling her, filled with gratitude, he gently brought her to the floor. He unpinned his brat and laid it over her, then stood. And he realized Moray was present.

The demon stepped out of the shadows, his eyes glowing and red.

And as Moray laughed at him, Malcolm knew.

Dread began. The maid lay motionless.

No. *He knelt at her side. He turned her face toward him and found her blue eyes wide and sightless.*

"Welcome, my brother. Welcome to the pleasures of death."

Malcolm stood abruptly, throwing his mug of wine savagely at the hearth. It was midnight, and he was alone in the great hall, except for a pair of prized wolfhounds. The dogs watched him, unperturbed.

He had not allowed himself to think of Urquhart in months. He had spent three years atoning for his sins, wrestling with his guilt. He had thought himself firmly in control. There had been a hundred women since Urquhart, yet there had been no temptation. But it was a lie.

He was not in control. He thought about Urquhart now. And then he thought about the woman who slept upstairs, another innocent maid, a woman who was so seductive, he wished to taste her life.

Three years ago, he had thought himself the hunter, but he had been wrong. Moray had been hunting him; Moray had been hunting his soul.

And now the woman tempted him in an unthinkable way. He had thought his soul safe, but he had been wrong.

CLAIRE WAS SUMMONED the following dawn. Her eyes barely open, she met the gaze of a small boy who poked her, grinned and mimed dressing and eating. He gestured rapidly at the door and grinned and left. Claire sat up, clutching a fur to her body, feeling as if she were terribly hungover.

But she wasn't hungover, not in the normal sense of the word. And her pulse quickened as she recalled that she was in medieval Scotland—and that last night, Malcolm had made love to her.

Claire felt the fist of desire slamming into her chest and belly. She stared at her chamber, at the small fire in the hearth, the rickety table where a jug of water sat, and the narrow window. The shutter had been thrust open and the sky outside was bloodred.

Although she hadn't believed she would be able to sleep a wink yesterday, exhaustion had swiftly claimed her after Malcolm had left. She had slept like a log until the knock on her chamber door.

The boy clearly wished for her to hurry, and she knew why. She was wide-awake now. They were going to Dunroch. Genuine excitement began.

But there was also apprehension. It was the light of a new day. She was about to see Malcolm, and yesterday—well, she had behaved like a woman she did not know. And damn it, she wasn't ever going to forget how he had pleasured her without asking her for anything in return.

Claire washed using frigid water, hoping he would be gentleman enough not to remark on what had happened between them. And what about Sibylla? Just how safe would their trek be? She threw Malcolm's plaid over her shoulders, her trepidation rising, and went downstairs. Only the serving maids were in the great hall and Claire was disappointed, even if she didn't want to be. Starving now—Claire wasn't sure when she had last eaten—she sat down to a huge tray of bread, cheese and several various types of smoked fish, as well as a bowl of oatmeal. She ate swiftly, using a two-pronged fork and a crude knife and spoon, eager to leave the hall. As she ate, she kept glancing at the great door, but it did not open.

She pushed the tray away. She had to face Malcolm sooner or later, and she didn't know what to say, how to act or what to do. But she had to face the fact that she did not have regrets. It would be hypocritical to pretend to have them. She had needed a night like that one.

She felt her cheeks heat. Malcolm was a generous lover. She was going to throw all stereotypes out. She would never think of him as some macho medieval jerk again. He was definitely complicated, intriguing and very, very sexy. She wouldn't mind really sharing his bed.

The mere thought made her feel weak and faint.

Do not go there, she warned herself, heading for the doors. She knew herself. If she ever really slept with him, she'd fall in love. And that was a very bad idea. She must not become fond of him. Only a fool or a madwoman would care for Malcolm, considering the circumstances. She warned herself to keep her interest in him purely academic.

She opened the doors and was met by a blast of chilling Highland wind, never mind that it was summer. She paused on the top of the steps. A dozen men were mounting their chargers by the other hall. Just below her, Malcolm stood beside two saddled horses, speaking with Royce. As one, both men turned to look at her.

Her gaze met Malcolm's and she blushed. This was, she thought, beyond awkward. They were virtually strangers. She started down the stairs, avoiding his eyes.

He probably thought her really fast and loose, although that couldn't be further from the truth.

Malcolm strode forward. "Did ye sleep well?" he asked. His gaze was direct and searching.

If he was referring to the fact that she had been so physically sated she had passed out, she could not tell. "Yes. And you?" She meant to be polite but the moment she spoke, she wished she hadn't. He'd probably tossed and turned all night.

His stare intensified. Then he shrugged, his gaze veering

to her throat. He began unpinning the brooch with which she'd awkwardly pinned her cloak. "Ye need garments," he said. "I'll see ye clothed at Dunroch." He swept the long, oddly shaped cloak from her shoulders, shook it out, folded it not quite evenly and draped it over her, pinning it to one shoulder. It now fell to her knees, securely covering her thighs and skirt.

She swallowed. "Thank you." The merest brushing of his hands caused a frisson of pleasure. How was she going to keep her focus on the books, the shrine, the secret society—everything but the man himself?

His gaze locked with hers. "I nay be the only man with eyes," he said with a slight smile. He nodded toward Royce, whose expression was wry.

Claire didn't care if his uncle had been openly regarding her legs or anything else. It was hard to think clearly with Malcolm hovering about, being possessive. She wished she could tell what he was thinking about last night. He probably had a different woman in his arms every night, which meant their little interlude wasn't a big deal for him. And that was for the best. Because it was far too big a deal to her, and she needed to keep a good perspective, no matter how hard it might be.

He helped Claire mount and turned to leap on his own destrier. Claire realized she had been given an older, quiet horse, for which she was grateful. She moved it over to Royce. "Thank you for the room, the bed and breakfast," she said.

"'Twas my pleasure, Lady Claire. Bon voyage."

His smile was utterly masculine and just a bit knowing. Claire hoped she hadn't been so loud that he had heard her crying out last night. "Adieu." She flushed and moved her horse past him.

Malcolm signaled to the cavalcade and the troops fell into line behind him and Claire. He turned to Royce. "I'll speak with ye after I return from Loch Awe."

Royce nodded but seized Malcolm's bridle. "Do nothing rash."

Malcolm smiled tightly. Then he lifted his hand and glanced at Claire, and they moved toward the passageway beneath the gatehouse. After passing through the dark, stone-walled tunnel, riding side by side over the trapdoor through the dark shadows, the sunlight outside was almost blinding.

For Claire, as they left the dank passage behind, a new tension began.

It was another medieval morning, her second day in the past. So much had happened since the leap that she felt as if she had been in the fifteenth century for weeks. While she did not know if the journey from Carrick to Dunroch was a safe one, she was too excited now to care. Dunroch had been her goal from the start and by that evening, they would be there. Soon she would be at Iona's holy shrine, because she was going with Malcolm, no matter what he said or what he wanted. She was not being left behind.

Because it was a holy shrine, it was guarded by the Masters. Malcolm had indirectly said so. She was about to discover a secret society that no historian had ever revealed.

She was living Highland history now. This was an incredible opportunity. Her fear had long since diminished. She had survived time travel, a brutal battle, a violent assault and Malcolm's lust—all in the span of twenty-four and some hours.

She did not know when she would be going home, although she was determined that she would. Until that time came, she was going to take advantage of this amazing twist of fate. She was going to focus all of her interest on the secret society, the sacred books and the political wars engendered by them, and on avoiding Sibylla, too. And she was going to forget last night had ever happened. Malcolm seemed indifferent. She would be indifferent, too. It was better to be detached from him in every possible way. Her focus on

Malcolm would be as a historical artifact of sorts, because he was a fifteenth-century laird and Master.

Malcolm was staring at her. She hoped he did not sense her thoughts. She smiled. "It's a gorgeous morning." As she spoke, an eagle soared overhead.

"Aye," he said flatly, his tone noncommittal, his gaze sharp. "Aye."

DUNROCH WAS AS GRAY as the towering cliffs it sat upon. Below were rock-strewn beaches and the vast enormity of the steel-gray Atlantic Ocean. Beyond, shrouded in mist, was the dark peak of Ben More. Claire inhaled as she rode her horse toward the Barbican.

Claire had only spent an hour at Dunroch two years ago, and she had not come by horse and then by galley, rowed through the sound and the ocean by six Highland men. She had arrived in a rental car, racing across unkempt roads heading south and west along the shore so she would make it to Dunroch before it closed. It had been a gray afternoon then, too—the island was often buffeted by the inclement ocean climate—but there had been cars parked just outside the castle's curtain walls. There hadn't been a barbican, just a few clumps of stone to indicate it had once been present.

Now the moat that surrounded three sides of the castle was full. The west side sat on sheer cliffs that dropped to the ocean. She and Malcolm remained astride their mounts, waiting as the drawbridge was slowly lowered over the moat by what Claire suspected was a pulley system.

She shivered, her mouth dry. It was so different; it was strikingly the same.

"Lass, the public rooms close in an hour. Ye can come back on Thursday an' ye won't throw yer money away," a toothless, white-haired Scot had told her, trying to be helpful.

Claire had been dizzy and faint, probably from driving at a breakneck speed across the island on the wrong side of the road. "I won't be here on Thursday, I'm going home tomorrow." She had bought her tickets, barely able to concentrate on the man selling them, wishing he didn't move with such infuriating slowness. She had been trembling with tension, excitement. And as she had hurried over the drawbridge, she had thought, "This is it."

Claire realized the bridge was down and Malcolm was waiting for her to join him. Dunroch's gatehouse was far less elaborate than the one at Carrick, and it comprised one wide, circular tower. It only took a moment to pass beneath.

She had forgotten the intense feelings she'd had then, but she was having the same feelings now. She drew her mare to a halt, staring at the face of the castle. And the same words whispered through her mind. *This is it.*

Claire stiffened, glancing around at the inner bailey and at the outer bailey that was north of it, inside the curtain walls. She knew Malcolm was staring but she couldn't look at him, because her mind was spinning.

Her entire vacation had been planned around this place, with the hope of meeting Dunroch's laird. If she could accept that this was fate, then there was one monumental question: *Why?*

Surely, surely it could not be about Malcolm.

"Ye be entranced, lass," Malcolm said. "Ye like me home?"

She tore her gaze from the goats and sheep in the lower bailey, wetting her lips. Her heart fluttered. "I was here before—two years ago. Why, Malcolm? Why do you think I am here now, in your time, not mine?"

"I ken ye dinna mean why did I bring ye back." He spurred his horse forward and Claire followed. Several men had materialized from the hall in the bailey. One tall, gray-haired Scot hurried toward them.

Malcolm dismounted in front of the castle's main entrance, a paneled and studded wood door set in another gated tower.

He handed the horse off to one of the men. "I be askin' the same questions, lass. The Ancients have strange, inexplicable ways."

Did that mean he thought it fate, too? "What about Sibylla? Do you think she might make an attempt to find me here?" She had been trying hard not to freak out over the fact that the other woman was running around the Highlands with an apparent agenda against her.

His face darkened. "She'd be a fool to do so. We be ready fer her an' her kind now." He offered her another smile, about to reach up to help her dismount.

Before Claire could ask how they were ready for her and what, exactly, "her kind" meant, a shrill cry sounded. Claire turned and saw a small boy fly into Malcolm's arms. It took her all of one second to realize this was his son, and her insides lurched with sickening force.

Malcolm swung the small, dark-haired boy around. Then they spoke swiftly, in French. "You obeyed Seamus, lad?"

"Yes, Father, I did. I also bagged a buck." He smiled proudly. "There'll be a fine supper tonight."

Malcolm caressed the boy's hair, smiling in approval.

The gray-haired man stepped forward. "There be a fine rack on the wall, Malcolm. A dozen points."

Malcolm smiled and clasped his shoulder. "Seamus, Brogan, I'd like ye t' meet our guest, Lady Camden. She be from the south," he added. His eyes twinkled when his gaze met Claire's.

Claire couldn't smile. Malcolm was *married*.

She felt faint and incapable of movement. She remained mounted on her horse. Of course he was married. Marriage was an important tool in the ever-shifting balance of power among the great nobles and the king. Likely he had married for political, geographical or monetary gain.

But he hadn't said a word. Not one damn word.

And she was an idiot, because she should have known.

She tried to tell herself this was for the best, but she was stricken with dismay. Still, if she was falling for this man, then this was a fortunate turn of events. His marriage would be a barrier between them that could not be breached.

Malcolm glanced at Brogan. "Go into the hall an' order the great chamber readied fer our guest."

The boy nodded eagerly and dashed off. Malcolm called after him. "With wine an' refreshments, lad, an' a fire. Lady Camden is a bit chilled. Seamus, I'll speak with ye in a bit."

"Aye." Seamus turned and strode off.

Malcolm took her hand. "Brogan is me bastard, Claire. I nay be married. But ye look as if someone has died."

There was so much relief.

"Come down," he said softly.

Claire slipped from the horse, beginning to think more clearly. She had just been devastated that he was not available, and now she was faint with relief. Oh, boy, if she was genuinely interested in this man, she was in big trouble.

She managed to gather some of her wits. "How did you know what I was thinking?"

He hesitated. "I told ye afore, yer thoughts scream so loudly, they be easy t' hear."

Claire folded her arms across her chest. "I am beginning to wonder if you have telepathic powers, too."

"I dinna ken all the words ye speak, lass."

"Can you read my mind?"

He stared.

"Oh, my God," Claire said, shaken. "You can read minds, can't you?"

"'Tis another wee gift I have," he said, but he flushed.

She would analyze the ramifications of this particular gift another time. Right now, she was furious. "You need to respect the privacy of my thoughts," she said harshly. "It's not fair that you eavesdrop on what I am thinking."

He smiled, tilting up her chin, turning his potent gaze on

her. "But if I had nay heard ye, loud an' clear right now, ye'd be in tears an' thinkin' o' denying what's between us."

Her eyes went wide. He'd been acting as if nothing had happened all day. "What's between us? I didn't even know you recalled yesterday morning," she said tersely. "And I wouldn't care if you were married!"

"Liar."

She felt her cheeks heat. "Well, maybe I'd care—a bit. But only because, in my time, it's wrong to sleep with a married man." Then she added, "It's wrong in your time, too, and you know it."

"I be glad I have not made such vows, Claire," he murmured very seductively. His thick, dark lashes slanted down. "Ye think I did not hear yer cries all night? I didna sleep, Claire, because of ye."

Her heart turned over, hard. "Well," she managed to say thickly. Desire surged. "Well."

His smile was as beautiful as the rising sun had been earlier that day. "I dinna ken why ye wished to go to Dunroch in yer time. I dinna ken why I want ye as I do. But I think there are answers t' be found, maybe on Iona."

"Iona," she repeated, instantly diverted.

"The MacNeil be almost as old as the Ancients, lass," he said. "I'll find the answers there. An' do not think o' Sibylla now. Ye be safe with me. Come." He walked beneath the portcullis, disappearing into the gatehouse.

Claire's mind scrambled. Were the answers to her presence in the past at Iona? God, she hoped so! And did Malcolm mean to pick up tonight where they'd left off yesterday?

She hurried after him. A very small courtyard was on the other side of the gatehouse and Malcolm was walking up the stairs to the great hall. Claire increased her pace, entering the great room.

The elegant seating arrangements were gone, as was the sword collection. Instead, there was only a long trestle table, benches and several period chairs. Tapestries covered most of the walls, their colors bright and new.

He was pouring ale from a jug on the table. Claire steeled herself as she approached. "We'll find the answers on Iona *together*," she said firmly.

He gave her an amused look. "I didna say ye'd come to the island with me, lass."

"I'm coming, come hell or high water," she snapped. "We agreed yesterday!"

He drained a mug and sighed. "I already spoke too boldly about affairs that are privy."

"You *know* you can trust me." It occurred to Claire that he trusted her because he could read her mind. "That is why you trust me, isn't it? You snoop about in my thoughts!"

He flushed. "Ye interest me."

She was thrilled, but now was not the time. "Malcolm, this is so important to me!"

"Yer not allowed on the island," he snapped.

Claire stiffened. "I don't believe it. A monastery always opens its doors to travelers."

He folded his arms across his chest and his biceps bulged. He seemed very annoyed, but there was no way he was winning this one. "If you return from Iona and I am dead—murdered by Sibylla in an unspeakable way—you will never be able to forgive yourself. First the maid, at your hands, and then me, your Innocent, at Sibylla's."

His eyes widened.

In that moment, Claire knew she had just won this particular war, and she regretted it. She hadn't meant to be cruel or ruthless. She hadn't meant to use his guilt against him and inflict even more pain.

He inclined his head, his mouth twisted in a way she now recognized, a sign of his inner torment. "We leave at sunrise," he said without inflection.

She bit her lip, wanting to say she was sorry. But a

woman's glad cry rang out. Claire did not like this turn of events.

With dread, she turned.

The woman rushed to Malcolm, beaming. "You are back! And safely, thank God!"

CHAPTER SEVEN

THE WOMAN WAS DARK BLOND, of medium height and pretty enough. Worse, her figure was lush and outstanding. She spoke French as if she had been raised in France, but she was dressed in the English style, her gown and robes a dark red. She wore gold earrings, a gold necklace and rings with stones Claire thought semiprecious. In short, she was a noblewoman of some means, and clearly she was involved with Malcolm.

Malcolm's dark expression did not soften. "Glenna, ye need welcome Lady Camden to Dunroch. Claire, this be me cousin, Lady Glenna NicPharlain o' Castle Cean."

Claire was rigid. He wasn't married, but he had a mistress. She had not a single doubt. Her smile felt brittle. She *hated* this woman.

"Speak in English fer our guest." Malcolm told his lover, who was staring at Claire with surprise. Then he glanced at Claire. "Glenna will show ye t' yer chamber. I hope it pleases ye."

She had no clue if he remained angry with her for her tactics. She somehow managed a brief, strained smile. "Thank you."

"Please come with me, Lady Camden."

Claire looked at her as Malcolm turned away. She almost wished she hadn't even come to Dunroch, but that was childish.

"Malcolm wishes you to go up." Glenna gestured toward the corridor beyond the hall.

Claire turned her attention on the blond woman as they went upstairs. She hated being petty and mean, but she didn't really get what Malcolm saw in Glenna. The woman was no spring chicken by medieval standards. She was probably Claire's age, but with her fair skin, and without the modern benefits of moisturizer, peels and dermabrasions, she had crow's-feet at her eyes and soft wrinkles in her brow. While pretty in the girl-next-door way, she looked faded and tired. Claire saw Malcolm with a raging beauty—someone like Catherine Zeta-Jones or Angelina Jolie. But of course, that ruled her out, too.

"So," Claire said when they were on the uppermost floor, "how long have you known Malcolm?"

Glenna looked at her as she pushed open a door. "Most of my life."

Great, Claire thought. Glenna and Malcolm had known one another forever; she'd known him for three days. They were probably best friends, as well as lovers; he probably loved her deeply; it was frigging classic. But it was better she found out now, sooner rather than later.

"And you are from the Lowlands?" Glenna asked. She sounded curious, and not all that bright.

"I have been abroad for most of my life," Claire said firmly, ducking the question.

Glenna paused, her hand on the door. "How do you know Malcolm?"

Claire hesitated. "We are distant cousins, too. Very distant," she added.

Glenna's eyes widened. "But I have never heard of your family."

Claire gave up. She was really upset and she had to admit it, which only proved that this turn was a blessing in disguise. What she wanted now was to be alone so she could get over her very brief involvement with a medieval macho man. She walked past Glenna—and fell in love.

From the upper-story window, the gleaming gray Atlantic Ocean stretched away into eternity. But if she looked a bit to the west, she could see the thickly forested shores of Argyll, the dark mountains beyond shrouded in mist. She tried to imagine the view on a sunny day and knew instantly that the water would be the color of sapphires, the forests of emeralds.

"Camden is a strange name. I have never heard it. Is it an English name?" Glenna asked. "Are you related to Malcolm's mother?"

Claire's mind raced. Was Malcolm's mother English? Many of the great Lowland families were. What tie could she claim? "My husband, may he rest in peace, was her cousin."

Glenna paled. "But you have remarried, of course."

Claire got her drift. "Actually, no, I haven't. I am unwed." She knew it was really petty to feel triumphant now, but she knew the last laugh wasn't going to be hers.

"Malcolm has brought you here to replace me, hasn't he?" Glenna trembled, tears filling her eyes. "Does he think to marry *you?*"

Claire tensed. Damn it, she felt sorry for Glenna. "We are not about to marry. We don't even know each other," she said slowly. Then she realized how ridiculous such a statement was in the fifteenth century, when marriages were for gain not love.

Glenna choked. "I am marrying him. I am his betrothed."

Claire went still. "Oh. I didn't know."

"I won't let you steal him from me," Glenna warned. "I have been here six months. Everyone knows we will wed."

"Is it official?"

"What?"

"When's the date?"

"Soon," she cried. "We will set a date soon!"

It was odd that a date hadn't been set and she felt relieved, although she knew she should not. Malcolm would probably marry his cousin. And if he didn't marry Glenna, there'd be someone else. It was the way of his world.

And Glenna belonged here. She, Claire, did not. She had to get over it—and him. There was no point hating Glenna; they were not rivals. Claire's kinder nature won. "Hey. You don't have to worry about me. I'm not hanging around for very long."

Glenna blinked back tears. "Who will hang you? What have you done?"

"I am not marrying Malcolm," she said seriously. She hesitated. What she and Malcolm had done wasn't right, although he would probably disagree. "Very soon, I am going home. You have nothing to worry about. At least, you don't need to worry about me."

"And where is home?" Glenna demanded, wiping her eyes. "And when will you return?"

"I am English," Claire said. "I will return to England. As for when, I don't know, not exactly."

Both women stared. Finally Glenna said, "And when he comes to you, tonight? Do not deny it—I know he will. I know him very well."

Claire's heart slammed. "I will bolt my door," she said. And she meant it.

CLAIRE HAD GIVEN HERSELF a tour of the keep, being careful to avoid the ramparts and the walls. Then she had bathed and brooded, and by the time Brogan appeared at her door, grinning, a baby tooth missing, and telling her in stilted English that Malcolm was waiting downstairs, she had come to her senses. She was now dressed like a Highland woman in a full-length leine with undergarments, and as she went down to the hall, she reminded herself that she was over Malcolm. In fact, she was happy for him and Glenna, really. She was *relieved.* He was a medieval macho man and there was no point in any kind of relationship at all. This was for the *best.* She could now focus on learning all she could about the shrine, the books and the secret society of Masters. She could focus on avoiding Sibylla and "her kind." She was eager for the morrow and their excursion to Iona—in fact, she could hardly wait.

She smiled firmly, patted down the surprisingly soft linen dress, making sure no material gaped over her belt—she did have a very narrow waist—adjusted her bra straps and her boobs, and started down the narrow stone stairs. The moment she approached the hall, she heard Glenna's voice, choked with sobs.

Claire stumbled and hesitated. Then, instead of going into the hall, she darted against the wall, near the entryway. She glanced inside.

"How can you do this to me?" Glenna wept. "And all because you have a new lover?"

"My decision stands," Malcolm said calmly.

"I hate you!" Glenna cried.

"If ye calm, ye be more than welcome to dine with us. But I willna have these tears at me table." A dangerous note had entered his tone.

Claire was in disbelief. What had Malcolm done? It almost sounded as if he had broken up with Glenna—and she was certain she knew why. Instantly outraged, she stepped closer to the doorway but did not go inside. Now she could see Glenna weeping pathetically, almost theatrically, Malcolm apparently unmoved, although he looked very annoyed.

"Good gods!" Malcolm finally snapped. "You act like a wife who is being sent to a French convent! The marriage is arranged, Glenna. Cease yer tears. 'Tis time fer ye to go home an' marry Rob Macleod."

Glenna shook her head, crying too hard to speak. Then she lifted her skirts and ran out of the hall.

This was unbelievable! Was this how he would treat her *if* they'd had an affair? He would cast her aside like a medieval tyrant? Use her and toss her out, handing her over to another man? Poor Glenna! What a macho jerk!

Malcolm started to smile at her, then he became wary. "Why do ye look at me with such accusation?"

"You are marrying her off to someone else?" Claire choked.

He stiffened. "Aye, an' it be a fine union fer Glenna."

Claire strode forward. "But she is your betrothed. Just like that, you give her the boot and send her to another man?"

His eyes widened with surprise and then became hard and dark.

Claire tensed. Why was she attacking him? This was the medieval way of things and it was not her affair. She didn't even like Glenna.

"Not that I must explain to ye, but I spent three months negotiating the match fer Glenna. I gave much consideration to the woman's future," he said tightly. "And she canna do better."

"She said she was marrying you," Claire told him. But if Malcolm had been negotiating a union for Glenna for three entire months, Glenna had lied to her.

"I never intended t' marry Glenna." He was angry with her now. "I dinna like bein' judged, Claire."

She had just made a huge mistake. "I'm sorry."

"Ye should be. She thought a few nights in her bed would change me mind. I will never marry. I told her so. 'Twill never change, not fer anyone." His face was cold.

Claire felt dread. "What, exactly, does that mean?"

He turned away, gesturing at her to come to the table, which was set with steaming platters of food.

Claire didn't move. Malcolm had no intention of marrying? What could that be about? All noblemen married.

Malcolm slowly faced her. "Dinna think to change my mind, either, lass."

"I beg your pardon?"

"Even ye willna entice me to the altar," he said. "No matter how much I enjoy yer bed."

She gasped. "You are so arrogant!" Jerk, she almost cried.

His gaze narrowed and he returned to stand directly in front of her. "Ye dinna wish t' marry me?" he asked very softly.

Claire knew she should lie and placate him. In the fifteenth-century Highlands, he was a catch. His eyes glittered. "No, I do not. I plan to marry someone from my time, someone brilliant and successful—someone with an open, intellectual mind!"

He stared, and a long moment ensued in which Claire knew he was considering her response. "Do ye call me weak an' foolish, Claire?"

Claire inhaled at his tone. Why had she lost her temper? "No, of course not," she cried, determined to undo whatever damage she had done to his pride. "You're strong and smart and rich, anyone can see that."

"Ye lie," he said.

"Don't you dare read my thoughts," she cried.

"Ye think me an arrogant *jerk*," he added as softly.

She was almost certain he did not know what a jerk was. "Not really," she began nervously.

"I'm nay the arrogant one in this hall," he said. "Ye stand there judging me all the time. Ye think I dinna ken? Ye think I canna hear ye callin' me a medieval macho man? I dinna ken macho, and I dinna need to. Ye be the arrogant one, Claire, thinkin' yerself wiser than me, lookin' down on all o' us."

She could barely breathe. "I don't think I'm wiser," she managed to say. "Not really. In my time, women are educated and independent of men. In my time, some women are actually smarter and richer than men. We think for ourselves, protect ourselves. We answer to no one."

"Aye, ye have said so often enough. In yer time, women are queens without kings. Ye need a king!" He strode abruptly from the hall, outside into the night, the heavy door slamming like thunder behind him.

Claire began to shake. How had that terrible battle happened? And he was right. She had patronized him from the first moment they met. Maybe, just maybe, she did think she was smarter than he was. But she also respected and admired him, because his courage and honor were amazing. She hated the fight they had just had.

Go and tell him!

Claire hesitated. Of course she needed to go after him and apologize. She needed to admit that she was partly wrong. Maybe she was *entirely* wrong. Glenna was an older woman by medieval standards, and Claire felt certain she had lands, due to the wealth her manner of dress indicated. In the fifteenth century, a woman needed a husband and an overlord and there was simply no getting around it.

Damn Malcolm for using his sneaky gift all the time. But she had obviously hurt his feelings and she had better watch her thoughts.

Claire went outside. It was twilight and she hesitated, recalling Sibylla's assault in its grotesque entirety. She did not want to be alone, not outside, after dark. She stood but a few steps from the door to the hall and glanced around. Malcolm stood above her on the ramparts above the nearby gatehouse. From his stance, she saw that his back was rigid.

Claire hurried up the stone steps and paused beside him. He glanced briefly at her. "I be proud o' bein' the Maclean," he said quietly, "an' if that makes me arrogant, so be it."

"You should be proud," Claire said softly, meaning it. Her heart turned over with dangerous haste, as if she really cared about this man. She touched his bare forearm and felt the muscle there tense. "You are the most courageous man I have ever met, and you are a Master. I don't know much about that world, but the vows you have taken are beyond admirable. Men like you don't exist in my time," she added. "And sometimes I am confused—I don't know what to do."

Their gazes had locked. "Ye need to trust me," he said flatly.

Claire started. "When it comes to my life, I do trust you."

He smiled at her. "That be a beginning, then, fer us."

What did that mean?

"Yer an arrogant woman, lass, but I dinna mind very much," he added even more softly.

Claire bit her lip, her pulse leaping. She wasn't arrogant, and there wasn't going to be a beginning or an "us." But she wasn't about to get into another argument now.

"Glenna has been widowed twice," he said, and Claire was stunned that he was going to explain himself to her. "She has lands, Claire, an' she needs a husband to protect them. Macleod is a widower with two children himself. He needs her wealth an' a mother for the boys."

Claire was filled with regret. "I'm sorry. I immediately jumped to the wrong conclusion."

He nodded, his expression remaining solemn. "Ye jump afore ye look, Claire, an' one day it may hurt ye badly."

She did have a tendency to act in haste, without forethought. "I'm also sorry I have called you names. I don't mean it, you just infuriate me sometimes."

"Nay, ye mean it. An' it's nay anger. I scare ye," he said bluntly.

She met his gaze, stunned. He was right. She did mean it when she called him a jerk, but he was obviously secure enough not to really care. And he did scare her, a lot. He scared her because he was so sexy and so powerful and she didn't know what she should do with herself—and her heart—while around him.

He smiled at her now. The smile was warm, but not knowing or promising. It was not seductive. But it didn't matter; it was too late. A different kind of intimacy had somehow begun—and she didn't want it. They had shared a battle and a bed, but they did not need any kind of emotional connection. That was dangerous. Impossible, even. Admiring him was okay. Liking him was not.

"Ye think too hard." He grasped her hand, pulling her back to face him.

Claire couldn't breathe. "It's w-what I do," she stuttered, because desire was flowing like honey. This was the problem—her attraction—and she wasn't going to complicate it with any feelings, not even friendship. "I had better go," she began nervously. Except, walking away from him was the last thing she really wished to do.

"I ha' never met a woman like ye, Claire," he said quietly.

It was an intense moment before she could speak. "Don't!" She managed a quick, tight smile. "Don't complicate things. I hate words!" She blushed at that because words were her life. "And if you want to seduce me, you don't have to do it with declarations of affection. We both know a simple entrancing look will do." She hesitated. "Making lo—I mean, sharing a bed is one thing, friendship is another. I don't think we should combine the two *ever*."

"But ye were friends with the men ye loved," Malcolm said, appearing skeptical.

"Damn it," she cried. "You must allow me my secrets!"

"I want to understand ye, lass. And we both ken 'tis only a matter o' time afore we become lovers."

She inhaled. "Not fair. Remember, I am going home, hopefully sooner rather than later. You swore it."

He smiled. "What does yer goin' back to yer time have to do with our being lovers? Ye want me, an' dinna deny it. I want ye. There are complications now, but I am hopin' they will soon be gone. An' ye may not be so eager t' leave when ye've passed an entire night in me bed." His smile became cocky.

"I told you," she said, entirely hot, "I can't give you my body apart from my love."

His lashes lowered, then slowly he looked up. "Will ye nay try?"

"No!" she snapped, shaking.

"An' if I tell ye I dinna mind if ye love me?"

Her eyes widened. How could she have even forgotten, for one minute, that he was an arrogant medieval jerk? "I will not be tossed aside like Glenna at your tyrannical whim!"

"Did I say I'd toss ye aside?"

She froze.

His eyes were wide and watchful. "I gave ye my word I'd take ye home when 'tis safe, an' I will keep it."

Claire couldn't even breathe. "But?"

His eyes flickered but he did not look away. He murmured, "But ye need nay go if ye dinna wish to."

"What does *that* mean? Is that an invitation? Or are you suggesting I will be so smitten with your performance in bed—or so deeply in love with a man I will never understand—that I will decide to stay in the fifteenth century? There's no way, Malcolm, no damn way!"

His face was hard, his gaze terribly intent. "Ye like it here," he said softly. "Ye like me. I dinna mind—I like ye, too. Ye hope t' fight me, but I willna fight ye, lass."

Claire shook her head, dismayed. "I only came up here to apologize. It was a terrible idea. Why are you doing this?"

"Because when the time comes, mayhap ye won't be wantin' t' leave Dunroch—or me."

THEY BOTH DINED in silence. Malcolm ate with ravenous intent, apparently unperturbed by their conversation, while Claire was determined to fuel up and not look him in the eye. She was shaken, but she was glad that conversation had ensued. She had been mistaken to think, even for a moment, that they could have any kind of understanding or a physical affair, much less an emotional connection. His arrogance was mind-blowing. Of course she was going home! She was leaving his time the moment it was safe to do so. And in the interim, there would be no more sex, not even kisses, damn it, *nothing!* And she was not going to have any more intimate conversations with this man, either. Friendship was as bad an idea as anything else and she didn't think it was possible anyway. Not when he was so certain he'd screw her brains out and she'd be dying for more. Not when he was so certain she'd want to stay with him in this god-forsaken time.

Malcolm finally pushed his plate away, but he refilled her glass and then his. He had been filling her glass all night. She didn't care—she could handle her wine—and she refused to glance up and thank him. She did not trust herself to look into his eyes—he would probably entrance her the moment she did so.

Suddenly, after twenty minutes of silence, he spoke. "I ken ye be tired an' it be late. But we ha' matters to discuss."

Having no choice, Claire looked up warily. She knew what he wanted, oh, yes. "Last night was a mistake." And even as she spoke, she felt her cheeks heat and her flesh swell. This was it, then. The moment she had been worrying about—and waiting for. The moment when he'd look at her, mesmerize her and take her to his bed.

But he did not react as she expected. He looked amused. "I dinna wish to speak o' last night."

She was confused. "You don't?"

He folded his arms authoritatively across his chest. "I trust meself less now, after last night, than I ever did," he said firmly.

Claire realized her brain was working a tad slowly. She was just a bit tipsy after all.

His gray eyes turned silver. "Dinna look at me with so much hunger, lass. I'd pleasure ye," he added softly, "if we were in the light o' day. But the moon be bright an' I want to come inside ye. There's more I'm wantin' than yer body."

Claire was ready to faint with the desire pooling beneath her leine and skirt. Faint, or come. "Damn it," she said softly. All willpower was gone.

"'Tis easy to play ye, lass." His eyes gleamed and he smiled. "An' I'll play ye again when the time is right."

It was so hard to think. She clasped her burning cheeks. She knew she had decided to avoid him sexually—and in every way—but none of that seemed to matter. What mattered was the gut-wrenching desire in her body, the moisture trickling down her thighs, the urgent throbbing of her distended flesh. What mattered was Malcolm. "Guess what?" she said thickly. "I've changed my mind—a woman's prerogative."

And he was reading her thoughts, because he darkened. "Dinna try to seduce me, lass, I won't have it."

"You really don't want to go upstairs?" She was shocked.

"Ye've had too much wine." He stared.

It finally clicked. He was still afraid she'd drop dead in his arms. "As powerful as you think you are," she said huskily, "I am not about to die in your bed."

His eyes widened. "Ye think I think that I killed the maid with my cock?"

She blushed. "I think she died of heart failure but I think you believe yourself pretty unusually endowed!"

He suddenly laughed, and the sound was warm and rich and beautiful. "Lass, that be sure an' strong, but the maid died another way." His smile faded.

Claire did not like the serious expression crossing his face. "I'd give a fortune for an espresso," she said grimly.

"I dinna ken."

"No, you wouldn't know. Why are you looking at me as if a firing squad is standing behind me?"

He reached for her. Claire was surprised when he took her hand in his. "Ye dinna wish t' ken the truth."

Claire tried to pull her hand away. "You know what? I did have too much wine and I am damn tired. I am going up to bed. Alone…I guess." She tried to stand, but he hadn't let her go, and she wound up sitting on the bench again.

"In yer heart," he said quietly, "ye ken the truth already."

"Like hell I do." Now she tugged hard, and he released her.

"Whatever you want to tell me, it can wait." She felt panic, and it was making her far too sober.

"There be no safe place to hide, lass, nay even in ignorance."

A shudder of dread swept through her. "Damn you."

"Ye wish me to hell?" He was incredulous.

She inhaled. "No."

"Ye don't want t' ken the way o' the world," he said softly, laying his large hand over hers again. "I ken because I hear ye thinkin' all the time, an' ye choose thoughts that please ye. Ye need face the truth, Claire, about Sibylla and her kind."

Claire couldn't quite breathe. She knew she did not want to hear his next words. "Sybilla is unnaturally strong, that's all."

His grip tightened. "She licked yer skin. Yer throat."

Claire cried out, leaping to her feet. "She's a sicko!"

"Pleasure crimes be ancient history, Claire," Malcolm said grimly, rising to his feet. He never let her go. "The Deamhanain be the source."

Claire was shaking. No! Malcolm did not know anything about pleasure crimes—he had been reading her mind! Death by pleasure was the result of the breakdown of *modern* society. It was not a part of the Middle Ages, too.

"The Deamhanain have been killing the Innocent fer pleasure fer thousands o' years, long before Christ," he said.

She knew what the Gaelic word *Deamhanain* meant without having to be told. "I don't believe in the devil and I don't believe in demons," she cried desperately.

"But yer mother an' yer cousin were killed by Deamhanain…fer their pleasure."

"Stop! Please! They were killed by madmen, human madmen!"

"True Deamhanain can take life from anyone. They can suck life from a human until he has no power left t' live. But fornication adds to the pleasure." His nostrils flared. "The rapture be called Le Puissance."

"Stop!"

He finally released her hand. "Yer afraid o' the night, an' ye should be, 'cause evil walks openly in the night while it hides in the day. Ye need to face the truth, Claire. There be nay safe place t' hide, ever."

She struck him, hard, across the face.

He jerked but remained rigid. "Yer world is nay different from this one. The Deamhanain be everywhere, in every time, in every place, and they want yer death—an' mine."

Claire couldn't speak. She was sick. The floor felt off kilter and it was spinning. *This could not be happening.* The world could not be the way Malcolm was describing it.

His tone became kind as he steadied her. "Sibylla be human, like ye. But her powers are not. Moray has possessed her. 'Tis why she be so strong, so evil."

Claire shook her head. Tears fell. "So Sibylla is a possessed human? Now you'll tell me Moray is the devil?"

"Long ago," he said softly, "a great warrior goddess came to Alba an' lay with kings. One o' her sons was Moray. He became a great Master…until Satan stole his soul."

She met his gaze. His features were blurred. "You believe," she gasped, "but I don't…I won't!"

"In Alba, Moray be the lord o' the darkness, Claire. His spawn be the Deamhanain."

Claire stepped back and hit the table. The devil. Demons descended from ancient deities. Possessed humans. Pleasure crimes since time began… On some gut level it made absolute sense.

Moray, a demon who had once been a Master….

And Malcolm, a Master who had killed a maid…

Claire felt the room swim. She was in a nightmare. And she knew that, for the first time in her life, she was about to faint.

She reeled. Malcolm caught her. She whispered, "Then what does that make you?"

Malcolm lifted her into his arms just as her world went black.

CLAIRE CAME TO CONSCIOUSNESS, choking on a foul odor. She was in the bed of the chamber she had been given. Malcolm sat beside her, his face grim. In that terrible instant, the nightmare returned and began all over again.

Her head pounded, hurting like hell. Malcolm was wrong. He had to be, even if Sibylla had had the strength of ten men.

He hesitated. "Lass, I be sorry."

"Get out," she gasped. She could accept that some men were genetically programmed for evil and that evil was as ancient as the Bible. And she could and would accept that crimes of pleasure existed in the Middle Ages, just the way crimes of passion did. What she would not accept, not for an instant, was that those crimes were being committed by beings with supernatural powers, beings that were not really human.

Malcolm walked out.

Claire lay back against the pillows, feeling sick in her soul. Evil was human. This was a medieval myth. The devil did not exist, and she was going to repeat that litany until she went home. Moray was probably an extraordinarily ruthless, ambitious and clever man, propagating the myth that he was a master of evil. This was a primitive time and men like Malcolm were resorting to superstition and religion to explain things they could not understand!

Claire felt tears falling down her face.

But the perpetrators of pleasure crimes were never caught. Their ability to seduce their victims had never been explained. All the victims died because their hearts stopped. And it was an epidemic....

The shutter on her window suddenly swung open.

Claire leaped from the bed, shaking with fear, but Sibylla did not appear, nor did any supposed demon. She reminded herself that the window opening was too small to admit even a child—and Sibylla didn't need a window to get inside.

Claire cursed, terrified. She ran to the window and

slammed the shutter closed. As she did, black shadows danced on the ramparts above her head.

Claire reminded herself that it was the night watch. A log fell in the fire, hissing. Claire's heart exploded and she ran from the chamber, instinctively going directly to the end of the hall. The door was wide open and she glimpsed Malcolm inside. She seized the door, breathing hard.

He turned. He'd stripped off his clothes, every single garment, and his entire body bulged with rippling muscle. He was hugely endowed. His eyes widened, but she just stood there.

Now she failed entirely to breathe, but desire wasn't the issue. Tears crept out from her eyes. Claire swiped at them, thinking about blood and demons and Masters and Malcolm, all at once. *The maid died takin' her pleasure from me.*

Claire swallowed the urge to retch. *No.* Malcolm was human and good and he had not committed a crime of pleasure. That woman had died from too much hot sex. According to Malcolm, it was subhuman demons with superpowers who sucked the life from their victims.

"Lass."

She looked up slowly, aware that she was at her emotional limit. "The shutter opened," she whispered.

"It be the wind. There's nay evil here. The walls were anointed with holy water before we supped." He had wrapped the brat around his waist like a towel, but it bulged.

Claire trembled.

"The Deamhanain do not enter holy places, lass," he added softly, but he didn't slide his arm around her. She wanted to be in his big, strong and very safe embrace.

She hugged herself. "How can you be excited at a time like this?" she whispered.

"Ye'll always excite me," he murmured. "Come here." And he pulled her into his arms.

Claire found her face pressed against the strong crook of his warm neck and shoulder, her hands flat on his broad chest, over his strong, pounding heart. She ignored the powerful organ that throbbed between them. "I don't believe it," she insisted desperately. "Not any of it. But what I do know is that you are good."

His grip tightened and he stroked her hair as it flowed down her back. "Yer chamber be safe, Claire. But I ken ye dinna like t' sleep alone. Ye can have the bed. I'll watch over ye t'night."

Claire laughed hysterically. This from a medieval macho man? "Thank you."

"Why do ye nay sleep now?" He smiled. "I'll sit by the fire."

"I can't sleep!" she cried, looking up at him. And she hated the look in his eyes of concern blended with pity. She banged her fist on the slab of his pectoral muscle. "Moray is not the son of Satan. He can't be."

His arms tightened and he pulled her close. Claire thought she felt his mouth on her hair. "We'll discuss such matters t'morrow."

"There can't be demons, Malcolm," she whispered against his chest, meaning it. "There is evil…but it is human."

He stroked her hair again, remaining silent.

Claire started to really cry then. She had worked so hard to rationalize the frightening epidemic of pleasure crimes— as had every intelligent person she knew. Everyone knew that city life was dangerous, but it was explicable. Crime was the result of poverty, broken homes, drugs and a culture of violence, and while some lunatics ran loose, causing murder and mayhem, relishing every violent sexual act, it was on a random basis. As bad as society was, as decadent, as chaotic, the loonies were a small minority, and they were human. There was always hope.

Claire didn't know what to think now.

CHAPTER EIGHT

THE FOLLOWING SUNRISE, Claire waited to mount her mare, shivering. A dozen men were preparing to mount up, as well, and the gatehouse doors had been opened, the portcullis raised. Through it, she could see the shadow of the drawbridge as it was lowered. She turned her gaze and instantly found Malcolm.

He had yet to mount and was speaking with Seamus by the castle's interior entrance. Claire's heart turned over, hard.

She had had one of the worst nights of her life. She'd barely slept, tossing and turning, her mind racing, but every time she'd opened her eyes, she'd seen Malcolm seated by the fire, awake and watchful. He'd watched over her the entire night.

Before Malcolm's terrible declaration last night, she had been eager to go to Iona where she would see the shrine and hopefully the Cathach, as well. But how could she be excited now when her world was unraveling at the speed of light?

Moray be the lord o' the darkness.

His spawn be the Deamhanain.

Claire had spent the entire night convincing herself that evil was human. She had prayed that demons and the devil did not exist. But it had been impossible to convince herself that she was right and Malcolm wrong.

What if everything Malcolm believed was actually true?

Claire did not want to go down that road, not today, not ever. But that's what scholars did—they asked, *what if?* She stared at Malcolm. He looked exactly the way a man dedicated to vanquishing evil should. He had the charisma of a leader, the power of a warrior, and he was so damn gorgeous. He looked as if he was the one descended from the gods.

Malcolm turned. His gaze was as concerned as it had been last night, but she did not want his kindness or his concern. She was very ashamed of her hysterical and cowardly behavior. It wasn't going to happen again, no matter what. Panic and fear weren't going to solve anything. And she already knew that bad things went bump in the night.

Claire thought about Amy, who had to be worried sick about her by now. How many times had Amy stressed how evil criminals today were? God, did she know something? How could she not, when her husband was in the Bureau, even if he was in counterterrorism? He had to have inside information; all cops talked, including feds.

If the world was as Malcolm claimed, then evil was deliberately and purposefully stalking its innocent victims, seeking destruction and death.

If Malcolm was right, evil had a terrifying new face.

Malcolm approached, his men now mounted. He smiled at her, but his gray gaze was searching. "Ye didna sleep well."

It wasn't a question. "Neither did you." Claire noted that he didn't look tired at all. She wouldn't be surprised if he could go days without sleep and remain unaffected.

"'Tis a short trek to Iona," he said. "Ye can rest there."

Rest was not on her mind. "I am sorry about last night," Claire said tersely. "It will never happen again."

He shrugged. "Yer a woman, lass. Ye need a man to protect ye."

Claire smiled grimly. She did not want to fight with him. The fight had been knocked out of her last night.

A moment later, she was mounted beside him and they were riding through the gatehouse, the portcullis slamming down behind them. They crossed the drawbridge. The moment the last rider cleared the bridge, Claire heard it being raised. The trail down to the beach was as steep as she recalled, forested ridges on their right, the cliffs on their left. And then the temperature dropped.

Instantly, beneath the horse's hooves, in a single heartbeat, the dirt turned white with frost.

The leaves and thistle on the sides of the trail turned white, too, and her breath made puffs in the air.

And Claire knew.

So did Malcolm. He shouted a command in Gaelic. He glanced at Claire. "Ye stay back!"

Before Claire could exclaim or protest, he was on his charger, galloping down the road with his men, one warrior having seized her reins. She tried to jerk her reins back, because all she could comprehend was that evil was hunting them and Malcolm was not going to face it alone.

"Let go!" she screamed.

The man was young, huge and annoyed. He reached for her—and Claire jammed her Taser into his arm. He collapsed.

She seized her reins and kicked her horse as hard as she could, galloping headlong down the trail, holding the saddle horn, determined not to fall off. Malcolm's war cry rang out in all its bloodcurdling intensity. Her heart went wild. She rounded a corner and saw Malcolm's men furiously battling their attackers. Already, bloody bodies littered the road. She saw him whirl his charger, meeting a vicious assault with his shield. A moment later his attacker lay on the ground, face-first. And as suddenly as it began, the battle seemed to be over.

She sawed on her reins. Five men in mail lay prone on the ground. Huge relief began.

The mare halted, flinging her head about in protest. Claire didn't want to go closer, not yet. She wanted to see what Malcolm was going to do now, because they'd taken three prisoners.

Malcolm dismounted and handed his shield off. His

swords sheathed, he approached the three prisoners, who were being held by his men. Claire tensed, uncertain. She had a very bad feeling. Malcolm's expression had never been so ruthless.

Malcolm paused before the trio. She saw him look at one man, dismiss him mentally, then look at another and finally face the third. A terrible light flickered in his eyes.

The third man, a tall, fair-skinned giant with blond hair, paled as if with pain.

Malcolm said something to him in Gaelic. Claire knew he was demanding answers.

The other man gave the most evil smile Claire had ever seen and her gut turned over with dread.

Malcolm spoke again.

The giant stared coldly back. Malcolm didn't move a muscle. He skewered the giant with his stare and the man went down on his knees, as if pushed. But Malcolm hadn't touched him, and his men stood behind the prisoner to prevent his escape.

Claire's skin crawled. What was happening? The giant seemed to be in some pain. Malcolm's stare burned and the prisoner went abruptly down on his back, as if flung by a huge force.

Malcolm pressed one booted foot on the man's throat.

Claire bit off a cry.

And now, although Malcolm spoke in Gaelic, Claire understood. *"Moray neo Sibylla?"* Moray or Sibylla? He wanted to know who had sent them.

The giant sneered.

Malcolm smiled with such menace that Claire froze—and then she silently begged him to stop. He did not. A terrible crack sounded as he stepped harder on the man's throat. Claire cried out.

But the giant, his neck now bent at an impossible angle, spoke. In French, he said, "Your lord sent me and he'll send others. There is no place for her to hide." He snarled, very much like an animal, spittle on his mouth.

Claire couldn't breathe. Her heart raced with hurtful speed.

Malcolm removed his boot from the man's neck. A terrible expression formed on his face and his stare never wavered.

"Stop, Malcolm," Claire cried instinctively, but it was too late. The giant's snarl had frozen. His face was a stiff mask, his eyes wide and lifeless now.

In utter shock, Claire slid from the mare, walked over to the woods and knelt. As she tried to vomit, she heard Malcolm giving orders and the men mounting. What had just happened? What had he done? Then she heard him come to stand behind her.

"Ye were t' stay behind."

She couldn't throw up, she realized. She turned. He held out his hand, his expression no longer utterly ruthless, just harsh and grim. She refused it, staggering to her feet. "What did you do?"

He stared, his eyes glittering. "I be sworn to vanquish evil. He be a Deamhan. We do not allow Deamhanain to live. He'd kill ye the moment I turned me back."

She panted. "He didn't die from a broken neck!"

"Nay."

Oh, God, she thought. "What did you do? Suck his life out?"

Malcolm turned away, then back. "We need ride." He was angry now.

Claire had seen it with her own eyes. "You killed that monster using some kind of kinetic power, didn't you!"

He didn't answer—and it was an answer enough.

"What are you?" she cried.

IONA WAS JUST a few miles long and as wide, with low, lush green hills dotted with sheep, and pearl-white beaches. As the galley they were in approached, Claire huddled in her brat, chilled to the bone.

Malcolm had killed that creature with a look.
He had superhuman powers, too.
What did that make him?

She glanced at Malcolm where he stood in the galley's bow. Last night he had spent the entire night making certain she was safe. He had done so more to comfort her than to protect her from evil beings.

But evil was out there. That creature hadn't been human.

Claire closed her eyes. She wasn't ready to use the word *demon,* not even in her own thoughts.

And then she felt him stand above her. She looked up. He stared down at her with that concerned expression she was becoming so familiar with. "I be sorry," he said grimly, "that ye saw what ye did."

"Tell me," she whispered.

"'Tis forbidden."

"You've told me everything else!"

He hesitated and she saw he was truly uncertain.

"Who am I going to tell? The pope?"

"'Tis nay amusing t' jest in such a manner." He was harsh.

Claire reminded herself that, in this time, heresy was the most serious offense in Christendom, more so even than witchcraft. Any Catholic clergyman who had witnessed what she had would believe Malcolm was both a heretic and a sorcerer. He'd be prosecuted ruthlessly. If fortunate, his punishment would be excommunication and exile. "I am trying," she said, low, "to keep it together. And maybe I can remain sane, if you just tell me what I need to know."

He sat down beside her on the bench. His voice as low, he said grimly, "The Deamhanain be nay the only ones descended from the goddess Faola. Every Master can claim her blood."

She made a sound, almost a laugh. *He was also descended from ancient gods.* Of course he was. How could she have thought otherwise? She clasped her cheeks, which were hot. A nervous breakdown wasn't going to help her now!

Staring at the bow, he said grimly, "Evil was born with Adam and Eve, as ye ken. Long ago, the Ancients saw the need fer a race o' warriors t' fight the evil, Claire. Faola was sent to many kings."

Claire choked on shock and fear. Her determination to dismiss his beliefs had become frighteningly fragile.

She stared at him, trying to think clearly. Malcolm had powers that were becoming harder and harder to rationalize. And he was good. "So you're half god and half human."

"Nay. There be three generations between me an' Faola, lass. I be her great-grandson."

He might believe he was the great-grandson of a goddess, Claire told herself, but that didn't make it true. Maybe there was a rational explanation out there, somewhere. "Did you suck the life out of that thing the way the Deamhanain do?"

He stood. "Canna a god take life an' give it? A Master can take life, lass. And some, a very few, can give it, too."

"Great! You can give life, too?" she cried, shaken all over again.

"Nay. I canna heal. But all Masters have the power t' take life. Otherwise, we are nay chosen."

Unfortunately, he had finally made sense. The power of life and death was the greatest power of all, a power belonging to God or the gods. This race of warriors, *if* given by the gods to fight evil, would obviously have such a power, too.

An odd calm began. Wasn't it better that the Masters had the same immortal blood in their veins as the demons?

She breathed hard and bit her lip. "That...*thing* was a demon. You broke its neck."

"Aye. The Deamhanain dinna feel pain the way we do."

Claire searched his gaze. "You don't feel pain the way we do, either, do you?"

"I be strong." His gaze held hers, a question there.

Claire knew what he was asking. He wanted to know how she felt about him now. She didn't have that answer. "Why did you let the other two demons live? Why are they on this galley?" They were up front in the bow, tied up.

"They be humans, Claire, that be possessed. The monks have spells an' mayhap they can be freed."

She started. "You mean the monks will try to exorcize them?"

He nodded. Then, hesitantly, he smiled at her. "I need t' help the men."

Claire saw that they were pushing up to a pair of wooden piers. She couldn't quite smile back.

As Malcolm leaped from the galley to the first pier, two other Highlanders leaped out, as well. Ropes were tossed at the pilings, the other four men remaining at the oars. Claire finally turned her attention to Iona. She'd come by ferry last time, so her vantage point was the same. Otherwise, nothing was the same at all.

Two walled enclosures were visible, and she knew they were the older, fortified monastery and the medieval abbey. Both had been ruins in the present, and a newer cathedral existed in their place. The famous Celtic Cross that stood before the present-day cathedral was gone. The abbey was not far from the pier, clearly built recently. The monastery was farther up the road and built in paler stone.

The galley dipped as Malcolm climbed back inside. He returned to Claire and held out his hand. "Lass."

Claire met his penetrating gaze, wishing she could keep his world at bay. "I think I believe you," she said harshly. "I don't want to, but I think I do."

"'Tis better if ye do."

Claire stared at him and he regarded her steadily. And she wondered where that left them.

CLAIRE BECAME INTERESTED in her surroundings as they waited for the monastery's paneled wood door to be unlocked. She was about to enter an intact, working, fifteenth-century monastery. Here, there might be answers from an abbot named MacNeil. Her guidebooks had claimed that the monastery had been built centuries earlier than the abbey, although the original buildings, made of wood, would have been built by St. Columba in the sixth century. No wood buildings remained now, she saw, glancing over the monastery's walls. The walls were too low for comfort. They could be so easily scaled.

Many religious houses had been fortified in this time period, but this one was not. There were no high, crenellated walls, no defensive towers, no gatehouse, no moat or barbican. "Malcolm, this is such a flimsy door."

"No Deamhan enters a holy place, Claire," he said.

"Why not?"

"They lose their powers an' we can easily destroy them."

Thank God for small favors, she thought. Claire heard a bolt being lifted and the heavy door opened.

Claire preceded Malcolm inside, glancing curiously around. The monastery was a small village, really, with a dotter and refectory where the monks slept and ate, cookhouses, breweries, a church and many other buildings, as well as gardens and orchards.

Then she looked at the man who had admitted them and her heart almost stopped.

It was like looking at Matthew McConaughey playing the part of a medieval Highland warrior. He was dressed almost identically to Malcolm, except his brat was green and black, thinly striped with white and gold. He was tall and powerfully built, with dark gold hair, bulging biceps and quads, and he wore gold cuffs on both arms. She quickly revised her opinion—he looked like a bigger, stronger, sexier version of Matthew McConaughey.

His very green, very intense gaze swept her from head to toe and then he smiled slightly at Malcolm. That was all it took for his dimples to be revealed. "Ye break so many rules, Calum."

Malcolm did not smile back. "This be Lady Claire," he said. "I ken ye have seen us on our voyage."

This could not be the abbot, Claire thought, trying not to ogle his thighs and arms. Abbots were short, fat and old. Abbots were bald.

"I have expected ye," Matthew said flatly. His gaze slid very sensually over Claire again. A slight smile began. "Welcome, Lady Camden."

Claire tensed. Malcolm had not uttered her last name.

"Niall MacNeil, lass," Malcolm said tersely. "Niall? I dinna care how great yer powers be, keep yer eyes where they belong—in the head upon yer shoulders."

Niall MacNeil smiled, amused. "I dinna chase yer Innocent, Malcolm. An' ye can ease yerself. I ken ye'd come, an' the Ancients have allowed it." He sent another very seductive, very indolent smile at Claire, and she instantly decided that he enjoyed his blatant male sensuality far too much.

"You were expecting me, or Malcolm?" she asked, shaken.

"Both," he said, gesturing for them to start walking up the path.

Claire didn't like games, especially not now. "Did you mean that the Ancients don't mind my being here?" What did the old gods want with her? If there *were* old gods!

"Aye, lassie. Odd as it may be, the Ancients dinna mind yer presence amongst the Brotherhood."

Before she could respond, she started, glancing past both men. A pair of huge, armed hunks was leaving one of the adjacent buildings.

The red-haired man was dressed like a Highlander in brat and leine, the other, a swarthy dark-haired man, like an Englishman in dark hose, knee-high boots, jeweled spurs, and a doublet and short-skirted burgundy jacket, which barely covered his upper hips. Claire had read all about codpieces but had never seen one—and she had never expected to see one on a six-foot-three- or four-inch walking billboard for manhood.

She stared at the bulging laced-up pouch of fabric attached to his hose, then knew she flushed. She turned away, but not before the Englishman gave her an inviting smile. That attire was shocking and indecent on a man built like that. Women in her time would go nuts for it and him—for all of them!

"So now ye like Englishmen?" Malcolm asked dangerously.

Was he jealous? She took one quick look at him and saw he was irate. She remained too shaken from the morning to be even slightly pleased. "This is a monastery?" She was entirely disbelieving. Except now, the chapel bells were ringing and she saw actual monks leaving the refectory—normal men in robes, some thin, some fat—all utterly silent as they made their way to the church. Then another gorgeous giant, also dressed as an Englishman, appeared from a smaller building and crossed over to the gardens behind the church. And then she saw several other Highlanders coming toward them from another building, all huge, powerful and frigging gorgeous. There was so much testosterone in the air now that she was dizzy. She stared after the trio, her heart racing. Malcolm gave her a dark look.

She met his gaze, thinking that she was undoubtedly surrounded by the most gorgeous, sexy, virile men in the history of the world, but none of them compared to Malcolm of Dunroch.

"A small chapter o' monks remain," MacNeil said, lowering his incredibly thick lashes, "to keep the grounds holy. The monastery became our sanctuary long ago. Most of the monks have gone to other cloisters. 'Tis a secure haven fer us, when we choose to come." He suddenly grinned, dimples deep, his gaze direct. "An' sometimes they are summoned fer the orders I give them."

She swallowed and glanced at Malcolm, who was now royally pissed with his buddy. MacNeil was showing off by letting her know who the boss really was there. "I need the truth," she said, aware of the desperation in her tone.

His gaze moved slowly to her mouth. "Ye have so many questions," he exclaimed softly. "Malcolm has told ye the truth. 'Tis spinning in yer mind, like a top."

"He is really the great-grandson of a goddess?" she cried.

"Aye."

Claire stared at the tawny Highlander. He just smiled at her. Then he said softly, never removing his gaze from her, "Calum, lad, I wish a few moments alone with the lass."

Malcolm turned to Claire. She didn't hesitate. "Please."

He nodded grimly and strode off.

She was alone with the so-called abbot now. "So it's all true. This is a world of good and evil, demons and Masters. The demons have superpowers, and so do you. You're both descended from old gods. Malcolm is descended from that goddess, Faola. And this is a secret brotherhood."

"Aye."

Claire stared, finally accepting reality—or the ultimate nightmare. He stared back, patient but intent. It was so hard to bend her mind around the fact that Malcolm was the great-grandson of a deity. She finally said, with dread, "Is he immortal?"

MacNeil smiled. "None of us be immortal, lass. Brogan Mor died in battle from mortal wounds. He was two hundred and fifty-two."

Claire had almost forgotten. "Can Malcolm die in a battle, too? The way his father did?" That thought made her even more distraught.

"O' course he can. Any Master can die from the worst wounds, if no one heals him—or if he doesna heal himself."

Claire had to know. "And if he isn't hurt, how long will he live? Two hundred years? Five hundred years?"

"I dinna ken."

"Take a guess!" she cried, trembling.

MacNeil sobered. "My guess would be hundreds of years." His expression was searching now, as if he wished to understand the turmoil in her heart.

Claire turned to gaze at Malcolm. She wanted him to have a long life, but this was too much to bear. What if he lived a few hundred years? But it wasn't as if they would be together. When she died at ninety or so, he wasn't going to know about it—or even care.

I will care.

Malcolm's voice sounded loud and clear in her mind, although he stood so far away she couldn't hear him if he spoke to her. "This is really hard," she heard herself say. She forced a smile that felt ghastly at MacNeil. "I wonder if I'll wake up tomorrow in my bed in New York—in a sane world filled with criminals who are sociopaths and perverts, nothing more."

Compassion flitted through MacNeil's emerald-green eyes. "We both ken ye canna return yet."

Claire thought about Sibylla and the demon on the road to Dunroch. She shivered. "I have a major question. Why haven't you guys brought all kinds of modern inventions back to this time? Why are you fighting with swords and not guns? For that matter, why not just suck the life from each other?"

His smile flashed. "I can take yer life away, but not the life of a powerful Deamhan—he'd use his great power to thwart mine. But if I wound him badly, I can take his life very simply, for he'll be too weak to stop me."

Unfortunately, that made sense.

"It takes a great effort to take life, lass. 'Tis often easier to take a man's head with a blade. Besides," he added, "we're Highlanders. Even though we can travel to yer time, we live here."

"What about the rest?"

He became serious. "There be many rules, Claire. When we make our vows, we swear to obey the Code. There be debate to some meanings, but certain rules are clear. A Master shall *not* change history. A Master shall *not* corrupt the present people. A Master shall *not* defy fate. Bringing your guns here would do all o' that."

"And the demons? Surely those time-traveling twerps are into guns and gas."

"We destroy them when they come, whether they bring the future with them or not. When they do, we destroy their weapons." He added softly, "The Deamhanain do not take pleasure in using poison, gas or guns. They take pleasure in torture and pain inflicted with their own foul hands, in rape and then the murder o' innocent life."

"Got it," Claire breathed. She turned away, sick to her stomach. Is that what Sibylla intended for her? Torture, rape and then death?

She touched her throat and walked toward a pair of fir trees, pausing in the shade. She gulped air. Her mind was ready to shut down. "What other powers do the demons have? What is the worst they can do?" *What is the worst Sibylla can do?*

MacNeil's gaze darkened. "If there be a power, there be a demon, somewhere, who has it." His mouth hardened. "But there be a Master, somewhere, who has it, too."

She was swept with unpleasant chills. "Great. Something to look forward to. Invincible demons." Claire sat down on a small, handsomely carved bench.

"I just told ye, there be a Master to vanquish them." He continued, revealing that he was reading her mind, "Sibylla has been given great powers o' evil. She truly enjoys torture, takin' life."

She stared grimly at him. "Lucky me."

"Ye have Malcolm to protect ye. He willna fail, lass."

She began to tremble. "Why? Why am I here, MacNeil? Little old human, scholarly, cowardly Claire!"

"Ye have yearned to be here fer years," he returned. "Ye have yearned to meet Malcolm. Why do ye complain?"

"That is not an answer!" she cried. "And how do you know this? Why was I expected? Damn it, what do the Ancients want of me?" And she realized she considered her journey through time to be fate.

"I have the gift o' sight at times, but I dinna ken what the Ancients intend fer ye. They have nay let me see." He stared intently at her. "My suggestion be this. Dinna fight yer fate."

She stared. "Is Malcolm my fate?"

"I canna answer ye."

"Like hell!" she cried, fists clenched. "You can't—or you won't?"

His face hardened, and in that instant, there was nothing pleasing or reassuring about him. "I willna."

Claire retreated. He could be affable, even flirtatious, but now, there was no mistaking he was a powerful, authoritative man. Like Malcolm, he was a Highland laird—and on Iona, he was a virtual king. "Gotcha," she said.

His face eased slightly.

Claire bit her lip. She wanted to know if she would make it back home and if Amy, John and their kids would live long, healthy lives.

"Ye will return, lass," he said softly. "I be allowed to tell ye that much."

Claire had expected to be thrilled. Instead, she was dismayed. Her stare wandered across the gardens to Malcolm, whose gaze was riveted upon them. Her heart lurched. One day, she would leave him.

She swallowed. "Can you please tell me about my family?"

"If I tell ye yer cousin doesna need ye, will ye believe me?"

Claire hesitated. Could she really trust this man's interpretation of the future when it came to Amy and the kids? It hit her then that Amy had to be told everything. She might know that evil wasn't as random as it seemed, but she couldn't possibly know about inhuman demons, could she?

Or could she?

If the war between good and evil had gone on since time began; if cults existed like this Brotherhood to fight it; if she,

Claire Camden, had uncovered the truth; then damn it all, others had to know, too.

"When will ye ask me what ye really wish to?" MacNeil said softly.

Claire became rigid and her gaze flew to his. Then she glanced at Malcolm. Suddenly, she felt as if Malcolm was listening to their every word, but that was impossible. She was sure that he was listening to her every thought, though.

But there was no avoiding the most frightening subject of all. It was hard to get the words out because she dreaded MacNeil's answer. Her voice was hoarse when she spoke. "He is supposed to protect the Innocent, but he killed an innocent woman during sex. Was it an accident?"

"Aye."

"Then explain it to me," she cried softly. "Because it sounds like a crime of pleasure!"

"He was seduced into the crime by Moray."

Claire felt all the blood drain from her face.

"Evil always hunts the young Masters, those who dinna ken their powers well. Moray wanted Malcolm to take pleasure in death—and then wish to take such pleasure again. He wanted Malcolm to turn demon, Claire."

"Oh, my God," Claire whispered. "He wanted Malcolm's soul."

"Aye. Moray lured Malcolm to Urquhart, battled him there an' left him dyin'. Then he sent a beautiful maid to him—to tempt him to evil."

Claire's mind scrambled. "I don't get it."

He was very serious now. "The Ancients gave us the power to take life from others, not just to destroy evil but to enhance our powers an' to save ourselves from mortality. We are meant to live, Claire, for we are the salvation o' mankind. Malcolm was dyin'. He took life from the woman to heal himself—as he should. But he didna realize he'd taken all she had until it be too late, an' she lay dead."

Claire was on her feet, partly horrified—and partly mesmerized. "I would understand this, except they were having *sex,* MacNeil."

"Ah, lassie, well, power be the ultimate pleasure. Power makes men hot," he said softly, "an' there be no rapture like havin' more power swellin' in the veins."

Claire went still, a very graphic image coming into mind. Taking power was sexually arousing? Taking power and a life force made a man want sex? It was orgasmic?

"Aye," he murmured, and he grinned.

His tone had become so seductive that she instantly knew he'd taken power during sex. She looked from his smoking green eyes toward Malcolm. He was now striding over, appearing enraged.

MacNeil said, his gaze sparkling, "When ye add sex to Le Puissance, there be even more rapture."

When he grinned, appearing very much a naughty boy, Claire knew he had wanted to make her hot. It had worked. In spite of the dire nature of their conversation, every inch of her was inflamed.

She walked away from him, too stunned to be angry with such antics. In a way, this also made sense, because since time began, power was as much an aphrodisiac as beauty, if not more.

She whirled with sudden comprehension. "The women— the victims—they get off on it, too, don't they?"

MacNeil nodded. "Like yer telepathy, lassie. What the man feels, the woman does, an' the other way around."

Malcolm seized her arm. "She's had enough words with ye," he told MacNeil furiously. "But I'll be havin' a few words with ye, meself."

MacNeil shrugged. "Ye be very fortunate, Calum. An' I be a man, as well as a Master. I canna help but admire such beauty an' want it fer meself."

Malcolm was ready to explode and Claire knew it. But

before she could try to defuse his anger, MacNeil said, "I'd never betray ye, lad." He shrugged as if he'd done no wrong and walked away.

Malcolm pulled on Claire, dragging her aside. Claire turned into his arms instead. His eyes widened, and then he gripped her shoulders. Claire stepped closer, knowing what she would find. His huge arousal hit her hip.

"Is that what happened?" she whispered.

"Aye." His gaze held hers searchingly.

"But you were hurt—dying. With me, you're fine. Why do you think you'll lose control?" she cried, touching his cheek.

"Because I've known Le Puissance. Any man who has will want such rapture again. When I be with ye, lass, I have the urge to take one taste—*one taste*—o' yer power."

Claire stared into his heated eyes, aware that his desire, which should have frightened her, was having a very opposite effect. Her heart pounded far too rapidly now. "I trust you," she said, and dear God, she did.

In spite of what he was saying, she moved deeply into his embrace, laying her cheek on his chest, listening to his thundering heart. Her body throbbed against his. Malcolm's hands moved over her back. "Damn the MacNeil fer makin' ye so hot."

"You make me hot," she managed to say. She looked up. "I do trust you. I am certain we can make love without resorting to…" She hesitated. "Le Puissance."

And the moment she had spoken, she felt his body jerk and swell impossibly. "Nay."

"Malcolm!"

"Canna ye try to ken? Moray wanted me to take pleasure in death. He wants me to lust fer Le Puissance."

Claire stared back. Dread arose, and with it, fear. "You do want it again," she said thickly. "You want it from me."

"Aye," he said as roughly. "Yer my test, Claire."

CHAPTER NINE

"MY LORD," his steward said carefully, but his eyes were filled with fear, "the earl of Moray is downstairs and he has requested your presence."

Aidan already knew that the lord of darkness was in his castle. He had felt his dark, chilling presence while he was buried deeply inside the woman who was his most recent lover. He glanced at her with regret. She lay beneath a cover, waist-length blond curls spilling past her naked shoulders, beyond any doubt the fairest woman in all of Scotland. Her beauty was breathtaking—and now she was his. When it came to beauty, he never denied himself. He had been prepared to battle her father for her favors, besieging his keep if necessary until the man came to heel, but that hadn't been necessary. Isabel's father had understood the lengths he would go to have her. There hadn't been bloody battles, just a swift negotiation. Aidan would see Isabel properly wed when he was done with her, providing a very generous dowry. As MacIver lived on land adjacent to Awe, Aidan would marry her off to one of the lesser lords who served him. In the end, Isabel's father would be a new lieutenant serving Aidan, and his daughter would be lady of her own small keep.

Aidan bent over her. He was hardly sated but she was exhausted. "Sleep well, my beauty, ye deserve it." He stroked his thumb over her swollen mouth, when he would prefer to caress her lips with his tongue.

Her eyes shone with adoration. "My lord."

His reputation as a lover with infinite stamina and as much generosity was well established and deserved. He turned away, very pleased. Maybe this time it would be different. Maybe this time the ennui would be slower to come. Thanks to his damn father, he had blood that was always hot but his interest always waned, and quickly. Isabel had been at Awe for five days. He wished he could enjoy her for many months, or even longer, but knew it would be only a matter of weeks before he moved on.

Of course, it didn't really matter. There would be someone new to replace her in his bed. There always was.

Clearly, he had not inherited a single trait from his mother, a noblewoman of great character. She was a woman capable of undying love and loyalty. He could not imagine pining away for a deceased spouse as she did. But she had loved her husband, and she preferred the cloister now that he was gone. Until recently, he had never loved anyone—not his mother, whom he did not know, and not his foster parents, who had raised him only because they had not been given any choice. That had changed, though, with the birth of his son, whom he cherished and adored.

"Shall I tell his lordship you will be down shortly?" Rob asked, his face flushed.

Aidan was still. Briefly he imagined denying the most powerful and dangerous man in the realm. He would relish thwarting Moray, but was hardly foolish enough to do so over such an insignificant issue. He smiled coldly. "Nay. I'll speak with him myself."

His gut twisted as he went downstairs. No one could instill as much tension in him as the earl of Moray. He hated the game they played, the war they waged. There was no other choice. However, there was one small consolation. Moray had yet to kill him, and Aidan had begun to think that he never would. Moray intended victory over him, at all costs. It was a matter of the devil's pride.

The closer Aidan came to the great hall, the more frigid the castle became. He was used to it, but he shivered anyway. The shudder was filled with distaste and dread.

Moray was alone in the great hall, admiring an oil painting by John Constable. No one knew the earl's true age, but he appeared to be in his midthirties. He was so beautiful, blond and blue-eyed, that women fought to share his bed, even though they rarely survived the night. Men fought to enjoy such "favors," too.

He was dressed in the current court style of long red robes and crimson hose, his short, skirted jacket black. And of course, he wore the red, black and gold brat of Moray and many jewels. Moray had furnished the hall over the centuries before handing Castle Awe to Aidan, in the hope of buying his loyalty, aware of his preference for great beauty. Aidan had continued the endeavor, and the vast room was filled with treasures from all over the world and many different centuries, including those in the future.

"I believe you have something for me," the lord of darkness said.

Refusing to reveal his tension, Aidan guarded his mind so Moray could not read his thoughts. But of course the earl would somehow know he had found the missing page in the New York bookstore. Moray had spies everywhere. And he probably spied on Aidan's thoughts when they were not guarded, as well as his dreams.

"Aye, I have found the page from the Cladich. But what good is it to me if I hand it to ye?"

"You will remain in my favor," Moray said softly, his pale eyes gleaming. "You curry nothing but disfavor with your reckless, ungrateful and independent behavior."

"Ye can always take off my head an' be rid of such a nuisance," Aidan said. Moray was undefeated in battle. He could probably do such a thing before Aidan could even unsheathe his sword. Aidan walked to the trestle table and poured claret into a beautiful crystal wineglass made by someone named Baccarat. He handed it to Moray, who accepted it, then poured a glass for himself.

"We both know I am never defeated. In the end, I will win. You will realize you have wasted the first years of your life on the Brotherhood. You are destined to be one of the most powerful demons of all time. You are destined to serve me."

Aidan saluted him and drank. He was not a good man, but he was not evil, either. He had protected Innocence in spite of his ambivalence about his vows, and would continue to do so, although he much preferred seducing it. What he would not do was take pleasure in death, even if at times his loins screamed for such fulfillment. He would kill himself first. He hated Moray that much.

"We both know you will enjoy your new lover even more if you taste her pure life, if you take her power while you are fucking her," Moray murmured.

He stiffened. "Aye, fer a moment." He turned away, aroused and hating it, going to the locked chest on the room's far side. It was from a place called India, and was made of solid gold and silver. He removed the key from the chain on his neck, unlocked it and handed Moray what he wanted—a page from the sacred Cladich. Maybe then the lord of darkness would leave him in peace.

This particular page had great powers, for Aidan had had his priest translate it. The third verse could give life back to the dying, if the wounds were inflicted by sword, or a similar weapon that cut a man in that way, such as a dagger or knife. Considering the nature of most battles, there could be no more important page in the entire book of healing.

Moray took the page instantly, his eyes turned red with fury. "This is useless! Its power is gone."

Aidan smiled, pleased. "Aye, 'tis worthless. I tried it meself on one o' me squires who fell on his sword, impaling himself instantly. But he died from the wound."

Moray let the parchment fall to the floor. "You think to deceive me?"

Aidan's heart accelerated. "I found this in the bookstore. 'Tis nay my fault it be useless. I believe it to be a forgery."

Moray smiled, his eyes still glowing. "You played me and enjoyed it."

Aidan tensed, aware of his fear escalating. He was afraid of Moray, but not of dying, although he very much preferred to live. "Ye didna ask if it be potent." He shrugged.

Moray reached out and cupped Aidan's cheek. Aidan tensed. He leaned close enough that his lips brushed his skin. "Then I'll be taking the woman." He added, his mouth a caress, "This time."

Aidan jerked away in horror, for he understood the threat. Moray would take Isabel, taste her, fuck her and kill her, shouting in pleasure as he did so. And Isabel would die in pleasure, too.

This time.

Next time, there was Aidan's infant son.

Aidan saw red. He grasped the hilt of his sword, bracing himself for battle, his heart thundering now. It was his duty to protect his lover, but he would die for his son. Moray was far more powerful than he was and his victory was certain, but if the Ancients forgave him his many sins, maybe he would discover a new power. Moray must not escape unscathed.

Surely Malcolm of Dunroch, a noble man, would protect his son from the darkness.

A serving wench he sometimes took to bed, a very beautiful fifteen-year-old lass, hurried into the room. Her eyes were glazed and Aidan immediately knew she was entranced.

"My lord." She knelt before Moray.

Aidan drew his sword. "Nay!"

Moray looked down on her and she crumpled slowly to the floor. Aidan did not have to kneel by her to know that she was dead. His power was so great he could take an entire human life in the space of a single heartbeat.

Moray turned, but he did not look sated. Lust burned in his red eyes. "A small warning. I lose patience with every rising moon."

Aidan breathed hard. "One day, someone will send ye to hell."

Moray laughed, and Aidan was flung against the far wall by his invisible force. He had not expected the energy blow and he'd had no time to use his own power to dilute it. His head hit the stone and he saw stars.

When the stars vanished, Moray stood over him. "Next time, Isabel."

Aidan struggled to his feet. "I am done with her," he lied, careful to keep his thoughts blank. "There be someone new. Ye can take her now."

Moray stared, and Aidan knew he was trying to lurk. Aidan changed his thoughts. Moray had fresh power now, making him even stronger than when he'd walked into the door. But that was his way. He took life the way a man took his bread. And until a great Master arose, he would continue his reign of evil, scorching the earth with fresh blood wherever he passed and turning other Innocents into demons for his hordes.

"You remain the same stubborn fool," Moray murmured. "Your hatred does not serve you well. You know the truth. I can give you the power you dream of."

Aidan tensed. His single ambition was power—but not for the reason everyone thought. Power was a necessary bulwark against Moray. Power was protection for himself and his infant son.

"Soon, Aidan, you will bend to me." The red was fading from his eyes. He smiled and vanished into thin air.

Aidan shook with rage and hatred. Then he whirled and raced up the stairs to make certain Isabel was where he had left her—and that she was alive. She lay as still as a perfect statue. He went to her side and touched her breast, only to find it rising and falling in the rhythm of life. His relief knew no bounds.

He straightened.

Aidan had never hated anyone the way he hated his father.

CLAIRE DID NOT WANT to be a test, not of any kind. Not where the outcome was the possession of Malcolm's soul. Malcolm had to be wrong. If they made love, he was not going to lose control. She turned away from Malcolm, staring out at the ocean, over the lower-lying monastery walls.

It was almost unbelievable how quickly she had bought into this terrible new world. She was grim. She wondered if she'd ever feel lighthearted again.

He came to stand behind her. "Dinna brood," he said, his tone lighter, but with an effort. She knew he wanted to offer her some comfort. "Yer on Iona, lass, an' I ken this be what ye have wanted. I'll ask MacNeil if ye can see the Cathach."

She turned. "I'd like that." She hesitated. "Malcolm, it's eerie. It's almost as if Moray is hunting you now."

His eyes flickered, but his expression did not change. It was impossible to read. "'Twas three years ago, Claire. He's nay huntin' me now. He's huntin' other game."

Claire wished she could believe him. "What's three years in the life span of a demon like Moray?"

Malcolm stiffened.

"What is he, five hundred years old? A thousand?"

"I dinna ken. No one does."

Her anger finally erupted. "I hate them! I hate them all! They murdered my mother, Lorie, thousands of others, and they want you, too! Except they want you to turn. Is that the word? Turn? Is that what they call it when a Master is seduced to evil?" Her rage knew no bounds.

"I'll nay be seduced to the dark side, Claire," Malcolm said, his gray eyes flashing. "I'd die by me own hand first."

"That is not reassuring." She hugged herself. "I keep thinking about life back at home. About the hints Amy was always dropping whenever the news featured another pleasure crime. Did she know something? Or did she guess?"

"I dinna ken yer cousin, Claire."

"MacNeil said I am going home. He didn't say when."

Malcolm looked away from her, his face set in harsh lines.

She seized his arm. "When I do, I have to protect my cousin and her children somehow. I need to tell her the truth about evil."

Malcolm grasped her elbow. His eyes blazed. "I must ask ye, how will ye protect them, Claire?"

Claire hesitated. That was a damn good question. "Can you teach me how to fight—no, *kill*—the bastards?"

He stood there, looking very unhappy with her request. "I dinna think so."

But Claire barely heard. Now that she understood the world she lived in, she had damn well better be able to protect herself. This *was* a world at war, and Malcolm was right. There was no safe place to hide. She was terrified, but fighting back was better than hiding. Surely, with some skill and a lot of wit, a human could take down demons.

He was lurking. "Nay! Yer a woman, and a mortal one, at that! Ye have no powers!"

She realized there was no other choice. It was do or die, literally. "They murdered Lorie and my mom. I'm strong. Teach me how to kill demons. You said yourself that Moray dispenses powers from the Duaisean. Why can't I be given powers, too?"

"We be Masters, not magicians! We're born with our powers, Claire. They be in our blood! An' we dinna ha' the Duaisean, Moray does. Even if we did, its powers be fer the Masters, an' only the Masters!" he exclaimed, flushing. "Ye might be able to kill the lower Deamhanain like ye did the other day. Ye might even find a way t' kill Sibylla. But a real

Deamhan like Moray will read yer thoughts! If ye somehow managed to attack him, ye'd have to stop his mind, otherwise he'll suck yer life dry, laughin' as he does so."

Claire trembled, getting the unspoken message. She'd be sexually seduced, too. "How can I stop a powerful demon's mind?"

"Well, let's see," he mocked furiously. "Ye can wield a sword an' behead him, or stab him through the heart!"

A demon had to be instantaneously killed, she thought. "What if I managed to make him unconscious? He couldn't entrance me then or take my life."

"Nay! I willna ha' ye fightin' demons. I'll do the fightin' fer ye."

Like hell, Claire thought. "Teach me to use a sword."

"It takes *years* o' practice! An' even so, ye dinna have the strength to sever a man's head from his body."

"Shit," Claire said. "And damn it, too." But she could do this. Carotid arteries could be slit. Hearts could be punctured. So could lungs. Wrists could be cut. There was no choice. "I'm going to do this, Malcolm, with or without your help."

"I shouldna ha' told ye the truth."

It was too late, Claire thought. Images were flashing in her mind now. The medieval world, the modern world. A world at war...demons and Masters...

A terrible idea began. Eyes wide, she looked up at Malcolm. "Malcolm."

He stared back with dismay.

"I want to find the demon who murdered my mother."

CLAIRE FOLLOWED MacNeil down the very short nave of the chapel, which was set behind the church and apart from it. She hadn't noticed the chapel upon first entering the monastery. The stone building was centuries old, the ceiling low and round. Claire immediately saw the shrine.

A recess was set in the stone wall behind where the altar had once been and an ancient iron reliquary was there, trimmed with gold, the design Celtic. Claire's pulse pounded.

As they stepped up to the shrine, their footsteps echoing, Claire became aware of the power and beauty that cloaked the chapel, heavy and tangible, weighing down the air.

Claire faltered as MacNeil went to the reliquary. There was something so silent and so deep in this church, so vast, so awesome. And if it wasn't God's presence, what was it?

She met MacNeil's gaze and he smiled at her, clearly aware of what she was feeling. Because the ceiling was so low, he stood stooped. "The Masters make their vows here, Claire. Yer feeling more than eight hundred years o' power an' grace."

Claire had never been religious, but he was right. "The Brotherhood came into being when St. Columba founded the monastery here in the sixth century?" she asked.

He dimpled. "Nay. There ha' been Masters since the beginnin' o' time. But the Sanctuary moved t' Iona with the great Saint."

She faced the shrine as MacNeil took a key from the ring chained to his belt and unlocked the reliquary, raising its lid to expose the Cathach. Claire stepped closer and gasped.

The Cathach on display in Dublin was a manuscript. She was staring at a bound book, its cover encrusted with hundreds of blazing gems—rubies, sapphires, emeralds and citrines. A gold lock kept the pages concealed. "It's beautiful!" she said in a low whisper.

"Aye."

Claire gazed at him, her mind racing. "The Cathach in Dublin—it's a copy St. Columba had scribed. This is the real deal, isn't it?"

MacNeil smiled. "The pages were scribed fer us on Dalriada, lass, afore Columba was even born."

Oh, my God, Claire thought in awe. "And it was bound

recently." She wasn't asking a question. Bound books were an invention of the Middle Ages.

"A century ago." MacNeil unlocked the padlock and opened the book.

Claire's heart went wild. Instantly she saw the pages were parchment, hide that was intricately treated in order to be thinned, softened and preserved.

MacNeil was lurking, because he said, "'Tis the hide o' sacred bulls. The Ancients told the shamans how to cure it when they gave us their wisdom an' power."

Claire licked her lips. "The book won't last forever. It needs to be placed in a very sterile environment with precisely the right amount of humidity."

MacNeil grinned at her. "The book has been blessed by the gods, lass. It be eternal."

Claire fervently hoped he was right. She stepped closer. Like the copy on display in the twenty-first century, it was written in old Irish Gaelic. There were no spaces between words, and it was decorated with trumpet, spiral and guilloche patterns, distorting the letters. She could not tear her gaze away. She was staring at a holy Celtic relic—one her peers didn't even know existed.

Claire desperately wanted to read the book, but as she didn't know Gaelic, she couldn't. A translator would be the next best thing. "Read it to me, MacNeil. Just a page."

His eyes widened. "'Tis forbidden—but ye have guessed that already."

She slowly met MacNeil's intense green gaze. "Historians believe the Cathach was used before battle to empower armies. If I recall correctly, a Scot carried it into battle and then it was fought over by clans."

"They are wrong. A Master carried it into battle centuries ago. A demon fought him fer it."

"Of course," Claire murmured. History had been misinterpreted.

"Ye be wise, Claire. Ye dinna need the wisdom o' the Cathach."

She stared at him again. "I need power. I need the kind of power you guys have, so I can hunt demons—so I can hunt the demon that killed my mother."

"I be sorry, lass, but I canna give ye such powers. Only the devil can."

Claire shuddered.

Giving her a sidelong glance, he closed the bejeweled cover and locked it. Then he slid the book back into the reliquary chest, which he also locked.

Wisdom was even stronger than power, Claire thought. She wished to get rid of MacNeil and somehow open the chest and the book. As she couldn't read it, she'd touch the pages and pray. Maybe it would give her the wisdom to find her enemy. Maybe it would give her the wisdom to defeat him, too.

But she wasn't going to try to break the lock of such a sacred relic. She needed the key. She looked at MacNeil, wondering if she could seduce him and take the key as she did so.

He grinned. "Ah, lass, I'd love to be seduced, but ye'd still fail to steal the key. Yer entranced. Ye'll feel better when ye leave the shrine." He laid his large palm on her shoulder. "I need to speak with Malcolm. Stay here if ye wish. We trust ye, lass."

She nodded. His green eyes were warm and amused as he dropped his hand and left.

She trembled. She had actually been thinking of violating a sacred shrine. She did not want to be entranced by the Cathach, but it was hard to think clearly. The power and grace in the chapel felt stronger than ever before.

Claire didn't hesitate. She stepped closer and ran her hands over the gold-filigreed iron chest. She was going to find and kill the demon that had murdered her mother or die trying— with or without enhanced power and wisdom.

But a little help would go a long way.

Claire hadn't prayed in years. Long ago, she had decided God didn't really care about her and her problems. But it felt like He might care now.

Her temples throbbed. So did the iron box under her hand, and her mother's pendant burned her chest. Claire whispered, "Is this why I am here? Am I here to help the Masters somehow? If so, am I supposed to use my mind—my education? Or am I supposed to pick up arms and engage the enemy, the way Malcolm does?"

She inhaled. "I need help. Help me do this. Help me find the strength, the courage, to fight evil. Please keep Amy, John and the kids safe." She bit her lip, thinking of Malcolm, her heart accelerating. "Please help Malcolm. Help him fight evil—help him stay in Your light."

The chapel felt as if it were spinning, like a carousel. "Faola. If you are listening, thank you for sending Malcolm to me." She faltered. Did she believe in the goddess? "Help Malcolm and me. Help us fight evil, help us fight Moray." She shuddered. Moray was Faola's son, if all was to be believed. "And if it's not too much to ask, help me make the right choices. I want to help Malcolm, not hurt him."

She had one more request. "A little superpower would be appreciated." She grimaced. "Amen."

Claire stared at the reliquary, which was as blurred as the rest of the chapel. She fought to breathe slowly, deeply, as she fought for calm. The heaviness in the chapel was suffocating.

And then the air lightened.

Claire realized the reliquary no longer burned her hand and she felt lighter. She felt that He had listened. Maybe the goddess had listened, too.

"Halt!"

Claire froze at the sound of the sharp command, spoken in French.

"Take yer hand from the chest."

Claire slowly turned.

A towering Highlander faced her. Dark and handsome, his eyes blazing with the wrath of gods, he exuded authority and danger. His hand was on the hilt of a two-handed broadsword. Claire knew he wouldn't hesitate to use it. "Step away."

Claire obeyed. "MacNeil said I could spend a few minutes alone. I needed to pray."

His eyes widened. They were spring-green, lighter than MacNeil's. "Yer an American."

Claire was surprised. Had he traveled to her country in her time?

But he had not relaxed. Suspicion filled his strong features. He gestured now. "Come forward."

Claire did so. "I am with Malcolm of Dunroch," she said tersely. This man appeared to be about forty, which meant he was older even than MacNeil, didn't he? His eyes were hard, terribly hard. He did not look as if he had ever smiled, not once in his entire long life. He made Malcolm, Royce and MacNeil look like charming playboys.

His eyes narrowed, sliding over her in a cursory inspection, and then it veered abruptly to her throat. He met her gaze. "If ye be friends with Malcolm and if MacNeil truly left ye alone here, then I will only advise ye to never touch the shrine."

"I'll go."

"Ye be from a foreign land, but ye wear a Highland charm."

Claire froze. She touched her pendant, which was shockingly hot again. First Malcolm had been fascinated with the stone, now this stranger. "Yes. It was my mother's. Who are you?"

"Ironheart of Lachlan."

When he didn't elaborate, Claire said uneasily, "I should go. I bet Malcolm is looking for me."

"How did your mother get the stone?"

"I don't know."

"May I see it?"

Claire stiffened. She rarely took the charm off, and then only to clean and polish it. She didn't want this stranger touching it.

"Lady." He smiled now. His eyes had become warm and friendly. "Mayhap a proper introduction is in order? I be the earl of Lachlan, an old friend of Malcolm's." His tone had softened and Claire had no doubt he often used it on women to lure them to his bed.

"I am Claire—Lady Claire Camden," she amended, relaxing.

He nodded, his gaze holding hers. "My brother had a similar stone once. It was stolen. I canna help wonder if ye wear his stone." His regard became intense.

Claire was stunned. It was impossible to look away.

"I should like to see the stone more closely," he murmured, his stare turning to smoke, yet it remained direct, penetrating. "I ken ye dinna mind to give it over to me, Claire Camden."

Why would she mind? she wondered. She reached for the clasp and undid it, handing the necklace over.

As he held the pendant up to the light, the fog lifted. Claire realized she had been entranced and she shook her head to clear it. She had just handed her mother's necklace to a medieval stranger! Ironheart's power to mesmerize was far more potent than Malcolm's. She hadn't been able to even think about what he had asked her to do until he turned away.

She bit her lip, shaken.

He handed it back to her, ruefully smiling, his eyes soft. "'Tis nay my brother's, but then, 'twould be a miracle if it was." His tone was offhand, but his gaze was searching.

Claire put the necklace back on, avoiding his eyes. "Malcolm is looking for me," she said firmly, wanting to get away from this man. He had so much power. Didn't the demons have this kind of power, too? She must never let her guard down again, not in this time or any time.

"I'll take ye to him," Ironheart said. "'Tis my pleasure."

"If Aidan has the page from the Cladich, I be confident he will bring it here," MacNeil said. The two men were strolling in the orchard, where no one, not even another Master, could overhear them.

"An' I nay be confident," Malcolm said flatly. "I go to Awe immediately."

"Give Aidan a chance to relinquish the page," MacNeil said softly, but it was an order and they both knew it.

"How many chances will ye give him before ye ken he be as evil an' twisted as Moray?"

"Is that what ye really believe?"

Malcolm tensed. The truth was, he didn't know what to believe about the Wolf of Awe. Aidan had been sworn to uphold the Code, but as often as not he ignored his orders, chasing his own ambition. While his father, Moray, had given him Castle Awe, clearly forging an alliance with his rebel son, Aidan had turned around and married a great heiress, vastly expanding his lands and his power. It was uncertain if he supported Moray or not. His wife had died a few months ago in childbirth, his son surviving. Malcolm knew Aidan would find another heiress, and soon. Aidan had also somehow convinced the king to pass on his wife's title to him, when the title should have passed directly to his son. He was now the earl of Lismore.

What Malcolm did know was that Aidan could not be trusted.

"Aidan can bring the page to ye, under my protection, by my escort, or he can hand it over to me. One way or another, ye will have the page." Malcolm meant it. He relished the coming confrontation.

"I see ye will harbor yer grudge. When will ye speak of what ye really wish to speak of—the beautiful woman?" MacNeil smiled with knowing amusement.

Malcolm's blood swelled in his veins. He could not control his mind, his desire or his rising cock. In a few hours, it would be dark....

"I ken what ye wish to be asking, Malcolm," MacNeil said with a laugh.

He faced MacNeil angrily. "Will it amuse ye when I take the woman t' bed and at dawn she is lyin' there dead?"

MacNeil's smile faded. "Ye have not strayed a single time since Urquhart. Why do ye think to stray into the dark now? Ye tasted unholy pleasure once. Ye can master the urge to do so again."

Malcolm knew he turned red. "I fear my lust is unholy," he flashed. "Because I want her more than I have ever wanted any woman or anything. I think when I am comin' inside her, I will want more than her body."

"Then ye'll have to fight temptation," MacNeil said, his tone dry. "Will ye not?"

"Yer enjoyin' my discomfort!"

"Aye, I am. Go fuck a chambermaid. That should help."

"I dinna want another! An' I ken ye have the power t' help me, MacNeil." He was angry and frustrated enough to throw a primitive blow at him, but he managed to restrain himself. "Mayhap ye be thinkin' to deny me, as I have denied ye!"

MacNeil's eyes widened with mock innocence. "Have we ever fought over a woman?"

Malcolm stared. He finally said, with warning, "I will never fight ye. But she is *mine*."

MacNeil sighed, but his eyes twinkled. "Yer young an' hot, an' I barely recall such days. What kind o' power do ye think I have?"

"The power t' take my powers, just fer a day an' a night. Find a spell."

MacNeil grinned. "Not too greedy, are ye, lad?" He laughed. "Canna ye not ask me nicely? And canna ye manage with an hour?"

Malcolm was in disbelief. MacNeil would only suspend his powers to take life for a single hour? Was he mad? That was worse than not taking them away at all. He'd be better off avoiding her entirely than spending a single hour with her. "Do ye wish fer me to grovel?"

MacNeil became serious. "Malcolm. I can see yer as frustrated as a green lad. I can suspend the power. But for a day an' a night? Are ye mad? Has she stolen yer reason? You'd be defenseless against the likes of Sibylla, much less Moray, for far too long. He'll sense your weakness if ye go for so long without powers."

"An hour is not enough. And my patience be gone."

He had never meant anything more. He had to get her beneath him. He wanted to taste her lips, her skin, her sex, to push deep inside hot, wet, tight flesh and sheathe himself there all night. He wanted her to come a hundred times. He could see them together in his mind's eye. She would match him in lust, aye, stroke for stroke, climax for climax. He somehow knew it.

"I need the spell *now*," Malcolm said, flushing. After they were finally sated, he was going to hold her in his arms until dawn broke. Maybe she would tell him more about her world. Maybe they could speak lightly about unimportant matters, as if the real world and all the burdens he carried did not exist. Maybe she could explain why the fashion in her time was rags and strings. He smiled.

"If yer beginning to care fer the lass, ye had better think carefully about what that means," MacNeil said softly, cutting into his thoughts.

He had lurked. Malcolm was not a gentleman. His interest in women was basic. He provided for those under his protection, and those he lusted for, he seduced. Warm embraces and casual conversations were not a part of any relationship he had ever had.

"Dinna become fond o' the woman. She'll be used against ye. She'll make ye weak."

"I be nay fond o' her." Malcolm was uneasy. "Did ye tell Claire she'll go back to her time?" He kept his mind closed now, so MacNeil could not lurk. He shouldn't care, but he did.

"Aye," MacNeil said, staring closely. "Mayhap ye should avoid that road."

"An' which road is that?" Malcolm said, fists clenched. MacNeil had the power of sight. At times it refused to come to him, but when it came, he was never wrong. No matter how Malcolm protected her, and no matter how well he pleased her in bed, she was going to leave him in the end.

He could barely believe it.

"Forget what's betwixt yer legs." But MacNeil choked on laughter, as no Master was going to forget his needs.

Malcolm debated using his fist to erase all of MacNeil's amusement.

"Ye be so intent!" MacNeil exclaimed. "How can I nay be amused? She's only a woman, Calum—pretty enough, but there be thousands more."

"Will ye give me the spell?"

"Aye, I will, because I feel how much yer hurtin'." He grinned again.

Then he became utterly serious. He placed both hands on Malcolm and murmured in such an ancient tongue that Malcolm did not understand it. When he had finished, he released him, smiling. "Ye can begin yer lovemaking at moonrise, but the spell won't last once ye can see the sun."

Malcolm nodded, a savage excitement beginning. "I'll be owin' ye."

"An' I will collect." MacNeil's gaze moved past him. He followed his gaze and saw Claire as she entered the courtyard beyond the orchard. His pulse leaped. In a few hours, he would be allowed to make love to her as passionately as he wished.

He saw that she was accompanied by Ironheart. While Malcolm did not know the enigmatic man well, his reputation preceded him and Malcolm respected him greatly. Very pleased, he left the orchard with MacNeil, seeking out her thoughts as he did so. Malcolm instantly recognized Claire's unease.

"He be a friend, lass," he said when they had approached.

Claire sent him a slight smile back. *I want to talk to you, alone.*

Then, *I saw the Cathach!*

Reading her thoughts was a good thing, not a bad thing, and he didn't understand why it always annoyed her when he did so. Her excitement made him soften somewhere in his chest. He faced Ironheart. *"Hallo a Alasdair."*

"Hallo a Chaluim," Ironheart returned.

He reverted to English. "We go t' Awe as soon as me affairs here be finished."

Ironheart was clearly interested. "Since when do you visit the Wolf? I didna ken ye be comrades."

"We're nay friends," Malcolm replied softly, thinking about the page Aidan surely had. If Ironheart could be convinced to go with them, he would be a useful ally if Aidan was unwilling to part with the holy page.

Ironheart absorbed that. "Mayhap I'll return to Lachlan in a more leisurely manner."

Malcolm smiled. "I had hoped ye would say as much."

Ironheart nodded at Claire and he and MacNeil walked into the chapter house, leaving them standing alone outside.

Claire stared after the pair, distressed. "I hope that doesn't mean what I think it does."

"Aye, lass, he will come with us t' Awe." Seeing her grim expression, he brushed her shoulder, well aware that what he really wanted to do was pull her close. "I can use his help if I must fight Aidan."

Claire's expression paled. "Aidan is at Awe?"

"Aye." He instantly read her thoughts. "He's nay a Deamhan, lass. He be a Master, too."

Her eyes widened. "But the two of you tried to kill one another!"

"He be a rogue. He dinna obey the Code. He dinna have any conscience, any heart. I dinna trust him with the page. He'd as likely give it t' Moray as us."

"Great! A Master who is turning!" she cried. She rubbed her temples. Malcolm could feel them throbbing. She was scared and worried about him, and not just because he might fight Aidan. She was afraid of Moray—which was as it should be.

But her concern pleased him greatly. *Maybe MacNeil was wrong about the future, this one time.* "Lass, I be pleased when ye care fer me, even a little," he said softly, giving in and pulling her close. He bumped her hip and wanted to moan. He did not.

But she had felt his arousal, too. She gasped, her gaze seeking his.

He was proud of his virile erection. "Aye, I be needin' ye, lass," he murmured, sliding his hands down her strong back. He pulled her closer, throbbing with growing urgency against her belly. He wished they were back at Dunroch and the hours had passed. He knew she was ready for him—he could feel her desire expanding at an uncontrollable rate.

And he also felt her mind racing in circles, debating whether she should give in to him and join him in bed or not. And as his control was still fragile, he released her. "I willna hurt ye, Claire."

She was breathing hard. "It's not that."

She hesitated, and he felt her thinking, not about the fact that he'd spent many nights in a lover's bed without losing control, but about her inability to guard her heart from him if she shared his bed. She was afraid to love him. But he had told her, he didn't mind. He would like it if she did. He was never going to genuinely understand her fear of loving him, because he was a powerful lord and other women happily fell in love with him. Other women did not mind having his favors just for a short time.

And he would never understand her absurd need to love a man in order to have sex with him. "Ye willna be sorry," he tried, smiling into her eyes. They mirrored her conflict. "I intend to please ye greatly. However ye choose, lass."

Her eyes widened and he felt her body flame. There was so much desire in her he could not stand it.

He leaned closer, touched her face. "Ye like it when I talk about it, do ye not? Dinna refuse me, lass. MacNeil has suspended my powers for the night. We mayna have other nights so soon. I need t' come inside ye, an' ye need to have me there. I need t' see ye takin' yer pleasure, Claire, an' I need to hear an' feel ye comin', too."

She nodded, and he felt her hollow hugely, enough so that he could fill the space, right then, right there.

"We'll leave fer Dunroch as soon as the galley returns," he murmured. He reached out, reeled her in. Like an adolescent boy, he could no longer think straight.

She gasped and reached for his shoulders. "Malcolm. Okay."

Triumphant, he kissed her, deep.

CHAPTER TEN

THE SUN WAS SETTING as they trekked up the short, steep ascent to Dunroch from the port below. The galley had been portaged halfway up the road and then laid on wood blocks. Claire chose to walk far behind Malcolm, hoping for some privacy for her thoughts, even though she wanted to get inside Dunroch's walls before dark. No day could have been longer. There had been one stunning revelation after another, without respite. She was mentally and emotionally exhausted.

Claire glanced ahead toward the drawbridge and gatehouse. In another hour or so it would be dark.

Claire's desire flared. And Malcolm knew, because he halted and turned to look at her.

There was no longer any decision to make about their relationship. She wanted him acutely, so much so that she could almost feel him inside her now, hot and strong, the friction insane. She had a frightening attraction to him, one she no longer believed she could resist, even if she wanted to. But she didn't want to resist. There was no point.

Her world had changed. She didn't know if she was going to live for very long, and the values she'd clung to her entire life seemed frivolous now. Waiting for love in order to be with a man like Malcolm was absurd, given the probability that her life span was going to be really short, despite what MacNeil had said.

She'd had time to think about that. If he had seen her imminent demise, he would not tell her. That might only lead

to a self-fulfilling prophecy. And Claire was pretty certain
that, unless she was given superpowers, she wasn't going to
survive for very long as a Deamhan hunter. The Deamhanain
were just too damn strong.

As for falling in love with Malcolm, she'd fight her heart's
ridiculous need for love before having sex. And if she failed,
so what? A broken heart didn't seem like the worst deal. It
seemed pretty mundane, in fact.

The men vanished through the gatehouse. Malcolm waited
for her by the drawbridge. As she came up to him, his gray
eyes gleamed with anticipation. Claire walked past him.
Acutely aware of him behind her, she went through the gatehouse and into the bailey. The men were veering off toward
their hall, glad cries sounding from some children as they did
so. Claire was relieved to be inside the curtain walls, more
so when she turned to watch the drawbridge being raised, the
portcullis slamming closed. Malcolm smiled with so much
promise that her heart turned over in response, as if to say,
"Tough luck." Her world had changed but her heart didn't
seem to care.

She followed Ironheart into the hall. Malcolm paused to
close the studded front door behind her, and his gaze was not
directed upon her now. Claire was very surprised to see Royce
sitting before the fire. As they all walked into the room, he
rose, quads rippling, biceps bulging.

Malcolm strode forward, meeting Royce halfway across
the hall, clearly surprised to see him. "What brings ye back?"

Royce said, his tone noncommittal, "I decided a visit to
Aidan be in order. I will join ye tomorrow."

Claire saw Malcolm's expression become as blank as
Royce's. She wondered what the hell was going on.

She hesitated. Both Seamus and Irohheart had sat down
on the benches at the long table, taking up mugs of wine. She
could smell roasted game and knew a meal was about to be
served, and in spite of her worries, she was starving.

But Ironheart continued to make her uneasy. She had felt his eyes on her repeatedly during the journey back to Mull and knew he did not like or trust her. Now, she smiled at him, helping herself to a mug of claret, as well. "May I?" Claire asked.

"Lady Claire, o' course ye can sit. Ye be Malcolm's guest."

Claire sat down across from him, aware of Malcolm glancing at her. "Thank you."

Ironheart stared. "Why do ye wish to go to Awe with Malcolm?"

Claire met his flat gaze. "Why not?"

"There may be battles ahead."

"I can protect myself." Claire grimaced. She needed a weapon. But Malcolm didn't seem all that worried about facing off with Aidan, and that was comforting. On the other hand, nothing was comforting about the earl of Moray, whom Claire had learned was Defender of the Realm, the Highland equivalent to commander in chief. "Refresh my memory—who is king?"

Ironheart gave her an odd glance. "James be king an' afore ye ask, his queen be Joan Beaufort."

"Are they on our side or—theirs?"

"The king spent most o' his life a hostage o' King Henry V in England. He has but one side—his own."

Claire translated Ironheart's words to mean that King James was human. If he'd spent most of his life held at the English court, he was probably interested in his own power and his own throne. Most of Scotland's kings had had huge problems bringing the Highlands under control. That would explain the summons.

On the other hand, a new source of power existed, and it was evil. She did not like where her mind wanted to go, but all James had to do was sell his soul and the kingdom would be his—with Moray at the forefront of his troops.

Moray was already there.

Her temples ached. Maybe James had sold his soul already. "I need a weapon," she said seriously, looking up. Going to Awe unarmed was insane. "I need a dagger—and Malcolm must show me how to use it."

"An' that will help ye do what, lass?"

Another medieval chauvinist, she thought. She decided not to bother to fill him in on the state of modern women. "Well, I was actually thinking about staying alive, and defending myself when my *protector* isn't about. There's the little matter of the Deamhanain. They seem to appear out of nowhere— whoops, out of time—and I am not looking forward to facing Sibylla again." That was a gross understatement. But if she couldn't vanquish Sibylla, a human possessed by evil, how would she ever get the demon who'd murdered her mother?

"Lass, ye will never find the Deamhan who killed yer mother. Leave it to a Master."

"Like hell," Claire said softly. "I just need tools, weapons, knowledge. And it's rude to read my mind!"

Ironheart stared. Then he spoke grimly. "If Malcolm will nay teach ye, I will."

"You? Why would you do such a thing?" She was incredulous.

"I have spoken the same vows as Malcolm, Claire. 'Tis my duty t' protect ye. If ye think to hunt a Deamhan, then ye need some skill. But," he added darkly, "ye willna succeed alone. Ye had better sway Malcolm to yer cause."

She had already reached that exact conclusion. "Thank you."

His attention was diverted as two women began placing streaming trays of meat and fish on the table. Both men began to heap their trenchers with game and fish.

Claire was also diverted, for Malcolm and Royce were coming to sit down. Royce smiled at her. *"Hallo a Chlaire."*

"Hallo a Rhuari," she returned swiftly in Gaelic.

His smile widened as he sat down besides her. *"Ciamar a tha sibh?"*

Claire had heard this phrase several times since arriving in the past. She had also heard the response. *"Tha gu math,"* she said.

Royce grinned and Malcolm turned to stare. Royce murmured, "An' you might also say, *Tapadh leibh.*"

He was flirting. Claire didn't mind, and why would she? His chest rippled beneath the leine and his biceps bulged. Today he wore a huge, wide gold cuff on his left arm, one with a citrine cross in its center. Besides, maybe he was only half the chauvinist that Malcolm was. She might need an ally down the road. *"Tapadh leibh,"* she said.

He smiled, revealing the fact that he had dimples, too. "Ye have a fine ear, lass," he murmured.

"Did you just ask me how I am?"

"Aye, and ye said, 'Fine, thank ye kindly.'" His gray eyes were warm—too warm.

Malcolm sat down beside Ironheart, facing them, his gaze narrowed. He was not pleased.

"O' course, if we be familiar," he said softly, "I'd ask ye differently. *Ciamar a tha thu?*"

He *was* definitely flirting. And Malcolm was jealous. Claire was pleased. She also understood. She'd caught quite a bit of Gaelic in the past few days. *"Tha gu math, tapadh...leat?"*

Royce's eyes gleamed. "Ye learn fast, lass."

Malcolm slammed his fist on the table. "An' I'll be the one teachin' her now."

Claire grinned, enjoying his primitive jealousy. There was an upside to medieval chauvinism. "But Ironheart has already offered to teach me how to fight with a dagger and a sword," she said innocently, batting her lashes at him.

Ironheart choked.

Malcolm turned red. "Like hell. We already discussed this. Ye'll wind up dead. I ken ye wish t' fight the Deamhanain, Claire, but ye canna. Yer a woman, an' a mortal one at that."

Claire became dead serious. "Do you think I think I will

succeed? But I have to try! My days are numbered—I know it. But I will do what I have to do. Which is why you must help me by teaching me what I need to know!"

Malcolm recovered his composure. "Lass. Yer too brave fer yer own good."

He meant it and even though he was wrong, his praise moved her to no end. "Malcolm, I'm not brave. I'm afraid. But you need to try to see my side."

"A warrior without fear be a very foolish man," Malcolm said. "Men fight because they are strong. Women stay safe behind stone walls t' bear their bairns. 'Tis the way o' the world. If I can, when we are done here, I'll find the Deamhan who murdered yer mother."

He wasn't going to even try to hear what she was saying, she thought. It took Claire a moment to respond. "Is it your vows? Do you think to protect me even when I leave because you swore to do so? Because when I go back, my life is my own."

His jaw flexed. "I ha' told ye again an' again, I dinna wish to see ye dead."

She reached across the table for his hand. "Do not get me wrong. I am grateful for the protection you have given me, Malcolm, I am. But it might take *years* to find the demon who killed my mom and you're pretty busy right here in 1427." She hesitated. "I know you'll never understand me—what I want, what I need, what I have to do—or my world." The comprehension hurt.

Anger entered his gray eyes. "Ah, lass, ye be arrogant again—annoyingly so!"

"You listen, but you refuse to hear a word I am saying!" she cried, upset as she realized the extent of the cultural gulf between them. "It's not even the way of this world, Malcolm, because in a few years in France, Joan of Arc is going to lead her people in battle against her enemies. And in the time of your ancestors, women were great warriors, fighting alongside their men. In my time, women are soldiers. They go to war and they fight and die beside men."

Malcolm said softly, dangerously, "As long as I can breathe, I will keep ye safe. 'Tis the vow I took t' protect the Innocent and ye be *my* Innocent, Claire. Even when ye leave me, that canna change."

She tensed, because he had spoken of her returning to her time in such a personal way. And she knew that she had come up against a brick wall. "There's a bottom line. If you want to protect me until I die, I guess I can't stop you. But my life belongs to me. If I want to avenge my mother, no one can stop me. Now that I know the truth, how can I sit back and do nothing? If that demon is alive, I have to try to avenge my mother. You would do the same damn thing for your mother."

Malcolm paled.

And Claire knew she had said something terribly wrong, because the three other men at the table stilled. Abruptly everyone turned their attention to their plates except for Malcolm. She looked at him and saw that he was stricken.

"Malcolm," she said carefully. "I'm sorry. Whatever I just said, it was a mistake." But she didn't have a clue as to what she had done to upset him so.

Malcolm shoved his empty trencher aside. For one moment he stared at it, clearly grappling with his emotions, and then he stood. He walked out into the night.

Claire looked at the men. "What just happened?"

Royce said softly, "His mother be a sore spot, lass."

Claire remained utterly clueless. Then she leaped up and ran after him.

Outside, the night had settled, a Highland darkness filled with a billion bright stars. She saw Malcolm walking up the stairs to the ramparts. He wanted to be alone, she was certain. Claire went after him anyway.

"Nay now, lass," he said, not turning, his gaze directed across the ocean, an expanse of shimmering ebony.

Claire paused behind him. "Can you tell me what I said to distress you so?"

"Ye be right. Vengeance be proper. Yer a warrior in yer heart, and ye burn to avenge yer mother."

Claire wet her lips. "Glenna told me your mother is English, but that's all. Is this about your mother—or about your father?"

A silence fell. "Aye. 'Tis about them both."

And Claire knew something terrible had happened. She took his hand and held it.

He shrugged free. "Moray raped my mother," he said suddenly, quietly. "When she was a bride."

Claire made sure not to gasp, but she was horrified. And then she became afraid. "Moray isn't your biological father, is he?"

His jaw tensed. "I was born three years later, Claire. Nay. I be the son o' Brogan Mor."

Claire bit her lip, beyond relief. "Was it a pleasure crime?"

He shook his head. "It be rape. Brutal, sadistic, hurtful rape. It be torture, Claire. Moray raped Lady Mairead when my father went to battle, many times. He could have murdered her, but he wanted to spare her, to worsen the torment. My mother tried to hang herself, but her maid found her in time." He added, nostrils flared, "She's cloistered now."

Claire felt tears well. "I am sorry! That's a terrible story!"

He faced her, eyes blazing. "I didna ken the truth until I'd made my vows." His laughter was harsh, angry. "The night afterward, my uncle told me exactly why Moray be my mortal enemy. An' he begged me to leave the man who raped my mother *alone,*" he said sarcastically.

Claire began to realize what had happened. "Oh, God. That's when you went after Moray. And he toyed with you, didn't he? That's when you fought, when you almost died, when he entrapped you with the woman."

He faced her, his expression harsh, ruthless. "My father spent his life seeking revenge an' he failed. I sought revenge.

I failed. I dinna want t' see ye raped, Claire, or worse! I dinna want t' see ye die."

Claire wiped an errant tear, heartbroken for him, his mother and father, but dread was blooming. Moray hadn't killed Mairead—he wanted her to spend a lifetime suffering. And he'd used her as bait in the trap he'd set for Malcolm.

He said roughly, "Do ye ken? I must protect ye. I canna fail ye."

Claire swallowed hard. "Yes. I get it." *Was Moray done with the Macleans—or not? Was he done with Malcolm?*

His gaze held hers. "Yer world may be different. I dinna ken. But in my world, I protect women. In my world, I protect ye. Or I die in the tryin'." He softened. "Will ye nay allow me t' protect ye, lass?"

Claire nodded, overwhelmed. But she could not change her mind about what she had to do. She wasn't Mairead, or anything like her. No matter how strong Malcolm was, she couldn't rely on him as if she were a fifteenth-century woman. She didn't even have a choice, not anymore. Maybe Malcolm was right about one thing. Maybe in her heart, she was a warrior, because she had to have vengeance.

But she wasn't going to argue. He would never change his mind, that was now clear. He was filled with guilt, and his failure to avenge his mother was something he'd live with forever. Except the man standing in the dark before her was burning with determination. "You were young and rash," she said through stiff lips. "But it's different now, isn't it?"

His eyes flickered; he looked away.

"Oh, God. It's not over. You're biding your time. You'll never rest—not until you've vanquished Moray or somehow paid him back, equally."

He faced her, his gray eyes burning. "One day, we'll meet again. I may die. It won't matter. Because I will take him with me—this time."

Claire panicked, not for herself but for Malcolm. "Is your

power equal to his?" She already knew that answer. "Haven't Masters tried to vanquish him for centuries? Two wrongs don't make a right!"

"The day will come," he said, so softly chills swept over her. "Dinna fear fer me. The day I die, if Moray dies I be pleased, Claire, very pleased."

Claire couldn't speak. Impossibly macho, impossibly heroic. Damn it, he was the one who was going to die.

He reached out. "Canna ye have some faith in yer man, lass?"

Her man. She looked up and he met her gaze, his regard sweeping and intense. "I have faith. I'm just so worried now."

His smile began, so soft and so beautiful it left her breathless. "Ah, lass, ye have a care fer me." His grasp tightened. "But ye will fight me anyway."

She bit her lip. It wasn't a question and they both knew it. "Sometimes," she said carefully, her heart slamming so much she thought she might explode, "a difference of opinion between a man and a woman is a good thing."

He reeled her in with another soul-shattering smile. "Aye," he whispered. "A very good thing. Ye let me worry, Claire. Let me worry—let me fight—let me please ye…now."

She was in his arms, her breasts crushed by his iron chest. The night was velvet on her bare calves, her cheek. And Malcolm was as hard as a rock against her belly, her waist. *This was it,* she somehow thought. And now, there was only one possible conclusion to their opposing world views. "Malcolm," she breathed.

His gaze moved over her face, his large hands sliding over her back. He smiled, touching her lips with his mouth, just once. "Aye, lass, I ken what ye need from me. An' ye ken what I need from ye."

Claire inhaled as his hands slid lower, firmly grasping her bottom over the denim skirt and linen tunic, pulling her entirely against a very impressive erection. "Oh." His arousal was burning hot, even though her clothes.

He ran his tongue along her full lower lip. Claire gasped, while his hands delved lower, beneath the brat and leine, over her miniskirt, fingertips perilously close to where she wished them to be, on the back of her bare thighs. He licked at her lips, the tip of his tongue relaxing, murmuring, "Ye still wear the rag."

"It's...a...skirt."

"Nay," he breathed. And he took her mouth with his.

Claire forgot about everything except the man she wanted. She moaned in pleasure, holding on to his huge shoulders as he turned her, pressing her against the wall, his mouth firm and commanding, forcing her to part her lips for him. His tongue swept deep. If he could make her throb greedily in a near climax with his tongue down her throat, she knew she'd die and go to heaven when they made love.

So much heat ran through her, swelling her sex impossibly, that she could not stand it. But before she could beg him to either take her down to bed or take her there, against the wall, he reached between them, beneath her skirt. The moment his fingers found her turgid flesh, spreading her there, she flung her head back and sobbed as pleasure exploded over her. And then she felt the massive tip of him, bare, hot and slick, pressing against her swollen lips. He rubbed himself back and forth, breathing hard, and she dug her fingers into his shoulders, spinning mindlessly, so much pleasure cresting. He seized her thigh, helping her wrap it around his waist.

His face pressed to her ear, he murmured, "Hold on *tight*." And he thrust hard and deep.

Wet, hot, huge strength. Claire gasped, blinded by having Malcolm finally inside of her, stretching her wide. His size was shocking, and she felt the power bursting from his erection. Claire felt a violent climax begin, making the first one pitiful in comparison, rolling over her in greater and greater waves. Pleasure escalated impossibly, until there was only mindless ecstasy, spasm after spasm, as he slowly and deliberately moved his massive length and breadth inside her. He gasped and she sobbed and keened.

Malcolm began thrusting with real urgency. The waves kept building. Claire thought she might die. This must be what he had been talking about, pleasure in death. She was shattering over and over in a black universe of ecstasy and she was never coming out. She didn't want to ever return to reality again.

Malcolm gasped. She felt him expand, lengthen, explode. Hot seed scalded, going deep. And it didn't stop…

Claire did not know how long she had been in the throes of either multiple orgasms or a single endless one, but at some far point in time, her body finally softened, giving up its greedy grasp on pleasure, and she began to float back into Malcolm's arms. He kissed her cheek. Still dazed, she realized he remained hard and engorged, his entire body shaking, as if he hadn't come. But that was impossible—except—she wasn't imagining things. In fact, unless time moved differently here, she was beginning to think his orgasm had been extraordinary in duration, as well.

He kissed her cheek again and Claire realized she rode his waist, her back pinned to the rough rampart wall. And to make matters even more interesting, her body was warming to his once more as he impaled her still.

"Let me take ye to my bed, Claire," he murmured in the sexiest tone she had ever heard.

Desire flamed. "We don't need a bed," she said thickly. She could not manage even the briefest separation.

And he started moving inside her again, long and slow. "I canna fuck ye properly against a wall."

She smiled against his face. She couldn't imagine what that meant. "Then hurry."

He pulled away, holding her as she came to her feet. "Lusty wench," he murmured, his eyes ablaze.

No man had ever looked at her with so much heat. Claire

hollowed, desire fisting in her gut, her knees useless. And then she froze.

They hadn't used protection.

"Claire?"

"May I assume that you might get me pregnant?" she managed to say.

Instantly he swept her up into his arms, smiling. "Yer not in yer time o' month, Claire. If ye were, I wouldn't be filling ye with my seed."

"What?" she cried.

"I can sense when yer fertile. Can ye imagine how many bastards a Master would have otherwise?"

"Are you certain?"

"I am very certain," he said with a wicked smile as he carried her down the narrow stairs.

She was so relieved. "Can you put me down? I'm not a feather. I'm five foot ten, for God's sake!"

"Aye, and most of ye be legs. I be a fortunate man, especially when ye have them around my waist."

He kicked open the door to his chamber, thrilling Claire. Elbowing the door closed, he swiftly crossed the room and laid her on the bed. His smiled re-formed as he tossed his brat aside. Claire sat up against the pillows, highly interested now. He grinned, removing each boot in turn. "I like yer eyes on me that way."

Claire didn't answer; she couldn't. She was interested in one thing now—the object that had given her so much extraordinary pleasure. As he tossed the leine aside, she inhaled.

He sat down beside her, laughing. "Ye have nay shame."

She wet her lips and ran her fingertips down his incredibly thick length. His smile vanished. She looked into his eyes, then abruptly stood.

Claire fumbled with the brooch.

Malcolm became still, watching. His eyes were molten silver now.

"I like your eyes on me that way," Claire whispered. He didn't smile and she knew he couldn't.

She shed the brat and belt, and then tugged the leine over her head. She faced him in her miniskirt and tee. His eyes were so hot she expected a fire to break out in the room.

He nodded. "Go on, lass."

She trembled, heat dripping down her thighs. That had been an order and just then, she liked his macho ways. She stepped out of her boots, her skirt riding high over her ass as she bent over. Malcolm didn't make a sound but she felt his lust escalate.

She faced him, slowly tugging off the tee and pausing with the hands on the snap of her denim skirt.

Malcolm was breathing hard. His penis looked fuller, bigger, but that was impossible. "What do ye call the chemise?"

"A bra," she said softly. It was sheer and lacy and Malcolm seemed mesmerized. She unsnapped her skirt and let it pool to the floor.

Malcolm's gaze flew to what the lace thong contained. "Turn around," he ordered. "Show me the entire garment."

Claire didn't laugh. She was ready to have an orgasm just standing there. She slowly turned in a circle, and before she had finished, he stood behind her, his huge erection pressing between her buttocks, his mouth on the side of her neck, his hands beneath the soaking-wet thong, covering her sex. Claire cried out, throbbing in his palm.

"Ye be so very beautiful, Claire," he whispered harshly. And then he lifted her up abruptly and Claire fell back into the pillows.

He spread her thighs. Claire went still as her heart lurched and raced in wild anticipation. Braced up on all fours, Malcolm met her eyes with his hot silver gaze. "I need ye now. I'll use me tongue on ye later, lass." He tugged the thong to the side.

Claire moaned, looking down as he posed to take her, restlessly throbbing over her. "I can't wait," she choked.

"Aye, ye can." He slowly lowered himself and when she felt his slick heat stroking against her, she cried out, clawing his back.

"'Tis better slow," he breathed, beginning to press against her.

Claire dug her nails deep. "I hate you," she wept.

"Aye, fer a moment." He kissed her briefly and then began a slow entry, inch by single inch.

Pleasure cloaked her mind. She couldn't breathe. He smiled, pushing four inches deeper, then five. Claire felt herself begin to shake. She heard herself panting and she realized she was begging, but he did not accelerate his pace. And before he was through, she felt herself break.

She met his gaze and as he watched her, she came. So much ecstasy shattered over her, sweeping her into that dark scintillating universe where waves of pleasure begat even greater waves, and Claire cried out, eagerly embracing the vortex. "Malcolm!"

He smiled once, triumphant, and he moved more swiftly, joining her in that mindless frenzy now.

"Claire, 'tis almost dawn."

Claire barely heard as Malcolm left her, moving onto his back beside her. She was in a daze of ecstasy and agony, the evening spent in pure frenzied hedonistic passion. She had long since lost the ability to think. She closed her eyes, absolutely breathless, waiting for the tremors and trembling of her aroused body to cease, waiting for her heart to finally slow.

And when she was coherent, she was in disbelief. Malcolm was an insatiable but superb lover, and his prowess in bed was clearly not human. No man could arouse and continually pleasure a woman as he had done for hours and hours, without tiring or even flagging. She was finally aware of being exhausted. She was also aware of a level of satiation that was impossible to define. And there was even more than that. Her heart began a little dance inside her chest. No, she thought quickly, don't you dare go there!

They were lovers, that's all, and clearly that made her one very lucky lady.

Slowly, she turned her head to look at him in the gray light of the coming dawn. And she inhaled at the tender look in his eyes.

He had one arm under his head and he was regarding her intently. "Ye be pleased, lass?"

She had to smile. "Are you kidding?" And before he could tell her he did not understand, she said softly, "I am very pleased, Malcolm. I have never been so well pleased."

To her surprise, he abruptly reached out and pulled her against his side, smiling in satisfaction.

Claire was amazed. He wanted to cuddle? She pressed her cheek against his chest and was rewarded with the slow, strong thudding of his heart. It would be so easy to fall for this man, she thought.

His hand stroked down her arm, then he toyed with strands of her hair. *"Tha ur falt brèagha,"* he said softly.

Claire looked up. "You said that to me in my store. What does it mean?"

"Yer hair be beautiful," he murmured, his gaze holding hers. "Almost as beautiful as ye."

Claire felt a rush of pleasure. She ran her hand down his magnificent torso. "You are the beautiful one."

He laughed. "One o' us needs be dressed." He got up, reaching for his brat, which was on the floor.

Claire shifted so she could ogle him openly. He smiled at her as he deftly wrapped the brat around his bare hips. Amazingly, Claire felt her mouth water. "That is sexier than nothing at all."

He smiled and returned to the bed, instantly taking her back into his arms. "It pleases me that ye like my manliness." He hugged her.

Claire's heart danced anew and she reminded it to stop. "All women like your manliness," she said with a smile.

"Aye."

Claire decided not to go there. She had just been made love to as if there was no tomorrow, in ways that weren't really possible, and she was floating with satiation and happiness. If he made love to other women that way, she didn't want to know.

"I ha' never wanted any woman as I do ye," he said gently, clearly having listened to her thoughts.

"You haven't?"

"Nay." He tilted up her chin. "An' ye, lass?"

It took her a moment. Claire started. Was she supposed to confess that she had never wanted a man as she did him? And that she never would? After last night, she doubted she'd ever want to go to bed with someone else. God, when she went home, she'd spend the rest of her life in celibacy. Claire had not a doubt.

He pulled her close and stroked her hair and she felt him smile.

He had listened to her thoughts! Claire jerked away from him. "I hope you're happy," she said tersely.

"I couldna be happier. But do we have t' fight again? Ye were so pleased a moment ago."

Claire sought the covers and pulled them up to her chin. "Let's not." This was really unfair, she thought with dread. Eventually he would be with other women, having impossibly great sex, and her fate was to live like a spinster when she got home. But that *was* fate. He was a supersized, superpowerful Master. And if she was smart, she'd enjoy this for as long as she could.

Claire wondered how long that would be. "Were you faithful to Glenna?"

He looked like a boy caught with his hand in his brother's piggy bank.

"I didn't think so," Claire said slowly. She had to be mature about this. They were literally from different worlds. She could not have the expectations she would have if he was the guy next door and they were lovers in her time.

He spoke slowly. "Do ye wish fer me t' be exclusive with ye?"

Her heart slammed hard. "Er…ugh…I…what?"

He pulled her close, sitting up beside her now. "I dinna mind."

"What?" Claire said again. Had he hit her over the head, she could not be more stunned.

"I dinna mind bein' faithful t' ye," he said seriously.

"Why?" she managed to say.

He smiled. "I dinna want another woman, lass, an' if it's important t' ye, I dinna mind." He sobered. "Even though it willna be easy at first. I'll have to go to Iona every afternoon fer MacNeil's spell, until I am sure I willna use me powers on ye." He darkened. "He will love to see me grovelin'."

Claire remained absolutely shocked. "You are offering me a committed relationship?"

He smiled at her, that beautiful heartwarming, body-melting smile. "Aye. O' course, ye need to be faithful t' me, as well. An' stop ogling the Masters an' thinkin' about what's betwixt their legs."

"Okay." Claire didn't have to think about it. She jumped from the bed, reaching for her scattered clothes, turning off her thoughts because she knew he would listen if she did not.

"Yer in a rush t' leave my bed?" He chuckled.

She faced him, holding her clothes, absolutely unashamed of her nudity. His eyes wandered, warming. "We're going to Awe," she reminded him.

His face closed. "I go t' Awe with Royce an' Ironheart. Ye'll be safe at Dunroch with Seamus."

"Like hell!" she cried, fists on her hips, clothes falling.

He took an eyeful as he stood, his refusal in his eyes.

Claire blocked his path to the door. "If you *ever* want to enjoy my favors again, you are taking me with you."

His gaze narrowed. "Ye make threats? I dinna think I need to worry about seducin' ye."

"Then I will travel with Black Royce," she said tersely. "Or Ironheart. One of them will take me."

His eyes widened and turned hard. "Dinna think to seduce them to yer ways when we have just concluded our bargain!"

"I have no intention of seducing anyone—except you. It's not my style." She softened. "Malcolm, how can you even think to leave me here? What if Sibylla comes back for me?" She clasped his shoulders. "And what about tonight? We just started something wonderful."

"I willna be under MacNeil's spell t'night an' without a spell, I willna risk yer life." He was final.

"I am safer with you than alone." She was not the kind of pitiful female to use feminine wiles on a man, but she batted her lashes at him and implored, "Please," using a breathy tone she hadn't even known she possessed.

And she saw his resolve to deny her crumble. "Are ye entrancin' me now, lass?" he asked in disbelief.

"I wish." She smiled.

He pulled her into his embrace. "I never want to argue again, Claire. I mean it. Ye be stubborn an' headstrong. Ye annoy me to no end. Damn it all! Ye have eyes that go past me soul. I want to please ye, lass, an' nay just in bed."

"Then do so," she said, thrilled. She cupped his face. "I don't understand why you want me to avoid Awe?"

His expression hardened. "We spent the night pleasin' one another, but that does nay give ye the rights to ken my life."

Claire flinched. That hurt deeply. "Well, I'm glad we cleared that up," she inhaled. "In my time, lovers are also friends. Clearly, you do not want me as a friend. But you're right. That's for the best. That way, when I leave no one gets hurt." But it was too late and she knew it. She had crossed that emotional line yesterday on Iona.

His jaw flexed and he reached for her. Claire meant to

dodge but failed, and he reeled her into his arms. "I be sorry," he said. "An' yer right. 'Tis Awe. I swore on Brogan's grave I would never go there. I swore I would never give that bastard the time o' day or even a passing nod, I swore that, fer as long as I live, he wouldna exist."

Claire's eyes were wide. "Who? Aidan? Why?"

A ripple of tension went through Malcolm and he released her. "Because he's nay just my enemy. He be my brother."

CHAPTER ELEVEN

CLAIRE HAD SPENT the morning in shock. Strong southwesterly winds had meant a swift sea voyage up the Firth of Lorn, but Claire had barely paid attention to the incredible scenery—the sapphire sea and jewel-toned forests, the white beaches, the stark mountains against the robin's-egg-blue sky. They had disembarked near present-day Oban, having transported their horses with them, mounting there. The sun was high, indicating it was midday, as Claire grappled with the fact that Malcolm's half brother was the son of one of the most evil men in Scotland. She recalled Aidan's shocking beauty and the mischievous light in his eyes when he had smiled at her. If he was as twisted as his father, she hadn't felt it. She prayed he had somehow escaped such a genetic fate.

Claire nudged her mount forward, trotting toward Malcolm as the column continued, leaving the bay behind, a sparkling loch below on her right. In every direction except behind her, there were forested mountains. She caught up to Malcolm. "Where are we?"

He smiled at her. "Ahead is the pass that will take us through the mountains and t' Awe. 'Tis nay far now. Another half day, nay more." He was clad in his mail, as were all of the men.

Claire managed a smile in return, but her gaze was searching.

His face changed. "Ye dinna need worry as if I be a child."

"Of course I am worried. Malcolm, what do you plan? In

my time, we have a saying. You get a lot more with honey than vinegar."

He glanced at her as they rode up the narrowing trail. "I willna beg fer the page."

"I didn't suggest that you beg. I think you should ask nicely."

His face hardened so much Claire thought it might crack. "If I wish fer yer opinion, I'll ask." He jabbed his stallion forward, setting a more rapid pace and leaving her behind.

Claire understood his touchiness, but his rude rejection hurt. Her worry escalated. Was he going to barge into Aidan's castle with his sword drawn, demanding the page? Was that why everyone wore chain mail and plate? That was going to engender another terrible sword fight. And no matter how skilled and powerful Malcolm was, if Aidan was Moray's son, then his powers were far greater than Malcolm's. Claire pulled her mount aside so she could fall into place with Royce. "May I ride with you? My champion is in a foul humor."

Royce smiled, a gleam in his eyes. "I canna think why. I hope ye'll fergive me nephew fer bein' such a foolish man."

Claire knew exactly what he meant. She had received enough knowing glances that day to assume that everyone realized she was now sharing Malcolm's bed. "It's my fault, not his. I pried. I know about Aidan, Royce."

"He told ye his privy affairs?" He seemed stunned.

Claire nodded.

Royce stared, unsmiling. "An' what else did he tell ye while ye shared his bed?"

Claire tensed. Had Royce become hostile? "I sensed he was very distressed, and I guessed it was about Awe. As it turns out, I was right. I want to help, Royce."

Royce finally nodded. "O' course. 'Tis a terrible fate fer both brothers."

Claire remained somewhat taken aback by Royce's initial

hostility. Until that morning, he had been nothing but pleasant, and at times flirtatious. "Why is it terrible for Aidan? He seems to hate Malcolm as much as Malcolm hates him. He wanted to kill Malcolm in my store."

"Aidan has no wish t' see Malcolm dead. Dinna think otherwise—ye be wrong. I dinna think Aidan would be so hateful if Malcolm accepted him," Royce said bluntly. "Aidan dinna choose this life. He has no family except Moray. He has never done more than glimpse his mother. She wanted nothing t' do with him once he was birthed. Yet he chooses good, not evil. Aidan needs his brother an' Malcolm needs him."

Claire was surprised that Royce would defend Aidan. Considering they were not related at all, it meant a lot. She wasn't sure she should have any sympathy for Aidan, but she did. "Have you said as much to Malcolm?"

"A thousand times."

Claire thought about that. "He is the most pigheaded and stubborn man I have ever met," she said softly, but she had to smile.

"His will makes him a powerful man," Royce said firmly. "An' one day, a great Master."

Claire looked at him and their gazes locked. Malcolm's iron will could be exasperating, but she was terribly proud of him. He was a hero in every sense of the word.

I'm going to fall in love with him if I don't stop this, she thought. And maybe it was already too late. Then she realized Royce was staring. "Can you read minds, too?"

His pleasant expression had vanished. "Aye, but I willna read yers. I dinna have to. Ye be fallin' in love with my nephew."

Claire paled. Did Royce suddenly disapprove? "Malcolm and I are impossibly different. He doesn't understand me and I am certain he never will. Obviously you know we spent last night together. That doesn't mean I am falling for him." Well, if he read her mind now, he'd know that she was. She added, "I have no intention of falling in love with a fifteenth-century knight."

"Every woman falls in love with him after sharing his bed."

Claire tensed.

"I dinna wish to be rude. But he be the Maclean, he be pleasing to the eye, an' he can pleasure a woman well enough. He will never love in return an' he will never marry."

That was a warning if Claire had ever heard one, and she was angry. "So you are his keeper?"

"He be my brother's son," Royce said flatly. "I will make sure he doesna repeat my brother's mistakes."

And Claire thought about Mairead, who had been raped by her husband's enemy while still a bride and had then had Moray's child. She thought about Brogan, who had hunted his enemy but failed to destroy him. Instead, he had died in a very human battle. And Mairead had retreated from the world to live as a nun when her legitimate son was only nine. She had also rejected Aidan, the child of her rape. She could barely begin to imagine the suffering of husband and wife.

"Claire, dinna mistake my meaning. Ye be a fine, strong woman. An' if Malcolm were just a laird, even though ye bring no dowry, I'd bless the union."

"You are getting ahead of yourself!" Claire cried, but she was pretty sure she was getting his meaning.

He reached across his saddle and seized her wrist. "The Masters who marry—or love—always regret it," Royce said. His gray gaze had become as dark as thunderclouds. "Look at the fate o' my brother an' his wife. There be a reason a Master lives alone, fights alone, dies alone."

Claire pulled away. "How sad," she whispered, still angry, but far less so. Because Royce was right. A Master by his very nature had the vilest and most powerful enemies in the land. A wife and a family were an invitation to tragedy. She thought about Malcolm's bastard son. "What about children?"

His harsh expression remained. "We need sons. They be the next generation o' Masters, if they're chosen."

"A child makes a man as vulnerable—more vulnerable—than a wife."

"Aye, but we have nay choice. Malcolm has Brogan protected day an' night. If he wished, he could send Brogan to Iona. Children have been raised there."

She absorbed that. "Is this why you are alone? Because your oh-so-cool head rules your heart?"

He became dangerously cold. "I was married once, long ago, before the Choosing. My wife be dead."

Claire saw she had hit a raw spot. "I am sorry, Royce. Look, how I feel doesn't matter, because I am going home after we find the page and it is safe for me to do so. It never occurred to me to stay here."

"It may never be safe fer ye to go back."

Claire stared, shaken. "I hope you're wrong!" Why would he think such a thing?

"Most women wouldna have the power to leave him," he said skeptically.

"I'm not most women. We come from different worlds, in case you haven't noticed. And I have to go back to avenge my mother. I also have family there. I worry about them."

"Ye should." Royce's gray gaze drifted to her throat. "The stone bothers me."

"It seems to bother—or fascinate—everyone."

"Ye wear a Highland charm. I can feel its power—I felt it the first time we met. Why were ye, a lass from York City in the future, given such a stone? I ken the stone was yer mother's, so who gave it to her? Were ye meant to be sent here? Do the Ancients wish to see if Malcolm will make the mistakes his father did? Because there be some reason ye be here, Claire. I can feel it. Ye became far too close to Malcolm, far too soon an' too easily."

Claire was shaken. In the back of her mind, she had almost

been thinking that her fate was Dunroch—and Malcolm. Damn it, she had secretly wondered if she was the love of his life. But that was the romantic in her, who had seen every single version of *Pride and Prejudice* and who, once in a while, locked herself in her room to read a really juicy romance novel. But Royce was right. There had been a connection from the moment he'd seized her in her store. And from that moment, everything had happened so damn fast.

MacNeil had said that the Ancients didn't mind her presence on Iona. The Ancients shouldn't even know about her!

Malcolm thought her a test for his soul. Royce thought her a test of his loyalty to the Brotherhood and his determination to uphold his vows. But wasn't it one and the same thing? Either way, she didn't want to be any kind of test.

Royce cut into her thoughts. "But the real question might be, how did the page come t' be in yer store?"

Claire tensed. If the page hadn't been believed to be in her store, she wouldn't have been burglarized by Sibylla, she wouldn't have met Malcolm and she wouldn't be in the fifteenth-century Highlands now.

And the truth was, they didn't even know if the page had ever been in her store, except that Malcolm was certain Aidan had it, and that he'd found it there. "Do you have any ideas as to who started the rumor that the page was in my store?" Claire asked uneasily. But she had a very bad inkling.

"Let us hope it was nay the lord o' darkness," Royce said. "He used Mairead to torture Brogan—and to trap Malcolm."

Claire felt sick. "He can't use me that way. Malcolm and I have just met."

"Ye love him. He be sworn to protect ye. If he comes to love ye, ye can be used, just like Mairead."

Claire began to shake.

"In the end, ye canna help Malcolm, ye can only weaken him. If he does start to care fer ye, ye canna allow it. He be a Master, Claire, an' he must live an' fight alone."

She was dismayed. She wanted Malcolm to care for her—after last night, she wanted it a lot. "Like you," she whispered.

"If ye truly love him," he said tersely, ignoring that, "when the time comes, ye will go." He spurred his horse forward, leaving her alone between the troops.

HOURS LATER, with the sun hanging low in the sky and threatening to vanish beneath the western ridges, Malcolm rode his destrier up to Claire. "Castle Awe be below," he said as he halted the huge gray beast. "Ye must be tired. If Aidan permits, we'll spend the night outside his walls."

He had gotten over her offering him a bit of advice, Claire thought, relieved. "I am sore," she admitted, pulling her mount up. They had spent hours riding through the pass. For Claire, it felt like days. And she wasn't just sore from gripping the horse with her legs; their vigorous lovemaking had taken its toll on her, as well. She was also bone tired. After all, they hadn't slept at all last night. But she knew her fatigue was more than physical. Every day seemed to bring a slew of new challenges. Royce's advice had felt like a warning. She didn't want him set against her now. They needed to stick together.

"Dinna grip so with yer legs, lass," Malcolm said softly.

Claire had the distinct feeling that he was thinking about just how strong her legs were. "It's a reflex. Fortunately, this old boy doesn't seem to care what I do." She could not be diverted from what Royce had just said.

Malcolm smiled. "Brogan learned t' ride on Saint."

"Is that what you call him?" Claire stroked the brown gelding's neck.

"Aye, Saint Will, as he takes care o' his rider."

Claire looked at the horse's neck, thinking about every instance in which Malcolm had taken care of her since they had met. His fate was clear. He was a Master, meant to protect people like her and battle evil like Moray.

Of course a real relationship would make him weak and vulnerable to his enemies. On that point, Royce was right.

Claire slowly looked up. "I never want to fight with you." She bit her lip as his eyes widened. "Especially after last night. I know you've read my mind. You know I don't take what we did lightly. No matter what I say, what I do, you can trust me. I'm your ally and your friend, Malcolm. I want what's best for you."

"A friend," he echoed. "An ally? What nonsense has Royce been whisperin' to ye, Claire?"

She flushed. "I don't want to make you weak."

His eyes widened. "Ye make me strong, Claire. Yer my woman."

She wasn't going to argue over his use of words and she certainly wasn't going to change his possessiveness. She wasn't sure she wanted to, no matter what Royce had said. "If I'm your woman, don't you expect me to be loyal?"

"Ye ken I do. An' ye be very loyal. Aye, I lurk all the time."

She couldn't be angry. "I'm sorry I told you what to do in regards to Aidan," she said. "I don't want you to get hurt. And in my time, women boss men around all the time. In fact, wives usually rule the roost."

He smiled grudgingly. "Ye be right," he said flatly, the last of his men passing them on the trail.

"Highland women dominate their men?"

"Nay. I wanted t' charge into Awe with my sword raised. But I'll ask Aidan nicely fer the page."

Claire smiled widely, filled with relief and happiness. He had changed his mind because of her. "Maybe he'll surprise you and turn it over without hesitation."

Malcolm's face hardened. "He wants the page fer himself. An' maybe fer Moray."

All pleasure disintegrated. "Royce would disagree. He says Aidan is good."

Malcolm's brow rose. "Good? He does good when it be his interest to do so. Nay fer selfless reasons. I am tellin' ye, Claire, and this one time ye will obey me. Dinna trust him, not ever."

Claire was not going to argue with him now. Besides, this was a promise she could easily make. "If it's that important to you, then I give you my word. I will never trust him. However," she added as he started to move his horse down the trail, "I hope you are wrong about your half brother."

He darkened. "Dinna remind me o' the miserable fact o' his life. We may share blood, but he is nay my brother, half or otherwise!"

Claire followed him down the trail, wondering how Mairead could have left Malcolm at such a tender age and how she could have turned her back on Aidan, just after his birth. She didn't want to judge the woman, as she had suffered a heinous crime. But both Aidan and Malcolm were the most innocent victims in the tragedy engineered by Moray. It was a damn shame they couldn't become friends.

The pass had wound through high ridges, most of it at elevations just above sea level. Suddenly, the forests opened up onto a brilliant green expanse of marsh, grass and shrub dotted with thick pine trees and blooming with yellow and pink wildflowers. The wooded fields ended in the sparkling azure waters of Loch Awe.

And rising from the loch was Castle Awe, a huge walled castle of red-brown stone with numerous towers, high ramparts and a central building four or five stories tall. Twice the size of Dunroch, Awe was surrounded by water. White swans floated near its walls. There was another island, also walled, connected by a bridge of land, where she saw stone buildings and peasant huts, and where some scrawny cattle grazed. The scene was picture-postcard perfect.

The drawbridge was down.

"He waits fer us," Malcolm said grimly.

"How would he know that we're here?"

"Aidan has very strong powers o' the mind. Ye stay back in the midst o' the men," he told her. He galloped ahead, joined by Royce and Ironheart.

And that was when the thundering of hoofbeats began.

It was déjà vu. That terrible, ominous sound, an invitation to death, was one Claire was never going to forget. She had hoped to never hear it again. The sound of an oncoming army of Highland warriors intent on battle and death was a nightmare come true. She turned, seized with fear, and saw *hundreds* of mounted men galloping upon them.

Malcolm, Royce and Ironheart drew to a halt at the head of Malcolm's men. Instantly, they were surrounded by the warriors. Claire realized not a single sword was drawn, not even Malcolm's.

One of the opposing men rode forward and faced Malcolm. He wore full armor, but his visor was up. Claire strained to hear, but the exchange was in Gaelic. Instantly, the giant signaled everyone forward to the lowered drawbridge.

Claire's fear escalated. Was Aidan taking them prisoner?

Claire prodded Saint into a trot to keep up with the men as they were herded over the drawbridge and through the raised portcullis. This land bridge seemed to form an outer bailey, as she saw buildings for the garrison there. She could only see Malcolm's back now and, while aware of his tension, could not discern anything else. They were urged through another gatehouse, a middle ward, and then a huge gatehouse with four high, defensive towers. The moment the last of Malcolm's men had entered the last inner bailey, the portcullis slammed closed behind them.

Claire flinched. They were certainly prisoners now. She looked carefully around at her surroundings. The castle inside the bailey was huge, with a half a dozen buildings built into the walls. Her gaze flew to the central keep facing them.

The dark wooden door of the hall opened and a man stepped out, standing two stories above them.

It was Aidan. *"Hallo a Chaluim."*

Malcolm rode his gray horse past the giant and to the stone stairs leading up to where Aidan stood. Claire expected him to stop there but he did not. He drove the gray right up the stairs until the steed stood beside Aidan, making Malcolm, still mounted, tower over him. "We come in peace. I wish a word with ye," Malcolm said tersely in French.

Aidan laughed, clearly not at all perturbed by Malcolm's actions. "I ken why ye have come, Malcolm. Please, my home be yer home...brother." His gaze moved past Malcolm, who was flushed with a rising temper, and settled right on Claire, never mind that a half dozen Highland men surrounded her, each one taller than she.

He smiled. "I wouldna leave the woman alone with my men, Malcolm," Aidan said softly in English. "She be far too beautiful." With that, he sent her a courtly bow and turned to go into his hall. "Leave the stallion in the stables." He strode inside.

Malcolm wheeled his gray, looking dangerously pissed, and galloped it down the stairs. Claire didn't blame him. Aidan was provocative, to say the least. Malcolm moved through Aidan's men. Halting his blowing steed beside her, he held out his hand. Claire understood and leaped from her nag to his charger. She wanted to whisper to him to take a few deep breaths, but decided this was not the best time to try to tell him how to proceed. Instead, she laid her hand on his shoulder, hoping he would find some composure before he went into Aidan's hall.

He looked back at her.

Claire hoped he was reading her mind this one time. It's all right, she thought. He hasn't really done anything except to be as annoying as a spoiled brat.

Malcolm made a sound and turned away, riding through

Aidan's men. At the foot of the stairs, he urged her to dismount, then vaulted to the ground, as well. One of his men ran to take the stallion from him and they started up the stairs.

Claire looked down into the bailey at the assembled troops and she shivered. Then she glanced toward the front door, which Aidan had left open. The sun was setting behind the hall, so she could not see inside, and it gaped at her, a black void.

Malcolm was right. Aidan was not to be trusted. Claire didn't know what he wanted or what he would do if Malcolm decided to be belligerent. She was afraid of what his comment about her looks had meant. He was as dangerous as a cornered tiger.

Now, too late, she wished they hadn't come.

CLAIRE FOLLOWED MALCOLM into a huge hall and blinked in surprise. She was faced with so many beautiful furnishings that did not come from the fifteenth century or any century even close to it. Then she saw a Picasso on the wall. Her eyes widened as she recognized a Renoir, a Constable, a Pollock. She stared at the room again. Aidan's home could have been furnished for the twenty-first century with the finest European antiques and furniture, except for the fact that there were no lamps.

He stood at a towering dark walnut buffet with clawed feet and gilded leaves creeping up the unit's sides. He was pouring wine from a crystal decanter into crystal wineglasses. Claire saw a modern corkscrew.

It made her dizzy. He was dressed in boots, bare legs and a leine and brat of emerald green, blue and black, and his attire was a glaring contrast to the room. Having poured several glasses, he faced her with that seductive and frankly amused smile she remembered just a bit too well. He knew he was irresistible to the opposite sex, she thought.

"A glass o' wine, Lady Claire," he murmured, approaching her as Royce and Ironheart came inside.

"No, thank you," Claire said, flustered. His eyes were gray

like Malcolm's, and filled with the same appreciative heat. Worse, he slid his gaze over her from head to toe. Claire was certain he was stripping away every item she was wearing and was mentally enjoying a very private view.

His smile widened. "'Tis from Bordeaux," he said softly.

She met his gaze, aware of heat in her cheeks. His tone was silken and she was sure he used it on women to get them into bed. She somehow knew he was thinking about what she would be like in his bed, too, and that his thoughts were terribly graphic. "I'm sure it's wonderful," she said hoarsely, turning away, uncomfortably shaken. His beauty and masculinity did not help matters.

Malcolm stepped between them. "Ye look at my woman that way again an' I'll take yer head an' send it across the floor, then put it on a pike." His eyes glittered with rage. He carried his helmet now, but his right hand rested on the hilt of his longsword.

Claire couldn't even think about calming Malcolm now. Aidan had thoroughly discomfited her, and he had known what he was doing. He had enjoyed making her uneasy and embarrassed.

"How can I nay look at a beautiful woman?" Aidan said softly and Claire knew his gaze had drifted back to her. "I have eyes in me head, Malcolm."

Glass broke.

Claire whirled and realized Malcolm had struck the wineglass from Aidan's hand.

"Ye show respect," he said tersely.

Aidan's smile remained, but his eyes had turned cold. "I have invited ye into me home. I chose not to throw ye in the tower. I dinna care fer red wine to be spilled on me fine rugs."

"I'll clean it," Claire cried, but she did not leap between the two men. Malcolm had his hand on the hilt of his sword and she was afraid he was going to unsheathe it. If he did, she knew Aidan would welcome the fight.

Ironheart settled into a chair to watch the drama, apparently nonplussed. Royce strode forward and laid a hand on Aidan's shoulder, stepping right between the two men. "Enough!" He was annoyed. "Ye provoked Malcolm. Ye deserve a cuff on the head like a lad of ten, not a grown man o' yer years."

Aidan looked at Royce without hostility and walked away from them both. He paused to stand before the hearth, staring into its flames. Terribly relieved, Claire went to Malcolm and took his hand. "You must try to ignore him," she began.

He gave her an incredulous look.

Claire leaped away, realizing her mistake. In this man's world, a woman had better keep her mouth shut until the appropriate time. Later, when they were alone in the chamber they would share, she could try to get him to see things her way. It was so hard to control her impulse to tell him when she knew exactly what he should do. Couldn't Malcolm see when he was being manipulated by Aidan? He had to take the high road.

Aidan had returned to the sideboard, pouring more wine, his hands rock steady. He handed a glass to Royce, who accepted it, and then he looked at Ironheart. The earl of Lachlan shook his head, otherwise not moving a muscle.

"Have ye met Lachlan?" Royce asked.

"Nay formally," Aidan said, not taking wine for himself. "His reputation is great."

"Then 'tis time. He'll be a good ally fer ye, when ye decide yer too old fer tricks an' ye decide to obey the Brotherhood more often than not."

Aidan looked at Royce without hostility and Royce stared back. Claire realized they knew each other better than in passing, and that Aidan would accept criticism from Malcolm's uncle, although they were not related at all. She felt certain that Royce had cultivated the relationship out of his love for his nephew. The tension in the room softened and she breathed.

"Actually, I'd love a glass of wine," she lied. She smiled at Aidan and Royce and walked over to the sideboard to help herself, hoping that an act of normalcy would further lighten the atmosphere. Having poured it, she faced the room. "You have a beautiful home," she said to Aidan. She was uncertain as to how to address him.

Aidan's smile began. He was pleased, and somewhat amused. "'Tis made far more beautiful by yer presence," he returned.

Claire glanced at Malcolm, who just shook his head in disgust. Claire felt like telling Aidan that in her time, women would laugh at such lines. But maybe not; he was so seductive, no woman would want to miss her chance with him.

Malcolm gave her a dark look and said to his half brother, "Ye ken why we be here."

Aidan faced him. "Aye." He set his glass down and reached inside his brat, producing a rolled-up and tied parchment page.

Claire gasped. "Is that what I think it is?"

Aidan handed the page to Malcolm. "Aye, Lady Claire, an' I can see yer entranced. But the page be worthless."

Malcolm untied the ribbon and unrolled the single page. Claire put her glass down and rushed to him. A page of beautifully but very stylized and heavily decorated script faced her, the letters even more distorted than in the Cathach. "I canna read the Latin. Lass?"

It was written in Latin, not Gaelic? "Yes," Claire breathed, taking the page from him. Her heart was thundering and she felt faint. "Thank you!" She kissed his cheek and ran to the fire, sitting down on a velvet bench there. She stared at the words, realizing that only a single paragraph was written in Latin. The rest was in old Irish Gaelic. It was hard to read because of the stylized script and the lack of spacing between words. And then she understood. It was a prayer, but not the likes of any she had ever heard. A Celtic goddess of healing whose name she had never heard—Ceanna—seemed to be the subject matter. "I wonder why a Latin insert is in such an old Celtic manuscript," she said, not looking up. The question was rhetorical, and no one answered her. "Are there Latin inserts in the Cathach?"

"There be two," Malcolm said. "When the scribes put the wisdom of the Ancients on the pages, one scribe preferred Latin. 'Tis said he was a Roman."

The Romans had conquered Britain, but not Ireland. On the other hand, a Roman could have easily crossed the Irish Sea. "This is an incredible discovery, with all kinds of implications," Claire breathed.

She looked up at Malcolm. "Can you translate the Gaelic for me?"

He hesitated. "I nay be as learned as the monks an' priests. I can try. It willna be easy."

"We'll do it together." Claire smiled brightly at him. "There's no rush. This page has to be translated. We have all night, don't we? We are spending the night, aren't we?"

His gaze held hers. It was a moment before he spoke. "Aye." He turned to Aidan. "Lady Claire wishes t' translate the page. She'll need light, parchment, a quill an' ink." He spoke in the tone of one giving commands.

Aidan just looked at him, clearly not about to obey.

Claire had finally translated the first Latin line. She looked up, aware that her hands were shaking from her excitement. "How can you say that this is worthless?" she exclaimed. "This is some kind of prayer to heal. Why do you think this is worthless? Where did you find this, Aidan? It is *priceless*."

He strolled over. "I found it in yer store, Claire," he murmured.

Claire wished he would stop trying to remind her that he was sexy. "Where in my store?" she demanded.

Aidan started to laugh. "In a King James Bible."

Claire stood up, stunned. There was one King James Bible

in her inventory, and it had been published in 1728. She had acquired the Bible just a month ago from an estate in London.

"There was a hiding place in the back cover," Aidan said. "I dinna ken how I found it. Sibylla had looked at the Bible first. I felt her prints on it. I be followin' her trail."

Claire stared at Malcolm's half brother. He could *feel* fingerprints? She focused. "This is a *huge* find," she stressed. She turned to Malcolm. "The sooner we translate this page, the better. But how did this page get into my store? Was it hidden in the Bible all along?" She didn't look at Royce now.

"It could ha' been in that Bible fer centuries, Claire," Malcolm said softly.

"And fate brought me to the Bible—and the page to my store?" She finally looked at Royce.

His gaze skidded aside.

"I can take ye back if ye wish t' do some searchin'," Aidan said, grinning.

Before Claire could politely refuse, Malcolm barked, "Ye'll take Claire nowhere, Aidan. *Nowhere.*"

Aidan shrugged, his eyes gleaming. "'Twas only a suggestion." Then he sobered. "The page doesna have power, Lady Claire. I can read well enough. 'Tis prayers an' a blessing to keep the mortally wounded from dyin', if the wounds be inflicted from a sword or a similar cuttin' weapon. My squire impaled himself. I tried to protect him from dyin' and I failed. There's no power in that page."

It took Claire a moment to understand what he was telling her.

But Malcolm looked at Aidan and spoke. He said, "Yer half Deamhan. The Deamhanain destroy. They canna heal. Yet ye tried to heal?" He was scathing.

Aidan clearly did not wish to speak, but he said coldly, "I may be half Deamhan, but I be Faola's *grandson.* An' I have healed, Malcolm, with these two hands an' a great white light." He held up his hands, which were shaking with his anger.

Royce walked over to stand between them. "I be pleased ye can heal a bit, Aidan." He glared at Malcolm. "Ye need set aside yer privy battles now. There be more important matters to attend."

Claire sat back down on the bench. Aidan had some ability to heal and Malcolm did not. That was interesting enough. Did it mean that the various Masters inherited traits in the same manner that people did?

Aidan's mouth was hard. "The power be new to me. I healed a very sick lass once. I didna ken it well an' it made me weak." He flushed, looking at Royce. "I didna think t' use such a weakening power again."

Claire was riveted. He'd healed a woman, and in doing so lost some of his strength?

"Mayhap the power will grow an' be easier to use, in time." Royce clasped his shoulder. "I be glad ye saved a life."

Claire stood. "Malcolm." She walked over to him and smiled earnestly. "It doesn't matter whether this page has healing power or not. What matters is that it might be from the Cladich. This page is incredibly valuable if it is genuine. It needs to be enshrined or go back to my time with the rest of the recovered manuscript, so it can be preserved."

Malcolm shook his head. "It matters if it doesna have powers, Claire. It matters greatly. If it be genuine, it will heal."

He didn't get it, Claire thought. Twenty-first century scholars would beg to have the opportunity to study this page.

And she didn't get its value to him, either. "You can take life to heal. Why is the Cladich so important?"

Malcolm made a sound. "Because we dinna need take life if we have the powers in the Cladich, Claire. The book can heal on its own."

Claire breathed hard. "So the book can heal the dying?" A Master would never have to take life if he was dying in order to survive. She got it now, all right. The book was beyond priceless.

And no wonder Moray wanted it. He could heal his demonic hordes with it. *Holy shit.*

"Aye. If ye read the right pages. Each page has its own cause."

And Claire suddenly shivered, because an icy chill had settled over the hall. Someone must have left the front door open.

But as the temperature dropped, just the way it had in the glade when they had first arrived in the fifteenth century, Claire began to realize what was happening.

Malcolm stepped beside her, filled with so much alarm and urgency Claire felt it. With dread, Claire followed his intense gaze to the open door. A black shadow filled it.

Death, Claire thought, unable to breathe.

But the black shadow parted to reveal a golden man in crimson robes. And the earl of Moray smiled at her. "Hello, Claire."

CHAPTER TWELVE

CLAIRE FELT HER KNEES SHAKE. She did not have to be intro-duced to know she was looking at Moray. *"How do you know my name?"* She was vaguely aware that everyone in the room had closed ranks, standing beside her and Malcolm.

"I know everything," he said, his white teeth flashing. No human being could be more beautiful. He had the face of a Greek god—no, a Celtic god, but then, that was what he was, or nearly so. Claire knew he was physical perfection, beauty in its most reverent form—just as she knew he had no soul and that death followed in his wake while he relished it.

And as she stood there, paralyzed by fear, the last clouds in her mind lifted.

The front door opened. But it wasn't Mom. A dark shadow drifted in.

In terror, Claire ran into the closet, slamming the door, but not before looking over her shoulder. A man stood in the center of the living room, staring at her.

Claire sobbed in fear.

The door opened.

Claire hid her eyes behind her hands, cowering beneath the sweaters and jackets hanging there. And he reached out, taking her hand. Claire was pulled into the light. She looked up—into his black, bottomless eyes.

I will come for you soon.

Claire choked on the horrific recollection.

"Ye have no affair with Claire." Malcolm's harsh tone cut

into her thoughts. He was standing directly in front of her now. "Yer affair be with me. Only with me."

"Actually, you are wrong," Moray said softly with a beautiful smile. "Claire's destiny is in my hands. Like father, like son," he added.

Claire froze.

Malcolm unsheathed his sword and Royce seized his arm.

Moray laughed at them all. "There is so much fear in this room that my power grows." He wet his lips, looking at Claire, and she felt his arousal and was horrified. "I will enjoy you far more than I did Mairead."

Malcolm started forward, enraged.

Aidan stepped in front of him, almost skewering himself on Malcolm's blade in the process. Royce and Ironheart seized him, but Malcolm tried to fling them off. Claire would have screamed at Malcolm but her vocal cords were also frozen. She could only think about the fact that Moray had mortally wounded him once and he could do so again.

"Ye will never touch her," Malcolm roared.

"And who will stop me?" Moray purred. "A weak Master like you? Your own father spent eleven years hunting me—or so he thought. I led him a merry chase and all the while Mairead mourned her treachery, her disloyalty, her faithlessness."

Malcolm broke free of Royce and Ironheart. "*A Bhrogain!*"

Claire screamed.

Aidan turned and seized his sword arm. "'Tis nay the way!" he shouted.

Malcolm threw him off, only to have Royce and Ironheart leap on him, dragging him backward to the other side of the room. He somehow shook them off, too. Moray laughed.

Claire cried out in horror as Malcolm staggered as if struck. But he stood alone, and there had been no physical blow.

"Dinna try," Royce said fiercely, and she saw Moray pale and grunt as if he had just been struck, too. "There be four o' us," he added coolly.

Claire looked around. So much power swirled in the room, male and hot. She realized she was standing in the midst of some kind of kinetic stalemate. Sweat dripped from Royce's temples and his eyes blazed. And every man in the room had an identical expression, even Moray.

Aidan confronted Moray, legs braced wide and hard. "I grow tired o' yer visits," he snapped. "Ye be in my home now. I be lord here an' I dinna give ye permission to enter my hall. Get out."

Moray smiled with no mirth. "Three years ago I chose to let Malcolm live when I could have ended his life. He tasted the wonderful pleasure we find in death, as was my wish, and soon, he will taste such pleasure again. *He will be mine.*"

Moray took Aidan's face in one hand and stroked his cheek with his long fingernails. He murmured, "And you, my boy, will be mine, too. It is but a matter of time." He released him and smiled at Claire. Then he vanished.

Claire wanted to run to Malcolm but she couldn't move. What Moray intended for everyone was worse than death. He was Satan, after all.

She was ready to retch and fell to her knees.

And then Malcolm was kneeling besides her. "'Tis over now," he said harshly, pulling her into an embrace. He held her hard.

"Over?" Claire gasped, barely able to speak. "It's not over, nothing is over. It has only begun!"

"I will protect ye," he tried, his arms tightening, his gaze hard.

She jerked away and her fear became outrage. "How? How will you do that? Did you not hear him? Me, he will rape and get with child. You, he will turn into a master of evil! Aidan? Aidan is marked, too! Unless there is a way to destroy him, we will all suffer fates far worse than death!"

Malcolm was breathing hard. "Ye have every right t' be afraid, Claire. Ye ha' just seen the lord o' evil fer the first time. I ken how distressed ye be."

"Distressed?" That, Claire thought, was the understatement of the ages. She looked at Malcolm. "Are you all right? What just happened?"

Malcolm hesitated. "He struck me with his power. I was braced fer it, an' he didna knock me down. With all o' us together, usin' our powers against his, he canna do great damage."

Claire shuddered. "Then why didn't the four of you combine your powers and zap him dead?"

Malcolm's eyes hardened. "If he could be vanquished in such a way, we would have done it."

"Great! He has enough power to withstand the four of you!" Claire tried to breathe deeply and evenly. She failed. She hadn't realized until that moment what evil really was. It was omnipotent, horrible, horrifying, and it intended to wreck total annihilation on everyone. More specifically, evil wanted to use her—and it wanted to use her against Malcolm. It wanted Malcolm's soul.

Royce's suspicions had been right.

Malcolm said, "I'll die before I turn evil. An' I'll do ye the same favor afore I let him touch ye." He stood and held out his hand.

Malcolm was promising to end her life before allowing Moray to use her. She was trying to think rationally now. His words were not helpful—because he meant them. But death was better than ever suffering that man's touch. She continued to shiver uncontrollably as she stood. "You said so yourself. No Master has been able to vanquish him for *centuries*."

"Aye, but there will be a first time. I asked ye t' have faith." His face hard and determined, showing no sign of fear, Malcolm turned and stalked out into the night.

Claire stared after him, impossibly cold. She wanted to have faith in him, but that seemed like suicide. It was better to err on the side of caution. This was a new reality and it defied the imagination.

Moray was hunting Malcolm.

Her heart lurched with sickening force.

Aidan walked over to her. "He sold his soul to Satan a thousand years ago, mayhap more, an' his power is protected by the devil. Many Masters combined cannot take it. We have tried. Some Masters have more power than others. Moray has taken the lives o' the lesser ones. He'll weaken a Master with mortal blows an' then do the evil deed. I be certain there be a mortal blow that can weaken Moray." Aidan's eyes burned. "*I be certain.* He lives in a half-mortal body. He *bleeds.*"

Claire stared at him, realizing that if Aidan was right, it wasn't entirely hopeless. On the other hand, Moray was so powerful, how could such a deadly blow be wielded?

Someone handed her a glass. It was Ironheart. "Take some wine, Claire," he said firmly. "'Twill clear yer fear. And yer wrong, lass."

Claire met his gaze and saw nothing but resolve. His expression was identical to Malcolm's. There was no fear, just courage.

"Malcolm has great power fer a Master so young. He will protect ye. Dinna judge him so poorly. An' I will protect ye, too. But mostly, if there be a way, Malcolm will find it. He burns with his ambition."

Claire took a breath. "I don't want him to burn with ambition and wind up dead," she said harshly. She looked at the men's faces. For them, this was just another moment in the line of Brotherhood duty. "As you said, he's young—too young to die. Or worse!" She swallowed. "Moray has to be stopped. Are you sure there isn't the knowledge we need to do just that in the Cathach?"

MALCOLM STOOD on the ramparts, no longer furious, just sick in his soul.

He had brought Claire back to his time to protect her, but now, in hindsight, he knew he had made a terrible mistake. She would have been safer in her store, facing the likes of Sibylla and Aidan, than she was now. Aidan would have done nothing worse than seduce her, and armed with her modern weapons, Claire was strong enough to have fought Sibylla, perhaps even triumphing over her. Moray was an entirely different matter.

It was entirely his fault that she was now an object Moray lusted for. If he dared to closely inspect his reasons for bringing her back with him, he would have to admit that the powerful attraction he had felt for her had been as much a factor as his desire to protect her.

Moray's threats had been clear. He planned to use Claire against Malcolm as Mairead had been used against Brogan. Royce and MacNeil had both warned him not to become fond of her, but it was too late. Suddenly, he saw Claire naked, beneath Moray, in the throes of pleasure as the other man used her and took her life.

What had he done?

What could he do now?

He needed more power and more wisdom. Three years ago he had hunted Moray, cornering him in the tower at Urquhart, and he had been easily defeated. He did not have enough power to vanquish Moray—no Master did or the Deamhan would have been sent to hell long ago. Moray had set a trap, but maybe he could be the trapper now.

Moray laughed, behind him.

Malcolm braced his power against the Deamhan and he whirled, sword ringing as he unsheathed it. It felt terribly familiar, as if that fatal dance at Urquhart was playing once more.

"Think harder, Malcolm, and you will see her begging me

for more and more pleasure, which I will gladly give her. She will beg me for my seed in a frenzy of mindless need. I will come inside her a hundred times every single night. And when I send her back to you, her belly swollen with my child, she won't want to leave me. She will hate you for taking her back."

All reason vanished. Malcolm roared, *"A Chlaire."*

Moray unsheathed his sword and met the vicious attack, smiling in delight.

Malcolm swung again and again, and it was déjà vu. In the back of his mind, he knew Moray had wanted this battle and he knew exactly why. Three years ago Moray had chosen to let him live.

He knew this was a trap.

He did not care.

Bloodlust consumed him.

He struck and Moray's blade met his own. The swords screamed.

THE WINE HAD the precise calming effect Ironheart had hoped for, Claire thought. She had stopped shaking and she was breathing normally. The fear remained, but it was controlled. *Moray was half human. Moray could bleed.*

She took another sip and exhaled, closing her eyes. She was an intellectual woman. There had to be a way to reduce Moray's powers, or to mortally wound him. Malcolm had said the demons never entered holy places, as they lost their powers there. There was an obvious conclusion to be drawn, but Moray probably knew better than to wander into a church or chapel. If he could have been lured to such a place, he would have been destroyed long ago.

Her mind turned over Aidan's frightening words. She had been ready to believe that Moray was Satan himself, but Aidan said he had Satan's protection, which was why his power couldn't be taken by the Masters. Well, she believed in everything else, and she was ready to embrace Aidan's world view now, too.

Damn it. If Moray could not be mortally wounded and thus weakened, then the gods were their only hope.

That was not particularly comforting. She wondered if any Master had recently seen one of the Ancients. They probably hung out in the Dalriadan version of Mount Olympus, the way the gods in Greek mythology did.

And where was Malcolm? Did he have to be outside, alone, at dark?

Claire trembled. She was afraid for Malcolm, really afraid. Claire opened her eyes, taking long, deep breaths. Malcolm was a great hero, a champion for all that was good in this world, and Moray was trying to turn him. She had to help him somehow. She couldn't imagine the world without Malcolm in it, a Master protecting Innocence through all ages.

There had to be a way.

She stared across the room. A beautiful oval dining table that sat twelve, its chairs upholstered in sapphire velvet and studded with nails, had been set for supper with gilded china and flatware. Ironheart and Royce were eating as quickly and efficiently as possible. As fueling up was probably crucial to their well-being—and power—she did not begrudge them their intent, nonsocial behavior. Aidan sat at the table's head, removed from the other men, drinking wine, his plate empty. He was obviously brooding.

Suddenly Claire felt a terrible searing pain in her side. She gasped, about to faint, her hand on her waist. For one moment, she thought a sword had gone through her side.

Aidan leaped to his feet. "Claire?"

Claire looked at her hand, expecting to see it covered with blood. There was none. *Malcolm.*

She staggered to her feet. "Malcolm is wounded!"

Claire moved first, running across the hall and flinging the door open. The night was blue-black, but the sky was filled with Highland stars and a waxing moon, which was golden and bright. Her eyes went right to the ramparts, just to the left and above where she stood, and she saw the two figures there.

One figure collapsed while the other stood tall and straight. Even in the starlight, Claire saw his perfect, bronzed face, the flash of white teeth and the sun-gold hair. He smiled at her, their eyes meeting. And Moray vanished.

Claire screamed and ran up the stairs, Aidan on her heels. She tripped and stumbled and fell to her knees where Malcolm lay prone. For one second, he looked so peaceful, as if asleep. She looked at his left side, and saw only the heavy wool brat that he wore over the mail hauberk. Then she saw that the wool was unusually dark, soaked with blood.

Malcolm's eyes opened, meeting Claire's. She recoiled. His gaze was silver and glittering insanely and his hand seized her wrist. For one terrible instant, Claire thought he meant to harm her.

"Get her gone!" Malcolm cried harshly, his face ravaged with pain.

Aidan knelt beside her, moving the brat and mail aside. He unlaced the leather vest to reveal a blood-soaked leine. "Leave now, Claire," Aidan said firmly.

"I am not going anywhere!" Claire cried as Aidan ripped open the linen. She gasped when she saw the horrible wound. There was so much blood. If Malcolm was hemorrhaging, or if an organ had been damaged, or become infected, he would die.

"Get her...gone," Malcolm repeated, his grasp on her wrist shockingly brutal, his eyes ablaze.

"Yer going to die if ye keep movin'," Aidan said tersely. "Lie still an' save yer strength."

As Malcolm held her wrist, Claire looked into his burning eyes and she recognized uncontrollable lust. He had already killed one woman to save his own life, and in that moment, she understood. He needed to live. He needed *life* to live.

Fear came, but she did not move. "I'm not going," she

whispered. Her heart thundered hard. "I want you to live. Take my life. Take...what you need."

"I...I willna...take ye," he gasped. His eyes closed, his head rolling to the side as he became unconscious.

Aidan cursed, glaring at Claire. "He's dyin'! Ye be an interference now—an' a temptation!"

"Then heal him!" she shouted back. "You said you had power—do it!" She pressed on the wound to stop the bleeding with her bare hands.

Booted steps sounded as Claire turned. "Hurry!" she screamed at Royce. "Get me bandages!"

Royce knelt, handing her his wadded-up brat. Immediately Claire covered the wound, put Royce's hands there and reached for Malcolm's pulse. She couldn't find it. She was on the verge of panic, but somehow she kept it at bay. "I can't find a pulse, Aidan," she warned. "If you don't heal him, he will die!"

Aidan had his hands on Malcolm's shoulders, a fierce expression on his face. Claire began to pray, Malcolm's head on her lap, his face in her hands. Ironheart knelt beside them.

Royce said thickly, "He's slippin' away, Aidan."

Claire saw fear in his eyes. She stared at Malcolm's face, which was so terribly pale now. The stone she wore was burning her throat and oddly she was reciting the prayer she had just read, that brief paragraph to some Celtic goddess. It was as if she had memorized it. The Latin formed on her tongue perfectly, making absolute sense, and nothing had ever been as comforting. She chanted silently to herself. It was as if she had no will of her own. She closed her eyes, sweating profusely, chanting quietly aloud now. The Latin litany was the only sound in the night.

Claire paused and looked at Aidan, who had released Malcolm. "What are you doing?" she gasped.

His gaze met hers. "I canna feel any life. I canna seem to

give him life. Moray has put a block on him. Royce, can ye
stop the bleeding?"

Royce didn't answer, almost as white as Malcolm now.

Claire fought panic. Malcolm could not die! She ripped the
stone from her neck and held it in her hands, shoving Royce
aside, who understood and moved away from her. The wool
beneath her hands was soaking wet. She chanted faster, fin-
ishing the prayer to Ceanna a fourth or fifth time as Royce
swiftly changed the wool beneath her hands. Her mind
screamed at her that Malcolm was not dead. She would feel
it if he was.

Royce had his face to Malcolm's. "He doesna breathe,
Aidan."

Aidan laid his hands on him again, sweat running down
his face. "I canna give him anything," he said. "If I had the
power, it's blocked or gone."

Claire sobbed. She seized Royce's hand and made him
staunch the wound and she bent over Malcolm's face. She
held his nose closed, opened his mouth and started giving him
CPR. He did not breathe.

*She had the Taser in the pocket of her skirt, which she wore
under her leine.*

Claire ripped open the neckline of his leine, tearing it
down to his ribs, her strength fueled by adrenaline. She was
about to lay the Taser there and shock his heart when she saw
his chest move.

It rose...it fell.

Claire held his face and leaned over him. She felt his
breath against her skin, and started to collapse, tears falling.

"Claire," Royce said sharply. "The bleeding's stopped. He
breathes. 'Tis shallow, weak, but he breathes."

She felt his lashes moving. "Don't move. You're hurt," she
managed to say, looking at him.

Malcolm stared at her, appearing somewhat dazed. Claire
wasn't sure he recognized her.

"Aidan, the wound is open an' deep," Royce said. "Ye need to heal him completely. I dinna think he can survive otherwise."

"I told ye, I didna heal him at all," Aidan said thickly. "'Twas Claire."

Royce looked at Aidan, who stared back. Then both Masters stared at her.

Claire couldn't focus on the two men. Malcolm was shockingly pale from the loss of so much blood. She was afraid he was going to die anyway. Claire sent him a smile she was certain was pitiful. "Royce. That needs to be cauterized." The bleeding might have stopped but how could he survive this kind of wound without modern medical attention?

"I go to MacNeil," Ironheart said, and vanished.

Claire began to shake. Apparently, they had stopped the bleeding and resuscitated him, but the crisis wasn't over. She was so afraid he was going to die at any moment. "Can MacNeil save him? Can he heal?"

"He has the power—if he gets here in time." Royce leaped up and hurried from the ramparts.

Claire couldn't fathom where he was going, when Malcolm said, "Come here, lass."

She jerked at his seductive tone. It went through her body, instantly causing warmth and heat. Stunned, she met his glittering eyes. His voice was hoarse, choked with pain. "I need ye, Claire… I'm dying…" And his intense regard held hers.

She could not look away. Claire went still, shocking desire crashing over and exploding inside her. There was no mistaking his meaning. He wanted to take life from her while he was buried inside her womb—the source of life. In that moment, there was complete comprehension and it made absolute sense. He needed her desperately—as desperately, she needed him. Her eyes went past the gaping bloody wound and she saw his manhood stirring, filling. Her gaze flew back to his eyes.

She should have been shocked but wasn't. She knew she

could heal him. She would give him her body and all of her being while he gave her impossible rapture. Her heart beat more frantically now. Somehow she knew what was in store. Le Puissance. The Power… She wet her lips, lowering her face to his. She gasped when her mouth found his. There was so much near-orgasmic pleasure in such a simple kiss. And Claire felt him grasp on to her life.

He gasped, and she reeled in a wave of brilliant, intense pleasure, ecstasy beckoning…

Suddenly, strong hands tore her away from Malcolm. Claire fought Aidan, her entire body throbbing relentlessly now. "No! Fool! He will die!"

"An' ye will die, 'cause he needs yer life an' he doesna ken what he be doing now. Ye give him yer life, an' Malcolm belongs to Moray," Aidan snapped.

Claire couldn't understand. There was too much desperation and too much lust, as if she were an animal in heat. She stared at Malcolm, who lay prone on the stone, consumed with pain, breathing hard, desperately needing her, urgently wanting her. She had to go to him. Furious, she tried to jerk away from Aidan. "I can help him!" She was enraged. "Leave us alone!"

Ignoring her, Aidan easily pulled her toward the stairs.

"What are you doing?" Claire cried, disbelieving, but some of the shocking lust eased. In the back of her mind, she became aware of coming out of a trance. "Malcolm will die if I don't help him! He needs me… Let go!"

"Yer out o' yer head…an' so is he. Moray has trapped my brother another time. He willna become a Deamhan." He wrapped his arm around her, the vise like steel.

Claire struggled and looked back. Malcolm remained prone, as still as a hunter in the forest, his glittering gaze on her, tracking her as Aidan forced her to leave.

I need ye, Claire…dinna go. Dinna listen to them… Come back to me…

His mouth never moved but she heard him as if he had spoken aloud.

The terrible urgency began all over again.

I'll come, she promised. *I will always come when you call...*

Royce bounded up the stairs, past Claire and Aidan, holding a red-hot iron that gleamed like hell's fires in the night.

And Claire fought Aidan wildly. "He doesn't need that," she screamed. "He needs *me!*"

Claire saw Royce hand Malcolm a dagger. She stopped struggling, panting in fear. Malcolm put the hilt in his mouth, biting down on the bone handle, his silver regard steady on her, unwavering there.

Claire held on to Aidan hard. Malcolm choked. The horrific smell of burning flesh rent the night.

Claire gagged, knees buckling. Aidan caught her, holding her tightly to his chest. "Oh, God," she gasped, weeping. She had to go to him now. "Please, Aidan," she cried, "Please!"

"He be unconscious. Ye canna help him now."

"I can," she sobbed. "I can."

Aidan looked back at Royce. Royce nodded. "The tower above," Aidan said. "There be but one way in an' one way out. I'll have locks put on the door."

They were going to lock him up like an animal, Claire thought, horrified. "I swear I will stay away from him," she lied. "Please, don't lock him up."

"I'm sorry, Claire. 'Tis best fer Malcolm," Aidan said. "And this be best fer ye, as well."

The blow on the back of her head took her by surprise. There was stunning pain and shocking comprehension. And then there was only darkness.

MALCOLM AWOKE.

He was burning in the fires of hell. He choked on the searing pain but could not move, the torment so terrible he couldn't even open his eyes. It took him a moment to fight the pain of the fire consuming most of his body and only then could he find any thought. He was dizzy, ready to faint.

He was close to death. He finally gasped, unable to hold back the sound, choking from the pain. Tears burned his eyes and he swam in his world of torment.

Lust began—the lust to live.

There were vows. He was a Master. It could not end this way.

He had to hold the pain back—he had to think. He tried to become oriented. Where was he? He needed life *now*.

His body knew what to do.

Malcolm became still, trying to scent life.

He lay on the floor, a pallet soft beneath his back, the stone cold beneath his hand. He heard himself moan again, and then he heard the pounding rain.

He turned his head. He saw an arrow slit on the far side of the small round chamber and the wooden door. Had they locked him in? He stared at the door, and suddenly, shockingly, he could see through it. A padlock hung on the other side. It didn't matter. Even if they'd left the door open, he didn't think he could stand, or even crawl to the door, much less break it down.

He had only felt so much weakness a single time in his life, at Urquhart, when he was skewered to the wall by Moray's sword, left there to die that way. But he hadn't died, he had taken the maid instead. Her life had saved him....

He burned for life. It was all he could think of. He tried to scent life again. And this time, instantly, he did so. *Claire was below him.*

Now, he had no other coherent thought. She was asleep, but he needed her with him.

Wake up, Claire. I need ye. Wake up...

He felt her stirring, he felt her shock. Malcolm inhaled hard. The need to bring her close and take power from her consuming. He tracked her with his mind as she stumbled from the bed. But something was stirring elsewhere, in his chest, his heart. A memory…

Whatever it was, he ignored it.

I be hurt. They ha' locked me up. When I come into yer body, ye will save me. Claire.

He felt her listening now. She was hearing him and that was good. He strained his senses and felt her desperation and then he felt her heat. He smiled. She was getting ready for him. His loins stiffened in anticipation and his heart began a new, stronger beat.

The memory tickled his mind now.

He didn't want memories; he only wanted her body, her life.

Find me, lass. I be waitin'.

She did not answer but he knew she had heard. He reached down and touched himself so he would be ready when she came.

Where are you?

Malcolm smiled, savagely pleased. *Claire. Upstairs. Above you.*

And he could see her now, two stories below, wrenching at the locked door of her chamber. She was only wearing that tiny chemise and the rag and her boots. Lust consumed him, as did impatience. He throbbed greedily now. He could literally taste her power, as he'd wanted to for so long. And his heart beat swiftly, too swiftly.

I dinna mind if ye love me, lass.

You are so arrogant!

Malcolm moaned. If he allowed himself this luxury, he would fight his need—and he would die. He closed his eyes, sweating, tasting what would soon be his, salivating, until his heart ceased all protest. His loins raged.

Le Puissance. There would be so much life and power, and rapture, unbelievable rapture.

Hurry, lass.

She was coming up the stairs. She was close now, just

outside the locked door, and his heart shrieked at him. *He cared for her.*

Images danced in his mind. Claire arguing with him, a woman who did not need her king. Claire clad only in the tiny beaded string. Claire posed to throw a rock at a Deamhan.

He moaned again. The memories should have dulled his lust, but instead, the urge to taste her power consumed him. *She was a woman like no other.* The distance between them was a hurdle but he somehow grasped on to her life, barely, and pulled power from her.

His veins swelled with hot force and a wave of terrible pleasure began to build. Breathing hard, so swollen it hurt, he turned his head and focused on her as she worked to break the lock.

She was frantic for their union. He felt her lust dripping on her thighs. She wanted to come. He pulled on her life again. Power. Strength. Manhood. Triumph began. He needed to come inside her and take even more from her…

The door burst open.

He pulled at her power, engorging even more fully as the rush of life came into his veins, growing. The wave of pleasure threatened to crest, break. He stared, slowly sitting up. Aye, he cared for her, but it was too late.

For she stood there, shaking and panting, swollen and wet.

"Come, Claire."

Claire stumbled forward. He managed to stand. She caught him, wrapping her arms around him, and instantly he pushed between her thighs, his mouth tearing at hers, and he felt her tears falling, filled with gratitude.

"Lass," he gasped, holding her in a viselike grasp. He flung his head back and began urgently taking her life, as hard and fast as he could.

So much power came. He swelled with it. And the wave broke. He howled his pleasure, pulling her down, thrusting deep into hot, wet flesh. She sobbed with her pleasure and so did he, the rapture escalating a hundredfold. It was blinding.

"Ye taste *good*."

She rode his thrusting length and she came again and again, weeping, but so did he. He had wanted to taste her life for so long and he had been right. Nothing could be as potent, as good. He wanted her riding his manhood this way forever—tonight was forever—and he drained her and came, time and again, while she whirled away, lost in her own pleasure and his. Aware that she kept wanting even more, as desperately as he did, he gave her orgasm after orgasm, allowing no respite.

More.

Aye.

Ecstasy crushed them both.

And Malcolm felt invincible. Total comprehension began. He had more power now than ever before and there was no more to take. This woman had given him everything—this beautiful foreign woman whom he loved. He came, roaring savagely a final time.

He thrust himself away from her.

Shaking from so much passion and power, Malcolm knelt over her prone body and instantly felt her slipping away. Sanity was returning, and horror began.

Claire had nothing left to give.

He'd taken it all.

They rushed into the chamber. Royce seized him, flinging him away from Claire. He was far stronger than Royce now but he let him push him aside. He straightened by the window, breathing hard, sick with fear. Aidan flung a cover over Claire as MacNeil bent over her.

What had he done? And to Claire? He could not lose her now! "Is she alive?" he demanded thickly.

"What the fuck have ye done?" Royce roared at him.

"Is she alive?" Malcolm cried.

MacNeil did not look at him. "Aye, she is, but barely." He had his hands on her, sending her life.

And Malcolm felt her return to this world. Her eyes fluttered and she murmured his name. "Malcolm?"

He was overcome with relief. *She was alive.* Their gazes held and she smiled at him before her lashes fluttered closed.

He had almost killed her.

The beast had raged freely, his intent murderous and evil. The soulless beast...

Royce slammed his hand onto Malcolm's shoulder, forcing their gazes to clash. "Which brother be Moray's spawn?" he said cruelly.

Malcolm flinched, but Royce had every right to wonder now.

She had opened her eyes again. She looked weak, disoriented and confused, but she sent him another beautiful smile. Did she not know what he had done? *How could he have done this?*

She should be afraid of him!

He was afraid of himself.

"Dinna move," MacNeil told her. "Ye have yer life but yer weak."

His horror and self-loathing must have shown because Claire said softly, "Malcolm, it's all right. I am not dead."

He could not respond. Malcolm turned and strode from the room.

MALCOLM SHRUGGED a leine on as he went downstairs. The image of Claire as she lay half-naked on the floor, as still and as white as a corpse, was engraved on his mind. He wanted it there. He had come close to killing her. He had taken her *life.*

He felt violently ill deep inside of himself, in his heart, in his soul. He strode into the hall, aware of Royce on his heels. He was determined to ignore him. He went to the sideboard and drank from one of the decanters, but no amount of wine could change what had happened—or erase the taste of Claire's life in his body and the unbelievable ecstasy of experiencing it.

Malcolm felt Royce's stare burning into his back. He slowly turned, grinding down his jaw. There was no one he hated in that moment as he hated himself.

"I see ye lickin' yer lips."

Malcolm tensed.

"Dinna deny it. Ye loved tastin' her near death."

He wanted to deny it but no words came forth.

"Ye'll fight it now," Royce warned, his eyes blazing silver. "Ye took vows t' protect the Innocent, not to destroy them."

Malcolm turned away. He had forsaken his vows, he had violated the Code. He had taken forbidden pleasure and enjoyed every damn moment of doing so.

Royce seized his shoulder and whipped him around. "If ye stray t' evil, I will kill ye."

Malcolm stared and Black Royce stared back. His uncle meant his every word. "If I turn to evil, I'll be expectin' ye to destroy me." He meant it, too.

"Ye'll fight it an' ye'll fight Moray," Royce snapped. He released Malcolm and stalked past him, looking as if he was ready to start throwing objects around the hall.

"I nay be evil," Malcolm said slowly, but he was uncertain. "I be sick with shame."

"Good. Ye should be ashamed." Royce walked away and began pouring wine into a crystal wineglass. His hand was shaking. Malcolm had never seen Royce tremble, not once in the entire lifetime he had known him.

"Ye canna ken," Malcolm said. "I was a beast, nay a man."

Royce slowly turned. "Why do ye think I wished to see ye locked up like a crazed animal?"

Malcolm stared. He was never going to forget what had just happened. "I almost murdered the woman I am sworn t' protect, Ruari."

"The woman ye are sworn to protect or the woman ye have come to love?" Royce was unsmiling and grim, and the question was an accusation.

Malcolm flinched. Royce was wrong. "I love no one," he finally said. He refused to recall the feelings he'd had in the heat of rapture.

"Ye love the American woman. It's written all over yer face an' I can hear it in yer heart."

"Damn it," Malcolm roared. Royce knew better than to invade his mind. "I be fond o' her, 'tis all. Fond, Royce, fond, like I am fond o' ye."

"Ye dinna think about fuckin' me night an' day." Royce walked away.

Malcolm felt like breaking something. "Yer nay pretty enough."

Royce faced him. "Malcolm, come t' yer senses. Ye have put her in mortal danger now. Ye controlled the takin' this time. What will happen next time?"

"There will be no next time," he cried, breaking into a sweat. He trusted himself even less now, but it was his duty to protect Claire. He would die doing so, willingly.

"I am hopin' so. But yer young, and yer blood is too damn hot. And Moray willna cease. Ye heard him, just as I did. He will take her, use her and send her back with child. Or, he'll trap ye again an' again, luring' ye t' evil, using the woman ye love to do so until ye do take her life."

Malcolm closed his eyes, trembling. He already knew this.

Royce softened. He went to him and clasped his shoulder. "I dinna think Claire should be near ye. Even if ye married her to one o' yer men in a pretense, he'd read her like a book—and ye, as well. No matter what ye think to do, Moray has marked her as a weapon against ye. The lass needs to go."

He knew this, too, instinctively, when he did not want to know it. "Nay. There must be some way to keep her safe."

"There is no way to keep her safe with ye!" Royce cried.

"I'll find a way," Malcolm gritted.

"There be no way," Royce said fiercely. "An' now I see I am right. Ye be a fool in love. Yer love will only kill her. An' her love will kill ye!"

It was almost as if he couldn't breathe. He had come to depend on Claire. He had come to expect her to be at his side, in his home and, after the other night, in his bed. He had come to look forward to their conversations and he anticipated her smiles, which pleased him so well that he tried to be the cause of them. Her arrogance could be annoying, but she was far too clever for a woman. He could dismiss her insults, because he knew she was in love with him. She didn't mean it when she called him a macho jerk. The only thing that really annoyed him was her disobedience, because he knew he was the smarter, stronger one. But he'd withstand every single flaunted command if he could undo what was happening now.

He needed her. It was astounding. He was aching at the thought of sending her far away. He would probably miss her when she was gone. "I will think on it," he said tersely. "Dinna push me now."

"There be nothin' to think on!" Royce was furious. "Ye either wish to find her dead one day or ye wish fer her to live. Make yer choice."

Malcolm stared, sickened. There was no choice to make. Because of the dark beast that lurked inside him, and because of Moray, who knew how to unchain that beast, Claire could not stay with him. She had become his Mairead. And like Mairead, there was only one safe place for her to go—the cloister.

"No Deamhan ever knowingly enters a holy place. I will take her to Iona." Malcolm said, and then he gave in, his anger erupting, and flung his arm out, knocking a beautiful chair onto its side, the arms breaking. His heart did not want her gone.

"She'll be safe there," Royce agreed. "But I will take her. It's late now, I'll take her t'morrow. We'll leave at dawn."

Malcolm turned, his heart thundering. "Ye dinna give the commands here, Royce," he warned. "I be yer liege an' lord."

"Aye, when yer not blinded by lust an' love." Royce stalked out of the hall.

More anger exploded. He leaned over another chair, breathing hard. The cloister would be safe for Claire. His mother was safe there and willingly wished to remain there until she died. Even Moray would not dare enter the sacred site. But Claire would not want to stay in the abbey for very long. In fact, he felt certain she wasn't going to wish to go there at all.

She was going to be furious, he thought. But he was lord and he was not going to give her a choice. He straightened and kicked a red-and-ivory damask chair halfway across the room.

Aidan strode into the hall. "If ye wish to break something, go into the woods, but leave my fine home alone!"

Malcolm looked at him. Unfortunately, this man was his half brother. Last night, he had tried to heal him. "How is Claire?"

"She be fast asleep. I wonder why."

Malcolm tensed.

Aidan's expression was closed, showing no emotion at all. "I didna heal ye. Moray put some spell on ye an' I was blocked." His eyes became hard. "Claire staunched the bleedin' with her hands. Claire breathed into ye an' gave ye back yer breath. She prayed to the Ancients fer yer life."

Malcolm knew what was coming next.

"An' then ye tried to take her life," Aidan said, his temples throbbing. "An' ye hate me fer being the devil's own?"

Malcolm flinched. "I hate meself more."

"Ye should." Aidan paused. "Claire can stay here."

Fury began. "I dinna share, Aidan. She goes to Iona."

"I have no wish to bed her," Aidan said firmly. "She deserves the chance to live."

"I take her to Iona at dawn," Malcolm said softly, enraged.

He knew his brother would never be able to resist Claire's allure. "Ye touch her an' ye die."

"Yer a dolt," Aidan said, striding past him. He picked up the broken chair. "Ye owe me a fine chair from France. Louis XIV, it's called."

Malcolm turned away. He couldn't find calm and he had to face why. His heart actually hurt, aching inside of his chest. Tomorrow he would take Claire to Iona. And then what? Moray could not be destroyed. Claire would have to spend years there, until she was forgotten. She would be furious at first, and then she would be miserable. He already felt miserable.

Aidan said quietly, "She's no Mairead."

Malcolm whirled. "Ye spy on me thoughts?"

"I dinna have to spy. Yer broken heart is screaming loud an' clear."

"My heart nay be broken." He smiled for emphasis.

But Aidan was deadly serious. "Malcolm, leave yer hatred o' me fer one moment. MacNeil didna heal Claire in the tower."

Malcolm stared. "What does that mean?"

"He told me that when he began to heal her, she was already healing *herself*."

Malcolm remained calm. "The stone?"

"I dinna ken. Maybe 'twas the magic of the stone, an' maybe not. I felt the power in the stone on the ramparts. Ye must have felt it, too."

"Aye, I felt the stone's charm last night an' I felt it the night we were attacked in Morvern. But that's not what yer thinking." Malcolm stared and Aidan stared back.

"Yer right," he finally said. "I think she may be one o' us."

CHAPTER THIRTEEN

CLAIRE AWOKE with a pounding migraine, the likes of which she had never before had. Pain consuming her, she staggered from the bed to a chamber pot, where she vomited helplessly.

She sat on the floor, trying to get her bearings and praying that she felt better. The terrible pain was gone, replaced by a less severe headache, but she felt nauseous now. In fact, she felt as if she'd drunk a whopping amount of wine last night.

But there hadn't been any wine last night.

Last night, there had been Malcolm.

Aghast, Claire glanced toward the chamber's two windows. Outside, it was a cloudy morning, the sun barely visible. She began to shake, becoming ill, not in her body but in her heart, her soul.

She was at Awe and last night Moray had dealt Malcolm a nearly fatal blow—for the second time. But he wasn't dead. He was very much alive.

Oh, God. What had she done? What had *he* done?

Malcolm had been near death. He had been locked up like a wild beast and she had been out of her mind, she thought, slowly standing. Now she recalled the terrible desperation, the shocking need to find him, be with him. Last night, she had been certain he was calling her, willing her to him. It had felt as if their minds were communicating. She had not hesitated to obey. In fact, to the contrary, nothing and no one could have stopped her from going to him.

She had not been in control of either her body or her

mind. Malcolm had been controlling her. But he hadn't been sane, either.

His savage roars filled her mind. *He had taken her life last night.*

Claire stumbled to a chair and sat down, horrified. Pleasure in death. That was the understatement of the ages. *Last night she had wanted to die for him. Last night she had wanted to die in the throes of an inhuman ecstasy.*

How close had she come to death? She vaguely recalled MacNeil and Aidan hovering over her. Claire's teeth began to chatter. Had Malcolm stopped…or had he been dragged from her like a rabid animal? She could not remember the details.

Claire could not believe she'd had no will of her own. That was terrifying.

But Malcolm had had no will, either. Being near death had turned him into something insatiable, determined to live no matter the cost.

Moray was about to own Malcolm's soul. Or was it too late?

A tear slipped down her cheek, followed by another and another. And Claire thought of his warm glances and affectionate smile as she lay in his arms after lovemaking, that one, single night, when he had stunned her by telling her he wished to make a commitment of fidelity to her.

Her heart shrieked in protest, demanding that she listen. Malcolm could not have turned evil last night. Malcolm hadn't really hurt her, because she was very much alive today. He was good, and she knew it with her heart, her soul. It was Moray who was evil, Moray and all of his kind. It was Moray who had left Malcolm to die, hoping Malcolm would kill Claire to save himself, hoping to entrap Malcolm into becoming a full-fledged Deamhan as he had tried to before. But Malcolm had regained his sanity before it was too late.

Claire was not reassured. Moray had almost succeeded in engineering her death and Malcolm's downfall. Her mind raced, pointing out that Malcolm had now violated his vows twice, even if she was alive. Was he on the brink of becoming evil?

What would she do if she went to Malcolm and found something else in his place?

Claire was ready to finally admit the truth. She was very much in love with a medieval man descended from a goddess. And last night, he had been insane with a barely comprehensible lust.

She went to the window and, realizing it pushed outward to open, managed to do so. As the fresh, damp air rolled in off the loch, she breathed deeply, her heart racing wildly. And she heard swords clashing.

Claire tensed. In the bailey below, Malcolm and Royce were dealing a series of blows against one another. For one moment she stared as the men locked swords, confused. They were so focused she would have sworn they meant to injure one another. Malcolm went after Royce with such an aggressive thrust that, for an instant, she thought Royce was doomed. But he blocked the blow and they braced there, savagely.

Claire ducked back inside, trembling anew.

Her heart was beating hard and fast. She might never forget what had happened last night, but she wasn't afraid of Malcolm. She was afraid *for* him.

As Claire crossed the room to leave, she glimpsed her reflection in the small mirror standing on the room's single bureau. Clad in her city clothes, she faltered. Her face was very pale, stained with two huge dark circles under her eyes. She looked ill, seriously so. And that was because she had almost died last night.

Claire turned away from the looking glass. She stepped into her cowboy boots and went downstairs. The hall was empty and outside, the Highland morning was wet and damp from last night's rain. The scent of summer rain, fresh flowers and wet grass was heady and intense but not enough to shake the ill feeling deep inside her.

Claire paused. Malcolm and Royce were so furiously engaged that she had grave doubts about the nature of their practice. As she took a good look at Malcolm and then Royce, she realized that both men were very angry. If this was practice, she did not know what a real battle would be like. Each was clearly intent on defeating the other. She could guess why Royce was so angry, but Malcolm looked just as mad. Her heart lurched and she started forward.

Blow parried blow. Malcolm's leine was soaking wet and it stuck to his powerful body, revealing every rippling muscle. His shoulder-length hair was dripping wet and sweat streaked his face. Royce matched him exactly.

Claire was certain that the events of last night were the reason for such terrible animosity. Malcolm needed to back down. Royce had been a father to him since Malcolm was nine years old. She understood Royce's anger. It came from fear for his nephew.

Malcolm glanced at her and Royce struck the sword from his grasp and then laid his blade against Malcolm's jugular. Malcolm tilted his head farther back, accepting his defeat but looking damn displeased about it.

"Royce!" Claire cried. Had Malcolm heard her thoughts? Surely Royce wasn't going to cut him!

Royce snarled and then flung his sword tip first into the ground, where it stood, quivering. He strode past Claire, brushing his wet golden hair from his face, spraying her with his sweat.

She breathed hard as Malcolm bent to retrieve his sword. She was ready to rush into his arms. Instead, she slowly went to him. "Are you all right?" Royce had left a thin red line on his throat.

He straightened, sheathing his sword. Then he pushed his wet hair straight back over his forehead and behind his ears. Claire trembled, realizing he wasn't looking at her. "Malcolm?"

He finally met her gaze, his eyes burning bright. "What, exactly, do ye ask? I should be the one asking ye if yer well."

She tensed. "I'm fine…upset…a little bit scared…but fine." She hugged herself. "Royce is angry about last night, isn't he? He doesn't really understand what happened."

He flinched, looking away, a terrible expression of revulsion on his face. "I dinna wish t' *ever* discuss last night. An' dinna try to defend me now."

"Of course I'll defend you! I will always defend you, because you are the most honorable man I have ever met! Honor won last night."

He faced her furiously, but he became stricken as he finally stared at her face. "'Tis time fer dinner," he said harshly. He started past her.

"We have to talk about last night!" Claire seized his wet forearm, but he whirled and leaped away. "Malcolm, we cannot ignore what happened! I almost lost you last night— and I almost died!"

"Will ye nay leave it alone?" he shouted. "I be here, do I not? Yer alive, are ye not?"

"How can I leave it alone? Moray almost turned you evil. I was ready to die last night in your arms, in pleasure—willingly!" she cried wildly, shaking.

He inhaled, and for one moment Claire thought he was going to shove her away. Instead, very gently, he removed her hand from his arm. "Aye, ye almost died last night. I took all o' ye that I could." His eyes blazed.

When he did not say another word, she whispered, "You were going to die. You're programmed to live, no matter the cost. And you didn't take all of me." Then, because she wanted to be certain, "You stopped, didn't you? Somehow, you stopped."

His face looked to be in danger of cracking. She wasn't certain he could speak, as he was breathing so hard. Finally he said, "Aye. I felt ye leavin' this world. I stopped the beast that lives in me. This one time."

"You chose good, not evil," she managed to say. "There is so much hope!"

He roared, "Ye had nothin' left that I wanted!"

She cringed. "Don't."

"Don't tell ye the truth yer so fond of?"

Compassion overcame her. "I understand your anger," she whispered. "And I understand last night. You know I do. I felt every explosive moment that you were having and it made me want more and more, too. It made me want to die for you. I get it, now. Who wouldn't want more of that kind of insane sex, that kind of unbelievable ecstasy, after trying it once? I get it. Even knowing the risks, it could tempt me to try it again! But you're not an average man. You were destined for good, not evil. You defeated Moray at the last possible moment. Malcolm, you *won*."

He became savage. "Ye should be afraid. I defeated no one! Ye wish to encourage my memories? When I look at ye, I see ye as ye were last night—near death, yer face filled with pleasure—and I feel ye flowin' in my veins. I feel ye even now!"

She recoiled, realizing that last night had changed everything. His control was very fragile, and she had spoken far too freely and in too much detail. She hesitated, uncertain of what to say.

"Aye. I can still taste ye, Claire. But ye want to 'talk' about it. Fine. We'll *talk*. I am close to bein' a Deamhan. Maybe I am already becoming one. Do ye still want to talk?" He strode away, toward the hall.

She had hoped, foolishly, that in the light of day the old Malcolm would be back. His anger told her that he cared about his fate. As long as he did, they could beat this terrible thing. But he was afraid now. She had never guessed that he might be afraid of anything, and he was afraid of himself.

Hearing her, he turned, eyes wide. "I be very angry, Claire. Aye, an' I be afraid. Ye need to stay far from me. And there be no 'we.' I fight Moray alone."

Claire knew she could not abandon him in this hour of crisis. She wasn't hiding in any more closets.

"Then yer a fool!" he cried, reading her thoughts. "Ye think to believe in me now, after what I did to ye?"

"I will always believe in you. You are the son of Brogan Mor," she whispered.

"Fer how much longer?" he demanded, their gazes colliding.

"Forever," she returned.

"Yer the most headstrong, foolish woman I have ever met," he said, disbelieving. "Ye think to trust me? Royce be right. Yer a temptation I dinna need, and yer nay safe with me. He'll take ye to Iona tomorrow."

Claire's eyes widened. They had planned to go to Iona together, to bring the page to the Brotherhood. However, those plans had been made before the events of last night. "What are you saying?"

"No Deamhan ever knowingly enters God's place. Ye'll be safe from Moray an' his Deamhanain there." His tone was cold, cruel. "If I turn Deamhan, ye'll be safe from me."

CLAIRE DIDN'T FOLLOW Malcolm inside. She turned, went over to the steps leading up to the ramparts and sat down hard. It was difficult to think, much less be rational now.

Malcolm was fighting terrible, dark urges. She wanted to fight them with him. But if evil was tempting him now—if *she* was tempting him—then maybe it was better that they put some distance between them for a while. Apparently, the abbey would be a very safe place for her to go. But this was a temporary solution at best. She couldn't stay at the abbey forever.

She glanced toward the castle. How could she let Malcolm fight evil alone?

Last night, Moray had gained ground, but Malcolm had been the victor in that single battle. He had to triumph over the dark urges consuming him now. How could she hide at Iona and let him do so alone? His future was at stake, and so was his soul.

She thought of her vivid recall of that night in Brooklyn. The memory had been so graphic, it could have been happening then and there. But while she knew she had seen a demon's face, she had not been able to imagine him.

He had said he would come back for her.

Fear slithered over her. Twenty years had passed, but to a demon who had lived for hundreds or thousands of years, that was like a second.

What had the demon wanted with her? And was it the same demon who'd murdered her mother?

Someone stepped out of the front door of the castle onto the landing above the stairs. "Claire?"

Claire jumped to her feet, facing Ironheart.

"Ye'll miss the feast. Ye need t' eat," he said without inflection.

He was right. She crossed the bailey, entering the hall behind him. Then she hesitated. Everyone was at the dining table, the great room hushed. A woman was seated beside Aidan, taking Claire by surprise.

Ironheart gestured at a vacant chair as he sat. She smiled gratefully at the older Master, aware that the other three men were actually ignoring her. Claire took the empty chair next to Royce, across from the blond woman. A quick glance showed her the next Swedish supermodel, if the woman ever wished to time travel. She was beautiful and very young. Claire doubted she was even twenty. Since Aidan's wife was deceased, she assumed this woman was his lover. Claire couldn't help stealing a glance at Malcolm to see if he was checking out the woman, but he was not. She was relieved.

Aidan looked up. "Isabel, this is Lady Claire," Aidan said in French. "She is my guest. *Cherie,* Lady Claire is from abroad."

The blonde smiled warmly at her. "I am so pleased to meet you, Lady Claire. It has been lonely here with no other ladies present."

Claire managed a slight smile back, thinking that her nights were likely not lonely. The young woman seemed besotted. Her French was stilted, and she had made a grammatical error. Although she wore a stunning gold necklace that looked as if it was set with sapphires, her leine was average in quality and a plain brooch pinned her brat. Claire decided she was from the lower ranks of the nobility. *"Enchantée,"* Claire returned. She glanced at Malcolm. He continued to ignore her but his plate was almost empty.

We need to finish our conversation, she told him silently.

His shoulder stiffened but he kept on eating.

Claire knew he'd heard her. She decided that the mind-reading thing was not such a bad deal after all. *I mean it,* she added for emphasis. Then she gave in to her heart. *I want to help! I know I can. I am not going to Iona.*

Malcolm threw his utensils on his plate, giving her an angry but incredulous stare. Claire thought he was going to storm from the table but he did not.

"Will you be at Awe for long?" Isabel asked pleasantly from across the table, preventing Claire from making a response.

Claire somehow focused on her. "I don't think so," Claire replied. She glanced at Malcolm, who had pushed his plate away. His face was hard, his gaze dangerously dark.

"Will you return to Dunroch?" Isabel smiled, making her beauty even more dazzling.

"That is the plan," Claire said pleasantly, aware of Royce now staring at her. Maybe a frontal attack wasn't the best idea. She heaped her plate and started to quickly eat.

"Actually," Royce said darkly, "Lady Claire misunderstands. I will escort her to Iona in the morning."

Like hell, Claire thought furiously. Was this Malcolm's new plan?

"Iona is a beautiful island," Isabel said. "Will you join me in the solar after we eat? I am almost finished with my needlepoint. I have a tapestry I wished to start, but you can begin it if you want."

Claire looked at her blankly. She was not going to Iona with Royce; she was going to Dunroch with Malcolm. "Actually, I don't sew."

Isabel looked at her as if she had the plague. "You cannot sew?"

"I'm afraid not," Claire said. She returned to her food, eating as fast as she could. Chairs were pushed back. Royce was pouring himself wine, but Malcolm was stalking from the hall. She took one more bite, preparing to run after him.

Royce seized her wrist. "Ye'll be his death," he warned in English.

"I thought we were friends," Claire cried.

"I like ye well enough. But ye ha' the power to turn him to evil, Claire, an' I willna allow it." His gray eyes blazed.

In that moment, Claire felt his authority. This man was a Master who could leap time, taking life if he so chose, and had other powers she had yet to comprehend. She had crossed the line and he was not her ally now. But at least he intended to protect Malcolm from the dark.

Still, Claire did not like his attitude. "Take your hand off me," she warned. "And I mean it."

His eyes widened.

Claire thought about taking her Taser and giving him a damn good shock.

Royce's expression tightened and he released her. "Ye be ready to leave at dawn. Ye go to Iona, whether ye wish it or nay."

Claire knew a threat when she heard one. "I guess you'll have to knock me out the way Aidan did last night. I also suggest you tie me up. I do not follow your orders." She stood, furious now, while Royce looked even angrier and taken aback. If he was expecting a meek and docile medieval wench, he had another think coming.

Claire strode across the hall in the direction Malcolm had gone. Her anger actually felt good. Anger, she realized, was empowering; fear and doubt were not. She was going to cling to it.

Malcolm was heading for the stables. For one moment she watched his back, all anger vanishing. She was afraid he was leaving, then and there. He disappeared into the stables. Claire lifted the calf-length brat and broke into a run.

He was saddling up his gray stallion as she burst into the stone-and-timber barn. "You cannot be leaving."

He faltered, his strong hands on the animal's leather girth. His back rigid with tension, he did not look over his shoulder at her. "I dinna want ye here. There is nothing more t' say."

"There's plenty more to say!" Claire cried, and she almost shouted, *I love you.*

She breathed hard, hoping he hadn't heard her.

He slowly faced her, looking just as taken aback as she felt. Hoarsely, he said, "Why canna ye ken? Ye'll be safe at the abbey."

He had heard her. "I understand that you are trying to protect me. But who will protect you?" she asked roughly.

He was aghast. "Ye canna protect me!"

Claire dared to reach out and touch his face. He jerked away. "Iona is a temporary solution—but it's no solution at all. You are important to me. I can't let you face Moray alone, Malcolm. I have to help. Your soul is at stake."

He shook his head. "Ye'll be my downfall, Eve to my Adam. Ye willna help, ye can only hurt. An' if I dinna hurt ye, Moray will."

That was one irrefutable point, she thought, but she was willing to take the chance. "I won't lie," she managed to say thickly, "not that it's even remotely possible with you eavesdropping on my thoughts. I am scared, but not of you. Even though that sexual animal last night is scary as all hell, he's a part of you—and I trust *you,* Malcolm." She tried to smile at him.

He smiled cruelly back. "And will ye trust me when the sun goes down? Will ye trust me now, if I tell ye I am thinkin' not about yer words, but your hot, wet body an' yer powerful life? I meant what I said earlier, Claire. I can still feel ye in my veins and ye dinna ken the power it gave me—or the lust."

She flinched, but her heart picked up a terrible different beat. Her skin began to tingle. An aching began, purely physical, purely sexual. "You are trying to scare me. Are you also entrancing me?"

"I want ye to be afraid! And I dinna wish to entrance ye, but the beast will have his way." He stared boldly at her, his eyes silver and hot.

In that second, Claire knew he was tasting every part of her all over again while thinking about being inside her, hard, strong and slick. In that moment, she felt his throbbing tension and knew that if she offered herself to him, he would accept. She was breathless now. Was the dark side of him mesmerizing her?

"Do ye still trust me now?" he asked softly, leaning toward her, the threat unmistakable.

She hesitated. She wanted to go into his arms and press up against his hardness. But she wasn't mindless or in a trance. She didn't want to die for him. She wanted to make love. "Yes, I do."

"Then yer in danger, lass," he said softly.

Oh, did she know that tone. It stirred her loins and licked her flesh. He was watching her with the same predatory intensity as he had last night. She found her voice. "Last night you were dying. You're not dying now. That animal is gone. I trust you. And you should trust yourself."

"That animal," he said tauntingly, "is raging t' be set free."

She did not want to tempt him or test him, but somehow she was doing just that. "No. I'm looking at Malcolm of Dunroch, a Master of Time, and what you want I am not afraid to give."

"Then ye dinna ken my needs, Claire."

She breathed hard, the tension growing hotter, seething between them. "You want sex, not death," she tried.

"I want to feel exactly what I felt last night," he said furiously. "But I dinna wish to hurt ye, not in any way! So ye will obey me command this single time."

He was in a terrible raging battle, she thought. It was worse than she had realized. "Fine. So you will go to Dunroch while Moray hunts you?" She was bitter, scathing. "And I will what? Languish at the abbey like Mairead? Hide in a new closet? For how long?"

"Aye," he said dangerously. "Ye'll hide there fer years, as long as it takes fer me t' forget yer taste, yer feel, yer look!"

She jerked, stunned.

He flushed. "Ye'll stay until Moray fergets ye have any use to him," he amended harshly. "An' that be the day ye go home to yer cousin an' yer books."

"That's not what you said," she said, her heart palpitating wildly. "And it's not what you meant."

He was grim, even savage. "Ye see what I'm thinking of! Ye ken an' ye dinna retreat! Ye want me to admit it? Ye want me t' admit the truth?"

Claire hesitated. She knew she wasn't going to like it. "You're going to hurt me."

"Aye, better I hurt ye now than fuck ye to death!" He pointed at her, his hand shaking. "Ye be an obsession, Claire. Not a passion, an obsession. I dinna love ye now an' I never will. I dinna want yer love! I want yer body an' yer life." He pushed his face close. "I want to push inside ye *right now* an' taste yer life until ye have nothing left to give. Until yer *dead*. Now get out."

She began shaking her head, refusing to move, and tears began. He could not mean it. She didn't expect his love, but she expected, wanted and needed his affection. "I don't believe you. I won't. I can believe I'm an obsession, but you do not want me dead. You want me alive and in your bed. I think you also want me in your life, because you care more than you can ever admit."

He paled.

"So if you think to terrorize or horrify me, well, I'm already terrorized and horrified and I am not about to forget last night. I will never forget last night. I am scared, Malcolm, but I am not dead! Because you stopped yourself from taking my life. And why is that?" She was shouting, crying. "Because there is good inside you. I am not looking at and speaking to an evil man! Moray set you up. I don't get the damn physiology of healing yourself with someone else's life, I will never understand what god made such a stupid plan, that kills innocent people to save great heroes. But life is about moral decisions, Malcolm. Throughout history, men make choices, men fight for good against bad, and they even fight against the bad in themselves! You made your choice last night.

"You beat Moray," she added more quietly, wiping her tears. "And I intend for us to defeat him again and again and again, however long it takes, *together*."

"Ye won't live t' see it," he said flatly, turning and mounting the gray horse.

Claire was dismayed. She had spoken with her heart, and she had passionately meant her every word. But Malcolm wasn't going to change his mind. His decision was set in stone. He was not going to consider that they could fight Moray together. He was not going to consider that they *should* fight Moray together.

Claire seized the reins. "I know there is a risk!" she cried furiously. "But I am willing to take it, because that is how much your soul means to me. This is my choice, Malcolm."

"No. It's nay yer choice. I am sworn t' protect ye, Claire, an' that is what I do. Ye be the most stubborn, pigheaded woman I ever met." His eyes blazed. "Ye'll go to Iona as I command. Let go o' my reins."

She inhaled, releasing the bridle. "I know you are king here, but in my world, a woman is free and she obeys no one, not even her husband. She only obeys herself!"

His laughter was harsh. "We be in my world, Claire, an' in this world, I be yer lord an' ye obey me."

Claire could barely think. This wasn't the best time to debate, not with their passions running wild, but if she did not convince him to trust himself, he was leaving without her. Maybe he was right and fighting for him was a huge and fatal mistake. But maybe he was wrong.

Claire decided to gamble her life.

And he must have sensed her intentions, because he turned white. The same horror she had seen last night covered his face.

She moved in front of the door, blocking the path out of the stable. "Malcolm, we have to believe in each other. And you have to believe in yourself. Please," she added desperately.

"How in God's name can ye do this now?" he roared, erupting into fury.

Claire's heart was pounding so hard she felt faint. "Make love to me."

CHAPTER FOURTEEN

IN HER HEART, Claire believed that if they could have a night like they'd had at Dunroch, without any spell, Malcolm would realize he could triumph over the darkness. But the moment the words were out, Claire wished she hadn't spoken them. Because what she was really asking was for him to love her.

Malcolm's expression turned from horror to fear. "Ye be mad," he said thickly. "Ye think to play with yer life. I willna play, Claire."

"You won't touch my life," she whispered. She was relieved. He hadn't made the connection. He thought she was asking only for sex.

"Why? Why would ye make me such an offer? Do ye belong to Moray now? Is this his plan to lure me to the dark?" Suspicion filled his eyes. "Is he in yer mind now?" Malcolm asked softly, dangerously. "Has he enslaved ye an' ye dinna ken?"

Claire cried out, shocked. "What are you saying?"

"Aye," Malcolm said. "'Tis his greatest power—to enslave weak minds. 'Tis how he turns good men into his evil soldiers. He can creep into a human mind an' do as he wills."

"No," Claire said in horror.

He shook his head, incapable of further speech, jammed his heels into the gray and galloped past her. Claire leaped out of his way. Dust and straw flew up in his wake.

Claire sat down on a bale of straw. Moray could control minds? Surely, surely, she was not being controlled that way.

Her heart had led her to make such an offer and had he accepted it, she would have gambled her life on Malcolm's will, strength and valor.

Claire couldn't stop shaking. She was certain her offer had come from her heart, because it had been motivated by so much love. Claire wished she had never admitted her feelings, because damn it, now she wanted Malcolm to love her back.

Hadn't she warned herself not to get entangled with this man?

Malcolm was not capable of love. He was capable of affection, passion, duty. But love?

He had promised her fidelity, but that didn't have anything to do with love. And they both knew she was going home, sooner rather than later, so it hadn't been a difficult promise to make or even keep.

Claire began to consider the fact that it might be some time, years even, before she went home. Everything had changed because they were both on Moray's radar.

Now what? It was one thing to want to help Malcolm fight for his soul, and it was another to be yearning for him to love her back, when the future of their relationship was doomed, no matter what.

She needed to get a grip on her heart, but she didn't think that was possible. She had always pitied women who fell hopelessly in love with men who did not return their feelings. Holy shit, she was one of those women now.

But she wasn't weak. Claire stood, resolved. She loved Malcolm in spite of their differences, in spite of what the future held, so she had one choice now. Fight with him, fight for him, and be strong enough to go home when the time came—with no regrets and no sorrow, with all of her pride intact.

And as for Iona, well, being a woman stuck in the Middle Ages had vastly reduced her power. If they insisted on it, she'd have to go, but she wasn't going to stay there for years and years. Royce had become hostile, but there was always MacNeil. And if she couldn't convince him to help her, there were all those hunky Masters coming and going. Claire smiled. She liked having a plan. It was barely formulated, but it was better than nothing.

"Claire?"

She jerked, realizing that Ironheart had paused in the doorway, carrying a small, rolled-up plaid, which she knew contained his gear. Her eyes widened. "Are you leaving?"

He smiled briefly, walking past her and leading his big bay stallion from a stall. "Aye."

She was dismayed. "How can you leave now? Malcolm needs you!" She thought, *I need you.*

He tied the horse and threw a blanket and saddle on him. "I'm going back to the Black Isle. I've been gone fer almost a month an' I have clan affairs to attend."

"The Black Isle?" she echoed.

"Aye. 'Tis my home in Lachlan." He finished saddling his mount and faced her. "I see ye fear fer Malcolm."

Claire hugged herself. "I am very worried about him."

"Aye, I ken. Claire, he is strong an' he is good. If he can stay alive, in time this war will pass. These wars always pass."

The first statement was disturbing, the second hopeful. "How much time will it take Moray to decide to stalk someone else?"

He hesitated. "A hundred years, perhaps more, mayhap less."

Claire's eyes widened. "Great."

Ironheart paused before leading the bay from the stable. "Ye are welcome at Lachlan Castle any time."

Claire was confused. What the hell was this? She knew it was not a come-on.

"The Black Isle will be safe fer ye an' ye are welcome in my home fer as long as ye wish. If ye dinna want to go to

Iona tomorrow, ye can come with me now." His green gaze became searching.

Claire was stunned. Should she leave Awe—and Malcolm—now and go with Ironheart? "Where is the Black Island?"

"'Tis nay far, a bit to the south an' west."

And Claire realized she wanted to delay her separation from Malcolm for as long as possible. Besides, Iona was mere miles from Dunroch and Lachlan Castle was not. And she hadn't been sent away yet. "Maybe, one day, I will accept your generous invitation. I'm not sure, though, why you made it."

"Ye be Innocent, Claire. I took the same vows as Malcolm." He swung up into the saddle.

Claire realized she no longer felt uneasy around him. He was an intense, motivated Master, without Aidan's and Royce's charm, but he felt like a very safe anchor. "Take care of yourself."

He nodded at her. "Think afore ye act, Claire, an' ye'll be fine. But if ye need help, summon me. God keep ye." He trotted past her.

Claire followed him from the barn, amazed by his words and his last directive. How on earth would she ever "summon" him? "God speed," she said. She liked the farewell and she lifted her hand. "And God bless."

He didn't respond, breaking into a canter. The drawbridge remained down from when Malcolm had left the stronghold.

Claire watched him vanish into the first gatehouse. That had been odd, but apparently she had an ally she could count on. Considering that Royce was no longer supporting her, and Aidan was an enigma, she was fortunate. But Ironheart had promised to teach her to fight. Obviously that would not happen now.

She needed another dagger, Claire thought, as last night she had broken the blade of the weapon Malcolm had given her. She still had her Taser, but in this world, that wasn't enough and the charge wouldn't last forever. Claire started toward the hall. Aidan surely had a stash of weapons at Awe.

The hall was silent when she slipped inside. She was glad Royce had gone off somewhere, as there'd been enough tension that morning to last through the day. Aidan hadn't been outside, but maybe he was going over Awe accounts. The castle was three times the size of Dunroch, and there was no point in trying to find him. Besides, Isabel probably knew where he was. The ladies' solar should be on the next floor, directly over the hall.

Claire went upstairs.

It never occurred to her to knock, since the heavy wooden door was ajar. Claire walked in and felt her heart drop to her feet.

Aidan was making love to Isabel, stark naked, except for his boots. Isabel was gasping in pleasure and Claire saw everything she shouldn't. He was a drop-dead gorgeous, powerful man.

He suddenly looked up, his gray eyes ablaze with lust.

Claire knew she turned red. "Sorry!" She turned and fled. In the hall, she leaned against the wall, breathless, trying not to envision Aidan with all that rippling muscle moving over that other woman. Isabel's cries intensified and Claire fled back downstairs. Her body had fired up and she couldn't help wishing she were in Malcolm's arms without the threat of evil hanging over them.

She remained acutely aware of the two lovers upstairs. Well, she didn't blame them. It was a great way to pass the afternoon.

Claire went to the table and poured a big glass of red wine. She drank some of it to relax and decided to look for Awe's arsenal. A weapons room would be below the hall, for all stores were kept on the ground-floor level. Claire went down into the "basement." It was stacked with barrels, chests and sacks. But on the east side, there was a door. It was locked.

Claire became excited. She would bet anything she had

just found the weapons room. Of course it would be locked and she should wait for Aidan to finish his afternoon of delight and ask him for what she needed. She looked at the chain and padlock and jiggled it, not that it was a test of any sort. Of course, the chain remained firm.

Last night she'd had shocking strength, but she knew she wouldn't have that kind of strength now. She had nothing to pick the lock with and breaking in would be rude, anyway, when Aidan had been the perfect host. She rattled the lock again, with some annoyance, thinking about the knives that had been on the dining-room table. She could probably pick this lock if she really tried.

Then Claire realized she was not alone. She tensed, turned.

Aidan's brows lifted. "Ye want something, Lady Claire?"

An image of him in far too much male glory flashed through her mind. "Ah," she began.

He smiled as if he knew.

She swallowed, banishing the image from her mind and her memory. "I am sorry about intruding." She felt annoyed. The door hadn't even been closed.

He shrugged. "I dinna care. Ye wish fer a weapon?"

He had a sly tone and an impudent smile. Claire smiled tightly back. If he thought for one second that she wished to share his bed, he was wrong. She thought about Malcolm and her heart ached. "Yes. I broke my dagger last night in your lock. You have been a gracious and generous host, and I have tremendous audacity asking you for another favor. But I have no real means to defend myself." And the one man who had promised to teach her to fight was gone.

Aidan's near leer vanished. He unlocked the door and pushed it open. "Ye need a weapon," he agreed.

Claire gasped. The small round chamber was filled with swords, shields, daggers and—holy shit—guns. She turned her shocked gaze to his. "You have weapons from the future."

"Aye, I do. I like the future an' I couldna help myself."

Claire had identified mid- to late-eighteenth century pistols. She also saw a revolver that she was pretty certain belonged in the nineteenth century. There were no modern revolvers, rifles or machine guns, which was too damn bad. "Isn't this forbidden?"

His grin flashed. "I dinna like rules, Claire, except when I be breakin' them." He walked to rows of neatly hanging daggers and chose a knife that was about twelve inches long with an exquisite ivory handle.

Claire bit her lip. "You have no guns from my time."

"I was in yer time fer that single day, an' I was lookin' fer the page."

"Aidan, in my time, there are guns that fire rapidly, a hundred times before a man can blink his eyes even once. Would a gun like that kill a demon?"

"It would depend on the Deamhan, Claire. Great evil, like Moray, becomes even greater if he has taken power from another afore a battle. And even if he dinna enhance his power first, if life was near, Moray would take it an' survive even if a hundred pellets struck him. But the lesser Deamhanain would quickly die," he added.

Claire thought about trapping Moray in such a way that he could not tap into anyone's life. But how would that be possible?

"It's nay possible, Claire. If ye be attackin' him with one o' yer weapons, he'll take ye. He might take ye afore ye can even attack the first time." He held out the dagger. "How does this feel?"

Claire wanted a nineteenth-century revolver, but she grasped the dagger. The hilt was comfortable in her hand.

Aidan took the dagger from her and replaced it with another. The second hilt was smaller and felt perfect in her grip. He smiled. "'Twill do."

"Is there any way Moray can be lured onto holy ground?"

Aidan laughed. "He can sense God the way we can sense evil. Nay."

Claire slowly lifted her gaze to Aidan's. "He's the devil, isn't he? Not the devil's own, but the devil. He is one of the faces of Satan."

Aidan hesitated.

Claire turned away. "Oh, God," she whispered, and it was a supplication. But the devil would not choose this land as his stomping ground, would he? "Why Scotland?"

"Why not? There be great Deamhanain everywhere, in every time—in yer time, too," Aidan said.

Aidan laid his hand on her shoulder. Claire tensed. "Ye ken, lass, 'tis an ancient belief that the devil chose Alba thousands o' years ago, for he be Lug's first an' eldest son. He wanted the power over all the gods that belonged to his father and that quest led him to evil."

"The fallen angel," Claire murmured, shifting so he no longer clasped her shoulder.

"They say in the land called Greece that the devil be the son o' their greatest god, too."

"Great," Claire whispered. "There are gods everywhere— and more than one devil."

He smiled somberly. "Aye. I'll teach ye how to defend yerself wi' the blade," he said quietly. "An' ye can have the gun ye covet."

She almost embraced him. "Thank you. Thank you."

"CUT ME WITH THE BLADE."

The sun was blazing down on them as they stood in the center of the bailey. A few of Aidan's men had paused as they passed to watch them train. Claire blinked. "You want me to cut you," she said.

His smile was arrogant. "I wish to see if ye have any skill, any speed," he said. "Ye canna cut me, Claire."

Claire wasn't sure he was right. She was unusually strong for a woman and far stronger than the average woman. Kick-boxing had made her light and quick on her feet; her balance was excellent. Of course, Aidan was superhuman. He would be a zillion times stronger and faster than she was. But that didn't mean she couldn't nick him if she tried.

He was impatient. "Cut me, Claire."

She hesitated. "I don't want to cut you," she said truthfully.

He smiled. "Ye willna succeed. But try."

This was a problem and she knew it. She wasn't into violence and in a way, he was a friend.

"Maybe ye dinna wish to cut me 'cause ye be thinkin' about me in Isabel's bed?" he said softly.

She was aware that he wished to anger her, but she was more annoyed than angry. "I am sorry I saw that, believe me!" she said. "Aidan, in my time, we frown on violence."

"Frown away, an' be dead," he said. Then he shrugged. "But ye'll die screamin' in pleasure an' likin' it, won't ye? No matter who the Deamhan be."

Claire grimaced.

He added, "I ken why ye dinna wish to cut me, lass. I dinna mind. Malcolm doesna wish to share, but I often do."

Claire gasped. *"What?"*

"Ye liked what ye saw an' ye like me too much now. Yer thinkin' o' me in yer bed now, nay Malcolm."

"You are a jerk," she cried, and she thrust the blade at his chest.

He seized her wrist, incapacitating her knife hand before she could blink. "An' ye are dead," he said. "Can ye move at all? Or are ye too tall an' awkwardly built?"

Claire jerked free, set up and side-kicked him hard. She was aiming for the chin but he jerked aside and a useless blow glanced on his shoulder. But he smiled, eyes wider. "I said cut me," he said. "Ye won't kill a Deamhan with yer feet." He reached for her.

But Claire was expecting it and she danced out of his reach. She was pleased when she saw respect flicker in his eyes. Now she would cut him, oh, yeah.

"Cut me with the blade, Claire," he taunted.

Claire feinted. She half turned and back-kicked him, but he dodged this time. Now that he knew she could kickbox, he was ready for her. She panted, determined to outthink him.

"Aye," he said, "yer first kick had better be the one that takes the Deamhan down."

"You're worse than your brother!" she said angrily. "Damn it, you have no right to read my mind."

"But any Deamhan who ken do so will do so," he said, backing out of the distance she could reach with her long legs. "Ye still haven't cut me, Claire."

He jerked his head toward the hall. "Ye liked watchin' me with Isabel, didn't ye, Claire? I saw the look in yer eyes. Ye got hot and excited, didn't ye?"

Claire was furious. The worst part was, there was some truth in his words.

He smiled knowingly at her. "I made ye hot."

"Fuck off!" She went to front-kick him in the ribs, but missed when he dodged. Without a pause, she shifted and followed up with a sidekick to his jaw. Claire was surprised when she connected solidly, but he only flinched. Triumphant, she dived at him with the knife.

He caught her wrist before she could sink it into his heart. Claire panted, struggled and gave up. He met her gaze, his eyes warm, and he nodded with a smile. "Ye have some hope," he said, releasing her.

Claire stepped back, breathing hard. "I want an apology."

He was rueful. "Aye, I be sorry." He hesitated. "Yer a great beauty an' I have eyes. But I ken ye love my brother an' that ye'll never come to me."

Aidan started, glancing past her.

In dread, Claire turned.

Malcolm's expression was thunderous.

Claire steeled herself for a battle. How long had he been

standing there? How much had he heard? But her heart ran wild at the sight of him. "I fought at your side in the woods and I killed one demon," she said tersely, in self-defense.

He strode over. "Ye had God's will on yer side—that one time." He turned a dark glare on Aidan. "I be her lord, not ye. I command her, not ye."

Aidan said quietly, "If she'll be alone, without ye, she'd better be able to fight."

"Aye, an' I'll be the one teachin' her," Malcolm said flatly.

Aidan nodded. "As ye should." He turned and walked off.

Claire slowly met Malcolm's eyes. "You've changed your mind!"

Malcolm smiled, but coldly. "I am not as pigheaded as ye keep sayin'."

If Malcolm was capable of changing his mind, there was hope for them, Claire thought. But he was still distant and upset. "What made you decide differently?"

"I dinna trust ye," he said bluntly.

Claire flinched. "What does that mean?"

"It means ye have no respect fer my orders, fer me."

"I respect no one as much as you!"

"I'm leavin' ye at the abbey, but I dinna trust ye to stay put. I won't be with ye to guard ye. Ye have the need to be able to defend yerself now—and t' kill evil, if ye can."

This was what Claire had wanted, but not this way, with him so angry. "Thank you." She hesitated. "Maybe one day, you will understand that I am exactly the kind of free-thinking and independent woman I should be," she said seriously. "Malcolm, just as you must do what you think best and right, so must I."

His face tightened impossibly. "And is being with Aidan best fer ye?"

"How long were you watching us?"

His mouth hardened. "Long enough."

Shit and double shit, she thought, panicking.

"Long enough to ken that ye like my bastard brother."

"That's not true! Not the way you mean. He's a friend."

"But ye bed yer friends, do ye not, Claire?" he asked. "Did he nay make ye hot?"

"How can you be jealous of Aidan!" she exclaimed.

"I'm nay jealous o' any man."

"I walked in on him and Isabel and it was a mistake. I didn't stay, damn it. *You* make me hot!"

He shook his head, a terrible look in his eyes, and started walking away.

Claire chased him, seizing his arm. "Don't do this," she cried. "You know how I feel—you eavesdrop on my thoughts all the time."

He halted and she crashed into the wall of his chest. "Aye, an' yer in guilt now."

"No! I saw them—and wanted you."

A terrible silence fell.

And Claire waited, because that was the truth. Aidan was handsome and he had his moments of charm, but he was not Malcolm and he never would be.

She saw the anger leave his eyes.

He said harshly, "I made ye a promise. Last night changes many things, but I always keep my word."

Claire realized he was referring to his vow of fidelity. "I made you the same promise, Malcolm." It was hard to breathe. "I am a woman of my word."

Their gazes finally locked.

Claire saw him breathing hard, too. No more than an inch separated them. His masculinity became overpowering. Claire wished she could go into his arms for a warm, hard embrace.

He slowly shook his head. "'Tis nay a good idea."

"What happens now?" she asked quietly. "We've made vows, but you won't come to my bed. If I respect your need to sleep alone—"

"Nay. I will keep ye safe."

He would still send her to Iona. They had just weathered another storm and she felt closer to him than ever. "You're calmer." Her whisper sounded urgent.

His gaze was unwavering. "Aye, I'm calmer. But ye willna be safe here. Yer nay safe from Moray. From me." His gaze moved to her mouth then lifted to her eyes. "We'll make our farewells in the morn." He nodded and turned to go.

She rushed to stride alongside him. "Where are you going now? What are you doing?"

"The sun sets in two hours. I'm going to the tower now."

She was incredulous. "You're locking yourself up?"

"Aye." He paused before the stairs leading to the front door of the castle. "Maybe in a few years," he said thickly, "there'll be a safe time an' a safe place fer us."

Claire cried out in protest. "A few hundred years?"

He gave her a long look and walked up those stairs.

CHAPTER FIFTEEN

ROYCE WAS WAITING for her in the great hall.

Claire's stomach was in knots. She had tossed and turned all night, acutely aware of the fact that Malcolm was above her in the tower. But he hadn't been summoning her. She had strained to listen for him but had heard nothing. She interpreted his silence to mean he was firmly in control of any lingering dark urges.

Royce strode over to her. "Break the fast. We willna stop until we reach Iona."

Claire met his gaze and saw no hostility, just quiet determination. She couldn't care less about breakfast. "Where is Malcolm? I have to say goodbye."

Royce said, "Outside."

She had been afraid they would not have a last word before parting. Claire hurried out. Malcolm's fifty men were already mounted, their horses blowing impatiently in the brisk chill of dawn. Instantly she saw Malcolm astride his big gray. He glanced her way and their eyes met. Malcolm moved the charger toward her.

Claire rushed over to him. "You wouldn't dare leave without telling me goodbye!"

He looked as tired as she felt, Claire realized, and that meant he'd had a rotten night, too. But she knew better than to believe he'd been tossing and turning over his undying affection for her. "I'll go with ye an' Royce as far as the sea loch," he said.

Claire was thrilled. She grasped one of his reins. "What changed your mind?"

His gaze held hers. "Dinna think so hard, Claire. I go back to Dunroch and 'tis the best way. I never said I wouldn't make part of the journey with ye." He turned his mount away.

Claire looked around for her mount. She knew exactly who she was riding through the pass with. Royce joined her, leading the brown gelding. "Mount up, Lady Claire."

Claire took Saint Will's reins and swung into the saddle, finding the wood stirrups. When she looked up, Aidan was handing her a revolver.

Claire grinned, briefly forgetting all about being in a situation in which she had no say and no control. "You didn't forget! Is it loaded?"

"If ye mean does it have six round pellets inside, aye, it does," he said with a grin of his own.

Claire would have kissed his cheek if she wasn't astride and if Malcolm hadn't been so jealous yesterday. "Thank you. Not just for the dagger and the gun, but for everything."

"I canna refuse a beautiful woman," he said, smiling.

Claire glanced across the troops and saw Malcolm watching her. She hoped he was reading her mind now. "That is obvious," Claire said. She leaned closer. "Be nice to Isabel. She's very young for your shenanigans."

His eyes widened. "Claire, she kens the way o' the world."

Claire thought it sad that she probably did at such a young age. She wasn't sure why she hoped to save Isabel from the broken heart that would be her fate, but she did. She moved her horse toward Malcolm, tucking the revolver carefully in her belt. Claire came abreast of him, uncertain. "Are you waiting for me?"

"Aye." He gestured that they should follow the men trotting under the raised portcullis and through the middle ward. A moment later, Claire was riding across the first drawbridge with Malcolm. The sky was turning pale blue, the sun shining faintly yellow as it crept over the still waters of the loch. To the north, Ben More and the lower, adjacent peaks remained shrouded in shadow and mist. As Royce and the first few men trotted onto the marshland, two does and a magnificent buck with huge antlers leaped out of the forest and across the road. Claire smiled at Malcolm. So much had happened since that terrible battle with Moray and she missed him.

He met her gaze. His eyes were unguarded, almost soft. "Are you eavesdropping?"

"Will ye shout?"

She almost laughed. "No."

"'Tis called lurking, Claire, and with ye, I dinna have t' even try to hear ye. Ye think so loud."

Her heart raced as they passed through the raised portcullis. "Then you know that I miss moments like this one."

His jaw flexed and his lashes lowered over his eyes.

"The rising sun, the crisp, clean air, the towering mountains, the scent of wood and pine…and you, here with me, like this."

"I canna change the past. 'Tis nay allowed."

"Malcolm."

"Aye," he said slowly, looking up at her. "I heard ye. But I willna say I miss the pleasant times. Dinna push me, lass. The affairs o' the court weigh on me mind now." He added, "'Tis where Moray has gone."

"Tell me what you are thinking," she said softly. "Do you have a plan for Moray?"

He gave her a look she could not decipher.

"Where does Moray fit in?" Claire asked. "He controls the royal armies. The king must depend upon him heavily."

"Aye, he does. But he controls Moray, Claire, not the other way. James be clever, ambitious and devout. An' ye can say a prayer o' thanks to any god ye choose that the king be so faithful."

Claire got his drift. James's religious beliefs were keeping him out of Moray's clutches. That was a relief.

"How devout is James? Is he fanatical? Is that what it takes to make a soul secure?"

"Ye think I should pray."

She wet her lips. "It can't hurt." And she started to think about the prayer she'd been saying when Malcolm had been dying on the ramparts. She hadn't memorized that verse, but it had come pouring out of her.

Malcolm hadn't died. And James wasn't Moray's soulless lackey. The gods were out there, and God had always been the bulwark against evil. She had to get religion.

"Ye want to use religion, Claire," Malcolm said quietly, "but usin' it, even fer a good cause, an' havin' faith be two different things." The words were barely out of his mouth when a terrible expression of alarm covered his face. And that was when Claire felt a chilling wind rush over the marshes.

Royce whirled his horse, shouting commands in Gaelic, and she heard the wild battle cries of the approaching army as they burst into the glen.

Fear choked her. She saw perhaps a hundred mail-clad foot soldiers, wielding pikes and shields, and two dozen fully armored, mounted men. Claire glanced behind her as the knights bore down upon them at a mad gallop. Castle Awe was a mile distant. The marsh was no more than a mile wide from side to side, surrounded by impenetrable forested mountains, the pass ahead. Claire wasn't a military strategist, but she didn't have to be one to know that they were too far from the castle to return safely to it, and that they were caught out in the open with no place to run or hide.

Royce galloped to them, slamming something at Malcolm, which he seized. "Take the page an' Claire," he said. "I'll hold them off here."

Claire expected Malcolm to protest as the first knights engaged his men, their bloodcurdling cries filling the dawn, lance against shield, sword against sword. But he seized her reins. "Claire!"

Claire grabbed the horse's mane as they wheeled and galloped back toward Awe. She looked back at the expanding battle. Everyone was now engaged, even the foot soldiers, making them terribly outnumbered. Horses screamed and men cried out, swords ringing, clashing, echoing. She turned ahead as they galloped toward the castle, breathing hard. The outer drawbridge was being slowly and cumbrously lowered. In minutes, surely, Aidan and his men would emerge. But her little gelding was on Malcolm's steed's flank, and she wasn't going to be able to keep up with his stallion for long.

She looked over her shoulder again. A dozen riders were pursuing them, ignoring the main battle. "Malcolm!" she screamed into the wind. The drawbridge felt as if it were a hundred miles away.

And Malcolm thought so, too. He slowed his gray, holding out his hand. *We'll leap.*

Claire reached out for him and their fingers brushed, but he missed grasping her hand.

"Claire!" He halted his stallion abruptly and it reared. Saint Will raced past the gray and was instantly flung backward by the rein Malcolm was holding, stumbling hard. Claire sailed over his head.

She somersaulted and landed hard right below her neck, where it joined her spine. For one moment, she just lay there, stunned, stars shooting in the sky above. Malcolm raced to her on foot now and Claire saw the pair of knights galloping toward him from behind, swords raised. She sat, pointing the gun, her hand shaking wildly. "Malcolm!" she warned him, firing.

She aimed at the horse. It went down, the knight rolling just out of the charger's way, avoiding being crushed. Malcolm whirled, sword and shield raised, to meet the other knight's attack. On foot, he swung hard at the rider, who swung as hard back. Malcolm staggered backward as their blades locked.

Three foot soldiers were upon them. Two wore mail shirts, one just a leine. Claire knelt, aimed, fired and saw one man fall. When he did not get up, she guessed they were men that Moray had turned to evil, not demons. Suddenly two knights were hauling their horses to a halt before her, cutting her off from Malcolm.

The first lifted her visor. "Hello, Claire." Sibylla grinned.

Claire froze, pointing the gun at her. Behind Sibylla, Malcolm was trying to fight three men at once. Her escalating heart rate made her feel faint. It was hard to aim straight.

"I wouldn't make me angry, if I were you, Claire," the redhead said, her smile widening. "You really don't want to get on my bad side." She rode at Claire.

Her heart slamming in alarm, Claire didn't hesitate. She fired. The bullet hit Sibylla in the chest and the impact through her armor should have sent her flying from her horse; it did not. Instead, she reached down and jerked the gun from Claire as if she hadn't felt the gunshot. From her eyes, Claire saw that she had felt some pain and that she was now angry, but it wasn't stopping her. Worse, as their gazes met, Claire felt a terrible sensation, as if her insides were being turned to jelly. Her racing heart slowed.

Sibylla was taking her life.

Claire's knees felt weak. She stumbled, aghast with what was happening. And she felt lust blaze in the other woman. Claire looked up to beg for her life.

Sibylla's eyes were hot and bright as she leaped from the horse to kneel over Claire. And the moment their gazes connected, Claire knew she'd made a fatal mistake. For Sibylla began to mesmerize her and Claire felt her body relax, even though her mind screamed at her to resist. The mushy feeling inside her increased—and to her horror, a wave of pleasure swept her body, and her loins swelled, aching for a caress.

Sibylla laughed softly. "You have so much power! But I

have known that for some time. Unfortunately, I'm not allowed to kill you, darling. And by the way, you won't need that."

And before Claire could understand, Sibylla leaned down and reached for her throat.

And Claire saw the other woman holding her mother's necklace. Disbelief and impotence vanished. Instead, there was rage. She howled, attacking the woman, intent on dragging her down—she'd get the stone back! But Sibylla caught her wrist, her strength shocking once more. In that moment, Claire knew she was toast.

Time stopped. Silence fell. Her eyes gleaming and crazed like a drug addict's, Sibylla thrust her shortsword deep into Claire's shoulder.

Claire had never known so much pain. She stiffened, blinded by the red-hot agony, incapable of any thoughts except a terrible awareness of the stunning torment.

"I'm not allowed to kill you," Sibylla whispered. "But maybe you'll die anyway." She released Claire.

Claire heard her but couldn't reply. She sank to the ground, her legs giving way instantly. The sky was turning black. She wanted it to turn black. She spun in a cyclone of pain. Vaguely she heard Malcolm's roar of rage. The pain made her want to die. Then there was nothing but silence.

Malcolm panicked.

As Claire fell, blood pouring down her chest and arm, he froze. Then panic exploded. Sibylla leaped onto her horse, sword raised, and charged at him.

He came to his senses. He parried her blow effortlessly and ran past her steed to Claire. He knelt as the sounds of battle died behind him. "Claire!"

She was unconscious and bleeding profusely, dangerously. He saw that the sword had gone through most of her shoulder. There would be no way to save her arm if she lived, but the rate at which she was losing blood made her survival questionable. She needed someone who had the power to heal her with ancient gifts. He roared for his brother. "Aidan!"

Royce jumped from his charger, running to him. "They're gone. Do ye have the page?"

"Aye. Get Aidan. Get Aidan here now!" Malcolm shouted at him, cutting off a long piece of his leine. She was turning white from the blood loss. He bound up the wound, aware of his hands shaking. She could not die!

Aidan leaped off of his black steed. Malcolm looked up and saw the fear in his half brother's eyes. "Ye heal her," he warned thickly. "Ye find the power an' ye find it now!"

Aidan knelt. "Get away from me," he said tersely, putting his hands on her wound. "Ye be a distraction I dinna need!"

Malcolm did not want to leave Claire. He stood, staring at her, unable to believe that this was happening. Fear made it almost impossible to think. He only knew he could not lose her. Not now, not like this. Not ever.

Aidan was sweating now.

Malcolm looked up at the heavens above and prayed. He prayed to all the old gods and, afraid they would not listen, offered them his own life in return for hers. Surely they would accept such a bargain! Then he looked down at his half brother. "What happens?" he cried. He could not find calm, no matter how he might try.

"I can feel her life," Aidan said tersely. He finally glanced up. "She be weak, Malcolm."

"Ye feel it returnin' or leavin?" Malcolm demanded furiously. He knew how weak Claire was!

Royce seized his arm and pulled him away. "Yer fear doesna help him."

"It be returnin' to her," Aidan said harshly. "She doesna need me. She be healin' herself. I can feel her force. Malcolm, she has *power*."

He felt no surprise. He had been suspicious of who she was from the start. Malcolm knelt and took Claire's hand. As he did so, he felt her life, weak but steady, flowing in her hand, around his. He tried to sense her power and slowly, he began to feel it, soft but strong, a clean and good white life force, so oddly familiar.

Aidan pulled the soaking red linen off her arm. He laid his hand on the wound. "She's nay bleedin' now."

As Aidan sat with her, his hands on her, Malcolm held her hand. He felt her pulse becoming stronger. Relief finally began.

Royce squatted and clasped his shoulder.

Malcolm looked at him.

"She'll need to stay at Awe fer a few days," Royce said. "I'll take the page to Iona." He hesitated. "I willna ask if ye'll stay with her."

"Good." Malcolm wasn't leaving Claire until she was well on her way to recovery. He reached into his brat and handed Royce the rolled-up page. Royce stood, his expression turning hard, and a moment later he had vanished into thin air.

Claire murmured his name.

Malcolm leaned over her. "Lass!"

Her lashes fluttered but her eyes did not open.

Aidan sagged to his hands and knees, his hands and forearms covered with Claire's blood. He was deathly white. "Get her inside. Ye can move her now," he gasped.

Malcolm realized Aidan had used his own power to heal Claire, so much so that he had made himself weak. He was dumbfounded. He signaled to the men surrounding them. "Help yer lord into the keep," he said sharply.

"I be fine," Aidan snapped, but he remained on the ground and did not appear to be capable of getting up.

He was a pigheaded man, Malcolm thought grimly. He knelt and lifted Claire gently into his arms. More relief made it hard to breathe. Two men had helped Aidan to his feet and he stared.

Malcolm gave in. "Thank ye."

Aidan nodded. "Ye be welcome."

CLAIRE REALIZED she was in a fluffy feather bed. Floating on down, she smiled dreamily, wondering whose bed she was in. Maybe she was dreaming, she somehow thought, as her own Doctor's Choice mattress was far firmer than this. Sunlight poured into the room. But such bright sunlight was nonexistent in Manhattan. Claire blinked, confused, and saw unfamiliar, crude stone walls that bobbed around her. Her shoulder hurt, the throbbing ache deep and intense. Then she realized that she was in someone's arms.

Claire pushed through the layers of fog. She was dazed, groggy. She saw a man's powerful forearm across her waist and felt his broad chest against her back, and realized Malcolm lay on his side behind her, and she was spooned against him. He felt incredibly right—strong, warm, safe. The room continued to slowly spin. She wasn't in the city or the present. She began to recall the terrible battle outside of Awe and Sibylla's vicious attack. Sibylla had thrust her sword into Claire's shoulder and she had enjoyed doing it. She had enjoyed taking some of Claire's life force even more.

Claire realized she was on some kind of medieval drug and it was hellishly strong. The bed seemed to be on a merry-go-round and it was hard to think clearly. She should be out of her mind with pain. But maybe there was another reason she wasn't in agony.

Afraid, Claire tensed and looked at her left arm, but it was attached to her shoulder. She sank against Malcolm in sheer relief. How long had she been unconscious? Days? Weeks? Thank God someone had saved her arm!

She somehow shifted, so she was on her back and could look up at him. She had assumed him to be asleep, but he was wide-awake and watching her closely. When she met his gaze, he smiled.

It was a beautiful, unreserved, heartbreaking, heartwarming smile. "Good afternoon, lass," he said softly.

Claire shifted to face him, pain stabbing through her, but

not badly. Malcolm seemed to bob, too, but not in tandem
with the walls and window. She laid her left hand on his
hard chest and shivered with pleasure. "These are wild
drugs," she whispered. "Why are you in my bed?" She
smiled up at him.

His hand clasped her waist. "I was tired. I thought to sleep."

Claire looked up into his stunningly gentle and uncompli-
cated gray eyes. Affection shimmered there. "You have your
own bed," she murmured. Was she seeing what she wanted
to see, as she was so heavily under the influence of whatever
potion she had been given?

He hesitated. "Do ye remember what happened, lass?"

Claire nodded. "How did they save my arm?"

Malcolm met her searching gaze. "Aidan worked to heal ye.
But ye have yer own powers, Claire. There's no more denyin'
it."

She knew that was absurd. "The stone has power," she
whispered, reaching for it with her left hand. She froze—it
was gone. Sibylla had taken it.

"I'll get it back fer you," Malcolm said, sliding his other
hand into her hair, the gesture entirely comforting.

But Claire wasn't comforted. In that instant, in spite of the
weaving room, Claire knew that stone had belonged to her
father. She recalled the way Ironheart had inspected it. But
it would be an impossible coincidence if her father had been
his brother. "It was my father's. I am certain of it now." Panic
began. She would be lost without the stone! It was her only
connection to her parents.

"Dinna worry about the stone."

But Claire was ill over the theft. "Why would she take it?"

"The stone may be givin' ye yer powers. Ye said ye wore
it since yer mother died. That's a long time to wear magic,
lass. I think that is why Sibylla took it from ye."

Claire thought that made a lot more sense than having
powers of her own, which she knew she did not. But she was

recalling something else, something she really didn't want to think too closely about. "Malcolm, I think Sibylla said she was not allowed to kill me."

He looked away from her now. "Ye be confused. Father Paul has given ye strong herbs an' flowers."

Maybe he was right, especially as the bed continued to slowly move around and round like a carousel. She used her left hand to touch his chest, beneath the veed neckline of the leine. His skin was warm, the hair there crisp. His eyes flickered and she knew he wanted her to continue touching him. Claire felt a stirring between her legs, a dryness in her mouth, and was surprised that she felt desire now. "You feel so good," Claire whispered. "Whatever he gave me, I like it. How long have I been unconscious?"

"Two days." His tone had changed.

Claire would have never believed it possible to feel this way after two short days. But she didn't care to analyze that, because Malcolm was having a very definite reaction to their proximity and her caress, and so was she. She met his gaze, watched it smolder, watched it go to her lips. She slid her hand up to his neck, shifting so she could arch sensually toward him. A very firm erection leaped against her hip.

"I'll go," he said, but he did not move, watching her closely.

"I miss you," she breathed in return. Damn, she might as well have been drunk. "I miss you so much."

Malcolm's breathing had deepened. He hesitated. "Ye scared me, lass."

"Why?" Claire asked, drifting her hand lower to his ribs, over the linen. He was such a beautiful man. "How could I possibly scare you?" She couldn't help it. The moment almost felt like a dream. She leaned toward him and pressed her mouth against his chest, in the gaping vee of the leine, near the heavy cross he wore.

He closed his eyes, not making a sound.

"This is so perfect." She vaguely recalled the terrible

events of the night he had been locked in the tower, but it felt like a lifetime ago and she knew it could not affect them now. She moved her mouth to his neck. She opened her mouth there, long and slow.

His body tensed. "Ye scared me 'cause ye almost died," he whispered roughly.

She stared into his eyes. He stared back and she smiled, because she was very much alive and there was moisture gathering to prove it. She stroked lower, to his navel, and met a thrusting head through the leine. She slowly looked up.

His gaze was bright silver. Claire slowly lifted the leine out of the way. She was expecting him to seize her hand to forestall her and jump from the bed. Instead, his hand tightened on her waist.

Claire gave in to swelling desire. She sighed and lay back against the pillows, leaving her hand on his bare hip, careful not to touch him now. Malcolm moaned.

"Do you like being teased?" she murmured, scrapping her nails gently over his belly.

"Nay very much," he warned.

She smiled and ran a nail around his burning hot head.

Malcolm turned toward her, his face as crimson as his member. Claire leaned low and used her tongue.

He fell onto his back. "Thank ye, lass."

Claire wanted to enjoy every possible inch of him, unhurried and unrushed. And when she came up for air, he was breathing hard, and their gazes met.

She inhaled when she saw the look in his eyes. "Come here," he said softly.

She slid her thigh over his in an unmistakable invitation, the chemise she wore riding high. She thought, this is so perfect, slow and hot and soft.

"I dinna mind slow, lass, but soft?" His smile came and went as he slid against her, probing there.

Claire gasped with pleasure as he slowly slid deep. "I

meant gentle," she managed to say as he filled her. Tears came. Pleasure rose, a growing wave.

"Ye meant this," he said roughly, pulling her closer and moving with excruciating care and deliberation, so slowly. "Ye did mean this?" A teasing note had entered his thick tone.

"Yes," she tried, and gave up. She closed her eyes and allowed a sweet, soft sensual release to begin. She cried out and pleasure rained down on them.

He gasped and she felt him smile. He began to move more swiftly, accelerating the pace. And suddenly an entirely new urgency began.

Claire tensed, holding on to one shoulder, instantly sensing the change in him. Every single muscle in his hard body had turned to steel, his heart rate exploding against her breast. A new, terrible ambition had arisen, and she felt his mind going to a dark, dangerous place. Malcolm went still.

"Come back," Claire whispered, holding on tightly, afraid in spite of her daze. "Don't go there. Come back to me."

Malcolm struggled with himself, the muscles in his arms bulging, his penis throbbing. "I want all o' ye," he ground out. He lifted his head and she met blazing eyes, eyes she instantly recognized, mirroring unholy, uncontrollable lust.

He knelt over her, pushing her onto her back. And as he loomed there, she saw his body thicken with more power, more muscle, while black shadows formed behind him and red fire burned there. Still buried inside, he threw his head back and panted and Claire felt him touch her life.

She gasped as the room whirled, a sudden vortex of pleasure sucking her in.

Malcolm cried out savagely, and then he jumped from the bed.

No shattering ecstasy came. The spinning eased. Claire somehow sat up. The room tilted wildly. She met fierce, glittering silver eyes. She blinked and saw Malcolm leaving the chamber.

Claire collapsed against the pillows, fighting for air. The spinning room slowed but did not stop. *Malcolm, don't go,* she begged.

If he heard her silent cries, he did not answer.

She somehow sat up again. She cursed the herbs and flowers, but that did not clear her mind. They had been making love and he had turned into that raging beast. She had felt him touch her deeply, she had felt him touch her soul. She stumbled from the bed.

Claire reeled but made it to the door. She pushed it open. "Malcolm."

There was no response.

She felt him leaving, not just her but Awe. Alarmed, Claire rushed to the stairs. She tripped, falling against the wall. Strong hands seized her.

"Let him go," Aidan said firmly, a command. "Ye need to rest an' he needs to go. He's huntin' Sibylla now."

Claire shook her head. "I am…going with him!"

"Dinna make me cuff ye in the head a second time," Aidan warned.

Claire couldn't answer. The stairs were lurching toward her. For one moment, she really believed it was an earthquake. Then Aidan caught her and the stairs leveled and settled where they belonged.

Exhausted, despairing, Claire started to weep.

THREE DAYS LATER, Claire stared at her shoulder in the looking glass in her chamber. The potion had finally worn off and she felt as healthy as ever. Her shoulder had a vivid and unattractive pink scar, but miraculously, otherwise, there was no sign of the recent wound. Yesterday when it had rained, her shoulder had ached. Today it felt fine, but when she reached overhead she was aware of a slight strain.

Ye have yer own powers, Claire. There's no denyin' it.

The stone, which Sibylla had stolen, had somehow imprinted her with its power to heal. Claire pulled her sleeve down and glanced at the vase of wildflowers that Isabel had brought to her room. Several days old, they were dying.

She stared at the flowers, thinking about seeing them rehydrate, grow, even blossom. She should have felt foolish. She did not. Nothing happened.

Claire picked a small pink blossom up and held it in her hand. She tried to focus. Instead of returning to its brilliant state of days before, a petal fell to the floor.

She sighed, putting the flower down. Whatever power she might have had, it was gone. Besides, Aidan had helped to heal her, and there was no question that he had some abilities, even if he wasn't adept at using them all of the time.

Claire became grim. Malcolm was hunting Sibylla. Maybe she was paranoid, but she was afraid it was another trap.

She'd had three days to think about him—about them. It was dangerous feeling about him as she did. It was probably hopeless for her to want him to return her love. Claire knew she couldn't control her own feelings or her yearning. They were in a relationship, as difficult and strained as it was. It wasn't going to last forever. At some point, she was going home. But while she stayed in medieval times, she wanted it to work.

Every couple had differences. Arguing because of those differences wasn't going to bring them closer together. So far, arguing hadn't accomplished anything positive at all.

Like any couple, modern or not, they were going to have to figure out how to understand each other and compromise.

However, she wasn't going to blindly obey his orders.

Claire went downstairs and into the great hall. It was early morning and bright light was trying to flood the great room, but unsuccessfully, due to the depth of the numerous windows. Isabel was breaking the fast alone. She smiled at her. "I am so glad that you are up and about," she said.

Claire smiled back. "Whatever potion they gave me, it kept me weak, tired and in bed, which was the point, I guess. But I feel like myself. Isabel, where is Aidan?"

Isabel started. "He left last night, Claire. He said he had affairs in Paris."

Claire sat down in sheer dismay. "He left us here—alone?"

"He said he would be back today."

Her eyes widened but she instantly got it. He was leaping over to Paris and back, never mind the rules—unless, of course, he was hunting evil, in which case he wasn't breaking any rules. She was about to ask Isabel if she was certain, when Aidan strode into the hall, smiling.

Claire's eyes widened. He was wearing a cloak that wasn't remotely a part of the fifteenth century, not even in France, and he was carrying a beautiful gold velvet, gilded rococo chair.

He grinned at them both. "What do ye think?"

Isabel blushed. Claire stood. "You went to France for a chair?"

"Aye." He set it down next to a table and sofa. "Malcolm owes me the chair but I dinna think he will ever replace it. He can pay me back another way." He stroked the gilded, intricately carved back. "'Tis a great beauty."

Claire went to him. "So much for only using your powers to uphold the Code."

He waved dismissively at her. "Rules, Claire, are made to be broken. What is it yer dyin' to ask me?"

Claire hesitated, glancing at Isabel.

Aidan walked over to his mistress. He bent, kissed her cheek, murmured to her and she dutifully got up and left the room. Then he faced Claire.

Claire thought about the fact that she actually liked him when he was both a heartbreaker and a chauvinist in the worst way. "Aidan, how can I convince you to take me to Malcolm?"

His eyes widened briefly. "Ye canna."

She went over to him. "I have to go. Malcolm cannot face Moray alone. This is a battle for his soul. He has to win. You know he must. If he loses, he will be a Deamhan and he will be dead to us. *Please.*"

"No." His tone was absolute. "Malcolm has asked me to take ye to the abbey, where ye'll be safe. Sibylla has gone to court. The court is nay safe, nay with Moray there, thinkin' to use ye against him. Malcolm has Royce to look after his soul." His gray eyes had become hard.

"He's followed Sibylla to court?" Dismay began. "If you take me, I will go with you back to my time and show you more beauty than you have ever seen." If Aidan had a weak spot, it was his love of beautiful women and beautiful objects. She would take him to the Met, Tiffany's, Asprey's…. She could think of a hundred places to go.

His smile was wry. "I can find beauty meself, Claire. Anytime, anyplace."

Claire took both of his hands in hers. "I am begging you. I am begging you to help me help your brother."

He shrugged free. "I dinna worry about my *brother,*" he said.

That was a lie. Claire felt it. She stared, thinking about the fact that Malcolm seemed to hate Aidan and vice versa. But in the past few days, the brothers had become civil and they had been allies. Malcolm, Claire knew, remained distrustful, but Aidan had tried to heal him, then had locked him up for his own good. And he had tried to heal her. He had been nothing but helpful since they had come to Awe. And why?

Claire suddenly had a terrible inkling. His mother had abandoned him at birth. Moray he despised—and possibly feared. He had some kind of relationship with Royce, but they were not related. His wife was dead. His only personal adult and familial relationship seemed to be with Isabel, and Claire knew that was a fling. Malcolm, however, was his half brother.

Aidan needed Malcolm.

"What would you do if Malcolm admitted you were his brother, if he treated you like his brother, if he came to care for you as a brother?" she asked softly.

He paled, then a flush of anger began. "Treachery, Claire?" he asked coldly.

She had struck a nerve. "The two of you should be great friends!" she cried. "You are as much a victim as Malcolm of what Moray did to your mother!"

Aidan was furious, his eyes blazing. "Ye go too far," he warned. He turned away.

Claire seized his arm. "No. Take me to Malcolm and I swear on my mother's grave, I will make him see that you are his greatest ally! Aidan, I like you, even though I do not care for philandering men. You are a good and, at times, kind man, and I will make Malcolm see that."

His face remained flushed, his eyes glittered. "I dinna care if we be friends or brothers or not."

"That is such a lie!"

He shook his head.

"You need Malcolm and he needs you, now more than ever," Claire tried passionately.

He flung his hands up, the fur-lined cloak flying back like wings. "He doesna want my help."

"But I can change that—I want to change that." She meant it. "When I go home, I want Malcolm to have you in his life as a brother, an ally, a friend. For God's sake, it's a dangerous world. The two of you should stand together."

He appeared distressed now and more grim than she had ever seen him. "I'll take ye," he finally said. "But ye dinna breathe one word o' our negotiation to Malcolm."

Claire gasped. *He would take her.* Somehow she would fulfill her part of the bargain. "When do we go?"

He shrugged. "Anytime."

"Now?"

"If ye wish."

"I need to get my gun and dagger." Claire impulsively kissed his cheek and raced upstairs. The sooner she got to court and was reunited with Malcolm, the better. Because Moray was there—and so was Sibylla. She seized her weapons and securely tucked them in her belt.

Turning to leave, she faltered.

Claire whirled to stare at the wildflowers.

The flowers in the vase remained dead. But the pink flower she had removed from the bunch lay on its side at the base of the vase—in full bloom.

CHAPTER SIXTEEN

LINLITHGOW MANOR HAD BURNED to the ground several years earlier in a fire that had also destroyed the burgh, but King James had built a magnificent palace in its place. Malcolm stood with Royce in the large courtyard, their mounts left behind in the stables on the other side of the small loch just beyond the castle's red-brown walls. Three four-story ranges with ramparts enclosed the courtyard, while the main part of the palace was five stories high, a grand tower in its midst. Other towers were on the corners of the walls. Courtiers and servants were coming and going as Malcolm glanced cautiously around. He'd been to Linlithgow when it was but a manor. The new stronghold was imposing, but instead of being impressed, he had a distinct feeling of unease.

"Have ye been here afore?" Malcolm asked quietly as they crossed the courtyard, a pair of departing noblewomen smiling at them as they did so.

"Six months ago," Royce said. He turned to look after the redhead. "Ye know I hate the intrigue o' court."

Malcolm almost smiled. "But nay the intrigue o' the wives."

Royce smiled grudgingly.

A ranking steward met them as they entered a vast hall, the far wall consisting entirely of hearths. A hundred lords and ladies mingled, many of them awaiting an audience with the king or queen. Malcolm recognized every Highland chieftain in the great room. He did not see the earl of Moray, but he felt his dark presence and knew he was at court.

He was very glad he had not brought Claire with him, he thought. She did not need political intrigue, royal treachery and demonic conspiracy heaped upon her plate. But his heart hurt when he thought of her. He had been trying not to do so. He had begun to understand why she called sex "making love." He cared deeply for her when he did not want to, and his feelings had been inextricably entwined with his desire the other day. Thinking about it made him uncomfortable and uncertain. He had to gain control of his affection. He must think of her as another Glenna—a pleasing mistress to use and eventually tire of and send away.

Except, he had no interest in her leaving. Even from the first moment of their meeting, he'd wondered if she might stay in his time with him. But she had made her intentions clear. MacNeil had seen the future, too, corroborating that her will would prevail over his. By the gods, it was shocking.

And he could not even use her as he would a mistress. He had wanted to hold her and touch her as they mated, yet his desire had turned to demonic lust in moments. When his excitement had begun to escalate out of control, the beast had leaped from its lair to take her life.

Except, oddly, he had not touched her life—he had touched and felt her soul.

It had been as beautiful and desirable as she was. He could not understand what had really happened, but it had been different from that time in the tower—blinding in pleasure, but somehow different.

Royce clasped his shoulder. "Yer at court. Ye wish fer passion, pick an' choose, but forget Lady Claire. The redhead in the courtyard was pretty enough."

Malcolm smiled tightly at him. He wished he could do just that. "She was inviting ye to her bed."

And suddenly Malcolm felt evil approaching. He turned, tension vibrating within him.

"Surely you will not be faithful to Lady Claire?" Moray said, the tone laced with amusement.

Malcolm tensed. Had Moray read his thoughts?

"You've healed well," Moray murmured. "And I take it yer beautiful mistress has also survived Sibylla's inopportune attack?"

"I am going t' kill Sibylla," Malcolm said. "Ye should ha' kept yer bitch leashed."

Moray shrugged. "And I will replace her," he said indifferently, "but that you already know."

"Ye keep *yourself* leashed," Malcolm warned, filled with hatred. "Ye stay away from Lady Claire. Ye'll not use her against me. I warn ye now. For if ye touch her, ye will face such a war as never afore. I dinna care what the royals command."

"Such treasonous speech," Moray murmured. "And how can I manage such an impossible feat when she is so…hot beneath a man?" Moray laughed, teeth flashing.

Malcolm moved to strike Moray but Royce held him back. Malcolm flung him off.

"Aye," Moray said, smiling. "I know her passion. I know it very well."

Malcolm stared, filled with dread. Had Moray spied on them in their most private moments? Or had he lurked in their minds, his favorite means of gathering his intelligence? For that was how the devil's own knew everything he wished to know.

Then Moray's smile was gone. "I am impressed, Malcolm, with your determination to deny your lust for such a woman. Have no fear. I will happily make up for your neglect. If you do not want to taste her impressive power, I do. If I cannot turn you, I will simply destroy you as I did Brogan, while she begs me for more, just as your mother did." His eyes hard, he left.

Malcolm was shaking in rage. Sick fear spoiled his anger. He had never been more afraid for Claire.

Royce took his arm. "He taunts ye apurpose! And dinna think o' Mairead now! Dinna think o' Claire!"

"He means his every word! And damn it, he be right. He could nay turn Brogan, but he destroyed their marriage and to this day, my mother suffers! Now, if he doesna turn me, he will attempt t' use Claire and destroy her." And for the first time in his life, Malcolm felt despair. He felt trapped and impotent, shocking feelings, feelings he hated. "All I wish t' do is protect her from evil. Instead, my every action brings her closer to its shadow and its strangling hold."

"Ye made the mistake o' allowing yerself to love her," Royce said grimly. He pulled him to a corner of the hall. "I dinna expect ye to change yer heart. I ken ye will love her till ye die."

"I swore to protect her, Royce," Malcolm said grimly. "Wanting her an' protecting her are nay love. Ye made the mistake o' lovin' yer wife an' look at yer life, hundreds o' years later! I willna be such a fool."

Royce shook his head, clearly not convinced or impressed. "I expect ye to stand true to the Code and God. Ye need to start praying, and not just to Christ. The old gods will awaken an' listen if ye mean it."

This was a subject he could manage. "I've already started praying," Malcolm said. "I've prayed fer strength in my soul to control what I dearly want to unleash."

"Ye have controlled the evil. Ye won. Ye beat Moray. It will get easier in time. And Moray will hunt another."

"In how much time?" Malcolm exclaimed. "How long does it take to find control, *real* control o' the dark?"

"Yer too young," Royce said, shaking his head. "An' no leap can change yer real age. The control comes with time. All young Masters want Le Puissance. Ye'll grow stronger; it will be easier to ferget it. Ye need to avoid Claire. Take a different wench to bed, a woman who willna tempt ye to stray."

Malcolm shook his head. "I dinna wish to bed another maid! I wish to bed Claire! You're over eight hundred years old! I'm twenty-seven! I canna wait eight centuries to love Claire properly." The moment he realized his choice of words, he felt his cheeks heat. He did not want to love Claire, ever—he merely wished to pleasure her.

Royce sighed. "I meant what I said earlier. Ye need to stay away from her, not others, as she is yer temptation. I am pleased ye left her at Awe."

"I dinna ken how long I can stay away from her."

"Ye fight yer lust. Ye fight it like ye fight Moray. The lust is Moray," Royce flashed. "An when ye ken that truth, ye'll win."

Royce was wrong. The lust was evil only when it became a raging beast that wished for more power than any man or Master should ever claim. Because briefly, when Claire had been recovering from Sibylla's attack, there had been desire that had nothing to do with evil. There had been desire that had come from the heart. "Ruari, have you ever felt a woman's soul?"

Royce was surprised. "What in God's name are ye speakin' of?"

Malcolm felt himself blush, and avoided his uncle's penetrating gaze. "Never ye mind."

Royce clasped his shoulder. "When I said pray to the Ancients, I meant it. 'Tis a god who will give ye the power to stay holy, Malcolm."

Royce was right. He had been steeped in religion from the day of his birth. When Brogan had died on the battlefield, some of his faith had wavered. Maybe it should have strengthened that day, instead. He was glad he had started praying to the Ancients again.

The only problem was that the gods could be capricious.

THE PAIN WAS TERRIBLE. Even though Aidan had given her a potion to withstand it more easily, Claire wept, vaguely aware of being in Aidan's strong arms. He did not speak as her body tried to explode from the force of leaping time. Every bone felt broken; every limb felt wrenched out of its socket. Even her hair hurt.

But the agony lessened rapidly. Claire became cognizant of the fact that not only were Aidan's arms around her, she had her face pressed to the wool of his brat, against his chest, which rose and fell softly and steadily.

"Ye be better now?" he asked hoarsely.

She couldn't quite speak. She took a deep breath, flexing her fingers, wishing he would get up and put some distance between them. She had just become aware of a tension in him she could not help but recognize. It was desire.

Aidan released her, standing. The color was returning to his face.

Claire blinked and met his too-bright, very warm silver gaze. "What...was that?"

His smile was wry. "I only hold a woman when I'm about to bed her, Claire. I canna help it if my body was expectin' more."

"Jerk." She didn't quite feel capable of standing just yet. She saw that they had landed just outside Linlithgow Palace itself, but inside the outer bailey. She was seated on damp, soft grass. From their elevated position, she could see the small, perfectly blue loch below, where swans drifted, and the dozen riders crossing the bridge that spanned it, heraldic banners waving above them, apparently on their way to the palace. She looked above her and saw guards standing on the highest ramparts of the two towers facing the palace entryway, and then she glanced back, where more guards paced the ramparts between the corner towers. Her heart flipped over hard. Malcolm was inside—and so was Moray. She knew it with every fiber of her being.

Aidan extended his hand.

Still angry for his daring to become aroused by her, she ignored it and stood up. "Father Paul's potion really helped manage the torment of the leap," she said. "Do you take it, too?" He hadn't made a sound.

"I be a man. I dinna need potions fer pain. I suffer the pain." He shrugged.

"Right, as if a woman could forget how macho you are."

He seemed amused. "If ye stop thinkin' about my body, ye'll stop being so angry. But I don't think it's me yer angry with."

"Like hell. Don't even begin to think I'm one bit attracted to you. You cannot compare to Malcolm, not in any way."

He flushed and gestured at the court entrance.

Claire regretted her words. After all, she owed Aidan for being at court now, and he probably couldn't help his over-sexed nature. Worse, he was the son of all evil and Malcolm was the son of a great Master. "I'm sorry. You are a lot like Malcolm, actually," she began.

"I'm nay like him," he said with warning. "I use my powers to please me, not the Brotherhood or the Ancients." His eyes were impossibly hard. "I dinna care about any Code. I care about my pleasure."

She flushed, refusing to believe him entirely. Filled with new tension, she strode ahead of him into the courtyard, glancing around at the three long, narrow, high buildings enclosing it. In the twenty-first century, Linlithgow Palace had been entirely enclosed.

The tallest, most imposing building was directly ahead, where the great hall was. Her heart sped and she increased her pace, Aidan falling into step beside her, both of them now ignoring the other. Many courtiers were coming and going, some of them in Highland dress, others clad in the English-court style. Claire did a double take, recognizing one clearly ranking and very handsome Lowlander—the Master she had glimpsed on Iona.

This time he wore pointy shoes instead of boots and burgundy hose, a short, full-skirted blue velvet jacket with puffed sleeves, but like before, he was fully armed. She blushed again, because it was impossible not to look at his bulging codpiece.

He smiled at her, clearly recognizing her, as well, and as he walked by, he swept her a courtly bow.

"That be Alexander of Blackwood, Sibylla's brother," Aidan said darkly. "Dinna ogle him!"

Claire halted in her tracks and turned a full 180 degrees to stare after him. "But I saw him on Iona, Aidan," she said, trembling. "He's a Master."

"Aye," Aidan said softly. "An' he hates his sister, as he should."

He tapped her arm and strode ahead. Recovering, Claire ran to catch up. The two massive, engraved doors of the great hall were open, and as she followed him inside, she saw the crowd milling within, awaiting either a summons or an audience with one of the royals. Claire became still, her heart pounding with sudden excitement. She was at court in the fifteenth century. She seized Aidan's brat as she scanned the crowd for a glimpse of Malcolm. It had been only a few days, but she missed him terribly and she now anticipated a not particularly pleasant reception. "Is the king or queen here?"

"Nay." Aidan suddenly stiffened, his eyes widening in shock.

Alarmed, Claire followed his gaze, and she saw Isabel standing in the midst of a small group of noblemen, pleasantly conversing. "That's not her twin, is it?" Claire whispered.

Aidan could not tear his eyes from her. "She has no twin."

"What day is this?"

"July 31."

They had made the leap yesterday and Isabel had been at Awe, bidding them goodbye. There was only one way she could have made it to Linlithgow in the same amount of time as they had. *Moray had taken her.* Dread uncoiled, making

Claire feel sick. Aidan was pushing through the crowd, and she followed him.

Isabel saw him and her expression became one of terrible relief. She made her apologies to the noblemen and rushed to Aidan, flinging herself against his chest. Aidan put his arms around her. "Ye be well?"

She nodded, looking up, tears shining in her eyes. "I am so glad you are here!" she cried. "I am so afraid."

Claire tried to breathe naturally and failed. Moray had done this—and God only knew what else he had done and intended to do. He would use Isabel now, against his own son. And Isabel was not a woman of intelligence and fortitude. She was a lamb being led to the slaughter. Claire was ill.

"What happened? How did ye get here?" Aidan demanded, his eyes flashing with fury.

"Do not be angry with me! Your father insisted. I cannot refuse the earl of Moray—no one can! And I don't know how I got here!" She began to cry. "He used a spell, Aidan, and when I awoke, I was in one of the court chambers."

Aidan's eyes were wide, hard. "Did he touch ye?"

Isabel looked blankly at him, then cried out, drying her tear-stained cheeks with her hand. "No, of course not. He has been charming, nothing more. But I am so afraid of him! When I look into his eyes, I am filled with fear."

"I'm takin' ye home," Aidan said abruptly. He smiled, intending to reassure her, tilting up her chin. "Ye have no reason to fear. I'll manage Moray."

"You can't take me home. I've met the queen." More tears came. "She has ordered me to wait upon her, Aidan. I am to do so tonight."

Aidan's eyes turned hard. "Then ye'll obey yer liege."

Claire wasn't certain what this meant, other than the fact that Isabel would remain at court indefinitely, so Moray could cruelly play cat and mouse with her and Aidan.

Then she glimpsed Malcolm.

Her heart thundered as their eyes locked. His expression was one of shock and disbelief. And then it became one of sheer fury.

She had known he would be angry when he saw her. Claire moved toward him, promising herself that she would not become angry in return. But he turned and started striding away, leaving the room, entering the long gallery that ran the length of the hall. Numerous windows allowed sunlight to filter within.

"Wait!" she cried, hurrying after him.

He suddenly whirled to face her, standing by a window that overlooked the western hills. "Ye disobey me another time?" he asked dangerously.

Claire tensed, but her heart slammed with joy and desire. "Malcolm." She cupped his cheek, causing his eyes to widen. "I know you are angry. But I couldn't go to the abbey and twiddle my thumbs while you are hunting Sibylla with Moray here!"

He jerked away from her hand. "Will ye ever obey me?"

She inhaled. "I can't take orders from you if I do not agree. I am not a medieval woman. I am not like Glenna or Isabel. You can't expect me to be."

"Ye think I dinna ken? Yer like no woman I have ever met!"

"Do you really want me to be weak, mindless and dependent?" she cried.

He stared, mouth hard. "Nay," he finally said, looking as if it killed him to admit it.

There was hope. "Malcolm, why can't agree on an action together? Why can't we sit down and discuss plans and come to terms that way?"

It was a moment before he spoke. "Ye wish fer us to be our own parliament?"

"Yes," she whispered, praying he might finally understand. "Malcolm, you were raised to give orders like a king. I was raised to think for myself, to make my own decisions."

She felt him finally considering her words.

"I know you understand compromise. You negotiate with other lords, and your enemies, all the time."

"Aye. I do." He folded his arms across her chest. "But we be in battle now, Claire." His tone was calm. "In battle, every man in my command obeys me."

She didn't hesitate. "Point taken. I'll obey you while we're in battle. I'll even obey you at court, *if* you agree that we're from different times, and that you cannot treat me like you do other women. If you agree that we will be our own parliament. No more orders, Malcolm. We make important decisions together!"

He stared thoughtfully. "'Tis quite a talent, lass, that ye have." He softened. "Yer too clever fer a maid."

Claire waited, forgetting to breathe.

"Agreed. Ye give yer word. I give mine."

She could not believe that they had crossed over the biggest cultural gulf separating them. She hadn't gotten everything she wanted, but this was a beginning. "I'll write it in blood, if you want," she teased. She realized she was happy. A maelstrom of evil awaited them, and she wanted to cling to this brief respite.

"Ye spilled enough blood at Awe." He sobered. "How did ye convince Aidan to bring ye here?"

She decided to ignore the question. This was not the time to espouse Aidan's cause. "Isabel is here, Malcolm. Moray brought her. I don't know what he intends." Dread arose, huge and swift.

"Ye ken what he wants. He wants to use her against Aidan and he wants pleasure in death."

Claire felt ill. "Aidan wanted to take her back to Awe, maybe to Iona, but the queen has ordered her to wait on her tonight. Maybe that will save her from Moray."

Malcolm gave her an odd look. "The queen is a lusty woman, Claire. She takes many lovers, and the gossip is that she even enjoys the services of her ladies."

"She likes women?" Claire gasped.

"Nay, she likes pleasure, an' she has had many men in her bed. Isabel will have to wait on her queen. It may save her life."

Claire simply stared into his eyes, shaken. The injustice of the medieval world was glaring at them both. No one had rights. Freedom did not exist. Everyone was at the whim of tyranny.

The midday bells began to toll. And chills crept up and down Claire's spine. Malcolm's eyes hardened. She whirled.

Sibylla had entered the north end of the gallery. She obviously had sensed their presence, because she approached in her crimson velvet gown, trailing her embroidered sleeves. Her eyes gleamed.

Claire's heart turned over. That demon had taken her life. It had been sexual—and she had wanted more.

Malcolm stepped in front of her. "Ah, lady, I have been hopin' our paths would cross."

Sibylla paused, alarm flickering in her black eyes. "You can't be thinking of battle now, here at court. My lord is a favorite of the king. We do not war in the presence of the royals. Here, we have a truce."

Claire slid her dagger into her hand. Her heart pumped so hard, she felt faint. There was no rational thought now. She had one question: What would happen if she stabbed Sibylla in the heart? Would she die? Her body was human. It would have to let go if all the blood was drained.

Sibylla looked at her, her smile wary. "So much courage, *ma doucette?* The king will take your head if you take mine."

Claire heard her, but she didn't care. If she didn't destroy Sibylla, she was coming back.

Claire, dinna do it. Not here, with the royal guards in the hall. We'll find a way, later, when there be no chance o' public display.

Claire heard Malcolm. She wet her lips. She didn't care that two guards stood by the entrance to the hall and that nobles were coming and going. "You said you weren't allowed to kill me." Her palms were sweating. "I get it now. I know who wants me alive."

Claire, nay. Malcolm clasped her shoulder.

Leave me be, Malcolm! "But no one has forbidden me from killing you," Claire cried. And she lunged.

"Claire!" Malcolm shouted, seizing her wrist.

But Claire felt her blade sink into warm, living flesh.

CHAPTER SEVENTEEN

HOT BLOOD SPURTED over Claire's hand. Malcolm wrestled her away from the woman. Claire saw that she had missed Sibylla's heart, but she had stabbed her deeply in her chest. Sibylla reeled, turning pale, and then fury turned her eyes red. Malcolm pushed Claire against the window seat and seized the dagger, wrenching it from Sibylla's chest.

"Finish her!" Claire screamed.

But chaos erupted in the gallery before Malcolm could do as she wanted. Sibylla pushed past him, apparently intending to run, but the passing noblemen blocked her way and she collapsed against one man. Claire heard footsteps pounding as heated exclamations and accusations began. Suddenly Royce shoved into their midst, seizing Malcolm's arm. Just as she began to realize what she had done—and what it might mean—she was seized from behind.

She struggled to get free of her captor and Aidan hissed, "Fool!" Instantly she went still, realizing he had grabbed her.

Panting, Claire saw Malcolm and Royce exchange looks as Malcolm dropped the bloody blade. The two royal guards appeared, ordering everyone aside, marching up to Malcolm and Royce. And in that moment Claire finally understood she had made a terrible mistake. "Let me go," she told Aidan, wondering what was going to happen to her now. She was pretty certain one could not stab a royal guest in the heat of the moment, even if that guest was a demon.

Her gaze met Malcolm's. He was furious and she heard

him as clear as day, even though he did not speak aloud. *Ye gave me your word.*

"I am sorry," Claire whispered.

Aidan jerked on her.

Dinna speak another word!

"What happened here?" a guard demanded as the royal steward who had first ushered them into the hall appeared.

"Lady Sibylla has been attacked," someone said.

Claire began to shake. Before she could confess to her crimes, Blackwood strode through the assembled crowd, his expression ruthless. He took one look at Sibylla and paled. For Claire, his look spoke volumes. He did not hate his possessed sister at all.

Sibylla cried out as Blackwood went to her, taking her into his arms. She was pale and bleeding heavily. Spittle ran from her mouth. Most of the bodice of her red dress was soaked with her blood. She looked at Claire with vicious hatred.

Sibylla wanted to kill her, Claire thought, her heart lurching at the murderous look in the other woman's eyes.

"I'll take care o' her," Blackwood said, lifting her into his arms.

Claire wanted to scream at him to finish the job. She was pretty certain he was going to get Sibylla medical attention, instead. He strode away, his sister finally fainting.

Malcolm picked up the dagger and looked at the steward. "Here's the weapon that may have murdered Lady Sibylla," he said grimly. "I admit to the crime."

"Arrest him," the steward snapped.

Claire cried out in horror. He would protect her this way? But as she began to protest, Aidan's grasp on her became a tight, even cruel embrace. "Dinna speak," he hissed at her as the guards seized Malcolm.

"My nephew lies," Royce said calmly. "I have marked Sibylla fer the grave long ago. He thinks to protect me. I stabbed her."

Claire gasped, her knees turning weak and useless. Royce's actions were incredibly selfless, but selfishly she prayed he would be the one arrested now.

Malcolm turned a black look on Royce. "He thinks to protect me. Sibylla has declared war on me an' mine. The deadly deed was done by my own hand."

Everyone began to talk at once, in the excited tones of a crowd mesmerized by high drama.

"It was me," Claire cried.

But in the frenzy of gossip and speculation, no one seemed to hear. Aidan jerked on her, literally dragging her from the hall. "Let me go," Claire began furiously.

"Arrest them both," the steward ordered, "until this matter can be decided by the king."

Claire was disbelieving. "It was me," she shouted loudly. "Damn it!" Looking over her shoulder, she saw that no one heard or cared to hear.

Malcolm was set on taking the fall for her.

I am sorry!

Dinna worry. I will be fine.

What will they do to you?

He did not answer her and Claire saw the guards strip him of his sword and dagger as Aidan pulled her from the hall. She found herself outside in the bailey, so sickened in her heart she was nauseated. She had lost all control—and now, Malcolm might pay a terrible price for what she had done.

Aidan let her go. "What will they do to him?" she cried.

"Could ye nay hold yer temper? Ye canna murder a lady in cold blood in front o' witnesses!" Aidan exclaimed.

Claire hugged herself, choking on her fear. She had wanted to kill Sibylla; now she was afraid she would die.

Aidan was lurking, because he said, "Blackwood will have her healed."

It was a double-edged sword. "So Sibylla will live to do her evil another day."

Aidan's eyes darkened. "Ye ferget she's as human as ye, Claire. He'll take her to Iona fer an exorcism."

And suddenly her bitterness faded as she understood. "He wants to exorcize the demon."

"She be Blackwood's sister. She deserves a chance to live again. And he deserves the chance to try to free his sister's soul."

Claire could only stare. Sanity finally returned. She had wanted Sibylla to die. She had been entirely consumed with murdering her enemy, so much so that she hadn't thought once about the fact that Sibylla was a human being. Once, she had been as normal as Claire. She began to shake, ashamed of her own violent behavior.

"And what if the exorcism fails?"

Aidan said coldly, "Blackwood will kill her."

She inhaled, shaken all over again. Everything was spinning wildly out of control. She could no longer think— or care—about Sibylla's fate. "I have to go back inside and tell the truth," she pleaded. "I can't let Malcolm be punished for what I did—or Royce, for that matter."

"'Tis what a man does fer his woman," Aidan said grimly. "An' it be far too late fer regrets."

"They can leap," Claire finally said. "Thank God they can leap to escape if they have to!"

"If they leap they will be outlaws, an' they will never be able to come back to this time."

Another thought occurred. "Let's leap back in time—back to Awe before Malcolm left! Now that we know what will happen, we can convince Malcolm to leave Sibylla alone."

Aidan shook his head. "'Tis nay allowed. A Master canna go back to the past an' change it fer his own whim."

"You follow the rules now?" she cried furiously.

He gave her a look. "No god would allow the Code to be broken like ye wish, Claire."

Claire gave up, for she didn't understand that. "Then what are we going to do?"

"I'll do what needs to be done, Claire. Ye'll do nothing. Yer in my care now, until Malcolm be released. In fact, I'm takin' ye far from the court, as there be nothin' here fer ye."

"Malcolm is here—locked up and awaiting a verdict for what I have done. I am not leaving court without him." She had never meant her words more.

He stared.

"I am desperate, Aidan," Claire admitted, resorting to any feminine wiles she had left. She let tears fill her eyes— genuine tears of fear for Malcolm. "I love him and I have to stand by him, just as he has stood by me."

Aidan softened. "I ken ye love him deeply. I dinna think he'll be imprisoned fer too long. He'll probably pay a high price in coin and lands fer the assault. Very well. I'll find us rooms until he be released. But," he said fiercely, "ye'll do *nothing* to make matters worse."

Claire quickly nodded. "Agreed."

"Ye will obey me, Claire," he added.

Although she wasn't sure she meant it, she nodded again. "Okay."

Then she saw Moray, staring at them from steps leading to the hall.

Divide and conquer, she thought, her insides lurching with sick dread.

MALCOLM TENSED. Claire was looking for him, filled with desperation. He could sense her racing through the palace corridors, lost and confused. Alarm filled him. She should not be looking for him, as he was the king's prisoner. It was not safe for her to be searching for him now. Linlithgow was not safe.

Malcolm, where are you?

He had been lying on a thin pallet on the stone floor in his cell. He sat up. *Claire, go back. Do not come!*

But she did not answer him and he knew she hadn't heard.

She was too afraid to hear him, he realized.

He heard her calling to him again.

Malcolm, help me find you!

Claire, there be guards. Go back to yer chamber, he ordered. But he knew she would not obey him, as she never did, and he was afraid for her.

He felt her despair intensify. He sensed she was lost in the maze of hallways. But he felt her presence. She was closer now. And then he heard her scream and he saw her standing in a dark, shadowed hall. She had come face-to-face with Moray.

Moray was smiling in evil anticipation.

No!

She was running. Malcolm encouraged her to run faster. Claire screamed again, so loudly she must have been outside the cell door, and he heard Moray's laughter. Malcolm banged on the cell door, furious and desperate. He had to help her escape Moray!

And he knew Claire's strength was failing her. She was sobbing, trying to run, but her legs had become oddly useless. He seized the door to wrest it from its hinges. And before he could do so, the door opened and Claire stood there.

He had never been happier to see anyone.

She cried out in relief, throwing her arms around him and holding him tightly. He held her hard, unsure he could ever let her go, thanking the Ancients for sparing her life. As he held her, his concern changed, and so much warmth began, not just in his loins, which swiftly hardened, but in his chest.

She smiled at him, her green eyes sparkling with unshed tears.

"Ye shouldn't have come," he said, tilting up her face. He could not wait to kiss her, and every inch of him pulsed with explosive force. God, he had to take this woman and he had to do so now....

He claimed her mouth, trying to be gentle because he now

knew she liked to start slowly. Still, he was a man and he pushed her against the wall, spreading her thighs with his, urgency racking his body. He could not wait. He pushed her down onto the pallet.

He pinned her there. Her clothing had vanished, and so had his. He deepened the kiss and in spite of the urgency consuming him, he slowly slid into her, shaking and gasping as he did so, fighting for self-control. He loved her hot, wet, tight flesh.

Claire gasped with pleasure; so did he.

He was throbbing so greatly he was ready to come, and so was she. He lifted his head to smile at her, breaking the kiss. *I love ye, lass.*

Her eyes widened and then she flung her face to his neck, crying out in her pleasure. His joy began. And then the door slammed against the stone wall.

Malcolm woke up, instantly realizing he had been dreaming. But it had seemed real, and he was as aroused as if he and Claire were really in his bed together. He lay facedown on the pallet, and because Royce shared the high tower room, he breathed hard, fighting for composure.

"Get up."

Malcolm realized the command was not addressed to him. He had been using his brat as a blanket, and he threw it aside, sitting up. Royce was being singled out by the two guards. Alarm began.

His uncle stood in the tower's center, his wrists being bound in front of him. Malcolm stood slowly, warily. Four slits were spaced evenly on the round tower walls, and Malcolm saw a night sky filled with stars and a high moon. It could not be much past midnight. Prisoners were executed in the broad light of day with an audience, so no one could misinterpret the extent of royal prerogative and power. So this was not an execution. Malcolm's alarm eased, but not greatly.

For while his uncle's face was so expressionless it might

have been cast from stone, he felt a thrumming tension in him. Briefly, Malcolm was confused. The heat felt sexual.

"Yer t' come with us," a guard said to Royce.

"Where do ye take him?" Malcolm demanded in the tone of a laird of a great clan who expected to be answered at once.

One of the guards glanced at him. "'Tis nay yer affair."

Malcolm lurked easily enough and was stunned to discover that Queen Joan had ordered Royce brought to her privy chambers. Incredulous, he looked at his uncle again.

He was not a fool. Everyone except the king knew of his wife's extreme carnal appetites and her numerous affairs. There could be only one reason for the queen to summon Royce at such an hour. But in the name of all gods, when had Royce even attracted her interest?

He lurked again and saw Royce and the queen passionately entwined in the royal bed. Worse, he felt his uncle's amusement, his indifference, and he sensed his lust.

This was not the first time.

Royce's head could wind up on the block. Was he mad?

Royce looked him in the eye and murmured, "No man can refuse his liege."

Malcolm was horrified. Royce was correct, but if ever discovered, he would pay for such adultery with his life.

"I dinna care, Malcolm," Royce said. And suddenly he seemed every one of his 850 or so years. "I dinna fear my death."

Royce opened his mind completely. And Malcolm saw the vast chasm of his uncle's exhaustion and loneliness, and realized he was tired of his life.

Royce did not look back as he was led from the tower.

CLAIRE COULD FEEL Malcolm's presence.

But the palace was a maze of dark corridors lit by burning sconces. Outside every window she passed, the moon was fuller and brighter than it had been last night. *Malcolm, where are you?* she cried desperately.

But there was no answer.

She had to find him; she had to make certain he was all right.

Claire paused, breathing hard, her back against a wall in an upper floor gallery, absolutely alone. It was very late and any lingering revelers were in the hall downstairs, where there had been a huge supper feast. *Malcolm, help me find you!*

He did not answer. Claire trembled with despair. She hurried on, the corridor endless, the shadows lengthening, darkening. And then she felt his presence. He was nearby!

A door appeared and she seized it, filled with anticipation, certain Malcolm would be on the other side. She flung it open.

Moray smiled at her, white teeth gleaming, eyes red.

Claire screamed, slamming the door closed in his face and running down the hall. She thought he was following her and she turned a corner, entering another endless, black corridor. But Malcolm felt closer now. She saw a door ahead and jerked it open.

Moray laughed at her.

Claire whirled and ran back the way she had come, crying now in fear and desperation, but her legs refused to move. She was running, but she wasn't going anywhere and he was about to seize her.

She wanted to wake up. She ran into another black door. It barred her way.

A hand touched her from behind…Moray.

Claire seized the door's handle, afraid Moray was there. She told herself not to open it but she had to find Malcolm, and she flung it open.

Malcolm faced her, his eyes burning silver.

Claire cried out in relief, throwing her arms around him and holding him for her life. He enclosed her in his warm embrace, his body hard and powerful and safe.

She tried to tell him Moray was behind her, following her, and that their lives were at stake.

"Ye shouldn't have come," he said, tilting up her face.

And Claire felt his manhood stiffen. This was insane, she thought as desire overcame her. But his grasp tightened and his mouth covered hers and she did not have the chance to tell him that Moray was there, waiting to trap them both.

He pushed her down, not onto the stone floor, but into the soft bed she had fallen asleep in.

It was so real.

His hard body pinned hers and his strong thighs spread her for him. Her clothing had vanished and so had his. Claire ran his hands over his rippling back, loving the feel of his hot, slick skin. If she was dreaming, she didn't want it to end. He deepened the kiss and slowly slid his huge length into her.

Claire gasped with pleasure; so did he.

I cannot be dreaming, she somehow thought. It was too vivid and real to be a dream and the wave of pleasure was beginning, growing stronger and stronger as he moved inside her. Her body was stretched tight, convulsing around him, and he was engorging more fully, the way he so often did, and she felt him throbbing inside her. She felt him smiling at her, too.

He raised his head, breaking the kiss, throbbing with the need to come, and she saw love shimmering in his eyes. He smiled as he moved inside her again. *I love ye, lass.*

Claire could barely believe what she had heard. She shattered, the wave of delirium breaking over her, and he gasped. She held on tight, his words echoing, and joy began. She opened her eyes to tell him that she loved him, too, more than he would ever know—and dark shadows greeted her.

She was very much alone in her bed.

Claire sat up, gasping and breathing hard. She was covered with perspiration and the pallet was wet.

She had been dreaming, the most vivid, tactile dream she'd ever had. It had felt as if he had really been making love to her.

Panting, she leaned back against the pillows. She had

been allowed to use the chamber intended for Malcolm. Her eyes began to adjust to the dark as her arousal diminished. Her fear for Malcolm returned. She still didn't know where he'd been taken or what his fate was. Aidan had sworn he'd find out. A small fire burned in the hearth. She glanced toward it—and cried out.

A man sat there in the shadows.

For one moment Claire was paralyzed, afraid it was Moray. She grabbed the fur and brought it to her chin.

"'Tis I," Aidan said tersely.

Disbelief began. What was he doing there in her chamber? He was sitting a few feet from her bed, while she was having a very sexual and orgasmic dream. She hoped she hadn't been gasping aloud. "What the hell are you doing here?"

He stood, stepping into the light. As he stood, the pale leine swirled, revealing a very evident arousal. "I was watching over ye," he said thickly.

She could barely speak. "You bastard!"

He tensed. "Ye were screaming in pleasure. I was outside in the hall. I thought ye were with a Deamhan, maybe Moray!"

Claire could not find calm. Her cheeks were now on fire. "I was having a dream," she said harshly. "About Malcolm."

"Aye." He gave her his back.

She didn't like the sound of that single word, and a terrible inkling began. Claire jumped from the bed, taking the cover with her. "Please tell me you did not lurk in my mind."

He didn't answer, going to the door.

"Can you lurk in a dream, Aidan?" she demanded rigidly.

"I'll be seeing you in the morn," he said, reaching for the door.

Claire grabbed the water pitcher and threw it as hard as she could at him. It hit him square on the back. He turned.

"How dare you spy on me and Malcolm!"

"I came here to protect ye," he said harshly. But the fire's light played on one side of his face and he was flushing.

"You were lurking in my dream! You might as well have been watching us make love in reality!" She was aghast. "What did you see?"

His face tightened. "'Twas only a dream, Claire. 'Twas not real."

"You saw everything!" she cried. "You watched me make love to Malcolm!"

She saw his flush intensify. Finally, softly, he said, "I couldna help myself. Didna ye watch me with Isabel?"

Claire stared at him, and so much anger began. "I walked in on you accidentally and I left a second later."

"I'm a man. Yer a woman. No man could walk away from such a dream."

"Get out!" she screamed.

"Ye should be pleased I care fer ye. I didna go into yer dream an' change places with my brother, although that is what I wanted to do." He strode out.

Shocked, Claire let the fur drop. Naked, she stood there shaking, incredulous and enraged. His being medieval and oversexed was not an acceptable excuse! Then she grabbed the fur, covered herself with it and ran to the door. She jerked it open. "You have no morals!" she screamed.

But Aidan was gone.

Claire slammed the door.

CHAPTER EIGHTEEN

ROYCE ESTIMATED that it was an hour past midnight. He walked between the armed guards into the queen's antechamber, where two of her ladies eyed him, blushing furiously. He was angry, and blood filled his manhood because of it. He did not mind fucking a beautiful woman, but he despised being disloyal to his liege lord, the king. However, a year and a half ago he had failed to outmaneuver Joan Beaufort, who was very clever, and he had had the equally pleasant and unpleasant task of pleasuring her until she wept for mercy. He knew exactly what she wanted now.

The ladies whispered and giggled, ogling his bulging leine. Sometimes the queen preferred an orgy to a single lover, although he knew that would not be the case tonight.

He smiled at them, but his smile was as hard and tight as his body. What he minded was being summoned by Her Majesty as if he were her sexual slave.

Their affair had started six months after the coronation. The queen's lusty interest had begun as he was making homage to her and the king. There'd been no gossip about her voracious appetites then. He had knelt, making his vows, surprised to find her every bit as beautiful as the poets claimed, and then he'd lurked. He'd been shocked to find her thinking of the various ways she could suck, fuck and ride him.

Of course he'd been aroused. He had wanted nothing more than to leap on her then and there, but that was politically dangerous. He'd escaped court immediately after the coronation, but six months later, affairs of the Brotherhood had required he go back. There had been no escaping or denying his queen then. In fact, she had been waiting for him. She had manipulated the Brotherhood to have him sent there. He would not deny that he'd enjoyed every moment in her bed. But she had been very annoyed when he had returned to Carrick. Twice since then she had sent him missives.

In the first, she had requested his appearance at court. In the second, piqued, she'd summoned him. He had politely explained, both times, that great affairs of the earldom prevented him from returning to court. It had not been wise to continue an affair with her then, just as it was not wise to do so now.

But she was the queen, and she could not be denied. So he would let her use him—and he would use her in return.

He walked inside her private chamber, the door closing behind him, both guards remaining outside. The large, well-appointed chamber was lit with sconces, candles and the hearth's fire. The queen stood facing the fire, her back to him. She wore a long, golden-yellow chemise the color of her hair, which fell in soft waves to her hips. The chemise was sheer. He looked at her plump buttocks and hardened even more.

Her shoulders were rigid. "How dare you refuse us."

He went into her mind. She was dripping wet and riding him, shouting in pleasure. He walked up to her and raised his bound wrists over her head. Then he slid his arms down so she was in his bound embrace, locked there, and he pushed his cock against one hip.

She trembled.

"I ken ye have missed me," he murmured, lust now fueling his anger. "Admit it."

"You refused our summons," she gasped. "Your fate is hanging by a thread."

"Is it?" He laughed. "I dinna care if ye take my head, Joan. I dinna care if the king takes it." He lowered his arms and rubbed the rope against her swollen mons.

She gasped and leaned back against him, throbbing against the abrasive cord. "How dare you…"

"Did ye bring me here to converse?" he murmured, moving his mouth against her ear. As he did, he shifted her away from the hearth.

"You know what I want," she said harshly, her tone still filled with anger. "If you ever refuse me again—"

He pushed her to the wall and used one thigh to spread her until she rode the muscles there. "Ye dinna own me, Joan. Dinna ever mistake it. Ye have my favors only if I wish to give them. An' I am in the mood to give them tonight."

She was shaking wildly now. "Hurry, Ruari!"

He smiled and rubbed himself against her buttocks. "Untie the cords."

She instantly fumbled to obey. When his hands were free, he lifted the chemise out of his way and seized her sex. She began to pant, moisture dripping.

"But as randy as I be, I need a favor from ye in return fer my favors."

"What?" she gasped, outrage mingling with desire.

He lifted one of her legs high with his thigh, bent and pushed his huge head against her very wet, throbbing heat. "Ye want this to come in ye? Ye free Malcolm. Ye free him *now*."

She trembled in fury. "I negotiate with no one!"

He laughed and pushed a mere inch inside her. "Really?"

She gasped, moaning, trying to wriggle down his length. He stepped away from her.

It took her a moment as she stood pressed against the wall, shaking and near climax. She whirled and struck his face. He just shook his head, amused, and stripped off his leine.

She looked at him and choked on a sob. "How dare you bargain with me now!"

He flicked his hand over his length. "Order the guards to free him."

She watched him playing with himself. "He is the king's prisoner."

He gave her a look. "Do ye nay wish to fuck all night? Do ye nay remember that I never tire, never slacken? Do ye nay wish to put yer tongue here?"

Tears rolled down her face. "I can make you pay dearly, Ruari."

He ignored that. "I want to make ye come, Joan. I want to make ye come a hundred times." She gasped, and he knew she would come the moment he touched her. "But my duty is to my nephew. We both ken ye can control yer husband when ye wish to. Release Malcolm."

She was flushed with arousal and breathing so hard it was a moment before she spoke. "I believe you don't care if you die. But you must know that I can release him today and imprison him tomorrow."

"Yer right. I am an old, tired man who doesna care if he dies at yer hand or the king's." He wanted her to make up her mind. He was ready to go inside her now and enjoy himself immensely.

She understood what he meant instantly. Her eyes widened.

He no longer smiled. If he had to expose the queen's infidelity, so be it. He'd lose his head, but she would never recover her lost power.

"If you were not such a great lover," she managed, "I would kill you with my own hand."

"I want to fuck ye, woman. Hurry up."

She turned to the door, parted it. "Release Malcolm of Dunroch. He is free to leave the court tonight."

Royce began to smile, very pleased. He strode up to her as she closed the door and before she could face him, he put his arms around her, clasping her between her thighs. He lifted her higher. She went still, convulsively, eagerly, and he felt his arousal grow to a fever pitch. "Who be master now? Who be the slave?"

Red need blinded him; he drove deep.

The queen wept in her release.

CLAIRE COULDN'T SLEEP. The moon was high and she stared through her window at it. She had dreamed of trying to find Malcolm, and she was very tempted to try to do so now, in the dead of the night. On the other hand, she knew he would be under guard and she was fairly certain she would not be able to charm the guards into letting her see him. And then there was Moray.

The last thing she wanted to do was run into him in the middle of the black night while alone in the palace.

She turned away from the shining moon to stare at the fire. What was going to happen to Malcolm and his uncle now? Would they be charged for assaulting Sibylla? Did Sibylla live? And how were they going to deal with Moray?

And Claire felt Malcolm.

Confused, she glanced toward the chamber door, which was closed. And then the door was thrust open and Malcolm strode into the room. Claire cried out, rushing into his arms. He held her tight.

"Is this a dream?" she gasped, aware of his heat, his strength.

He smiled tenderly at her. "'Tis no dream. Royce is with the Queen. They be lovers. I imagine he has used his powers o' persuasion to order my release and his."

Claire could not think about Royce now. She touched Malcolm's cheek, and to her surprise he clasped her hand there. His eyes shimmered the way they had in her dream. Claire tensed. She would give anything to hear him say those three words.

"I be free to go."

He dropped his hand, only to let it settle on her shoulder. "You are?"

"Aye, but Claire, how can I leave my uncle now? As long as he beds the Queen, he be in jeopardy." He looked slowly around the chamber.

Claire hesitated, realizing what Royce's affair could cost him. "Malcolm, if Royce's affair is discovered, no one can help him. Only a leap will save him."

An anguished expression crossed Malcolm's face and he turned away from her.

"What is it?"

He shook his head. "He won't leap, Claire. I dinna think he cares much fer this world anymore."

What did that mean? She went to Malcolm, but he gave her a dark look.

Claire did not like it and she tensed.

"What happened in this chamber t'night, Claire?"

She recognized his dangerous jealousy, but she had not been thinking about that terrible encounter with Aidan. "Nothing," she began.

He looked at the bed. "I dreamed about ye a few hours ago. I dreamed ye were on the run from Moray," Malcolm said softly. He finally looked at her. "Then I dreamed we were in bed. I can sense ye had pleasure tonight, Claire."

"I was dreaming of you, too," she whispered, stunned. "It was so real."

"Why can I scent Aidan in yer chamber?"

Claire tensed. No good was going to come of this.

He began to tremble with anger. "I ken ye didna break yer vows. Why was my bastard brother in here with ye? Did he try to seduce ye while I was locked up in the tower?"

"No!" she cried. She seized his hands. "He was watching over me, Malcolm—for you." Impossibly, she was defending Aidan now. "I did find pleasure tonight," she whispered, blushing. "It was only a dream, but I was with you and it was wonderful. He heard me from the hall and thought I might be with a demon. He barged in to rescue me. That is all," she said firmly.

Malcolm stared at her. Claire hated lying by omission. "Please forgive him," she said hoarsely. "He's your brother. The two of you should be allies, friends."

Malcolm's gaze turned ice-cold. "He'll stay away from ye now. I've had enough of his lustin' fer ye."

"He doesn't lust for me," she cried.

He raised both brows.

"Malcolm! All the Masters are impossibly oversexed. Aidan lusts for anything young, pretty and female!"

Some of his tension eased. "Ye wish fer us to be friends?" He was clearly disbelieving.

"Yes, I do."

"He be Moray's *son*. He be a *rogue*." He was grim, and from his expression, she saw that he did not trust Aidan. And how could he, when Aidan chose to behave so erratically and selfishly? At times she liked him and trusted him, but at other times she did not.

Malcolm had pulled away. He lifted his gaze to her. "I need ye, Claire. In bed, the way ye want it. Slow."

Claire's eyes widened. Was he telling her he wanted to make love to her? Or that he wanted to have sex, just in a less frenzied way?

She began to nod. The tension that was pulsing now felt right, not dark, not evil.

"Well," she said softly, breathless now, "there's a few hours before dawn."

He slowly smiled, the most seductive smile she had ever seen. Her body erupted into flames.

Past his shoulder, through the open door, she saw Aidan coming down the hall. Claire was filled with dismay. It was too late. Malcolm turned. Aidan glanced inside and faltered, starting as he saw Malcolm.

Go away! Claire thought silently, praying Aidan might hear.

But he only glanced briefly at her as he stepped to the threshold of the room. "Ye been released?" he exclaimed to Malcolm, his relief evident.

"Aye." Malcolm smiled coldly. "An' I be tired o' watchin' ye lust fer what is mine."

Aidan's relief vanished. He smiled coolly. "I'd never touch yer woman." He turned and walked up the hall, toward the chamber he shared with Isabel.

Claire leaped past Malcolm and slammed their door closed. "I am proud of you," she began, when a sudden sense of dread began and she knew something terrible was about to happen.

Malcolm felt it, too, because he tensed, his expression becoming one of alarm, an expression she now hated.

"What is it? Is it evil?" she gasped hoarsely.

Before Malcolm could answer, a horrible cry sounded. It was anguished, a cry of protest, of outrage.

"Aidan!" Malcolm exclaimed.

He seized the door, flinging it open. Claire followed him, uncertain that he had correctly identified the cry, because she could not recognize Aidan's voice in that raw sound. And now there was only a terrible, frightening silence.

Malcolm ran past several doors, Claire on his heels. Aidan's door was ajar and Malcolm barged inside, Claire with him. She saw Aidan on his knees, head bowed. For a split second she thought he was praying.

And then she saw Isabel.

She lay on her back, naked, hair streaming, eyes wide and sightless.

Claire gasped in horror. And then she saw the slight smile on her face.

Malcolm knelt. "Can ye find yer powers?"

Aidan did not speak. He was as still as a statue, staring at his mistress.

Malcolm touched Isabel and jerked to look at Claire. "She's cold. She's gone."

"Close her eyes," Claire said harshly. She rushed to Aidan and knelt, carefully touching his shoulder. She saw shock on his face and looked at Malcolm. Moray had done this. She had no doubt. "Help him."

Malcolm lifted Isabel and laid her on the bed, covering her entirely with a blanket. As he did, Aidan stood. The shock vanished from his expression. He stared at Isabel's corpse, his eyes burning with hatred, and Claire knew he was lusting for vengeance.

"Aidan," Claire said. Resolute, she went to him and tried to take his hand. "I am so sorry. Come, sit down. You're in shock."

He jerked free, not looking at her; Claire wasn't sure he'd even heard her or knew she was there. He started for the door.

Malcolm ran in front of him and barred his way. "Ye canna defeat Moray. Ye'll die."

Aidan smiled coldly. "Get out o' my way."

"Don't let him go," Claire whispered.

Malcolm did not take his gaze from his half brother. "I canna allow ye to hunt Moray."

"Get out o' my way," Aidan snarled. His teeth gleamed very brightly, and saliva dripped.

His expression was odd and frightening. Claire had never seen such a savage look on a man's face.

Aidan snarled at Malcolm.

The sound was filled with menace and was unbelievably bestial. Claire's insides lurched. She had a very bad feeling, but she did not know what to expect.

And she saw Aidan's beard growing at an impossible rate.

Malcolm stiffened. "Aidan!" It was an alarmed cry of protest.

Aidan snarled again. This time there was no mistaking the sound—it wasn't human, it was canine. And before her eyes she saw a gray wolf appear in his place.

Claire cried out, backing away. The wolf stood very still, crouched to attack, hackles raised, growling in such a way that it was clear he would assault Malcolm and ravage him to death.

Claire was stunned, but she instantly understood. Shape-shifting was one of the most basic tenets of Celtic culture, so why wouldn't these Masters have the ability to change from man to beast? If she hadn't seen it with her own eyes, she wouldn't have believed it. What she didn't know was whether Aidan remained inside the animal at all, or if only a murderous beast was there instead.

"Malcolm, get out of his way," she said, her heart thundering.

The wolf snarled once again, fangs dripping. Claire was afraid it would leap on Malcolm at any moment.

Malcolm did not move. "I didna believe ye could shape-shift," he said slowly. "Even though I heard ye called the Wolf of Awe." He hesitated. "Don't do this. Claire be right. Yer my brother. We'll hunt Moray together, the way brothers should."

The wolf snarled and sprang. His assault was so powerful that Claire knew Malcolm could not defend himself against such a supernatural beast. She screamed.

But Malcolm got down on one knee and the wolf bounded easily over him. It raced into the hall at such speed its feet barely touched the floor.

Malcolm followed, as did Claire. The wolf ran down the corridor toward the window. They ran after it. "Aidan, don't!" Malcolm shouted.

Too late. It leaped through the window, breaking the glazed glass.

Claire could not control another scream, this one of horror. She ran with Malcolm to the window and looked down. They were on the third floor. She expected to see a mangled wolf lying below, or a mangled man. Nothing lay in the shadows of the courtyard.

Malcolm grasped her elbow.

She followed his gaze. Against the moon, she saw a hawk soaring rapidly into the distance.

Tears began. Claire wept for Isabel, and she wept for Aidan, too.

Malcolm pulled her into his arms.

MALCOLM POURED THEM BOTH mugs of wine. Claire stood at the window, watching the night sky fading, turning mauve. He handed her the wine and she thanked him. More tears fell.

He put his arm around her. "I ken ye wanted t' save Isabel."

"With all my heart!" she cried. "She was sweet, guileless, more child than woman. She reminded me of my cousin Lorie."

Malcolm pulled away, his expression dark and grim.

Claire wiped her tears. She wanted to grieve, but there wasn't time. "I think we should return to Dunroch. We can't help Aidan if the king throws you back in prison. We should leave while we still can."

He stared at her, looking damned unhappy.

"I know you are worried about Royce and Aidan." She took both of his hands. "Can you admit it?"

"Aye, I be worried fer them both. But there be truth in yer words, Claire. If I dinna leave, I may be returned to the tower. I canna help anyone then."

"So we'll go?"

"Aye, at first light."

She didn't let him walk away. "Malcolm, you promised you would teach me to fight. It's clear that I am at a disadvantage here, in your time, even at court, by not having some fighting skills. And we both know I will need those skills when I go home, because I won't be surrounded by Masters then." The thought of going home made her feel even sadder than she already felt, but she'd deal with her feelings another time. She had to learn to fight. She'd had enough of evil. She'd had enough of destruction and death.

He pulled his hands from hers. "I'll teach ye at Dunroch."

Claire could feel him thinking about her going home, but not his exact thoughts. "I have to go back some time," she said hesitantly, almost wishing he'd refute her words.

He turned away.

She retreated. They had enough burdens now, and she wanted to ease Malcolm's worries if she could, just a bit. "Look, I don't think Aidan is rushing after Moray this instant. After all, Moray is here. He isn't going to assault the Defender of the Realm at court. He's smart. He'll cool down."

"If Aidan hunts Moray, he will die. He doesna have the power to defeat his father."

"Will he ever have that power?"

"Moray's power comes from Satan."

Claire had a striking thought. "Aidan is Moray's son. I bet, genetically, his powers are close to his father's. Maybe he'll get the power he needs from God—if we don't nail the bastard demon first."

"Mayhap."

She had never seen Malcolm so grim. "So you admit he is not evil?"

He seemed reluctant. "He's nay evil."

Claire almost smiled. He was capable of changing profound beliefs. He was open-minded, and it meant everything to her—not that it changed their future.

A wolf howled.

Goose bumps began and Claire and Malcolm exchanged looks. The howl continued, a sound of anguish and loneliness. And Claire was certain that it was also a sound of guilt and regret.

She went to Malcolm, who was stricken. He put an arm around her. The wolf howled again. Aidan was entitled to his grief, even if Isabel had been a passing fancy. "He blames himself," she whispered.

"Aye. He be her lord an' he failed in his duty to her. 'Twas his responsibility to protect her."

Moray had done this to his own son, Claire thought grimly as a knock sounded on the door.

Malcolm's expression turned stoic, impossible to read. He went to the door, where a household guard stood. She tensed as the two exchanged words in Gaelic. Then the guard left, but she did not relax. "What is it?"

Malcolm went to her and touched her hair. "Dinna worry, but the queen has summoned me."

It took Claire one moment to become enraged and horrified. "She's summoning you in the middle of the night? For what purpose?" she cried. Before Malcolm could answer, she said, "Oh, let me guess! She's done with Royce and she wants to try you out in her bed!"

"Claire, we dinna ken what she wishes. But I canna refuse her summons."

And he couldn't refuse an invitation for sex, either, could he? "Where the hell is the king?"

"Dinna fret so. James be an early riser an' it's almost dawn. She willna be takin' a lover at this hour." And then he shocked her by pulling her close and kissing her lightly on the cheek, the way a suburban husband might before his daily commute.

Claire wasn't reassured. She watched him go, hating her helplessness and the tyranny of the king and queen. In that one moment she had never appreciated the freedom of an open, democratic society more.

She tried to remind herself that she didn't know what the queen really wanted. But damn it, if her suspicions were right, Malcolm would have to pleasure the queen when he belonged to *her.*

Claire shivered. The last thing they needed was for Malcolm to get on the queen's sexual radar. She pulled her brat closer to her body, wondering if they'd left the shutters open. But a quick glance showed her that Malcolm had closed the shutter.

The chamber became frigidly cold.

Comprehension began. Claire turned slowly, horror rising.

And the earl of Moray smiled at her, exactly as he had a few hours ago in her dream. "I said I would come back for you," he murmured.

Terror overcame her and she could barely think.

The Deamhan opened the closet door and held out his hand. Terrified, the child took it, and he pulled her into the light and she saw his face.

Claire cried out. "It was you!"

CHAPTER NINETEEN

MALCOLM STRODE toward the queen's hall, passing only a handful of solemn noblemen and taciturn royal soldiers as he did so. It was still early, the sun straining to rise, the sky outside only just blushing. Undoubtedly the revelry had gone on to the midnight hour last night.

He did not know what the queen wished and he was afraid the summons had something to do with Royce. As he could not deny the extent of his worry for Aidan now, he felt sorely pressed. But he had been given permission to leave when he had been released. The sooner he got Claire away from the palace, the better.

And then he saw Royce emerging from the queen's hall, two guards closing the door behind him and standing in front of it. Royce saw him, as well, and appeared as surprised as Malcolm felt.

"What are ye doing here?" Royce asked.

Malcolm gave him a cursory glance and decided he was in one piece. "I was summoned. I thought surely ye had annoyed Her Highness."

Royce smiled. "She be well pleased and is sleeping deeply. I doubt she'll rise before noon."

Malcolm started. "I was summoned by the queen."

Royce's smile vanished. "Malcolm, I just left her. Her orders were that no one disturbs her till she rises."

And Malcolm realized the summons had been a trap. "Claire!" He turned and ran down the hall, Royce behind him.

He rushed up two sets of stairs. The door to his chamber was closed but he knew before opening it that she was not here. As he flung it aside, he felt the terrible chill within.

Moray had taken her.

CLAIRE AWOKE.

She lay on cold, uncomfortable stone. It took her a moment to orient herself. She blinked, realizing she was in a round tower and, from the look of the gray sky outside, high above the surrounding land. She recalled Moray walking into her chamber at the palace with his frightening smile, and then there was only darkness.

Claire clawed the stone. She remembered everything about the night of her mother's murder now.

Moray had been the demon who had drifted into their Brooklyn home that night. He had been the demon who had opened the closet door and taken her hand—and told her he would return for her.

Claire choked on bile and fear. She no longer believed in coincidence. She knew, in that heart-stopping moment, that he was the demon responsible for her mother's murder; that he was the demon she had wanted to hunt down and destroy to avenge her mother.

She began to shake convulsively. *He had been hunting her instead.*

She turned on all fours and retched.

Was it Malcolm he wanted—or her?

Claire slowly got to her feet. Her dagger and gun were gone. She was defenseless.

But she was defenseless even with those weapons, because nicking him would not save her from whatever he planned.

She began taking deep breaths. Fear wasn't going to help her now. She looked around. The tower was larger than the tower at Awe, but only a small table, two chairs and a pallet graced it. Engraved on one wall was a symbol she recognized—the universal symbol for evil and the devil. A black pentagram in an odd circle glared at her.

There was a pitcher on the table. Claire assumed it contained water or wine—she wasn't going near it.

She walked over to one of the tower's two windows. The tower was clearly centuries old, and the opening was two and a half times the size of an arrow slit. She glanced outside and saw why the windows were large enough to accommodate a small man.

They were a hundred feet above the forest below. No one could scale the tower to get inside. The castle was on the top of sheer cliffs and the forest below was pine, thick and impenetrable. It was a gray, windy day. She smelled salt in the air. They were not far from the ocean.

She stared outside, trying to decide where he had taken her, but it was so gray and foggy out Claire could not decide where the sun might be. She had no idea where she was.

She hesitated, shivering with a fear that wouldn't quit. Then she turned back to the window. With her nail, she started scraping a cross in the stone. It was faint and white but oddly comforting. She needed God now. She needed the Ancients, too.

She felt him coming.

Claire tensed, the arctic chill coming from outside the tower door, not from the wind or the sea. The black door opened and Moray walked in. He did not bother to close the door and he smiled at her.

"Where am I? What do you want?" Claire said. And she saw that he was wearing her mother's stone.

"You are at Tor, Claire. My home in the Orkney Islands."

Claire's eyes widened. "You killed my mother."

"How clever of you, Claire. Yes, I did. She was too beautiful to resist." He touched the charm stone.

"Why?" Claire cried, fists clenched, as furious as she was afraid. "It wasn't random, was it? You chose her for some damn reason!"

"I was hunting Alexander," he said softly.

It took Claire a moment. Her father's name had been Alex. "What?"

"I was hunting your father, Claire, and he was hunting me. We'd been doing so for hundreds of years. He led me to your mother. Their affair was random, but clearly, like Malcolm, he dared to care. How foolish. A Master should know better."

Claire couldn't breathe. "Tell me who he is!"

"But you've met Alexander of Lachlan. I believe you know him as Ironheart."

Claire cried out. There was so much shock, so much disbelief. She recalled the way he'd looked at her stone, his choice to help her learn to fight, the surprising invitation to the Black Isle. "Oh, my God."

"The gods aren't here, Claire. No god would ever dare enter my home."

Claire began to tremble again. "Ironheart will join with Malcolm to destroy you," she cried.

"I gave up hunting him when he came completely into his powers. They are vast. I suspect you have some of those powers, too, but it will be decades before you realize them. Despite his power, he failed to destroy me a hundred times. Like the Masters before him, he has turned his efforts to the Deamhanain he can destroy. Even if he did come after me, he cannot vanquish me. There is no living Master who can."

She wet her lips, her heart racing frantically. "What do you intend? Somehow I don't think you'd go to all this trouble for an old grudge against Ironheart. I know this isn't about Malcolm, either. It's about me."

"Oh, of course I would go to such ends to provoke your father! And I do love turning young Masters, Claire. Never mistake that. They make the most powerful Deamhanain when they have matured. But you're right. I was toying with Malcolm. I did think he'd give in to his lust—and to me—

but it doesn't matter. There are other Masters to hunt. No, it's you that I want. I knew it when I saw you as a child."

Claire had a terrible sense of dread. "I am going to kill myself," she said slowly, "before allowing you to touch me."

"No, you will not. Because the daughters of Masters have a particular value to me. They bear me great, powerful Deamhan sons. I will even let you return to Malcolm with my bastard. You may raise and love him—and then one day you will watch him worship me."

"You're sick."

"No, Claire, I am the devil."

Claire backed up against the wall. She shook her head.

"I have many guises," he said softly. "Come, darling," he said, and his eyes began to glow, not silver but red.

Claire looked away. "Aidan is not evil!"

"Ah, well, he may have a genetic defect. His mother is far too devout and I think that is the problem. However, I have not given up on him. I will never give up on him. He is the only one of my many children to dare defy me. Look at me," he murmured.

Claire knew she was about to be used, and her life would never be the same. This man had murdered her mother. Helpless, she looked up into his fiery eyes, but as she did so, she started praying. And to her shock, the words forming in her mind weren't English or even Latin—they were Gaelic.

She had been listening to the Highlanders conversing in their native tongue for weeks now, but she wasn't a genius and she didn't know the language. She didn't know how she knew this prayer, but she knew every word she was saying. It was a supplication to Faola, the willful goddess Malcolm claimed was his ancestor, for her help and protection.

Moray seemed delighted. "She won't help you now. As bold as that goddess is, she would never dare to confront me here. Here, my power is absolute. Here, the Ancients fear *me*."

Claire was panting. From the corner of her eye, she saw the tower window.

"I told you, I won't let you die. You will not jump. You do not want to."

I do want to, Claire thought. And she steeled her mind against him.

"You can't block me," he said quietly, amused. "My powers are *vast*. Yours are pitiful in comparison."

She could and she would. And Claire decided to jump to her death.

"I will not allow you to jump," he said easily, clearly reading her mind.

And the window vanished, becoming stone. Claire gasped, dismayed. The certain death had been her only way out.

And suddenly Claire felt his thoughts. She had been clinging to the prayer with the back of her mind, but now she let it go.

"Haven't we had enough conversation? Now you know the truth. There is nothing left to tell. And you can rest more easily, my dear, for I will return you to Malcolm with my bastard in your womb when I am done with you. Come to me, Claire." He extended his hand. "You want to come to me now. You want my touch, my caress, my power. You want the pleasure I will give you. Come."

And Claire became dazed. For one instant, she saw herself in a handsome man's arms, in the throes of sublime ecstasy. Her body became heavy, her flesh began to swell. The air cloaked her, hot and heavy, swirling with so much strength, she felt as if she were being pushed forward by a powerful wind.

"I will give you more pleasure than Malcolm ever has," he murmured. "Night after day and day after night. Come here. That's a good girl."

And Claire felt her legs moving. Aghast, she realized she was walking toward him, her heart racing now, but not with fear—with excitement. She must not let him mesmerize her now! She must fight his powers of enchantment. "No," she said hoarsely. "I won't give in to you!"

He smiled at her, impossibly beautiful, and his lust thickened the air that had become her cocoon and cage.

The images replayed now in her mind, and she saw herself writhing in his arms. She forced her mind away from the horrific fantasy. She burst into the Gaelic prayer, whirling somehow, but she faced the stone wall.

He moved over her, spreading her thighs wide. In another instant, his huge hardness would be inside.

Claire screamed, wanting to rush at the wall, fling herself upon the stone, anything to get Moray out of her mind. And she saw Malcolm.

He stood transposed upon the stone, like an apparition, his hand extended toward her.

She reached for it. Malcolm vanished. Claire expected to touch stone. Instead, she felt nothing but air.

Moray hadn't built a wall of stone—he had built an illusion.

"Claire," he murmured seductively.

She felt his hand slither over her back. In her mind, he impaled her and she wept in pleasure.

Claire leaped.

It was a leap a tiger might make. But Claire's legs sprang with shocking power and she burst through the small stone window and into the damp, cold air outside.

Time stood still. As she was launched into the sky, she looked down at the trees far below, and she knew she was about to die.

"Claire!" Moray snarled in fury.

And time returned and she fell.

The trees rushed up at her. She fell with the force of gravity, faster and faster, and she knew she was dead. She was only sorry that Moray lived—and that she could not tell Malcolm how much she loved him.

Suddenly pine needles and wood branches tore at her. Claire cried out with pain as she fell through branches, wood snapping. Pine abraded her face, her flesh. She landed hard on a bed of pine needles and dirt.

Stars exploded. The sky turned black. And then it cleared and she saw fingers of gray daylight streaking through the thick forest canopy above her head.

In shock, she realized she wasn't dead at all.

She should have died on impact, her body broken. Claire lay still, panting, waiting to be consumed with pain. Agony did not begin.

She was alive.

In fact, she didn't seem to be even close to death.

She sat up, reaching for her necklace, but of course it was gone. *The stone hadn't saved her.*

Moray would hunt her now.

Claire crouched, amazed that nothing hurt—but then, she was the daughter of a Master. However, she wasn't a Master. Masters had to be summoned and take vows, and not every child born to them was chosen. MacNeil had told her that. She hadn't asked, but in the patriarchal Brotherhood, she bet there were no women Masters. Still, she had some powers, oh, yes, and she'd use them now.

A chill fell over the wood.

The hunt had begun.

Claire started to run down the steep, forested hillside.

MALCOLM STOOD on the other side of the loch across from the palace, alone in a field. His eyes were closed, his face turned up to the morning sun, and sweat poured down his body. He strained to sense Claire.

He wasn't sure he had the power to do so. Moray had taken her and they could be any place, in any time.

Moray wanted to use her against him. His various strongholds were impregnable, guarded by his Deamhan hordes. Malcolm thought it likely that Claire remained in Scotland, even in the Highlands, and in this time.

No matter where she had been taken, he had to locate her.

He strained to sense her. Time passed and he remained acutely attentive.

Claire! Where are you?

But there was only silence.

CLAIRE HAD REACHED low ground and she froze. The forest ended in rolling, grassy hills, and she could hear horses and men shouting. They were looking for her.

She had been praying to Faola and the other great gods, including Lug and Daghda, incessantly. She was almost certain her only chance of surviving Moray was with the grace of the Ancients. Now she crouched low as the first troops appeared on the hillside.

Claire didn't move as the riders galloped toward her, but she prayed harder, sweat covering her entire body.

The riders came closer still. It was as if they knew where she was.

Claire wished she had the power to become invisible. She hid at the base of the pine, praying.

The first dozen riders crashed into the forest.

Claire saw a pair of men heading directly toward her. A wave of ice swept over her as the riders galloped through the wood, passing by her so closely their horses' hooves shot clods of dirt at her arms and face. And then they were gone, the forest silent, the hills empty.

Claire stopped praying, and quickly thanked whoever had been listening for his, her or their help. She collapsed against the tree trunk, panting and in disbelief. Somehow, with the help of the Ancients, they had not discovered her.

She was soaking wet, freezing cold and scared out of her mind. And she was lost.

Malcolm, she thought, suddenly aching for him. *I'm lost. I need you.*

There was only silence. Claire listened acutely now for

him, but she heard nothing. The riders gone, she stood, walking out of the woods. And as she finally paused on a low grassy ridge, the sky began to clear.

Still thunderously gray, she glimpsed the darker steel of the ocean below, somewhere. She had to cross the hills first.

Claire, where are you?

Claire froze. Had she just heard Malcolm?

Malcolm! Help me! I'm lost!

She strained to hear, but there was only silence. Claire started across the hills, and as she did so, the sun appeared in the gray sky. It was faint, but the promise was there, and Claire realized she was heading southwest.

The Highlands were southwest.

Malcolm was southwest, somewhere.

MALCOLM STIFFENED. Claire was lost, but she wasn't hurt. And she was alone. Somehow, she had escaped Moray.

He felt her now. He turned to face the northeast.

Royce came galloping up to him, leading his charger. "Ye have found her?"

Malcolm nodded. "I dinna need the charger. See him home, Ruari."

"Where is she?"

"She be near Tor."

CLAIRE REACHED the edge of the rolling hills and cried out. Below her, the drop perhaps a hundred feet, was one final plateau. A circle of giant stones faced her. Beyond, she saw black rock beaches and the steel waters of the ocean.

Claire began scrambling down to the standing stones. She had never been to the Orkneys, but to the best of her knowledge, no standing stones had ever been discovered there. She stumbled and tripped as she took a steep, rocky trail down to the field. Claire ran the short distance to the first towering black stone, which was the size of four or five men. And then she paused, overcome and awed.

She touched the stone. It was ice-cold.

Claire realized she had been hoping to find holiness in this place. Demons would not enter a holy place. She walked past the first stone into the circle and stood still, trying to find the Ancients, God or even any unknown pagan gods there. She began to despair. The chapel at the Sanctuary had been filled with power and grace. This circle was only that, a circle of tall stones. The gods, like mankind, had forgotten this place long ago.

Claire wanted to cry. Instead, she knew she must not give up. She wasn't dead and she wasn't Moray's prisoner. She crossed the circle, her destination the beach below. And she sensed that she was not alone.

Stiffening with alarm, Claire turned.

For one moment, in the gray day, she thought she saw a figure, ghostlike, standing beyond the circle of stones. "Malcolm?" she breathed.

The light shifted. No one was there.

Claire stared, her heart lurching. She wanted to believe she had seen a ghost, or better yet, an Ancient. And then her eyes widened, for Malcolm appeared as he climbed up from the beach. She cried out, rushing toward him. He saw her and scaled the ledge. Running to her, he pulled her against his chest, relief written all over his face.

Claire held on, hard.

He held on as tightly.

She couldn't speak. She had never loved anyone this way and she never would. He didn't speak, either, holding her so tightly it was hard to breathe. *Thank the gods yer all right.*

Claire looked up. "Moray abducted me from our chamber at court."

"Aye. I ken. How did ye escape, Claire?" His eyes were wide and worried.

"Malcolm, I leaped out of a tower. I should have died. I didn't." She touched his face. "Ironheart is my father."

Malcolm actually gasped. "He told ye that? How can ye trust a word from the Deamhan's tongue?"

"He told me, and I know it's true." She suddenly stiffened, shivering from the cold, which had intensified. Fear began. "We need to get out of here, please, now. Let's leap to the Sanctuary."

Malcolm eased his hold on her, his gaze not on her but beyond.

Claire whirled and saw a hundred knights above on the northwestern ridge to their right. And then she saw one man riding across the field. Moray slowly approached.

"Malcolm!"

His eyes burned with the need for vengeance and destruction, for death. He had eyes only for the demon. "Give me yer hand. I will send ye back alone."

Horror began. "You cannot defeat him!"

"Give me yer hand," he ordered as Moray rode past the first stones, looking very pleased. "Ye go to the Sanctuary. I failed to avenge Mairead and Brogan, Now, I avenge ye all."

He was going to die. He knew it and didn't care. He was determined to take Moray with him, somehow.

She did not give him her hand.

He briefly turned an incredulous gaze on her. "Claire. Ye gave me yer word. Ye swore to obey me in battle."

"I know. But I can't let you face him alone."

"I want ye to live!" Malcolm cried, seizing her hand.

Claire steeled herself against him.

"A lover's quarrel?" Moray asked softly. "*Hallo a Chaluim.* Has she told ye what I intend?"

Malcolm faced Moray, moving to stand in front of Claire. "Get off o' yer horse."

Moray dismounted, laughing.

"Malcolm, please, leap away with me!" Claire begged.

He ignored her, unsheathing his longsword. Moray slid his blade free, as well. And Claire felt the blast of his power as she stood right behind Malcolm. Malcolm was shoved back a dozen steps, as she was. It was like being thrown back by a tornado.

Malcolm recovered. *"A Bhrogain!"* But he spoke softly, and he did not move.

Moray grunted, being forced three steps back. His eyes gleamed red. "You can't match my power, Calum."

"Nay?" Malcolm strode forward, sword raised.

Claire cut off her cry as Moray easily parried the blow. As the swords rang, she looked around for a weapon. She found a jagged stone with a point that she intended to be lethal. The swords rang again and then again. Claire tensed, because from Malcolm's expression, she saw that he was using all of his strength to battle Moray. His face was drawn into a hundred lines, his arms and legs bulged with muscle, and sweat drenched his body. The demon was fighting back, using great effort, but Malcolm's power was still less than Moray's.

Claire dropped her stone. Thinking to use it was absurd. She looked at Moray and tried to focus any power she might have on him like a dagger, into his back.

Moray grunted, meeting another vicious thrust of Malcolm's blade. He looked over his shoulder at her, his eyes wide.

Claire tried to stab him telepathically again.

He dealt Malcolm a terrible blow, one that cut into his shoulder, spewing blood. Before Claire could gasp, Moray glanced at her and snarled, "You'll pay."

"A Mhairead," Malcolm said, and with his shortsword in his left hand, he cut across Moray's chest.

Blood gushed.

Enraged, Moray cried out and Malcolm staggered backward from an energy blow. Then he quickly straightened, viciously parrying Moray's pointed thrust.

Claire felt someone behind her. She looked up in alarm... and went still.

Only a ghostlike outline of a transparent figure was there, hovering a few feet from her, but this time, the figure was distinctly female.

And the woman materialized, becoming a dark beauty in white, flowing, almost Grecian robes. She spoke in Gaelic. Claire understood her every word.

"The son shall avenge the father, the daughter, the mother, for the two are blessed. It has been written."

The light shifted.

The goddess vanished.

The circle of stones blazed with blinding light.

Malcolm and Moray were braced liked horned stags, both of them bleeding heavily. As one, both men looked at the sky, startled.

The sun was gone and the sky remained dull and gray, except in the circle, which was filled with golden, shimmering light.

Moray's expression changed to surprise and then fear.

"A Chlaire," Malcolm said, and with his left hand he seized his shortsword and thrust across Moray's neck.

Claire cried out.

Moray's head fell, severed, to the ground.

For one more moment, the halo of light intensifying, the headless body remained engaged against Malcolm, longswords braced. Malcolm plunged the shortsword daggerlike into Moray's heart. He twisted it viciously there.

Claire covered her mouth with her hands. Malcolm pulled the blade from Moray's chest and the bloody body collapsed. Stunned, Claire glanced at Moray's head.

Moray smiled tightly at her the moment before his head vanished.

His body disappeared an instant later. Her mother's necklace lay in the damp, bloody grass.

Malcolm sheathed both swords and strode to her. She seized his arms. "What was that? What happened?" Even as she spoke, the light dulled rapidly, until only the inclement day remained.

His face hard, he put his arm around her. "I think ye have caught the ear o' the Ancients, Claire." He slowly looked around, as if expecting Moray to appear from thin air. Then he bent to retrieve the necklace.

"Malcolm, is he dead?"

"If he's nay dead, he'll never die." He sighed and pulled her close. "Let's go home, lass."

CHAPTER TWENTY

CLAIRE LAY in a very hot bath, the water up to her chin and ears, eyes closed. They had just returned to Dunroch and she was in Malcolm's chamber. There had been no question of where she would go and where she would sleep, not now. Moray was probably dead—vanquished at Malcolm's hands, with her help and some very holy help, too. In spite of the heat, Claire shivered.

I have many guises.

She bet he did. She just hoped not to ever encounter that particular guise again. Claire turned her thoughts away from the master of all that was dark, ugly, demonic and evil. Malcolm was a great hero. He had finally avenged Mairead and Brogan and she was thrilled for him. *But it had been written.*

The goddess had said so. When she had told Malcolm about the brunette goddess, who Claire assumed had been Faola, he hadn't seemed surprised. But then, the gods worked in mysterious ways. Claire smiled.

It had been fated that they'd deliver the bastard together. Well, that's what they'd done, and she had a bit of a telepathic warrior power herself. Her smile faded.

She was Ironheart's daughter.

Her heart raced. Had he intended to ever tell her? What should she do? She had to speak with him at length before she went home. Did he care about her? And how had she been born? Masters apparently were adept at birth control. What about her mother? Had he loved her at all?

When she went home.

Claire opened her eyes and saw the roaring fire. Through one window, the moon was high and full and bright in the Highland universe, alight with so many stars. She looked at the pleasant, if sparsely furnished, stone chamber, and then at the four-poster bed. Her body tensed, swelling with anticipation. Very soon, Malcolm was going to take her to bed. She could not wait to be in his arms, using her body to tell him just how much she loved him. And afterward they could cuddle, argue, chat.

She didn't want to leave.

Claire sat up, stunned. The chamber was absolutely silent except for the soft sound of her breathing, the flames licking wood, and from outside, an owl's deep hooting. She didn't miss anything about the twenty-first century or New York City. She didn't miss Ben & Jerry's, Favio's thin-crust pizza, electric lights and running water, smog and rush hour, shopping in Soho or Colin Farrell movies. She didn't even miss her books.

But she missed Amy and the kids.

She loved them with all of her heart, even John, and she sure as hell missed them.

But she really, truly loved Malcolm of Dunroch, a medieval warrior who belonged to the Brotherhood. A Master of Time.

Claire became afraid. There were a million reasons why she shouldn't stay with him. She loved him, but so what? He didn't love her back, although he clearly cared. They'd exchanged vows of fidelity, but how long would those vows last? Supersexed as he was, how long before someone younger, prettier and new caught his eye? As arrogant and autocratic as he was, he could be surprisingly open-minded, but he was still a product of his times. If she stayed, she was going to be so badly brokenhearted, she'd want to die.

Of course, if they married, it would be different. Claire knew he'd be faithful until he died. Malcolm was a man of his word.

She wished she hadn't stupidly thought about marriage and Malcolm in the same breath. It was impossible. Secretly, like a pitiful, unliberated female, she'd love to swear to love him until death, but he had said he would never wed. And she knew why. A wife would be his downfall. He cared about her and they had just gone through hell, because his relationship with her made him vulnerable to his enemies.

So marriage was out. Staying behind in the past was out. She would never forget Royce's words on the way to Awe. *If ye truly love him, when it's time, ye'll go.*

She loved him as much as was humanly possible.

And could she ever sleep at night, worrying about Amy and the kids? They needed her. She understood the world of good versus evil. They deserved long, healthy lives, demon free. She had a major familial duty to them.

She was going to have to leave, soon…really soon. There was no reason to linger. Moray was gone and the page from the Cladich had been found. As for the Cladich itself, well, it had been missing for hundreds of years. It might never be found.

The door opened and Malcolm stepped inside, smiling. "We have guests," he said, and as their eyes met, his smile vanished.

There was only one reason to linger, she thought, her heart beginning to break apart. Claire knew her thoughts were written all over her face, her grief reflected in her eyes. She managed a bright, fake smile.

His expression became utterly impassive. She hated it when he hid his thoughts. "It's the black of night," she remarked. "Who would arrive at this hour?"

"'Tis a half day by sea from Lachlan."

Claire sat up, stunned. "Ironheart is here?"

"He said he'll see ye when yer ready." His tone had become as wooden as his face. Malcolm picked up a thick wool plaid and stepped over to the tub.

Claire stood and he settled the towel around her from behind, his strong arms going around her, as well. She turned in the circle of his arms so they stood face-to-face. He released her. His gaze was searching and grim.

"Yer leaving me," he said.

She inhaled. "How can I stay?"

He stiffened. She could not read his feelings, and she strained to lurk in his mind. It was blank. "Don't block me," she said softly.

"I'll be in the hall with yer father." He turned and walked out.

IT TOOK CLAIRE a while to dry her hair before the fire. As upset as she was about leaving Malcolm, she was apprehensive about seeing the man who was her biological father. Had she ever seen an expression on his face other than determination, resolve, ambition? He reminded her of a career general. When her hair was almost dry, she went into the hall, her heart scudding with the fear of rejection and some anger that he had left her and her mother to fend for themselves.

She realized they had quite a bit of company. Malcolm was brooding with a mug of claret. Ironheart sat across from him, his face expressionless. MacNeil sat there, as well, the only man in an apparent good humor. Claire was very surprised to see him.

MacNeil was first to leap to his feet, green eyes twinkling, dimples deep. *"Hallo a Chlaire."*

"Hallo a Niall. Ciamar a tha sibh?"

His eyes brightened as he strode to her and clasped her hands. "Very well, lass. Ye've had quite a day."

Claire glanced past him, unable to return his smile.

"Fer a powerful woman who helped vanquish Moray, ye dinna seem all that pleased."

She jerked to face MacNeil. "Did we vanquish Moray?"

He hesitated. "Only the Ancients ken, Claire. But ye seem to have earned their favor. Ye have Faola's protection now."

He had all of her attention. "Was that her?"

"Aye, she was there. She allowed me a glimpse o' the battle in my crystal stone."

She noticed what he was showing her, a chunk of milky quartz set in gold arms, which he wore on a gold chain around his neck, beneath his leine. The stone was the size of an apricot. "Is that your crystal ball?"

"When I'm allowed to see," he said with a grin. "I never ken."

She had to know. "Does Malcolm have her protection, too?"

"I dinna ken, but even if Moray comes back, he will never hunt him again, not after what Malcolm has done. I've known the Deamhan fer a thousand years. He hunts what is easy. He be a coward at heart, Claire."

"Why was it written that we'd defeat Moray together?"

"Ye ask me? I dinna ken the Ancients' plans fer the future, lass." His smile broadened. He was clearly in great spirits. "I'm proud o' yer lord. He's the youngest o' us all an' he defeated Moray, with yer help. Malcolm has proven himself a great Master, hundreds o' years ahead o' the time fer such proof." He said softly, to Malcolm, *"Calum Leomhaiin."*

Claire looked at Malcolm. He held her gaze for a moment and she didn't have to read his mind to know he was more than upset—he was hurt. She was hurting him now. "I'm so proud of him, too." She tore her gaze from Malcolm. "What did you just call Malcolm?"

"The Lion, lass. Malcolm the Lion."

He had earned the name, she thought, feeling her heart crack open even as pride swelled.

"I be proud o' ye, too. Claire, yer brave an' cunning, an' ye have power. Ye be the daughter o' Ironheart in every way."

"How long have you known?"

"I didna ken, but I had my suspicions."

"MacNeil, what about my powers? How did I prevent myself from dying in that leap from Tor? Did I make myself invisible when Moray's hordes were searching for me? Do I have healing powers? What does that make me?"

"Yer Ironheart's daughter." MacNeil was firm. "I dinna ken why the Ancients gave ye some gifts, but yer not alone in this world. There be thousands of men an' women born to Masters who have some power, but not the powers a Master must have before takin' his vows. Every Master is different, Claire. We all have the power o' takin' life and leapin' time. We all have the strength o' ten mortal men. No man is chosen to make his vows otherwise. Ye haven't been chosen, an' ye won't be—there be no women Masters—but ye do have gifts. Say yer thanks fer them."

Claire got it. She'd have to figure out her powers, day by day. At least she would have some supernatural stuff going on to help her when she got home.

He clasped her shoulder. "I came to say farewell."

For one dumb moment, Claire thought he was going somewhere. Then she realized and she inhaled, turning to look at Malcolm.

"I ken yer leavin' in the morn," MacNeil said. "Ye have the Ancients with ye, lass. Make certain ye dinna forsake them. Ye'll be fine."

Before Claire could thank him, he smiled, released her and vanished.

She heard the bench scraping the floor and she stiffened, turning.

Ironheart approached.

With a nod from Malcolm, they went into his privy chamber, closing the door. Claire walked to the other side of the small room, then faced him. Now she recognized the red glints in his hair. She was a natural redhead, but her hair was a dark and deep auburn, and so were the streaks in his hair. And she recognized his eyes. They were a vivid spring green, like hers.

He seemed uneasy and it was startling. "Ye have questions. I heard ye an' I came."

"You lurked?" She was instantly displeased.

"Nay, Claire. Ye've been summonin' me even if ye didna ken."

"When did you realize I'm your daughter? And why didn't you tell me? Surely you haven't known my entire life!"

He jerked. "I had no idea! Do ye think I'd abandon the mother o' my daughter that way? I have no other children, Claire."

Claire stared. "How is it possible? You've lived for hundreds of years."

"I stand alone, Claire, an' I'll die alone. I made vows."

That was tragic and heroic. His life was the Brotherhood. "I was a mistake."

He hesitated. "Aye."

Claire already felt rejected. She shook her head, incapable of speech, even though she wanted to know more about him and her mother. But what more was there to know? Mom had said it was a single night of passion.

His hand settled on her shoulder. "Yer a miracle, Claire," he said harshly. "I never dreamed to have a child, an' here I have a grown daughter, fearless, clever and beautiful."

She whirled, stunned.

Moisture had gathered in his eyes. "Ye look like yer mother," he said, turning away.

Claire knew he had lost his composure and she thought he had probably not done so in hundreds of years, if ever. "You cared about her?"

He tensed. "Aye. I was in yer time, huntin'. I had followed a Deamhan there. Yer mother was on the street, struggling to carry a heavy box upstairs to her apartment. She was 'moving in,' as she called it. Men were passing by, looking at her because she was so pleasing t' the eye, but no one was helping her. Not only was she beautiful, she was wearing the shortest skirt I'd ever seen. I didna think twice. I took the box from her, and she was offerin' me coffee." He smiled. "Suddenly,

I was moving a hundred boxes—and yer mother was makin' me smile. Did ye ken she had a clever wit?"

"Mom liked to joke," Claire whispered. The story was beautiful.

"I had a Deamhan to chase. Instead, I helped yer mother open boxes an' then I was tryin' to fix her lights." He looked as if he might laugh. "I ken nothin' about electricity, Claire. Yer mother thought me a fool."

Claire actually smiled. "I doubt it."

His smile faded. "I wanted her. She wanted me. One night wasn't enough."

Claire stared. "How many nights were there?"

"Seven."

Her mother had lied. "Did you love her?"

He flushed. "I didna ken. I have one mistress, Claire. My vows." He sobered. "I told her after the first night that I had taken sacred vows, vows she wouldna ken, vows that required me to leave her. I didna lie. I made no promises, an' the leaving was sad." He paced across the room restlessly. "She didna weep. I gave her my stone, to keep her safe." He met her gaze. "When I saw ye wearin' the stone, for one moment, I thought ye were Jan. 'Twas a trick o' my mind. And then I felt the truth."

Claire wondered how much her mother had really known about her lover. "She loved you," Claire said thickly. "She never said so. She didn't have to. And she never took the stone off."

"Can ye forgive me, Claire, fer not protectin' ye both?"

"Of course I can," Claire said. "You didn't know."

A moment passed. "What will ye do now? Ye love Malcolm, but he's a Master. He be displeased t'night an' saddened deeply."

Claire's heart ached. "I have family at home—my cousin, her two kids. Who will protect them if I don't?" She added hoarsely, "And I make Malcolm weak."

"'Tis yer duty to defend yer kin. But Claire? Ye made Malcolm strong t'day." He smiled at her. "If ye need me, ye summon me. I'll hear."

CLAIRE RETURNED to the hall and found it empty. Her father had gone outside for some air. Claire knew he was traveling down memory lane and that he wanted to be alone with his thoughts. She hesitated, desperately wanting to be with Malcolm now. She hated the look she'd put in his eyes and on his face. She hated hurting him, but there wasn't any other choice.

She hurried up the stairs. The door to the chamber was open and Malcolm sat before the hearth, staring into the flames. The moment she came to the door, he looked up, smiling sadly. He stood. "Did ye have a pleasin' conversation with yer father?"

Claire nodded. "I can't stand seeing you so sad," she whispered.

"Then dinna leave."

Claire wanted to cry. *If ye love him, if ye truly do, ye'll leave when it's time.* "I have a duty, Malcolm, just like you."

"Then stay a year—I'll teach ye t' fight. Ye need skills, Claire," he said urgently.

If she stayed a year, she'd never leave. "When I was on Iona, speaking privately to MacNeil, I asked about the future. He said I'd succeed."

Malcolm inhaled. Their gazes held, locked. She heard his heart beating, slow but strong.

"I want to make love to ye, Claire."

Claire cried out. He was telling her that he loved her, damn it. "That's not fair."

He walked over to her, his gray eyes reflecting anguish. "Ye've wanted me to say it fer some time now. I want to make love. I want to show ye how I feel with me body, in bed."

Claire couldn't speak. *Malcolm loved her.* He was wrapping her in his arms and she grasped his shoulders, laying her cheek on his strong chest. His mouth moved over her hair, her ear, slowly, softly, sweetly. She shuddered, the sorrow easing, her hurting heart racing with far different feelings instead. He cupped her face and tilted it up. That tenderness shimmered in his eyes.

Claire realized she was starting to cry. He lowered his face and brushed his mouth against hers.

Love vibrated in the caress of lips. His tongue finally touched the seam. "Open," he whispered. "Let me fill ye, lass, all o' ye."

Claire wanted nothing more and she opened her mouth for him, releasing the muscles of her thighs, too. His tongue swept in, slow and soft. He bent his knees and his engorged penis swept up against the length of her sex.

He unpinned the brooch and tossed her brat aside. Her leine quickly followed. Claire was wearing only the fifteenth-century drawers. Briefly, he cupped her through the slit, gazing into her eyes. The light of his grief was still there, but she saw silver heat rising. As he slid them down, she stepped awkwardly out of her boots, looking from his strong, scarred hand up to his strained, scarred face. Desire, affection, even love were mirrored there, in every taut tendon, every angle, and in his beautiful gray eyes.

He sank to his knees and spread her throbbing lips, gently easing his tongue against her. Claire gasped, all of her anguish vanishing. There was no room now in her mind for thought. There was only need and the promise of so much pleasure. There was only love.

She wasn't sure if it was hers—or his.

HE HAD NEVER known such intense feeling—joy, despair, affection, loyalty, love—and he knew he never would again. He lifted Claire and carried her to the bed, overcome with far more than desire. He could not find the beast he'd left chained in his chest. It felt as if it was gone forever.

But hadn't he heard someone say, once, that love healed all wounds?

"Hurry," Claire breathed. Her eyes were hot and bright.

Malcolm stripped off his belt and leine. "Ye said ye want me slow. I want to take ye slow, Claire, too." It was the truth. Although he was so engorged he was close to coming, he wanted to worship her body for an eternity, if she would only stay.

"I lied," she managed to say, restlessly shifting for him in an ageless invitation. "I want you hot and hard, and I want you *now.*"

A savage sense of elation began. He straddled her and clasped her hair behind her nape. "Yer so strong an' so beautiful…an' ye belong to me, Claire," he said flatly. "An' dinna think to argue now!"

Her response stunned him. "I'll always belong to you," Claire said thickly. Tears filled her eyes. He lurked easily and was pleased, because she meant it. "I'm glad you're a chauvinist," she whispered.

"Yer glad I'm a powerful man," he returned, and the bargain done, he slowly filled her, inch by orgasmic inch, refusing to thrust quickly or deeply.

And Claire was coming before he was done.

He held her in his arms, murmuring in her ear, stroking long and slow and deep. As they made love, his excitement escalated, and as he started to reach for her, just to stroke her soul, he began to realize the black beast was truly gone. Deep inside, he touched her power, her essence, her life. There was so much beauty. All thought vanished, except for one. *I love ye, lass.*

I love you, Claire tried to gasp. She wept in pleasure and joy, instead.

SEVERAL HOURS LATER, Malcolm moved onto his back, apart from her. Claire lay beside him, completely sated, smiling at the shadows dancing on the ceiling. She was so deeply in love she was floating.

And then she felt his sorrow returning, a huge and heavy cloud.

A dozen cracks radiated through her heart. After so much love, there was so much pain.

Are ye really leavin' me?

Coherent thought returned, along with her awareness of what they had just done.

They had made love. No demonic desire had arisen, either.

Claire moved to her side and laid her cheek on his chest, her hand on his abdomen, not far from where his beautiful manhood lay resting. *Malcolm had just made love to her.* She did not have any doubts. His every touch, every kiss, every stroke, had been filled with feeling and emotion. But there had been even more. She had felt as if they had been joined on a plane that was not physical. She pressed her lips to his skin in a kiss, her heart finally breaking in two.

He sat up abruptly.

Claire sat up, too, her chest aching.

He glanced at her, stricken, and slid from the bed. In that moment, she felt him closing to her. Claire panicked as he walked over to the hearth. He leaned heavily on the mantel.

She listened for him and heard silence.

Claire got up. "I can stay a few days. Maybe a week!"

He didn't look at her. "I'll never forsake ye fer another. But yer right. A Master stands alone. 'Tis best."

She choked on a sob. "Who will hold you in the dark of the night?"

He half turned. "I need no one."

Claire thought, *You need me.*

"Nay, lass. Ye have a duty to yer kin. If ye willna protect them, provide fer them, who will?"

Claire swallowed, her ability to breathe failing. Heartbreak consumed her. "I think I fell in love with you my very first night in your time, that night at Carrick. I love you, Malcolm, and I always will. There will never be anyone else."

He straightened and slowly turned.

Claire winced, because her words had brought tears to his eyes which he would never shed. Could she really do this? How could she leave this man?

How could she stay?

"I ken. Ye be an independent woman, an' in yer time women fight their own battles an' they be lairds. Ye be laird o' yer clan, Claire." His gaze found hers.

Claire nodded, crying. "There's no one else."

His nostrils flared. His nose was red. He stared, his eyes shining now. "I willna take ye back. Ironheart will do so." He struggled to speak. "If ye need me, summon me." He breathed hard. She had never seen him more stricken. "I'll come."

He released the mantel and took a brat from the pegs on the wall. He walked out, wrapping it around his waist as he did so.

Claire realized that he had just said goodbye to her. She panicked and ran after him. "Malcolm, wait!" It could not end like this. She needed to hold him one last time!

But he was striding up the stairs to the ramparts, his posture stiff and set against her.

And she knew he wasn't going to halt or turn back. He had said his farewell.

It was over.

CHAPTER TWENTY-ONE

New York City—The Present

CLAIRE LANDED in her kitchen, alone. She fought to swim through the pain of the leap through six centuries, willing a swift healing. Claire had no idea if her determination had worked, but when she finally sat up, still breathless but in one piece, she instantly realized that her store was a crime scene. Do Not Cross police lines were taped everywhere.

She was sore from the leap and her head ached, but nothing could compare to the agony of her broken heart. Claire realized she was still devastated over losing Malcolm—it was the hardest thing she had ever done in her life. She slowly stood up, wearing not only her city clothes but her leine and brat. Ironheart had sent her back to her time by herself, a power he had apparently perfected.

She walked over to the small TV on the kitchen counter and flicked it on. Disbelieving, she learned it was August 5. She had left Dunroch on August 5, too, just five hundred and eighty years earlier.

She walked to the wall calendar, finding a Kleenex to wipe her eyes. She had been gone for fifteen days. She had to call Amy and her aunt. She had to call the police. Her disappearance was probably more of a priority than the investigation into the burglary she had reported. Focusing on what she had to do now might help her get through the grief.

Fifteen days. It felt like fifteen hundred years—it felt like fifteen lifetimes.

Claire didn't go to the phone. She walked into her office, hitting the lights, and sat down, but her laptop was gone. Rage began.

She had to research the fifteenth century. She had to learn what had happened to Malcolm after she had left him.

But the police had confiscated the computer. Some of Claire's fury had eased. What was she going to tell them, exactly?

Claire reached for her office phone and dialed her cousin. Amy answered, her tone dull and depressed.

"Hey, it's me. Don't be mad—I'm fine!"

"Claire, where are you?" Amy choked.

"I'm home. Can you come over? And bring your laptop."

"Where have you been?" Amy was in tears.

"Scotland."

"We thought you were abducted. We were afraid you were dead—like Lorie!" Amy gasped.

Claire hesitated. "I was abducted, sort of. But I'm not dead. I'm very much alive. Hey, Aim? I'm sorry."

FIVE HOURS LATER, Claire was allowed to leave the local precinct. She knew she had been deemed certifiable. Amy and John were with her, the two of them looking as haggard and drained as Claire felt.

She had told the two detectives the truth. With Amy holding her hand, she had told them how a medieval Highlander had appeared in her store, looking for a missing page from a sacred book. Both detectives, one a Sonny Crockett type, had begun the first exchanges of many odd glances. She had then described Aidan's appearance and the ensuing swordfight.

Crockett had said, "So two guys on their way to a costume party decided to play knight in shining armor? Oh, wait. No armor, just leines and brats and boots? Oh, yeah, and swords?" His tawny brows rose.

Claire then told him about being swept back in time to the fifteenth century. When she described the bloody battle that had ensued, both detectives offered her coffee, which she declined. By the time she described her arrival at Dunroch, she glanced at Crockett's partner to see if he was really taking notes. He was doodling.

An hour later she was free to go—case closed.

John, a hunky guy who almost looked like Joey from *Friends* and had that thick Queens accent, said, "Helluva story, Claire." But his gaze was direct.

She avoided it. "I'm fine," Claire said. He couldn't possibly think she'd been telling the truth. "They have better things to do than investigate what happened to my store."

"You don't look fine. You look like shit. You've been crying," Amy said fiercely. Dark blond and brown-eyed, she wasn't quite as tall as Claire. "Do you want to tell me what happened?" Amy said quietly as they walked down the precinct stairs.

"I am so sorry for not calling you," Claire said, meaning it. "I made a mistake with my flights, Aim, that's all. I had no idea I'd come home and find my store burglarized and myself a missing person."

Amy didn't comment and Claire knew her cousin was aware that she was not coming clean. Later, as they dropped her off at her store in John's Lexus sedan, she asked, "Do you want to stay with us? I think you should, Claire."

Claire hugged her. "How about lunch tomorrow?"

After they'd made plans, Claire let herself into her store, Amy's laptop under her arm. More grief began. She reminded herself that this was what she wanted. She didn't want to be Malcolm's Achilles' heel, and she had to protect Amy and the kids. She waved at Amy and John as they drove off and then went directly into her office. Powering on the laptop, she went online.

At dawn, she fell asleep in her chair. She hadn't found a

single reference to Malcolm of Dunroch, not in the fifteenth
century or any other one. It was as if he hadn't existed.

TWO WEEKS LATER, the grief remained. Claire reminded
herself on an hourly basis that she was doing what was best
for Malcolm. She had moved in with Amy and the kids. Her
cousin believed it to be a temporary situation, but Claire
planned otherwise. She had enrolled in a martial arts course.
And she had dabbled with her "powers." She seemed to have
the ability to make the sniffles vanish, and she had actually
moved a spoon across the kitchen table with her mind, but
that was about it—for now.

Her store was open for business again, but it was late
August now and the city was deserted. Everyone who was
anyone had taken off for the most humid, hottest month of
the summer. Claire was glad. She spent her days online, at
the midtown library and at NYU, searching for a reference
to Malcolm. She'd interviewed some of the foremost au-
thorities on medieval Scotland over the phone. She was
becoming frightened. It was almost as if her journey back in
time had been a wild dream. If she didn't have the leine and
brat neatly tucked away, she'd start to think she'd had an incredible fantasy. But every day in the city newspapers, usually
buried in the midsections, there were reports of pleasure
crimes.

She hadn't been sleeping well, either. When she did sleep,
Malcolm came to her in her dreams and often they made
love. The dreams were so real that she wondered if they were
somehow making love telepathically across the gulf of six
centuries.

But mostly she read books and articles online, fanatically determined to uncover some single, minuscule reference to him.

Claire was cross-eyed from the strain of spending twenty
hours a day staring at her computer screen. It was only noon,
and she'd spent all morning searching. And she started to cry.

She had made a mistake. Malcolm hadn't wanted her to go. Hadn't they vanquished Moray together? What if she did make him stronger, not weaker? And did it even matter, when she had a broken heart—and so did he?

She couldn't live this way. She was in love with a medieval man who was probably dead. Well, maybe not. He *was* a Master. For all she knew, he was still alive.

And Claire froze, but her mind raced. *If he was still alive, he was at Dunroch.*

But there were no references to Malcolm at all. If he was still laird of Dunroch, surely there'd be local articles about him.

She reached for the phone. It was seven hours later in Scotland. Finally she tracked down the number for the bed-and-breakfast where she had been planning to stay, Malcolm Arms. The wife of the elderly couple who owned the inn was more than happy to tell Claire all she knew. Yes, The Maclean's surname was Malcolm, but that was an old family name. No, he wasn't elderly, not at all. He was in his prime.

Claire closed her eyes. This couldn't be Malcolm, could it? Was it possible a single plane ride separated them? "If you're interested in Lord Malcolm, miss, you should come out and visit us."

Claire agreed, wondering what she would do if she learned that the current laird was Malcolm. For her, they'd been separated two weeks. If he was still alive, they had been apart for almost six hundred years. He had probably forgotten all about her. And then she knew that was impossible. Malcolm had given her his heart. She would own it forever.

"Are there any stories about him in the local papers?" she asked, her heart slamming.

"The Maclean doesn't allow any press, Miss Camden. He is a very private man. He has a publicist to keep his name *out* of the newspapers."

Claire began to breathe hard. This was sounding more

and more like Malcolm! "So there're no articles—no photos, nothing?"

There was a hesitation on the other end of the line. "Actually, we took a picture of him and his pretty wife at a charity event they held to save the Highland forests. We could send it to you."

Claire froze.

He had a wife?

Her mind had slowed, becoming heavy and dull. Her heart had slowed, too. This couldn't be happening, she thought. "Last month, when we spoke, you said he was unwed." She could barely get the words out.

"That's impossible. He's been married for a very long time—and happily, I might add."

Claire reminded herself that this might not be her Malcolm. After managing to ask the proprietress to send her the photo by e-mail, Claire sat down, stunned and ill. She could hardly think, but she tried. A month ago, the twenty-first-century laird of Dunroch had been unwed. If he'd been affianced, she would have been told so. No, he'd been a bachelor and available.

And now he was married.

What did that mean?

In the ensuing month, she'd gone back in time to him and they'd fallen in love.

Claire felt ill. Her laptop beeped. She went to it and opened the e-mail from Scotland. Very dizzy now, she clicked on the attachment.

It was Malcolm—*her* Malcolm—looking forty, not twenty-seven, but he remained a gorgeous hunk, even in his navy blue sports jacket and tan trousers.

He had married someone else.

It was over.

She couldn't believe it. Claire looked at his wife.

Her vision blurred, she saw a beautiful, elegant lady from

high society, dressed very much the way the British royals did. She wore a sleeveless print dress, white gloves, high heels and a beautiful large-brimmed white straw hat trimmed with flowers.

And Claire looked at her face.

Her heart slammed to a stop.

The woman was herself.

AMY SMILED uncertainly at her as she came into Claire's store. Claire hugged her hard. "Let's go into the kitchen," she said breathlessly.

Amy was wary. Then her cousin saw the small duffel bag near the stairs. In it were two pairs of Claire's favorite jeans, a dozen thongs and bras, her sexiest little red cocktail dress with her Manolo Blahniks, and five super-warm sweaters. Her laptop was in it, too, along with eight batteries.

"What's this?" Amy asked very quietly, as if she already knew.

Claire took her hand. "I told the cops the truth. I really did go to Scotland."

Amy stared. "I know. Who is he, Claire?"

Claire smiled. Amy thought she'd had a rendezvous in the present. "Malcolm of Dunroch, the laird of Dunroch."

Amy's eyes went wide. "You fell in love with the man you were fascinated with from the start?"

"Yes, I did. And he loves me." Claire trembled. "I have to go back."

"Of course you do. John and I were talking about it last night and wondering when you'd tell us the truth and why you left the love of your life." Amy seemed relieved, but the last had been a question.

Claire said, "You should sit down."

Amy followed Claire into the kitchen and sat. "I'm so happy for you." She reached for her hand and grasped it.

Claire inhaled. "Amy, I meant it when I said I told the truth.

I went to Scotland, but not the Scotland you are thinking of. I went to medieval Scotland, to the fifteenth century, and landed in the middle of a battle between good and evil. That's where I fell in love with Malcolm."

Amy didn't bat an eye.

"Amy? Why aren't you surprised?" But now, an inkling began. Hadn't she always suspected that Amy knew more than she'd let on?

Amy covered her hand. "John doesn't work for the Bureau's counterterrorism unit," she said. "He works for CDA."

"I don't get it," Claire said slowly. "I've never heard of CDA."

"It's the Center for Demonic Activity. It's top secret, a need-to-know-only organization. He's an agent there."

Claire wasn't that surprised. She thought of all of her cousin's references to evil. Amy had known it all.

"He hunts evil, Claire, with some very sophisticated equipment, and he's followed demons into past centuries three times." She paled. "I hate it when he does that. I'm so afraid he won't come back!"

"You know, when I learned about the demons and the Masters, I figured I wasn't the only one who knew the truth. The odds were that world leaders and the government knew."

"They do know. The DNA left at the scene of pleasure crimes isn't human."

Of course it's not, Claire thought. "I guess the government's afraid to come clean."

"They're afraid of mass hysteria! The demons are so strong. Every century, it has gotten worse. In CDA, there's a department called HCU, which stands for Historical Crimes Unit. They research the crimes of the past and crunch numbers on the crime trends. Do you know that Stalin had aberrant DNA? This has been going on *forever*. It's scary."

"Is John a Master?" Claire asked bluntly.

Amy started. "The Masters are a myth—aren't they? I

mean, there are whispers and rumors of these old-world super knights—and I do mean super, as in supernaturally endowed with power—but no one has ever seen one. They've never been documented. It's legend, it's folklore, it's fantasy. But we can hope, can't we? It would be great if such a superhero really did exist."

Claire hesitated. "They do exist. I've met them."

Amy gasped, eyes wide. "Not Malcolm?"

Claire had to smile. "As superheroic as it gets." She blushed. And as superendowed, she thought. "They have great powers, Aim. Inhuman strength, telepathy, kinetic force."

Amy just shook her head, teary-eyed. "I am so happy for you! But John won't believe this. I mean, we both sort of wondered if you'd told the cops the truth. But he won't believe that there are Masters out there, fighting evil with extraordinary powers. But thank God! Claire, he'll want to talk to you."

"I can't stay here another moment." Claire meant it. "Amy, coming back was a mistake. Malcolm is at Dunroch right now, in the twenty-first century. A month ago, he was unwed. Now, he's wed—to me."

Amy started.

"I know you don't get it. But I wasn't supposed to come back. I was supposed to stay with him and live through six centuries with him. The proof of that is the fact that right now, we're alive and well and really old, living in the Highlands together as husband and wife. If I don't go back, I'm going to blow our fate."

Amy began shaking her head. "Claire, you can't live six hundred years."

"I forgot to tell you. My father is a Master, and I have that godly DNA going on."

Amy gaped. "Damn it, girl! You had better go back before you rewrite your history with your man. But God, I will miss you!"

"I'll miss you, too," Claire said and they hugged.

WITH AMY GONE, Claire sat down with her duffel, holding it tightly. She wasn't a Master but she was the daughter of one, and she intended to will herself back in time, the way Malcolm had done. If that didn't work, she'd try to summon Malcolm to come help her get back. He'd said he would come if she needed him. She wasn't worried—she could probably talk John into sending her back, although he'd balk at using his top-secret fed technology to do so. One way or another, she was going back to become Malcolm's wife and live a helluva long time with him.

She was beyond excitement.

As she sat there, Faola's image came to mind and Claire was certain it was a sign. Did the goddess want to help? Claire was under her protection. Maybe, after destroying Moray, Faola had become fond of her.

Claire smiled and hugged her knees to her chest. "If you can help, I will be eternally obligated to you." She closed her eyes and willed herself back into the past. Then she waited.

Nothing happened.

Claire opened her eyes and looked at the clock in her office. Fifteen minutes had passed. She grimaced. Maybe she didn't have the power to leap. She closed her eyes again and strained to put herself back in the fifteenth-century medieval world at Dunroch. She concentrated so hard she became dizzy. And she waited and waited.

Claire opened her eyes. She was sweating and the room was spinning. Clearly, leaping wasn't one of her powers. Maybe Faola hadn't been listening after all or didn't care to help her. Maybe she wasn't even that powerful anymore. After all, she'd been forsaken by most of Alba along with her godly kin.

And a huge force swept Claire through the hall, the walls, through time, through space.

CLAIRE LANDED so hard she wondered if she'd survive this leap. She looked up at a very familiar raftered ceiling. Still fighting the waves of torment, she began to rejoice. She had landed flat on her back in Dunroch's great hall!

Gasps sounded.

Claire clutched the duffel bag to her chest. The pain was receding and a dozen male faces stared down at her. Claire met Malcolm's wide gray eyes and her joy knew no bounds. Love ballooned in her breast. It was hard to speak and she couldn't move yet. "I am so…happy…to see you!"

His eyes gleamed as he knelt beside her. "Ah, lass, I be very pleased t' see ye, too." He reached to help her sit up.

His touch had its usual, immediate warming effect, but Claire was confused. He slid his arm around her as if she were a trophy he'd just won or a notch he was adding to his belt. His gaze was filled with heat, primitive and carnal, but not joy, and certainly not love.

Something was wrong.

He smiled seductively at her, murmuring. "'Tis not every day a beautiful woman appears in my hall. Ye have powerful magic, lass."

His arm was around her. But now Claire saw that he looked terribly young—and he didn't have a scar over his left eyebrow. Claire could not believe this was happening. "Do you know who I am?" she cried in disbelief.

His grasp tightened. "Nay, but I will. After this night, I will ken ye very well, lass."

Claire's disbelief escalated. What had Faola done? Did the goddess think this *amusing?*

He turned and barked orders in Gaelic and the hall cleared. He added softly, "I dinna fear witches, either, lass. After we have pleasured one another, I'll make certain ye can travel safely to yer home."

She inhaled, trembling. "What year is this?"

He slid his hand down her arm, causing a delicious thrill of pleasure to begin, smiling with anticipation. "Fourteen hundred an' twenty."

Claire cried out. She had leaped too far back in time. He was only twenty years old—he hadn't been summoned by the Brotherhood yet. She stood, stepping away from him. "Damn it, Faola," she cried. "Not fair! Not fair at all!"

He released her. "Are ye mad?" he asked, puzzled.

Claire seized the duffel and focused hard. She was going to leap forward now into 1427, anytime after August 3, the day she'd been abducted, the day they'd killed Moray. She quickly reprised her plans. August 10, 1427 was a good, solid, safe date.

Just as she vanished, she saw Malcolm's shock and anger. This time the agony was unbearable. When she landed she was crying. Leaping twice hurt so badly she felt stretched out on the rack. Her entire body felt as if it was coming apart and as if screws were being driven into her bones to splinter them into shards. And then she felt Malcolm's powerful presence as he knelt besides her. "Claire!"

She opened her eyes and saw his shocked expression—and then she saw the relief flooding his eyes. "Malcolm?"

"Dinna speak. Yer hurt." He swept her into his arms and cradled her gently against his chest. His heart thundered there. His mouth pressed against her hair and scalp.

She had made it. She relished the feel of his power, his strength, his life, and she thought she could feel an odd joining coming from her to him and him to her. A union of souls, she thought.

Silently, Claire thanked the Ancients and Faola for everything. "What year—what month—is this?"

"'Tis two weeks since ye left me, Claire," he said roughly.

Claire realized she had a bit of practicing to do if she was ever going to leap time again by herself. She'd been off by nine days. She didn't care. Malcolm's gray eyes were moist with tears.

He gazed down at her. "Are ye here to stay? Will ye leave me again?" he demanded harshly.

"No. I am here to stay." She caressed his hard, beautiful jaw.

He made a harsh sound, holding her again, more tightly this time, his cheek pressed to hers. Joy flowed. This was right.

He smiled at her. "Ye came back. Ah, Claire, 'twas only a few days but I didna think ye'd come back t' me."

She sat up, feeling infinitely better. "We are stronger together, Malcolm. I know it, and Faola knows it, too."

"Aye," he said softly. "Claire, we be written in the Cathach, by name."

Claire gasped. "Are you kidding?"

He smiled at her. "Buried in the hundreds of pages, there be a verse about us. Aye, Calum Leomhain an' his lady, Claire, victors o' evil."

This was fate. She moved closer into his arms, overcome. His mouth feathered her hair. So much need began, but only half of it was physical. They had a future to plan. Claire took a deep breath and looked up. "I missed you so much."

"Aye, lass, an' I missed you very much, too." He smiled.

She caressed his cheek and asked somewhat playfully, "How much?"

"Do ye wish fer a show?" he murmured as playfully.

"Yes," she whispered. "I want a big, splendid, prolonged show!"

He swept her into his arms and stood, chuckling. That was when Claire saw they had an audience. She had interrupted the evening meal. Brogan called out to her, waving, and Royce smiled at her, clearly bearing no grudges or ill will.

But there was one thing Claire had to know. "Wait!"

"I canna wait," he said in his most seductive and sexy tone. "I be a man starvin' fer his woman."

"It was only two weeks!" she said happily. He let her go and she slipped to her feet and ran to the duffel. She pulled out the laptop as Malcolm knelt besides her. "This is a long shot. But shit, if we can travel through time, why can't bytes?"

"I dinna ken," he said seriously. He touched her hair. "But this be important t' ye."

"If this works, it will be great," Claire said. His brows lifted. Claire shrugged, and having powered on, she hit the Internet button. After an interminable moment, the Microsoft Internet Explorer page came on. Her default page was www.weatherchannel.com, but it did not appear. "Oh, well," Claire said. It didn't really matter. What mattered was the future they would share—all six hundred years of it—at least.

"Aye," he said, lifting her to her feet and pulling her against his big, hard body. "This be what matters, ye an' me. I love ye, Claire, an' I want ye t' be my wife."

Claire threw her arms around him. "I think you know my answer."

"Ye dinna like it when I lurk," he protested with mock innocence. And he laughed, because they both knew he was reading her mind and neither one cared.

He tugged her toward the stairs.

Claire's skin tightened and thrummed. With the promise of so much pleasure—and so much love—she didn't look back.

Her laptop whirred.

The weather in New York City on August 19, 2007, at 11:15 a.m., was sunny with a few clouds and a torrid 101 degrees.

Dear Reader,

I hope you have had as much fun reading *Dark Seduction* as I have had writing it. I had a blast and fell head over heels for Malcolm, just like Claire!

Branching out into the paranormal genre has been an excuse for me to do even sexier, more powerful heroes—and to dabble in my favorite time period, the Middle Ages. I chose contemporary heroines because I can think of nothing better than being swept into the past by a medieval hunk!

As always, I started by doing a lot of research into medieval Scotland, because my muse said these Masters would be Highlanders. Knowing that, I began to search for my hero's name. I finally decided on Malcolm, the English version of Calum. I also dared to pick a clan for him, and my muse told me it would be the Macleans. Then I had to decide where in the Highlands his castle sits. I'd already made some decisions about the shrine being on Iona, so I picked the island of Mull, as it is an easy trip from one to the other.

I was still researching, and lo and behold, I learned that Mull was Maclean territory! I was really surprised and then thrilled. However, this kind of coincidence has often occurred for me when I write anything at all historical. It gets better. Duart is the seat of the Macleans of Mull. That is on the north shore. I decided to divide the clan up so Malcolm could be laird, and I still had to choose a location for Dunroch. I chose the island's south shore so it would be a very easy trip by sea to Iona.

And then I bought a contemporary map of Scotland. Thus far, I'd been using very specific maps in the historical texts I was reading—clan maps and historical maps. *Where I placed Dunroch are cliffs called Malcolm's Point.*

That is a fact. Coincidence? Who knows!

Malcolm is a fictional character, as is his father, Brogan Mor. Mull was not divided between two branches of the Maclean clan as I have portrayed. But Red Hector, the Maclean of Duart, did die at the bloody battle of Red Harlaw in 1411.

I have also taken great liberty with the ancient and respectable name of Moray. The lords and later the earls of Moray have played significant roles in Highland history and I have completely fabricated the demonization of the early-fifteenth-century earl of Moray, who bears no resemblance to any historical or living member of the Moray family and line.

Black Royce's story is next. As you know, Royce is very tired and very alone, in spite of his close ties to Malcolm and Aidan. He has spent more than eight hundred years fighting the Deamhanain and protecting Innocence, and he has seen the worst evil can offer. But most important, he has been tormented for all that time with guilt for his failure to protect his bride from evil when he was newly chosen. He has not allowed himself any intimacy with a woman since. But his world is about to be turned upside down, and the catalyst is named Allie Monroe.

Allie is tiny, beautiful, feisty and determined. The world thinks her an heiress devoted to charity, but she has a huge secret. She is a Healer, and she has vowed to never turn her back on any living being or creature in need.

At midnight Allie slips from her family's mansion to cruise the city, healing the victims of evil crime. But that isn't enough. Allie hates evil passionately and wants to vanquish it. That is, she is a wannabe warrior.

Because she is five feet tall and ninety-nine pounds, she is not equipped to do battle, not under any circumstance. It frustrates her that her powers are limited to healing, and she has an arsenal of weapons and gadgets to try to get the job done. When Royce appears during a political fund-raiser at her home, hunting a Deamhan, he is both horrified and mesmerized to see such a woman trying to battle the Deamhanain! And she is thrilled that a superhero is finally on the side of the good guys!

There are a few problems. Allie takes one look at Royce and wants him, badly. He takes one look at her and wants her even more, but he senses that if he starts with her, he will get involved. He was involved once; he will never make the same mistake. How should he protect her from evil, as he was told to do by MacNeil, and avoid any entanglements?

You can guess what happens next! Sparks and tempers fly! Passions arise. And Allie must fight far more than evil. She must fight for Royce's life and fight to heal his black heart....

Dark Rival will be on sale in October 2007.

If you wish to learn more about Malcolm, Royce and the other Masters of Time, please visit my Web site at www.mastersoftimebooks.com. Check out Profiles, where you can meet these sexy Masters in lots of fun detail. In The Lounge, you will find excerpts well in advance of publication, including sneak peeks of works in progress that no one has seen— not even my editor. You can check out my future publishing plans and if you have questions about Dunroch, Carrick and Awe, site plans and maps will be posted.

Finally, please check out *The Perfect Bride,* on sale August 2007. If you haven't tried one of my historical romances, let me assure you that you will meet the powerful, sexy heroes I am known for, along with emotionally intense story lines that will bring tears to your eyes and joy to your heart. For more information on my historical romances, please visit www.thedewarennedynasty.com.

Happy reading, and see you at Carrick Castle in the summer of 1430!

Brenda Joyce

Desire is the first weapon

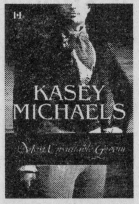

REQUEST YOUR FREE BOOKS!

2 FREE NOVELS
FROM THE ROMANCE/SUSPENSE
COLLECTION PLUS 2 FREE GIFTS!

YES! Please send me 2 FREE novels from the Romance/Suspense Collection and my 2 FREE gifts. After receiving them, if I don't wish to receive any more books, I can return the shipping statement marked "cancel." If I don't cancel, I will receive 4 brand-new novels every month and be billed just $5.49 per book in the U.S., or $5.99 per book in Canada, plus 25¢ shipping and handling per book plus applicable taxes, if any*. That's a savings of at least 20% off the cover price! I understand that accepting the 2 free books and gifts places me under no obligation to buy anything. I can always return a shipment and cancel at any time. Even if I never buy another book from the Reader Service, the two free books and gifts are mine to keep forever.

185 MDN EF5Y 385 MDN EF6C

Name _____ (PLEASE PRINT)

Address _____ Apt. #

City _____ State/Prov. _____ Zip/Postal Code

Signature (if under 18, a parent or guardian must sign)

Mail to **The Reader Service:**
IN U.S.A.: P.O. Box 1867, Buffalo, NY 14240-1867
IN CANADA: P.O. Box 609, Fort Erie, Ontario L2A 5X3

Not valid to current subscribers to the Romance Collection,
the Suspense Collection or the Romance/Suspense Collection.

Want to try two free books from another line?
Call 1-800-873-8635 or visit www.morefreebooks.com.

* Terms and prices subject to change without notice. NY residents add applicable sales tax. Canadian residents will be charged applicable provincial taxes and GST. This offer is limited to one order per household. All orders subject to approval. Credit or debit balances in a customer's account(s) may be offset by any other outstanding balance owed by or to the customer. Please allow 4 to 6 weeks for delivery.

Your Privacy: Harlequin is committed to protecting your privacy. Our Privacy Policy is available online at www.eHarlequin.com or upon request from the Reader Service. From time to time we make our lists of customers available to reputable firms who may have a product or service of interest to you. If you would prefer we not share your name and address, please check here. ☐

BOB07

***New York Times* bestselling author**

NORA ROBERTS

enchants readers once again with her
powerful, romantic stories about the beloved
MacGregor clan!

Discover a story of passion, fear, misunderstanding and
ultimate love, recounted by the beloved patriarch of the
MacGregor clan in FOR NOW, FOREVER. And for a
wounded minuteman and his nurse in prerevolutionary
America, a love affair blossoms, but not without a cost,
in IN FROM THE COLD.

Don't miss The MacGregors: Daniel & Ian

Where love comes alive™